PENGUIN TWENTIETH-CE

A LEGAC

Sybille Bedford was born in Charlottenburg, Germany, and was privately educated in Italy, England and France. She published her first book, *A Visit to Don Otavio: A Traveller's Tale from Mexico*, in 1953. Three years later she published *A Legacy*, which was described by Nancy Mitford as 'one of the very best novels I've ever read'. Since then she has also written the novels *A Favourite of the Gods* (1965), *A Compass Error* (1969) and *Jigsaw* (1989), which was shortlisted for the Booker prize. *The Best We Can Do: The Trial of Doctor Adams* (1958; Penguin 1989) started her on a new direction, and she attended some of the most important criminal and political trials of our times, notably the Auschwitz trial at Frankfurt, the trial of Jack Ruby in Dallas and the *Lady Chatterly's Lover* case. Her researches in England, France, Germany and Switzerland produced material for her book *The Faces of Justice*, published in 1960. She is the author of *As It Was* (1990) and the two volume authorized biography of Aldous Huxley. Sybille Bedford has contributed literary criticism and articles on travel, food, wine and the law to numerous publications, including the *Spectator, TLS, Observer, Harpers and Queen, Vogue*, the *New York Review of Books, The New York Times, Esquire, Life* magazine and the *Saturday Evening Post*.

Sybille Bedford is a Fellow of the Royal Society of Literature and Vice-President of PEN. She was awarded the OBE in 1981 and a C.Lit in 1994. She has lived in France, England, New York and Italy, and now lives in London.

Sybille Bedford

A LEGACY

PENGUIN BOOKS

PENGUIN BOOKS

Published by the Penguin Group
Penguin Books Ltd, 27 Wrights Lane, London w8 5tz, England
Penguin Putnam Inc., 375 Hudson Street, New York, New York 10014, USA
Penguin Books Australia Ltd, Ringwood, Victoria, Australia
Penguin Books Canada Ltd, 10 Alcorn Avenue, Toronto, Ontario, Canada m4v 3b2
Penguin Books (NZ) Ltd, Private Bag 102902, NSMC, Auckland, New Zealand

Penguin Books Ltd, Registered Offices: Harmondsworth, Middlesex, England

First published by Weidenfeld & Nicolson 1956
First published by Penguin 1964
Reissued with new Introduction in Penguin Books 1999
1 3 5 7 9 10 8 6 4 2

Printed in England by Clays Ltd, St Ives plc

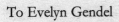

To Evelyn Gendel

Introduction

I began to write this novel as a sacred duty in a hot Roman August in 1952. I had turned forty and the sacred duty had nothing to do with the story, which must have lain for decades unregarded in my mind, but with the fact that Victor Gollancz had accepted the typescript of a travel book I had been working on for the last two years, and with my belief that I had attained at last the exalted *métier d'écrivain*. To write, to be a writer, had been the true goal ever since I began to think; which was early. My aptitude was not. The balance sheet of my literary past showed, beside some pompous essays, three novels, each perhaps a little less unsatisfactory than the last, each rejected (after some half-hopeful editorial dithering), each rejection followed by another year or more of doubt, despair and sloth. With equal naïvety I now regarded the promised leap into print – which in fact did not happen until the following spring – as an accomplished turnabout: GOLLANCZ ACCEPTE LIVRE the telegram (French text a compromise for both English and Italian post offices?) was brought up to me as I was doing the evening watering of my scented climbers on the Roman roof; I crossed myself, ritual rather than religion, and like the horse, Boxer, in *Animal Farm* I said aloud, 'I will work harder', tipped the messenger and there I was: a writer.

What a writer does is *write*. No more doubt, no more *sloth*, tough as it might be, and goodness knows it was and is and ever will be very very tough for me. So ...

However there were still some other duties before the new conscience allowed to roll that blank page into my typewriter. Duties, all of words, on paper – unanswered letters, work shirked, the monstrous task of a letter to Ivy

Compton-Burnett. I admired her work; intensely so and had spoken of it as 'an English secret' to the editors of the *Partisan Review*, the New York monthly, who commissioned me to do a piece under that title at my own length. *That* was in 1947. Blocked by inadequacy, the piece never got done. Now five years on, Ivy, even in America, was no longer a secret: whatever I might write about her would do her little public good; yet appreciation is always welcome (as she might have said herself); so driven by contrition I sat down, day after broiling day, writing to *her*: 'Dear Miss Compton-Burnett', explaining my omission and constructing a meticulous commentary on every of her seven – or was it nine then? – published novels, the letter running to some thirty pages. (She kept it, as it happened. Her biographers have quoted snippets.) Then, I could ill afford the time, one part of the penance being that there could be no question of remuneration, which I rather badly needed; I had no money, nor sources of income earned or unearned, other than the generosity of trusting friends. This was not going to last much longer (on whether Gollancz's deferred advance proved adequate, one might suspend judgment). A day came, we were well into mid-August, when the task was done, stuffed into an envelope stuck with huge postage and on a nocturnal walk dropped into an indifferent maw of the *Posta Centrale*. I kept no copy. That was part of the deal. Now I was free.

Free to write in earnest ... I had been conjuring, choosing, ordering words, tapping them into the portable Remington, re-thinking, re-setting, re-typing for a respectable number of daylight hours week after week: a discipline had been set up, next step – continue: *Begin*.

Tending my garden – handmade on the wasteland of a flat roof, out of tiles and string and terracotta pots and sacks of earth and goat manure – watching the sunset with the swifts' sudden covering of the sky, the first glass of cool red

Tuscan wine in my hand, at night walking, alone, criss-cross through Roman *piazette* and streets, elated by the beauty and the glory, the back of my mind had been seething with *Brothers and Sisters*, *Daughters and Sons* and the cutting acerbities of Burnettian dialogue; now that had stopped. I was on my own.

Next morning I wrote – fluently – the first paragraphs of a novel knowing it was going to be that. Abruptly resurrected from a fallow memory I had a framework, and possibly a point of view. I had a time, a country, I had people ... I knew who they were and where they were, of what they were going to become; what they were going to *do*, I had as yet no knowledge. That came slowly, gradually, one by one growing light in the tunnel – oh I got stuck so often, made what I call *fausse route*. This lay ahead. (The book took nearly three years.) But on that morning much seemed clear: the time was late nineteenth century and early twentieth, the country Germany, the people a triangle of three families who, somewhat unfortunately linked by marriages, were wholly unlike each other in habits, values and religions. They were divided by their ignorance or pursuit of politics, by geography and by money. All had a lop-sided perception of their time, taking their position as a norm, unaware that they could be seen (as by me, now) as eccentric, even anachronistic members of their respective milieus. One of the families was solid, upholstered, Jewish Berlin, the city of the disciplines, drives and deceits of the Protestant Prussian North; the other two belonged to discrepant realities of the Catholic South: one somnolent, agrarian, backward-looking; the other obsessed by ecumenical dreams of European dimensions. Each family and the individuals who composed it stood confident of being able to go on with what was theirs, while in fact they were play-things, often victims, of the now united Germany and of what was brewing therein. 1870–1914, as far as this novel goes. Much of what was allowed to happen in these decades was ill-conceived, cruel, bad (in simple terms); there was also a German dottiness, devoid of humour ... Is some of this a foundation of the vast and monstrous thing that followed? Did the private events I lightly draw upon leave some legacy? Writing about them made me think so. Hence the title.

Sometimes I am asked about my sources, and I have to answer that they were neither documents nor adult knowledge about German society and that epoch. In fact I did no research at all.

I *was* born in Germany but left it as a child (for good), first through circumstances, later on by choice, and had cut nearly all connections with the country which I did not see again until the 1960s (except for one brief visit on a motor tour with the Aldous Huxleys in the spring of 1932, some eight months, one should notice, before Hitler came to power). Thus what I know or feel I know about the places and the men and women in this story is derived from what I saw and above all heard and over-heard as a child at the age of roughly three to ten, much of which I managed to absorb, retain and decades after, to re-shape in an adult mode. The rest is invention and surmise. Some of the players' characters, notably Sarah's and Count Bernin's, are of my own devising. Just so, much of what I gathered as that infant had already been metamorphosed by imagination, turned into distillations of a past – expressed by rumours, innuendoes, half-truths, vengeful tales as well as pastoral set-pieces and fond recalls. Versions of these, often in the form of disapproval, warning or denial, were addressed to me – cut down to size; more was believed to be beyond my ear-shot or my comprehension. There was also a good deal of table-talk, literally above my head buried in a plate of soup. The purveyors of the talk were in disparate ways my father and my mother and, in their own modes, retainers, cousins, hangers-on, the cast to some extent of my fictional three families. Which brings me to another rather frequent inquiry: how much is autobiographical? How much of it did actually happen? Up to a point, quite a lot – privately and publicly. All the same that legacy is not my story; most of it happened before I was born. The first person singular, I perhaps clumsily employed, does a 'Cheshire cat' quite early on.

Well, yes, it was I who was bundled between two houses, one static and enclosed, the other not ungraceful. I *had* a father who may have been what I guessed or ascribed to him – a man brought up to pleasure, to staying on the sunnier side of life, who was trapped early and late between fears and events. I cannot know; he died early. And indeed I had a mother who might have been, but was not, the *rara avis* of another code and country who cuts into the story like an arrow: the catalyst who entrances and uncovers, seeks to heal, destroys, retreats defeated. She – Caroline – who shares some aspects with my mother – beauty, a way of talking, moral principles combined with a disregard for the morals of her time – is like her only to a limited extent. *This* is not her story either. As for the public, call it the historical, side of the novel: yes the evil schools, the Prussian Cadet Corps existed; the treatment of the boy Johannes and the numbers like him are a fraction of the human nightmare: ubiquitous, re-enacted ... And yes there was a family scandal that spilled over into a political one. Somebody did get shot. If my bureaucrats and priests, military dunces and grotesques are not exactly drawn from childhood encounters, I believe that they are not far off the actual mark. Germany *had* a Kaiser.

Enough. It is not my place here to re-tell or analyze my own book – anyway introductions that divulge are best read after the end – what I was asked to do was to say something about where I was and what I did and thought while I was writing it. Living in Rome during those years and more – seven in all – was an enormous privilege and for me the greatest and the most consistent of my visual experiences. In the mornings I worked in a shuttered room, pushing words about like stones for a stretch of road. Our flat was high in one of the side streets between Piazza di Spagna and Piazza del Popolo: when the shutters opened one saw the ochre facade of the Villa Medici and the dark trees on the far away Pincian Gardens. In the summer afternoons one remained enclosed and read; in winter, in slanted sunlight, I tended our flowered roof; in the warm seasons – mid-April to November with luck – if one didn't have dinner with friends in the street, one also ate and drank up there under the leaves and sky, having hauled dishes, cutlery, glasses and all in flat baskets to the top of the ship's ladder; later staying on in scented darkness, listening to music, dreaming, far into the night ... A good time that was to look back on. Yet what is still most indelibly held in my conscious is the walking, the hours and hours of walking, walking-seeing in the noontime glare and dramatic nights – Via Sistina, Quattro Fontane, Piazza Navona, Campo di Fiore, Foro Traiano, Tempio di Vesta, Campidoglio, Botteghe Oscure – exalted, feeling at one with the colour, the splendour, the grandeur and the clutter, the majestic jumble of Rome. For years I lived possessed.

That, and the excavation of my book: alongside these went another element, an agreeable, even-tempered and affectionate domestic life. A friend, Evelyn – Evelyn Gendel – pursuing her own discoveries during my solitudes, kept intruders away, went to market, played apprentice to my cookery and, like the British Monarchy, was on hand to encourage, warn, advise. She was a New Yorker who at another stage became a talented and respected literary editor. Then, she was young, enthusiastic, eager for exotic Europe which she tried to see through Proustian eyes; above all she was an admirable human being, all goodness, goodwill, *gentilezza*. I like to think that I emerged better for those years. *A Legacy* is dedicated to her.

The 1950s can be seen as an inappropriate time to be happy – I was – for many of us they were again years of forebodings and fears: the Bomb, the Cold War, the wars actually being fought; for others there had come a time of relief and release, of detachment – absolution – from the grief and gigantic horror of the previous decade: more of Europe than one had dared to hope had survived, was living again and this for the present at least was liberation. One often ceased to feel for what we now know cannot be forgotten: most of the days one was able to be light-hearted again.

I was certainly light-hearted about money, foolhardy rather, considering the improbability of my making a living in a future that loomed quite near. At one point of my precarious existence, Allanah Harper (a friend at the ultimate count for more than half a century) had made over a part of her income to me for three years. An act of generosity that ought not to be forgotten, and which I rejoice in making public now. Allanah was not well off and the money that went to me seriously clipped her financial wings. She gave me the peace of mind and time to write my first publishable book. (The Mexican one, *A Visit to Don Otavio.*) At the point when this was accepted and I had embarked on the present novel, the three years were well passed. I had been sensible and made the money last beyond them, living simply yet rather well as one could in Italy at that time. The rent always got paid. When the money actually ran out, *Don Otavio* had just been published and to my surprise was well received; very well though I say so. I had envisaged little beyond the Pride of Print; besides

Martha Gellhorn, a much looked-up friend of those days, had warned me that the book, if noticed at all, was more likely to be tepidly dismissed. (Martha cherished an enduring low regard for publishing.) When the cuttings arrived in fat envelopes through the slow Italian post bringing acceptance from the likes of Raymond Mortimer and *The Times*, I was as incredulous as I was pleased. All the same *Otavio* did not sell; the book had an unattractive cover, white, I seem to remember, with the photo of a cactus plant, and was full of my spelling mistakes in every available language. (Promotion, less vigorously pursued then, had certainly neither occurred to myself nor to Mr Gollancz in conjunction with me.) A few small royalty cheques did arrive and helped out for a while but there came other months – years – and the novel refused to be whipped along. Wisely perhaps, I remained unshaken by the preciousness of the situation. How we did manage to carry on, I can't quite follow now. Once we succeeded in getting a series of cookery pieces into an American magazine – the big French regional dishes: Choucroute Garnie, Bœuf à la Bourguignonne, Cassoulet – Evelyn did the writing, I the culinary step-by-step, unprofessional and impertinent since at this time we did not even have a proper oven for those exacting procedures. We got away with it – it was pre-Elizabeth David (just) and, more relevant to USA customs, pre-Julia Child; and we were hugely paid. (I *had* in fact cooked these classics more than once.) There were other critical times, other friends … Once Martha Gellhorn, in a most sensitive way, unprompted, unasked, lent me two hundred dollars purportedly coming from her mother, Mrs Gellhorn, a saintly woman from whom one could accept anything (Martha's ex-husbands went on adoring her).

By no means all of *A Legacy* was written in the Roman euphoria. I spent part of each year with my equal great love,

France. Holidays with another American friend, Esther
Murphy Arthur, an impressive Jeffersonian incarnation, the
fount of oratory and erudition, whose eccentricities dis-
guised a vulnerable and tender nature. She was the 'E' of the
long Mexican journey, my reluctant travel companion and
conversational butt. She lived in the 6ème Arrondissement,
rue Gît-le Cœur, where my half-sister sybaritically kept
house. There I wrote in an attic I fled to, my sister being
addicted to Radio Luxembourg. We enjoyed an amusing,
rather sociable life, and I often got stuck in Paris, no guid-
ing glimmer in the tunnel, hence half-despairing winter-
walks across the bridges and along the quays. Then there
was the summer month or longer in Provence, a few miles
inland from the Mediterranean. We stayed with Allanah
who by then lived there all year round. We led a sea-life of
long mornings, clear water, small boats, rock bays …
Afterwards I worked through the siesta hours, shuttered
again, invigorated by the unmoving heat. Here, one year –
already the third – the book had its worst hold-up. It was
well into midway: then all stood still. Two protagonists had
married and gone to live in Spain, very very unhappily, and
I had no idea of how to get them on or out again. Nothing
was happening. The story, if it existed, was veiled.

That autumn, back in Rome, I was beginning to write
with speed, the chiselling of words seemed to take care of
itself, at moments I was writing in the grip of deep emotion:
a passage would arise not out of memory or contrivance but
stream onto the page through sudden seeing and feeling.
Discernable to a reader? I wish I knew.

By December I had got very tired. It was then that Laura
Archera – eventually Laura Huxley, Aldous's second wife –
sprang into my existence with her voodoo. Aldous and
Maria had been to Rome early in the summer; it was Maria's
last time: she was already very ill and if we all knew this in
varying degrees, it was not spoken about. Laura Archera

was an Italian musician, quite young, who was practising her version of Ron Hubbard's 'Dianetics' in California. She, too, happened to be in Rome – the Huxleys very much liked her and Aldous's ever open mind was fascinated by her therapies. For some reason both he and Maria wished for Laura and myself to meet. This we did. On the tiles of our roof – 'Psychedelic', Aldous had said at first look, his tone half playful. Soon after I found myself, figuratively, on Laura's couch. I have never been quite clear as to the results. It should be recalled that at this stage of his life Aldous emanated an immense, benevolent, moral authority. However one might take his esoterics, if he suggested, one tended to fall in.

Around Christmas Laura Archera was in Italy again. On an impulse I drove up to Florence to see her for a few hours. It was a strange and emotional meeting, prompted, perhaps, by what was soon going to happen to Maria (Maria Huxley died the following February), an instinctive move towards a future. As I was leaving – early, to avoid the fogs of nightfall – Laura said that she had a pill for me which would help me to finish my book. It was a large pill, blue, transparent, wrapped in a piece of cotton wool. Not a drug, Laura said, a kind of vitamin, a potent one, its effect would carry me on for weeks. I was to take it slowly, quietly, sitting down with a bowl of something warm, soothing and substantial.

At home I told Evelyn and we were both a bit frightened. (I had never taken anything that could be remotely described as drug.) In the end we decided on porridge – we had found some oatmeal, not exactly indigenous to Italy – I sat with Evelyn standing beside me and, in a confused state of expectation and doubt, solemnly swallowed the pill. It was a very large pill. Nothing further happened that day.

Getting the last fifty pages onto paper went like skating. In January the book was done. It had to be typed once

more, polishing as I went. A laborious process. Then
Martha Gellhorn, on her way to England, took on the typescript and my future, enlightening me to the advisability of
acquiring an agent. Martha did not like the novel much, but
she did her best by it. She decided that it ought to go to
Weidenfeld, her meteor of the hour, and indeed persuaded
George to take it. Sonia Orwell, his influential reader then,
also didn't like it much. But Martha did her bulldozer. She
also got Elaine Greene to consent to be my agent. *That* was
a good decision. *Dear, dear* Elaine ... How she is missed
now. Here comes the sad awareness that nearly everyone I
mentioned is no longer with us. Elaine liked the novel;
thought it was not right for Weidenfeld and, transatlanticly
at least, got her way. So in due course young Bob Gottlieb
became my editor, I became his first autonomous editee, my
professional future became radically changed.

The year between delivery and publication was not a
happy one for me. Reactions ... I felt exhausted, then
depressed, sloth once more took over. I wanted to write
something, could not – did not. I was beginning to think
about leaving Rome – where I had moved to 'for good' in
1949 – there were various reasons and pressures. Evelyn,
too, facing emerging obligations, was planning towards a
return to New York. By the winter of 1956 I was more or
less living in London. In March *A Legacy* came out and fell
flat. Such reception as it had was mostly bewildered or
hostile or both. (The Critics on the *Third Programme* accused
me of having undertaken the book in order to get on to the
U – Non-U bandwagon. That hurt because nothing could
have been more stupidly off the mark.) George Weidenfeld
was in the midst of troubles of his own – wives and Cyril
Connolly – he gave me lunch at the Ritz on a bad day for
him and was openly sad. So we sat at that table by the door:
too downhearted to talk publishing. He, also, I believe
didn't like the novel over much. Notwithstanding, he

subsequently behaved very well towards me, extremely well when it came to our eventual parting – master-minded by Elaine Greene.

As I said, in England *A Legacy* seemed done for. Then chance took over. A friend in Paris lent a copy to Nancy Mitford; Nancy wrote to Evelyn Waugh, 'Do read this'. He did. 'I have written a tiny warm notice … for the *Spectator*', he wrote to Nancy. The notice, not tiny, and containing some reproaches – errors in Catholic dogma, too large a dose of Henry James – came to a judgment which I, ever self-doubtful, could not even have dreamed. Nothing that has been said about my work has given me so much pleasure. It has lasted me through life. 'I wondered …' Evelyn Waugh to Nancy, 'who this brilliant "Mrs Bedford" could be. A cosmopolitan military man, plainly, with a knowledge of parliamentary government and popular journalism, a dislike of Prussians, a liking for Jews, a belief that everyone speaks French in the home …' Well, I could happily put up with that identity. (Bar the military epithet.)

Part One

———

A HOUSE

I SPENT the first nine years of my life in Germany, bundled to and fro between two houses. One was outrageously large and ugly; the other was beautiful. They were a huge Wilhelminian town house in the old West of Berlin, built and inhabited by the parents of my father's first wife, and a small seventeenth-century château and park in the South, near the Vosges, bought for my father by my mother.

I was born, however, in a flat rented for the occasion in the suburb of Charlottenburg. My father and mother were living in Spain then (it was the beginning of this century); circumstances brought them to Berlin. My father's first parents-in-law, with whom he normally put up, were adverse to having any kind of bother underneath their roof; a nursing-home was not thought of. So a flat was fitted up, the main advantage of which seems to have been that it afforded space and access for their horses, neither of my parents liking the idea of the animals' being boarded out in some strange stable. A ramp from street level led to their quarters; these happened to be separated only by a thin wall from my mother's bedroom, and she later told me that she used to listen to their champing at night, and that she found it consoling.

The house in which I was not born was in Voss Strasse; it gave on to the back of the Imperial Chancellery and is, I believe, now destroyed.

There we all moved about three weeks after my birth.

My father's first wife had died young, leaving a small girl. The widower's continued position as a son of the

house, even after his marriage to my mother some ten
years later on, was not looked upon as anomalous by anyone concerned; his octogenarian hosts had formed the
habit of seeing him as a member of their family. Their
perceptions were not fine; and they were not struck by
the extension of their hospitality, on the same terms, to
my mother, her household and her child. Their name was
Merz. Arthur and Henrietta Merz. They were I believe
second cousins, and belonged by descent to the Jewish
upper-bourgeoisie of Berlin, the Oppenheims and Men-
delssohns and Simons, the dozen families or so whose
money still came in from banking and from trade, but
who also patronized and often practised the arts and
sciences, and whose houses, with their musical parties
and their pictures, had been oases in the Prussian capital
for the last hundred and twenty years. The Merz's were
direct and not remote descendants of Henrietta Merz, the
friend of Goethe and of Mirabeau, Schleiermacher and
the Humboldts, the woman who barely out of the ghetto
set up a salon where she received the translators of
Shakespeare with advice and the King of Prussia with
reserve. This celebrated lady had a tall figure and a greek
profile, a large circle, many lovers and an enormous
correspondence; like George Eliot, she spoke English,
German, French, Italian, Spanish, Latin, Greek and
Hebrew, and unlike George Eliot she could also read in
Swedish. No trace of this heredity survived in Grandmama and Grandpapa Merz, the name I was taught to
give them when I learnt to speak and the only one, I find,
I can now use with ease. They had no interests, tastes or
thoughts beyond their family and the comfort of their
persons. While members of what might have been their
world were dining to the sounds of Schubert and of
Haydn, endowing research and adding Corot land-

scapes to their Bouchers and the Delacroix, and some of them were buying their first Picasso, the Merz's were adding bell-pulls and thickening the upholstery. No music was heard at Voss Strasse outside the ball-room and the day nursery. They never travelled. They never went to the country. They never went anywhere, except to take a cure, and then they went in a private railway carriage, taking their own sheets.

They took no exercise and practised no sport; they kept no animals – except carriage horses – and none were allowed in the house. The caretaker couple kept a canary in their basement by the furnace, but no truffled nose had ever snuffed the still hot air upstairs, no padded paw had trod the Turkey pile, no tooth had gnawed, no claw ripped the mahogany and the plush, and there was a discreet mouse-trap set in every room. The Merz's had no friends, a word they seldom used; they saw no-one besides the family, the doctor and an occasional, usually slightly seedy, guest asked to occupy the fourteenth place at the table. They were never alone; when it wasn't the barber, it would be the manicure. Grandmama Merz had never taken a bath without the presence and assistance of her maid. They did not go to shops. Things were sent to them on approval, and people came to them for fittings. They never read. There was a smoking-room, and a billiard-room nobody used, but there was not so much as a courtesy library, and I cannot ever remember seeing a book about.

The only evidence of print on paper was a slender sheet, the *Kreuz Zeitung*, a Prussian daily long defunct and even then regarded as somewhat out of touch, a kind of limited *Morning Post* given over almost entirely to obituaries, marriages and births. Extracts from these were read to Grandpapa in the afternoon in the presence of his wife to whose attention items within her grasp would occasionally be brought. A middle-aged son—a real one unlike my father—who lived in the house often came in with a copy of the *Stock Exchange News*. In his younger days Grandpapa Merz had gone to board-meetings; now he still received at intervals the visit of a decent-looking individual who presented himself with a satchelful of papers to be signed, bank-notes and gold. This man was called the book-keeper. The money he brought was handed over to the butler, Gottlieb, who paid the wages and the house-keeping bills, had charge of his master and mistress's personal expenses, tipped my mother's cabs at the door and lent what were not always small sums to my half-sister. The banknotes were new. Money, like animals, was not hygienic, and no-one employed in the house was supposed to handle *used* notes. Thus everybody was paid straight off the press. The subsequent problem of change was not envisaged.

During the years when, intermittently, I lived with my nanny, my toys, and very much with myself, as a guest on an upper floor of the Merz's house, Grandpapa was turning ninety. He was a small, fraily made, dapper old gentleman, standing very straight and clean in a long old-fashioned coat and narrow, buff-coloured trousers. He had a smooth pink head, snow-white tufty side-whiskers and no beard, and a smooth pink unlined, almost polished, face. His feet were small, and his boots had stubby toes. He walked stiffly and slowly, but upright and without the help of stick or arm; and he spoke in a brief dry drawl, affecting the provincial accent and cab-driver's retort of the Berlin of his youth.

Grandmama Merz was a short bundle of a woman, all swaddled in stuffs and folds and flesh, stuck with brooches of rather grey diamonds, topped by an arrangement of rough grey hair. She had plump tranquil hands, and a waddling walk. Her face was a round, large, indeterminate expanse, not smooth like her husband's, though unlined for her age, with features that escaped attention and an expression that was at once querulous and placid. Her voice was a slow high quaver, and when she spoke it was not always certain whether she was addressing others or herself. She wore a dog-collar of pearls, a watch on a ribbon from her neck and a bunch of keys at her waist, and she saw the cook herself for half an hour every morning.

Grandmama had given up carriage exercise some twenty years ago; Grandpapa Merz still took his and kept up the diversions of his youth and middle-age to the extent of looking in at his club and of brightening his afternoons by the company of a shapely leg. This presented some difficulties to the family. Grandpapa was far too frail to be allowed out cavorting with the corps de ballet, and members of the corps de ballet at Voss Strasse were unthinkable. Where then could a shapely leg be found, this being literally the one perfection insisted on by the old gentleman. Certainly not in their own circle in which the acquaintance even of the younger relatives were past their seventh season at Marienbad. The answer was, in the Prussian aristocracy. Long, well-turned legs were natural to the ladies of that caste, and as a caste they were not well off. Thus a succession of stinted sisters of splendid cavalry brothers and thinly pensioned widows of line-regiment captains, long-limbed women of sparse figures and worn, closed, shiny faces, Fräulein von Bluchtenau, Fräulein von der Wahnenwitz,

Frau von Stein and Frau von Demuth, presented themselves at Voss Strasse after the luncheon nap to read the *Kreuz Zeitung* and to go for drives, clothed in plain, high blouses and long skirts that revealed sometimes the promise of a fine-made ankle. They were styled companions; and Grandmama used to shake her slow head at the turn-over. For none of these stiff women lasted long. The old gentleman had tried to push a bank-note under the garter of Fräulein zu der Hardeneck, and had called Frau von Kummer his little mouse. Gottlieb, who knew everything, saw to the successors.

"Young Reussleben owes everywhere," he announced at luncheon. Gottlieb took the initiative of speech whenever he felt like it. He was nearly seventy, and had entered the house fifty-five years ago as a boot-boy. He had a full, clean-shaven, florid face, small, shrewd blue eyes, and a bouncy senatorial bearing. He belonged to, and observed the conventions of, the Lutheran creed, and in this set the example to the servants of the house. "I understand he is being pressed by his tailor."

My father looked up. "Tailor?"

"Fasskessel & Muntmann, Herr Baron."

"Never heard of them," said my father, gently touching his coat.

"Expensive firm," said Friedrich, the son who lived in the house. "Much too good for poor lieutenants."

"What's too good?" said Grandmama Merz from the head of the table.

"Nothing, mama," said her son.

"The soufflé is dry."

My father cast about the table for someone to address. He had several subjects. He believed that fish should be whole and seen, not whipped into a soufflé, and he could not understand why a man should want to go to a

German tailor; he was also extremely polite. There were, besides the old couple and their son, Grand-uncle Emil and Cousin Markwald, two old gentlemen, one of them a hunchback and very sweet, who having lost or dissipated their own fortunes in their youth had come to live in the house some thirty years ago; and there were also my half-sister and her French governess. My mother seldom came down to luncheon, and nanny, who would not have understood a word of what was said, had hers on a tray upstairs. My father's look fell on me. I may have been four or five. He gave a slight cough.

"You see," he said evenly, "it is not that you cannot find a good man for boots in this country."

"Five sisters, sir," said Gottlieb. "Two of them grown-up. We might try the eldest."

"What's that?" said Grandmama.

It was explained to her.

"Isn't Fräulein What's-her-name coming today?"

"Fräulein von Kalkenrath has chosen to leave us, ma'am," said Gottlieb, sounding every syllable.

"Very inconsiderate," said Grandmama, her face on her plate.

"A change may not always be unwelcome, ma'am."

"I don't want a change," she said on a higher note.

"Did you say the elder sister?" said her husband, who had been following.

"I understand the younger has a limp, sir."

"All the same to us," said Grandmama.

"If I may be permitted to point out, ma'am," said Gottlieb in his ringing voice, "a lady steady in the leg would be of more use to Herr Geheimrat on his outings."

"That will do, Gottlieb," said Friedrich.

"I was only explaining our problem to Frau Geheimrat, sir."

My father raised his head with an expression of controlled despair. He was at once delicate and worldly, and much affected by lapses that were neither. He picked up his fork, stared at it, and put it down almost at once, reminded that he did not like the design and that Gottlieb, in his opinion, overdid the silver.

*   *   *   *   *

The old Merz's had not been happy in their children. Both daughters died of consumption in their twenties. These pretty, pampered girls were struck one after the other in the same year. Each went through a brief marriage. Their deaths made an impression in Berlin—the old Merz's had always been regarded as something apart from human kind: the loss of the daughters was invested with almost mythological significance and it was not forgotten in anyone's life-time. The girls who died had been called Melanie and Flora, and their names were not mentioned in their home.

The second son, Friedrich, was a leather-faced, idle bureaucrat of fifty-eight or nine, of whom it was said that he put by half his allowance and all his pay each year. He was supposed to have been a dull boy but a good son. He had been to a couple of universities, sat for his exams, and in due course entered the judicial branch of the Prussian civil service. He ruined his career by meeting a Frenchwoman, who though presentable was not respectable. One of the counts against her was that in an age of rubber tubs she travelled with a silver bidet. The old people put their foot down. They managed to prevent marriage, but they prevented nothing else. Friedrich brought the lady to Berlin; his parents finally regularized the position by setting her up in a hat-shop. I do not believe that Jeanne, as we came to call her, had any particular disposition for the trimming or selling of hats, but the provision was one regarded suitable for all Frenchwomen of not entire virtue. Friedrich went on living at home. His advancement, however, was compromised, and he continued into late middle-age in a junior and unexacting post at a Berlin tribunal. Jeanne was not received at Voss Strasse. Other houses opened to her; and as the years went on and the rumour of her being amusing as well as agreeable spread, younger members of the family began to seek her out. From an alien and faintly scandalous presence, Jeanne, in forty years, came to be looked upon in the town as a paragon of constancy, a victim of parental power, the representative of a more graceful world and an ornament at a dinner-party. When at last I was allowed to see her, she had blue-white hair extremely well done, kind eyes, and talked with an animation that lit up the surroundings. Her own clothes, like the hats she sold, were Paris, but a different Paris as my father said, who knew. Friedrich married her the day after his mother's funeral.

The eldest son, Eduard Merz, once the envy and model of the bloods, was a Clubman, a rake, a gambler, and at sixty a bankrupt and a by-word in Berlin. In the Eighties and Nineties his debts had been paid eleven times by his father and three times by his wife. She was Sarah Genz-Kastell of Frankfort, one of the aniline heiresses, a tall, cool, worldly, clear-brained woman, elegant rather than beautiful, who had complete *tenu* and a good deal of character. Her manner was not ungracious, but it was nothing more; she was neither sentimental nor expansive, and she could sometimes speak with a sting. Sarah was disliked and feared at Voss Strasse, and one might see her with their eyes, not seeing what met hers. It had been a love match, and she had been wearied by the dribble of flimsy infidelities as well as the inroads made on even their combined fortunes by her husband's glib irresponsibility. Every time Edu was caught up with he gave his word not to touch another card again. It used to be his word of honour, later they made him write it down. On the last occasion Sarah paid what there was to pay, then set out to protect the future of her children, indeed her own old age, by pressing through a legal separation of their property. She made an allowance to her husband which added to his salary as director in his father's firm, and she made it clear that he was not expected to contribute to their joint expenses. In fact, she made everything very clear; she stated the course she meant to take in a letter to her father-in-law, and warned her husband in detail as to what to expect in the event of his getting into debt again. She also offered him a divorce. Edu was put out. Then she published a notice declaring herself not responsible for her husband's future liabilities. A chill went through the clubs. Edu cried reform. Voss Strasse was outraged. Sarah disclosed the sums involved in the last clearance to Friedrich, who conveyed them to his father.

These were not easily met again, and the old Gentleman sat up.

"The lout's going to ruin us," he said.

"As Frau Eduard has already pointed out, sir," said Gottlieb who was present.

"Stick of money. Has he got something to show for it?"

"No, papa."

"Whist, I suppose."

"Not whist, papa."

"Well, some fool game. Good money out of the window. Daresay it's in the family. Look at your Uncle Emil. Wake up, Emil!" His brother-in-law, who was fifteen years younger and neither deaf nor napping, looked up. "Edu's lost more at the tables than you ever had a chance to spit at."

"Poor Sarah," said Emil, who was a nice man.

"Sarah is a rich woman," said Cousin Markwald, who was neither.

"*Well,* she forked it out. How much did you say it was?" said Grandpapa who knew, but wished to hear again.

Friedrich named a figure.

"Round," said Grandpapa.

"Has poor Edu been losing again?" said Grandmama. "He's always such bad luck. I'm sure they swindle him."

"*Him,*" said Cousin Markwald.

"The results do not point to *that* conclusion, sir."

"Well, yes, mama, I think the money-lenders take him in. It's hardly conceivable otherwise; no-one could stake so much in cold blood."

"I never heard of *anyone* staking in cold blood," said Emil.

"Money-lenders?" said Grandmama. "What should the poor boy want to borrow money for?"

"Has *my* son been to the money-lenders?" said the old gentleman, really stung. "I'm going to cut him off. Who does the fool think he is, a Goy?"

"Everybody goes to them nowadays, papa," said Friedrich.

"It does sound degenerate of us," said Emil.

Six months later Edu said to his wife, "I say, Sarah, you wouldn't let me draw the next quarter of my allowance now?"

"I'm afraid not, Edu."

"I wish you would you know. Just this once. You see credit's awfully sticky these days."

"Credit?"

"It's these damned notices of yours. Everybody seems to take them seriously. It takes me all day to raise a couple of hundreds, even at forty per cent."

"I see."

"Oh very well . . But I wish you were a bit more reasonable. Never does to keep a chap too short. Don't say you weren't warned."

Edu went to his mother, who directed Gottlieb to supply him out of household funds.

Edu Merz's values, manner and appearance ran very much to form. He wore an eye-glass, and he wore loose, tweedy, careless English clothes, and he had a tall, loose-limbed, slightly stooping body and a lined face with features of the faintly simian strain that went through all the Merz's except Grandpapa. He made clever women feel dowdy, and had a way with the others; and of course he never looked at one who was not pretty, and of course he was facile and arrogant and shallow, and of course he had charm. He always had a joke for me, and I used to stare at him from the bottom of the dinner-table with uncompromising distaste. My half-sister was devoted to him.

My mother once said that everything about Edu was impersonation: that his passion was not cards, but seeing himself at cards. She may have been right. It is certain that Edu adored his chosen personality; and its setting, in some measure, depended on his wife. Edu at race-meetings, at bachelor suppers, Edu with the duns, was one thing; Edu with Sarah was another, and as a couple they were something else again. Obviously their marriage was a failure, but that was something both were able to set aside, and if they had little else in common, they shared at least two things—a belief in the importance of society, and the habit of being rich. Both were at home in their time.

Edu was born in the same year as King Edward VII, and indeed he was lucky in his period as it allowed for the fulfilment of his second nature. For only by flourishing as he did in an era at once so friendly to the sons of jewish magnates and so unprejudiced about baccarat could he be what he was, and also be an Edwardian gentleman.

The life led by Edu and Sarah was a far cry from the congealed provincialism of Voss Strasse. The old Merz's dined at seven fifteen and had soup for lunch, the young Merz's were fashionable. They went to England a great deal, wintered on the Riviera, and Sarah went to Paris for her clothes, which was then neither usual nor approved of in Berlin. She also went, without Edu, to Florence and to Rome. They lived some ten miles out of town, in a large-windowed house built for Sarah by Hans Messel, and they entertained incessantly—sporting people, theatrical people, the Crown Prince, writers, critics; Sarah was accused of having long-haired friends, and pictures that might as well be looked at upside down.

At the same time the young Merz's went on doing their filial duties as they were seen, Edu calling on his mother every day, he and Sarah never failing to dine at Voss Strasse on a Sunday night.

Their children, two girls, went to boarding-school in England, to the horror of their grandparents who had heard that there was no steam heating in the bedrooms. Sarah was bringing up her girls in the *simple* way. They had no maid, did their own hair and went to cooking classes, and they were sent into Berlin for afternoon concerts and classical matinees on the public horse omnibus. Their mother ran the first electric brougham in town, and soon after bought a Delaunay-Belleville, but kept her coachman; Edu got himself a Minerva with a Belgian mechanic in the Nineties; his father continued to go about in a well-sprung landau drawn by two fat mares.

Edu scraped along for a few years. Two or three times he got into a hole and was helped out by his father; once he made a killing in roulette. Then, one night, he lost half a million marks in I O U s at the Herren Club. Within two days his other creditors closed in. Sarah did not pay. It could not have been easy. Grandpapa Merz cursed her, but did not pay either. Edu went bankrupt. He had to resign his directorship with Merz & Merz, and from all his clubs. He could not believe his fate. He promised sincere, complete and everlasting reform. When he grasped that what his wife had warned him of was true, that he could no longer enter the Rooms anywhere, he broke down.

Once more Sarah offered divorce. Once more Edu chose to stay. His mother sent for Sarah. The old lady was near tears. "Poor Edu tells me it's all up with him," she said. "Poor boy—so cold I hear, and very nasty food."

But she brightened at once on being told that her son still had the choice of two comfortable homes.

"They say Edu's bankrot, doesn't he have to go to prison?"

"Not any more, mama." The nature of modern bankruptcy was explained to her.

"Clink'd serve him right," said Grandpapa, who was at once furious with his son and delighted at his having come a cropper.

"He doesn't have to pay his bills?" said Grandmama.

"He can't."

"Sounds a very good idea to me. Why is he so upset about it?"

This, too, was explained to her, and from the standpoint of her son.

"Yes, yes . . Men like to go to these places. I don't see why Edu can't ask those people in and have a nice game of cards at home?" she said, foretelling, rather accurately, her son's future course.

Opinions as to Sarah's conduct differed. Germany in the early Nineteen-hundreds was a boom-country, and Berlin its capital. Standards of behaviour were fluid. Before union, the atmosphere and ways of living in the various parts and principalities had been regional and European; the changes afterwards were gradual and not complete. Except in Brandenburg. To that nucleus of Prussia, to that poor flat country of marshes and poor sandy soil and the city set among parade-grounds and sparse pines, to that border province of garrisons and unwieldy estates worked by Slav day-labourers and Huguenot artisans and ruled by the descendants of Teutonic

Knights, Bismarck's successful wars and the foundation
of the Empire brought at once a tide of big money, big
enterprise, big building, big ideas which blurred demar-
cations between castes, swelled military and domestic
discipline into Wagnerian displays and atrophied the
older traditions of economy, frugality and probity.
Trades-people were coining money, the middle-classes
were getting rich and the rich became opulent. The pay
of the bureaucracy remained lean, but its members were
puffed with self-importance. Sons of bankers entered
guard-regiments instead of their fathers' firms, and the
sons of brigadier generals resigned commissions in
favour of marriage to an actress or an heiress. Uniforms,
no longer the livery of duty, were worn like feathers, to
strut the owner and attract the eligible. Men still toiled,
but they also spent and glittered; women were still
expected to bring portions and mend socks, but they
often failed in the fulfilment of either of these expectations.

At the clubs some of the men said that Sarah Merz
was a mean hard bitch who could well afford to have
bailed poor Edu out; others said that no-one could
afford doing that for ever.

"She might have given him another chance though."

"Edu's had a good many."

"She ought to have put her foot down before. It was
paying up those other times that gave him ideas."

"When a woman's as rich as that she can't help giving
a man ideas."

"Odd, when you think of it, Edu falling for a clever
woman."

"Edu wouldn't know."

"He knew about Kastell Aniline."

"They all did that."

"Oh Edu was mad about Sarah."

"And Edu was no pauper either."

"Well he is one now."

"Yes. It hasn't turned out so well for Edu after all, has it?"

"It hasn't turned out well at all."

The older men said Edu was still snug enough. The house was Sarah's.

"And that allowance for pocket money."

"He couldn't—he's a bankrupt."

"Sarah could slip it to him."

"Not Sarah."

"No; I suppose not Sarah."

"She might at least have paid his card debts. Jolly uncomfortable for a man."

"Think of a woman being able to do that!"

"Has he still got that girl at the Lessing Theatre?"

"Her or another."

"Sarah can't have liked that part much."

"She can hardly like any of it."

"Oh it's a bad business any way you look at it."

"*A very bad business.*"

At the courts where Friedrich had his post they said, "Eduard Merz is in the receiver's hands. Shouldn't have thought to see that name on the bankruptcy lists."

"The old people must feel it."

"Feel is a strong word for that family."

"*There is money owing.*"

"Nobody had any business giving Merz credit."

"Not after the way his wife tied it all up."

"Yes, that was done quite properly—as far as that ever goes."

"Young Mrs. Merz took a great deal on herself."

"Any assets?"

"Only personal. Merz's got a motor."

"Not much prospect of a discharge!"

"Not a chance."

"Much the best thing for him."

"It'll look fishy though. If they go on living in that huge house of theirs—"

"*It will look damn fishy.*"

"Who acted for Mrs. Merz?"

"Benjamin & Bleibtreu. Her people's people."

"You can hear what the Socialists are going to say about it."

"Curious bankruptcy when you look at it—not an honest penny owed. All to usurers and old gamblers, and a few supper bills."

"Grist for the papers."

"Sort of thing does nobody any good."

"She ought to have paid up!"

"And *he*'d have them all in the gutter sooner or later."

"A wife can always be loyal and face the music."

"Not these Frankfort millionairesses, not the way they're brought up."

The people who came to Sarah's house said to each other, "She might have done it less publicly."

"This kind of thing can only be done in that way, or not at all."

"Then it cannot be done at all."
"It *is* one of those things."

The Kaiser was furious. He made a scene to Eulenburg. He said he was not going to have that sort of thing in Berlin among those sort of people. He said that for fifteen years he had tried to get rid of anti-semitism, he said those Kastells thought they owned the world; he said those debts would have to be paid.

But when the facts were put before him, he became furious with Edu. He would have him run out of the capital, he said, and how was he expected to put down gambling in the Guards while that kind of thing went on in civilian clubs. It became known that he meant to send a letter of sympathy to Grandpapa Merz, and everybody was all agog at the impending indiscretion until Bülow persuaded him to keep his oar out.

Edu's dentist bill happened to be owing. He and Sarah did not go to the same man. The lawyers told her that it would be fatal to meet any single liability. Sarah sent her protesting children to have their teeth seen to again. She was understood and the dentist sent her a comprehensive statement, which she paid.

At Voss Strasse as time passed and they realized that Edu was actually unable to put name to cheque or note, the sentiment was surprised relief. Of course when they remembered to think of it, they did not forgive Sarah. They also resented the gaps at the Sunday dinners, for the young Merz's had gone to live abroad. First they had tried a villa of theirs between Grasse and Nice, but the proximity of Monte Carlo made Edu too unhappy. A friendly yacht offered and bore him to less tempting shores. Sarah went to Paris. She asked my father to get her a flat and he found her one in the Avenue Rapp. Sarah sent the Henri II sideboards into storage, but said that the Louis XIII suite might do not at all badly with a picture she had an eye on; my father said that indeed he also did not like renaissance but what could one expect in these furnished places, and if really she was about to buy something, she had better have a look at a thirteenth-century relief of the Annunciation he had found, well he would not tell her where yet, and which he was sure came from Cluny. Sarah engaged the cook on my father's advice and bought the picture on her own. And it was in this flat, at a dinner-party, that my father met my mother.

Part Two

AUGUSTANS

Chapter One

JULIUS MARIA VON FELDEN was born about the middle of the last century in Baden, as second son of Augustus Matthias Joseph, Baron Felden, Freiherr zu Landeney, and after the continental custom inherited with his three brothers a version of the title and a portion of the estate. The family was old, landed, agreeably off without being in the least rich and of no particular distinction. At a period nearer to its origin it must have conformed no doubt to a tougher and a more acquisitive mould, and at least one Felden had been obliged to take part in a crusade, but for the last four centuries Feldens had looked after their land, diminishing rather than otherwise, filled diplomatic posts of a more decorative than political character and discharged functions at provincial courts. Yet they were neither backwoodsmen nor courtiers, but country gentlemen of cultured, if not general, interests. They drank hock and claret, but they also drank and knew how to make their own wine. They dabbled in the natural sciences; they enjoyed and contributed to those branches of the arts that increase the amenities of living–domestic architecture, instrument-making, horticulture. They were bored by the abstract, bored by letters, and their acceptance of thought was confined to thought about things. They liked new theories of acoustics, but turned from ones of government with suspicion and distaste. They played music like craftsmen, and made objects like artists. One went to Cremona; learnt; and became known as an amateur lute-builder. Some contributed to works of ornithology, some botanized. In their time several had experimented with alchemy, and my father's grandfather had been fascinated by steam. Physics held no terrors then and the laws of the universe were something a man might deal with pleasantly in a workshop set up behind the stables.

For an undilutedly Catholic family, few had entered the church, and of these most had remained country abbés. The French Revolution was still alive with them as a calamity, and of the Industrial one they were not aware. During the Napoleonic Wars they had favoured the Confederation of the Rhine, and though unenthusiastic about Buonaparte had fought a little on his side. No Felden, however, had borne arms as a profession since the Reformation, and not one was known to have borne them in a cause. They married their neighbours' daughters, they married women from Bavaria, from Piedmont, from the Tyrol, Lombardy, Alsace and France; looks were important in their choice, yet not once within the recorded memory of the Almanach de Gotha had they married outside the Catholic aristocracy. At the time of my father's birth, the language spoken in his family was French, the temper and setting of their lives retarded Eighteenth Century; their seat had always been in a warm corner of Baden, that mild bland rural country of meadows and trout-streams, small farms, low mountains and small towns; their home was Catholic Western Continental Europe, and the centre of their world was France. They ignored, despised, and later dreaded, Prussia; and they were strangers to the sea.

When I was born, Julius von Felden was already a man in his late fifties and his own parents, and their age, had

long been dead. I never knew my grandparents and I
never knew Landen, the house in which my father had
grown up. Yet something of the atmosphere of his youth
came through in his own person, and some of the facts I
learnt from talk. Not all of them. What my father chose
to remember was governed by his own sense of rele-
vancy, and his aim was to converse. He would have
preferred solitude, or rather a privacy of animals and
objets-d'art, yet thought it was incumbent on him to
spend a reasonable amount of his time—at dinner, perhaps—with his kind. His language was limited, he was
certainly not aware of words, but I believe that when he
spoke he saw what he had lived. From these set fragments, then, I knew the sheltered valley of Landen where
the apricots had ripened on the south wall every year; I
learnt the names of dogs and ducks and horses, and the
smells of seasons—of the scent that drifted across the
snow from where the sides of boar were smoked, of sweet
clouded wine drunk foaming off the press and stands at
sunrise immobile by a pond, of the tree that bore three-
hundred weight in plums and the swinging fall of rye
before the scythe. I learnt terms of bee-keeping and terms
of stag-driving; I learnt of clean straw, oats and clover,
of winter honey, walnuts and March wool, of the pig
killed at Michaelmas and Easter, and the hams baked
whole inside a loaf of bread; I learnt of demonstrations
held by travelling Mesmerists in the library, of quirks of
squires, discomfitures of tutors, and of the ruses employed by peacocks. Rural life under Julius's touch
emerged as composed as his own exquisitely turned-out
person and well-ordered day. I did not learn the name of
my father's mother, nor what the tutors had been supposed to teach; I learnt that at Landen they had dined at
exactly one hour after sunset and that my grandfather

(or was it *his* father?) explained this to his guests as a custom of the Romans; I learnt that Julius and his brothers rode any old how but were kept to be most particular about their dress when driving, that the boys were always given brandy and hot water when they came in from skating in the winter dusk, and that Johannes the third son had danced with a bear at a fair.

I learnt of the missal dropped by them from the choir of Karlsruhe Cathedral during high mass in order to prove Newton, and how in consequence they were all packed off for a term to the Jesuit Seminary where the Fathers had dined off hock, trout and hare, and the pupils had dined off soup. I learnt of holidays in summer with cousins in the Côte-d'Or, *en Bourgogne* my father called it, where he had been allowed to wax the furniture and given black currant syrup mixed in his white wine; I learnt that Cagliostro had once spent a night at Landen and was supposed to have left a secret; that Gustavus, the eldest (Julius never liked him), had a fine hand at water-colouring but disgusted the old Baron by not helping with the birds, persisting instead to paint in coats of arms; I learnt that the curé was asked to dinner once a year, on Saint Martin's Day, when they were served, in a length of courses, with two roast geese: one for the company, one for the curé, and how my grandfather *refusing* to speak German in his house except to tenants and domestics, and the curé *unable* to speak French, they had all had to get along in Latin; and I could taste the cakes that had no taste at all given to my father as a baby by the old Grand-Duchess of Baden, and it comes to me only now that she cannot well have been the same old lady, the Grand-Duchess Louisa, I was taken to in turn to have my head patted at the age of four.

Julius's mother died when he was a small boy. His

father did not re-marry, no female relative was called in and the house went on being run by an elderly major-domo. They were all taught early, Julius said, to order their own dinner. The boys, in fact, took their place at table at twelve, not as children but as sons of the house, drinking their wine and doing their share as hosts. They entertained their neighbours as little as possible. Baden, the old Baron said, had turned dowdy in the Sixties—the men dressed badly and the women were interested in nothing. Yet the house was always full; with scientists and travellers and collectors from all over Europe, with gentlemen of decided hobbies, with old beaux, with cousins and gourmets and the sons of the relics of the French Revolution, and there was always a warm welcome at Landen for quacks. In this household my father remained until he was seventeen years old.

Then he was asked to accompany a Prince of Baden of the same age on an educational tour. The rest of the suite consisted of the Prince's tutor Herr von L., one equerry, a courier and a valet, and they stayed away some years. They went to France where they were inscribed at the *Beaux-Arts* and Julius took lessons in furniture designing and began his lifelong siege of the *Hôtel des Ventes*, and met the women who pleased him among the *grandes cocottes* of the Second Empire. They went to Spain; to Portugal, and thence by sea to Italy. On Julius's insistence they went to Spanish Morocco, and on Herr von L.'s to Greece. They returned by way of Vienna, stayed at the Hofburg and the young men had their glimpse of the Empress Elizabeth. They did the usual things and saw the expected people. They sketched; looked at sights; went to dances. They hunted in the Guadarrama, were at Seville for Holy Week one year and at Venice for the Carnival the next; they called at the proper courts, had their fortunes told by a gypsy under the walls of the Alhambra and paid their respects at Rome; yet Julius's pursuits and will must have dominated the party, for they spent the best of their time looking at houses and browsing in antique shops. Julius always loved France, but he was swept off his feet by Spain. In Italy he knew already what he was looking for and found less of it; in Greece their travelling became more strenuous—he was enchanted by the ritual of Mediterranean living he found among goat-herds and fishermen, and hardly touched by anything else. He returned to Landen as a young man, with a lemur, some crates full of bric-a-brac, and a clear idea of how he wished to spend his life.

It was after 1870; the Franco-Prussian War had been fought while Julius was in Spain, Baden was now a part of Germany, and he found everything quite changed.

The Feldens, like many people in those parts, would have preferred to stay on as they were. They had not liked the idea of even a Southern-German Federation, and had it not meant giving up the monarchy they would not have minded being joined to France. The accomplished fact of a wholly German Union with and—worse—headed by Prussia in the wake of a French defeat in a gratuitous war, gave them a most unpleasant shock. No good would come of it, the old Baron said, and his tenants said the same; politics were an activity of plotters, of whom Bismarck was a fair example. They decided to wash their hands of the new Empire—it could not make any difference to themselves. And then all at once the most unlikely people were in uniform. Land values were going down and everything else became expensive. Anyone wanting the *quietest* post was asked for qualifications. Baron Felden believed himself on the brink of ruin; neighbours

came and badgered him about providing careers for his
four sons. He was seventy himself and, without realizing
it, had always done as he pleased; now they told him
one must swim with the times. There had never been
any talk of this kind at Landen; before his tour Julius
had wanted to be an amateur cabinet-maker and his
brother Johannes an animal trainer. The old man got
rattled and Johannes, at fifteen, was carted off to a cadet
corps to be made into an officer; Julius, who was too old
for this fate, was boarded with a crammer at Bonn to be
got through the new examinations for the Diplomatic
Service. The lemur died.

* * * * *

The old Baron's choice had not been wise. At any event
it was made too late. Johannes, rather unbelievably,
became a captain; my father never got beyond third
secretary, and at his chance resigned. But Johannes also
became simple and in due course the pivot of a *cause
célèbre*; Julius in most respects managed to fare better,
but the changes sprung on him gave him a distrust of
life and he adjusted himself with a twist that left him, too,
at odd angles with reality. He saw forces everywhere he
wished only to dodge, not understand, and existence
governed by a sequence of fortuitous blows. He had a
long run of successful elusion of what he feared, but he
believed it to be always at his heels, and his own great
talent for the grace of living was mined by that streak of
pessimism, gloom and caution which must have made
life seem to him such a precarious course, and life with
him so peculiar. One could never tell, he used to say, what
one might find upon returning from a journey. It was

most catching. And by his side, up on the box, about to turn into our drive, my heart too contracted and my hand stole to my forehead for a protective sign as we sat, my father and I, joggled, silent, trying each for himself to lay the vision of the house burnt to the ground.

The rigours of the Prussian cadet institutions were notorious and intentional. They were places where boys —the sons usually of military gentlemen, and sometimes from as young as nine—were left to spend seven or eight years in a formative atmosphere of organized hunger, brutality and spiritual deprivation. There they were drilled into rigidity on frosty mornings with small-arms, von Moltke, the Army Manual, Julius Caesar and the campaigns of Frederic the Great. Many died. Of dysentery or pneumonia in the infirmaries—no boy was sent, or after one experience would go, to these for less— of injuries, never reported, never mentioned, suffered in the dormitories after dark. The survivors were released at eighteen as career officers and defective human beings. Corps Benzheim on the Rhine, a recent foundation, was only newly Prussian but a good self-conscious copy of the originals. Johannes went out of his mind.

He could not have been less prepared. He, who in his ample home had always had a sunny bedroom to himself and his three large dogs, who had eaten fresh food brought in from their own farms, who had always been spoken to and been taught to speak with gentle courtesy to everyone, who had spent his days in the fields and his evenings round a polished table, Johannes, who had not even been a school-boy, but was shaped into an uncon- scious blend of fine animal, young gentleman and happy

child, was locked to sleep in a dormitory with forty
breathing humans, shouted at by corporals and prefects,
marched along corridors and dished-out slops in an
enamel mug. On his first night, at supper, he cried. As
the clatter of the refectory, the commands, the gaslight,
the fumes of thin soup and undrained greens broke in on
him, he burst into open tears. A Rousseau flavour still
lingered about Landen and the old gentlemen his father's
guests wept freely. Johannes did not know the century
had changed. He did not know, he could not know, what
tears meant at Benzheim. For an instant he was looked
upon with awe—this display of what no-one ever might
uncover could only be an enormous, an unimaginable
act of daring. Then they loathed him. The captain with
the game leg who was on surveillance limped by, eyes
averted. The word *later* went almost audibly through
everybody's mind. The head-boy of his table, a cadet of
seventeen, leant forward and stared at Johannes cold and
hard. The others followed. The faces of two or three
of the smaller boys began to work, one yelped out a
snicker. They subsided at once. Johannes, locked in his
home-sickness, lifted his childish streaming face, unseeing. Then there came a diversion: it was Thursday night,
and on Thursday night they were given meat-balls for
their supper. There were other meat days—Irish stew on
Wednesday at mid-day, beef-and-gravy for Sunday
dinner, all wolfed—but the Thursday meat-balls were the
big treat, the one good thing in all the week.

The story of Johannes's first evening at Benzheim was
a part of the experience of my childhood. I knew it at a
time when the turn of his affairs had made my father my
only companion and me the only company of his later

years. I was seven, then eight, then nine. By day I played alone; at night in a high-ceilinged room my father told a lighter version of his life, and I concealed my knowledge. Thus the memory of the boy who was a man and died before I was as much as born, and of the school I never saw, were part of the secret reality of my own past.

They called the meat-balls *klops*. An orderly went round and ladled out two grey pellets on each thick white plate. The cadets did not take up their forks. They tried not to look at the food, they tried not to look at each other; they did not know where to look. They did not know what to do with their hands. Then the prefect, *Stubenältester* was the unprepossessing term, went off like a firecracker. The sound was something like *Klawp/sah RHOWFF!* and it was an order. Twenty-three white china disks flew up, changed hands, whirled through the air, tilted on the same angle at the head, flew on—It was a dazzling manoeuvre, executed like a variety turn. Johannes sat up, friendly and captivated.

The prefect rapped *RrrrhALT!* and the plates grounded smoothly. There was a plate once more in front of every boy and about ten of them were empty; and there was now before the prefect's place a neat mound of meat-balls. He shovelled, fast as fast, a *klops* at a time. The boys kept their poses. Then he put down the fork and cracked his sound. The plates circled; six more were cleared. They landed with Johannes's full one conspicuous in their middle.

"You there, pass up your plate," said the prefect. "And mind you know how to next week. Tonight you may take it up to me yourself."

Johannes did not budge.

"Did you hear me?" said the prefect. He did not speak, he shouted.

"Yes," said Johannes.

"Bring up your plate!"

"No," said Johannes.

The walls did not come down.

"Oh it isn't that I want to eat it," said Johannes. Then, fearing he'd been rude about the food in someone's house, he said, "You see, I'm not hungry," and began to weep again. Johannes's German was deplorable, full of wrong inflections and French words, and he spoke it with the buzzing slur of the Baden peasants.

The cadets acted sniggers.

Johannes turned to a boy of twelve, "Have mine," he said, "won't you?"

The boy recoiled but knew it was too late. He had looked at the new monster's plate; he was included in his doom.

"I am waiting," said the prefect.

"You had enough," said Johannes. "It is disgusting to eat up other people's dinners. They look as if they wanted them themselves."

There was a swell of embarrassment.

"Stand up when you speak to me," said the prefect.

"Pourquoi donc?" said Johannes.

"STAND UP."

"This is very silly," said Johannes.

There was a stiffening—the captain on the round stood by Johannes's chair. "Get up," he said.

Johannes got up.

"Name?"

"We already met, *Monsieur l'Officier,* you very kindly showed me upstairs this afternoon."

The captain was the physics master. The masters at

Benzheim were Army officers, and a tricky lot; men whose physique was too poor for soldiering and whose talents or connections had failed to get them a staff appointment. "Name?" the captain said.

"Johannes von Felden."

"Cadet von Felden," said the captain, leaning on his stick, "I must remind you, One: your *Stubenältester* is your immediate superior; Two: your display of civilian humour is out of place at Benzheim, and will not be tolerated."

"Do I have to do everything he tells me, sir?" said Johannes.

"You heard me. In future you will address me as *Herr Hauptmann.*"

"Yes, *Herr Hauptmann.*"

"We have had enough of your Yes's and No's, Cadet von Felden. The correct form is 'At your orders, *Herr Hauptmann.*' That is all. Cadets, you may finish your supper."

Johannes picked up his plate and took it to the head of the table. He put it before the prefect with a slight bow. "Monsieur vous me dégoutez," he said, and returned to his chair.

The prefect resumed command; the plates circulated—four untouched lots remained. As he chewed he pulled out his watch, laid it on the table, then went, *Faaahll/T TSOOH!* and the four boys before whom full plates happened to have come down, ate. It was forty seconds to go till grace, they had long finished their bread and mug of cocoa, and the wretched minced meat was stone cold.

That night in the dormitory they fell on him. They did

not have an easy time of it, for Johannes was very strong. In fact anywhere else, his strength, his innocence and his beauty—"ah, il etait b e a u", my father had once said—would have saved him. He fought like a beast at bay—he sprang, he charged, he bit; he clawed, he bucked; but no-one accused him of fighting like a girl, and what unnerved them most was the noise he made. He growled, he covered them with injurious French, "Çà, alors çà—çà c'est trop fort!" He howled in the dark from the top of his lungs, great loud forest howls of rage and pain, and they knew that silence during these affairs was of the essence. But at the end they were too many for him. He mauled them, but they mauled him badly; and when rather sooner though than they had meant they let him go, Johannes was in a pitiable state. He leapt on his bunk with a cry of, "Vous n'êtes qu'une bande de mal-élevés!" trembling with fury. And so outraged was he, so aching and incredulous that, overcome, he fell asleep at once, and for the first time perhaps at Benzheim a new boy went to bed on his first night without a thought of home.

Next morning he walked out.

He was waked by an enormous bell. He was so beaten up that he could hardly move and it was very cold. He followed the others—washed before a line of tin basins, got dressed as he was expected, joined the stampede downstairs for early roll-call. He stood in the yard with them, at attention in the March wind. When they re-formed for tramping in to prep he walked off. He just walked off. A couple of officers looked up, Johannes walked on. A sentry called a question, Johannes walked by—across the square, past the guard-house, through the gate, down the hill, into the town—

He did not last long. He was picked up a few hours later at an inn as he was trying to get them to let him have a meal and advance the money for a telegram home, and was rather impressively arrested. The town of course was out of bounds, though permission was usually given to spend an hour with a visiting relative. It was one of those quaint German market-towns, all scrape-and-bow and nook-and-beam, and the inhabitants were making quite a good thing out of the hungry cadets, yet their hearts were with the authorities and the band, and the streets were full of cake-shops, sausage-butchers and spies. Johannes's full intentions were not grasped. The charge was absence without leave, and as he was new, and probably a half-wit, they let it go at that. He was arraigned at roll-call, caned and locked up for forty-eight hours in a cell. When they let him out he sprang at the lieutenant and bit him through the uniform. He was hand-cuffed, tried, sentenced and locked up again. After that he became more tractable. As he could not spell and hardly write, they put him in the lowest form and he held himself very quiet. The small boys never managed to keep all the rules, they were always having something buttoned the wrong way or staying in bed ten seconds after bell or dropping the soap because their hands were cold, and they were always being punished, and among them Johannes was rather less conspicuous. Even so discretion was not his strong suit: he yet had much to learn. He betrayed himself into an argument—disinterested, as he was not slow—against the Benzheim custom of penalizing every day and on all occasions the boy who happened to be last in any move. Johannes though under-educated was rational and he was struck by the point that someone or

other *had* to be last through any door, and he pressed it.
And when at the fortnightly half-hour he was told to
write his letter home, he covered a copy-book page with
his laborious scrawl in utter confidence. One can imagine
what followed. Later the letter was put into a dossier and
the poor scrap survived.

Ce Dimanche 28 Mars 187 . . .

Cher Papa,
Je suis fort malheureux. Tous le monde ici est fou. Mes
camerades sont des méchant. Quand je suis parti ils mon
prit et j'ai fait de la prison. IL FAUT ENVOYER ME
CHERCHER TOUS DE SUITE je vous embrasse Em-
brassez pour moi Jules, Ursus et Ulysse, Zoro et le Petit
Gabriel

votre bien *malheureux*

Fils
Jean

All in all he was much in trouble. His reputation had
become bad and he was watched. And so it took him
several weeks before he got away again.

Julius meanwhile did not fare too badly at his crammer's. The work surprised and bored him—"at my age!"
—and there was rather an amount of it. Unlike his brother's, his hand was formed and ornamental; but like
Johannes's it was illegible, and like Johannes he had never
learnt to spell. He was also vexed by the necessity impressed upon him to become correct in German, pointing
out that as he was supposed to be sent en poste elsewhere
it would surely be more sensible to learn *languages*. There

were compensations. Bonn was not at the end of the
world, and there was an excellent train service. Every
week he spent a day or two in Holland or in Belgium,
looking at Bruges and Ghent, eating oysters at Amster-
dam, gutting antique shops, walking evening streets in
Brussels and water-fronts at Antwerp and Delft. He
looked: he picked up things: he learnt. It was still a time
of finds, and he developed an eye and a shrewd manner
with the dealers. At Liège he stalked a table for three
weeks. "*Quel dommage,*" cried the shopman, "*qu'un
homme si élégant puisse être aussi radin.*"

I did not hear much about the crammer and his
family, but I gathered they were amiable enough. Julius
charmed them into disposing of their furniture and letting
him install his acquisitions in their dining-room; and
they seem to have put up with his tame raven—no cage
—French bull-dog and the cat who as least likely to mind
town or climate had been chosen to go to Bonn with
Jules. And he persuaded them to keep geese. Such
intelligent animals, he never failed to say, so rewarding.
He was shocked by the crammer's food and asked leave
to accompany the maid to market. And there he went,
six foot one, booted, gloved and hatted like Apollo,
buying fish, teaching to choose vegetables. Still, grey
roasts continued to appear in baths of flour gravy,
potatoes were boiled without their jackets, the haricots
verts were *sliced* . . . Julius bought a spirit lamp; found
that he could cook; took over. The old Baron sent a man
from Landen every week with game, smoked meats,
proper bread, butter, pears; and he wrote advice.
Always consider Texture . . . Order Every Step before-
hand in your Mind . . . Make yourself master of the
Basic Culinary Processes, and you will be *free* to do Anything . . . My grandfather held decided views; in his

youth he had known and corresponded with the great
Chefs Cuisiniers of the Empire and the Bourbon Restaura-
tion, and he was the author of a slim brochure entitled,
Quelques Remarques sur la Théorie du Braisage des Mets,
which had been dedicated to Carême and which is a lucid
and still useful manual.

Of course Julius had money troubles. His board and
tuition were paid for him quarterly; he had a letter of
credit from his father—enough for a young man to live
on as he should, and it was presumed that he would run
up some bills. He kept a horse, brought from Landen,
and a trap, looked after by a boy also from Landen, who
was boarded at the crammer's too. A barber came to
shave Julius in the morning, and to brush his hair; a
local tailor pressed his suits, and his linen was looked
after by the women of the house. He saw to his own
boots. Julius did not squander, but his ordinary needs
were not cheap, and he certainly did not have enough
left over for starting a collection. If he knew about prices,
he knew nothing about finance: various people were
disposed to accommodate him and he made some rather
injudicious debts.

He sought no company at Bonn. When he was not
travelling he spent the evening playing piquet and bézique
with his crammer, to whom he had taught these games.
The crammer's idea had been that they might use the
time for study.

"After *dinner*?" said Julius.

The crammer, conscientiously, wrote to Landen.
The old Baron, who addressed him as *Monsieur le Précep-
teur,* sent a dozen of Madeira and a note to the effect that
his son was not an Encyclopaedist but an *homme du
monde,* books at night Unhealthy and Exaggerated, time
of no Moment, and instruction to be pursued at a

Rational pace. After this plea, probably unique in his career, the crammer appears to have settled down to a long stretch of geese-training, *haute cuisine,* period furniture and games of chance, with the rest of his establishment given over to the care of Julius's clothes. What happened to his standing with the University of Bonn, what was his treatment of his subsequent pupils, indeed whether he found any, I do not know. It was not the kind of question my father would have understood.

Julius's mould set early. His range and frame were already fixed at Bonn. In his own mind that period of his life became his student days, and in fact he had yet to accumulate that knowledge of the objects of five centuries, find scope to feed his tastes, acquire more things in more places with more means, increase his skills—but the tastes and skills remained the same. They were the lines that enclosed his nature and laid out the always repeated pattern of the coming years : the daily care spent on his person and its setting; the existence built with money, unease over money; the guards against intrusion; the trick of living in Germany as though it were a vacuum; the side-stepping of self and life through a hobby; the lack of curiosity about the human world, and the absence, remarkable in so young a man, of the need for general human company. Women were the exception—he was susceptible and at periods believed himself involved. But these loves were not windows, only entrances into another decorated room. He only liked and knew one kind, the polished, the well turned-out, the agreeable. He valued liveliness; vacuity was no requirement; in fact he disliked what he called *l'esprit lourd*, but there were

bounds, and nimbleness of mind was acceptable only
when balanced by a steady level of manners and good
temper. Indeed, his rue-de-Rivoli standards were high
and he never deviated from them even in marriage.
At that time, when women in their thirties were considered old, the finished manner was compatible with
youthful charms, and Julius enjoyed all the success he
could have wished for among a number of married
beauties of the age of twenty-nine.

Johannes's escape from Benzheim must have been a
feat. He broke out of the dormitory after lights-out,
avoided patrols, climbed a wall. When he was free, he
began to run and he ran all night. At morning he lay
low. He did not know much geography, but he was sure
that he knew his way home, and he also knew that he
must not take it. He suddenly knew a good deal. He knew
that they would be after him, and he knew where they
would look. He was dead certain determined that he must
not be taken, and on this he concentrated with ferocity.
He hid in a wood for the whole of the first day; after dark
he started out towards the North. It was as much in the
opposite direction of Landen as he knew to make it, and
he stuck to it for seven nights. He had no money. He got
a tramp to let him have his clothes; then dug a hole for
the uniform with his hands, his knife and stones. After
this he avoided roads and humans; he never let himself
be seen. At night he streaked through fields and vine-
yards; in daytime he crawled from cover to cover where
he could, but mostly he lay still. It was an animated
region and people were about their work all day.
Johannes knew that he must sleep lightly or not at all, and

D

at once he learnt to sleep like a hare. Dogs and cows came
to snuff him in his hedge, but with these he knew how to
deal and they always walked off quietly. He did everything
with a purpose, and everything he did was right. He had
taken his watch and his knife with him, and the daguerreo-
type of his black dog Zoro—he left nothing he loved at
Benzheim—but he buried them with his uniform. Johannes had been a very open boy, now he lived like an
animal that is used to covering its tracks. Once he had a
shock: at morning he saw a river and a gabled town, and
he believed it was the Rhine. It was the fifth day, and of
course he had read his *Leather Stocking,* and he knew all
about walking in circles. It may or it may not have been
Benzheim; he never found out. But he was crazed with
panic and had to fight it—alone, without a hold, lying still
in grass; and that day exhausted his heart.

It was mid-April when Johannes had left Benzheim;
the days were often grey and wet, and the nights were
still quite cold. There was always ground-frost. The
tramp's boots would not have done, and Johannes's own,
unnecessarily perhaps, were buried; so first he walked on
socks and then he walked barefoot. He kept alive on
water. Sometimes he stole a little food. Eggs from farm-
house hens, beets and mangel from a barn, milk straight
from a goat. He tried to munch oats. There was nothing
edible yet in fields and orchards, and he never broke into
a larder. He had read in the Encyclopaedia at Landen
that man could live without food for twenty-seven days
provided he took plenty of water, and he had discussed
this riveting fact with his brothers. The Encyclopaedia
said that the subject would feel no actual hunger, and
Johannes, who didn't either, marvelled at such prescience
and it gave him confidence. All the same he was growing
weaker. He did not realize that the Encyclopaedia had

not assumed the subject to walk five-and-twenty miles a
night over rough roads.

He had been right. They were after him and with all
the apparatus of authority. How near he came to being
taken perhaps only his instinct knew. The Cologne
Constabulary drew a cordon round a twenty-mile radius
from Benzheim; the Country Police of Rhine-Hesse,
Württemberg and Baden were alerted; his description
circulated; Gendarmes patrolled the roads. They were
many; they used the means at their disposal; and they
could count on eager locals to help them in a man-hunt.
Against this mechanism Johannes set his solitary discipline. Two points were in his favour. The Cadet Corps
were not popular; atrocity stories were going round. A
cadet had been killed that winter by falling from an
upper-storey window at Lichterfelde where his comrades
had made him stand at attention on the ledge during a
freezing night. The Socialists, the Liberals, the yet not
very well-affected South were likely to pounce questions
at an opportunity. It was expedient, then, to keep an
escape quiet, above all not to let it leak into the papers;
and so, the eager locals' support could only be enlisted in a
round about way.

The Benzheim authorities also took one risk: confident that the boy would never reach them, they did not
inform his relatives.

The second point was the tendency of the Army mind
to follow past experience—they were still out-manœuvring
his last walk-out. Reports of what J. v. Felden was likely
to do were sent out to police captains. Instructions were
to look for an impudent and forward boy who would
throw his weight about at hotels, ask for what he wanted,

and speak in a thick Baden border accent mixed with French. All the same, this was not a wholly convincing character to the policing yokelry, and many a zealous *Wachtmeister* went about the countryside with his own ideas, asking farm-wives to keep an eye open for anything suspicious; and so indeed if Johannes had tried to help himself from somewhere to a sausage all might well have been up with him.

The tramp was never found; or did not talk.

On the eighth night Johannes changed his course to East. (He kept count of time, and he did this by biting notches in a stick.) It was dairy country now, cattle were already out at night, and he was able to get more milk. After four more days he turned at last south-west and risked a bee-line home.

He reached Landen on a Sunday afternoon in May. The old Baron, Julius, who was spending the week, and Gustavus were out driving. They saw a filthy matted figure rise before them from the ground. They did not recognize him, nor did the spaniel who was with them.

And then that ragged skeleton threw himself into the tilbury with a howl.

"Prenez garde au vernis," cried the old Baron. And then they knew it was Johannes.

But they could not believe it.

Johannes embraced them, and they were stunned.

"Mon Dieu, mon fils," said the old Baron, "qu'est-ce que cela peut bien dire?"

They really did have Tokay Essence at Landen, and they brought it up for Johannes. The cork bore the stamp of a year in the Eighteenth Century, and a spoonful of it appears to have had all the effect attributed to that fabled elixir. And when Johannes had had a bath and been put into clean linen, eaten a hot-house peach and drunk another nip of the reviving wine, the old Baron became indignant and affectionate. He clucked and tutted at Johannes's tale—Pas possible . . . Est-ce conceivable? Pensez-donc! Quel endroit sauvage—and Johannes told it freely. He still spoke then. Except for his appalling physical condition, he did not seem changed; he was himself. He babbled, he complained, he talked of Benzheim with simple indignation. Yet certain scenes he re-enacted for Julius every day. Julius and Johannes had been most close for years, as Gustavus was a stick and Gabriel a baby. Perhaps none of them was able to follow all; much of it must have been outside the grasp of Johannes's father who was getting old, and the range of Gustavus's sympathy who was growing up a pedant. The old Baron was put out by Johannes having what he called thrown away his watch; burial he rejected as dramatic.

"Such a *good* watch," he said every time he was reminded. "Your own grandfather made it, *so* exaggerated."

But Gabriel, who was twelve then, had nightmares about Benzheim; and on Julius, threatened as he felt himself, something of what Johannes had met with impressed itself for life. There was enough to upset them all. The old Baron got very angry with Benzheim—he said it was a great shame, a great pity, Johannes must have beef-tea every day, and the episode was closed. Julius stayed on at Landen for the time being and Johannes made a quick recovery.

Chapter Two

THEN several kinds of forces began to move all at once. They were not directly interested in Johannes; he was discounted and at the same time a factor in their calculations, and they crushed him. Gustavus had been trying to get engaged all that spring, and a week after Johannes's return he succeeded.

"Whatever next?" said the old Baron. "Quelle folie encore?"

Gustavus said he had the privilege of being accepted.

"By that young woman?"

"Indeed, papa."

"You *asked* her?"

"Well yes, papa. When I had her father's permission."

"How very rash. Well, you shall not have mine. At *your* age. You are much too young. How old are you?"

"Twenty-three in August."

"There you are! Who ever heard of a man marrying at twenty-three. Best years of his life. I did not. Your grandfather did not. Your Uncle Xavier did not. Jules a sa maitresse près de Namur. Une femme très bien. Why, I was fifty before I set eyes on your mother."

"You were married at forty-eight, papa."

"Quite. Nearly fifty. You *see?*"

It was true. The Feldens were susceptible, but prudent. They liked to live single and they liked to leave children, and few of them lived very old. So they married late and died soon. There were barely two generations of them to a century, and no Felden child had ever known its grandfather. Gustavus might have pointed out the

questionable wisdom of directing sons from the brink of
dotage; what he said was, "Things were different then,
papa, and I love Clara."

"Bien sûr. Tout le monde connait ce sentiment.
Pourtant ce n'est point une femme aimable. Et lorsqu'elle
aura trente ans elle sera fort laide. Et puis c'est une
dévote . . ."

"She's a saint!"

"Eh bien! cela te fera une jolie épouse. If you want
someone to drag you to mass seven days a week, engage
a chaplain. I see no reason for you to leave your home
now that I am old and have my experiments and my
correspondence and cannot be expected to think about
the harvest and those rascals my tenants and count every
cart of hay. None of you seem to know when you are
well off. Look at Jean."

"But papa, I'm not thinking of leaving home. We will
all live here. Clara thinks she would like to start a
school—"

"Ah pas de bonnes œuvres—surtout pas de bonnes
œuvres!"

"Clara says, the village needs—"

"Bring her *here*?" The old Baron pulled himself together. "Quite impossible. The house is too small. And
what would she do with herself? She cannot sit with us
at night. I daresay she would want your mother's drawing-room opened, and she would be very dull. No, no,
no, all quite impracticable . . . And believe me, no good
will come of marrying people like that. Mais oui, c'est un
beau nom. Mais le tien l'est aussi. Et si aujourd'hui il a un
peu moins d'éclat, c'est que depuis des siècles nous
avons bien mangé et vécu heureux! Le vieux Bernin a
toujours eu quelque chat à fouetter. Pire qu'un cardinal.
C'est presqu'un ambitieux."

"But Clara is an angel."

"No doubt."

The old Baron spluttered on for days. He complained to Julius, nattered to the major-domo, poured out letters. Gustavus sulked. He was disappointed by his father's reception of his news, but what he really minded was the attitude of the Bernins themselves, which was reserved. There was little they could decently take exception to in the engagement, and there was nothing to please them. It upset long laid lines and in return offered a young man with no prepared career or overt worth, and a connection with one of the least forward-looking elements in the Grand Duchy. The fiancée's father, Count Bernin Sigmundshofen, was an extremely able, extremely active man, the leader of a powerful Catholic clique, the head of one of the great South German families, and a public figure. He was President of the *Landtag* and for many years had been the envoy of the Grand Duke Friedrich to the Holy See, yet the range of his activities lay well beyond the narrow scope of Baden. He was one of those men who are supposed to have a friend in every chancellery, and he certainly had a relative in many; not only Baron Felden accused him of ambition. He now seems to have been something else: a disinterested man with a cause. He was also a meddler by conviction, had immense experience of motives and affairs, and, alas for Johannes, considerable charm.

Count Bernin's ends were dedicated to the Church, or rather to the unity and eminence of Catholic Europe for which aim he saw her as the instrument. The Reformation stood for him as the root of present evil and he no more accepted the split of Christendom than my grandfather accepted the German Empire. Yet while my grandfather went about complaining loudly morning, day and night, the Count was a man who prided himself on his long-term view; and if he was, as he may well have been, a fanatic, he also had the gift of urbanity, and he was a practical politician. He, too, deplored the new Germany, but he had seen it coming, and as the next step proposed to fight it from within. It could not have been a happy moment for dreaming of a *Pax Catholica*. For one thing there was no Catholic power. France was anti-clerical and defeated, Spain neutral, Italy not united, Austria embroiled with Slavs and Sultans and about to fall apart. Moreover the alliances of these decades—with Russia, with England, with Turkey, with Japan—were sought not on lines of denominational concordance but for purposes of colonial expansion, territorial adjustments and condoned aggression: to allay and inspire fears. Count Bernin, well aware, contended that given these facts, and given also the ineptitude of the Wittelsbachs, the dotage of the Hapsburgs and the push of Prussia, the lines for the politically amorphous German South and its slumbering nobility were laid; it must revitalize, take up its part, shoulder the Catholic burden and become dominant in Germany, the bridge to France, a link with Rome and one day perhaps the corner-stone of the Apostolic Hegemony of Europe. So Count Bernin went from country house to committee room, hinting, consulting, expounding, talking of profits and preferments and the dangers of being left behind, prodding lazy prelates, flattering supine civil-servants and lethargic land-owners into visions of their own importance, urging friends and colleagues to take office, bid for office, groom their sons for office. First one must beat the Prussians at their own game, he argued. They were making up at present to the South—very well then, one must take their plums. Let us become efficient; let us use that Prussian foible for the military: Bavaria, Württemberg and Baden had some excellent regiments full of uniforms and traditions—Let us send our sons to sparkle in the Guards.

Count Bernin was a rich man. Clara was his only daughter. She was then a woman in her mid-twenties who showed signs of character and integrity, and more than signs of will. She had great piety, and combined a staunch and simple orthodoxy of Catholic creed with a righteous line of conduct that seemed positively Protestant. She was long and spare, and was not, but seemed, taller than Gustavus, with features that were good and would become better with a more accordant age. Her clothes neither intended nor attracted notice. She had beautiful hands, and for the taste of the period not quite enough hair.

Her mother was dead; her brother was a papal chamberlain. Her father had found it necessary to impress upon her early that her duty lay in labouring the vineyard wherever it was most lacking, in short, that in the present century her call was in the world. As the years passed and Clara took no step towards that tiresome vocation, Count Bernin became more specific. He began to speak of the young man—young for his career—who was already Under-Secretary for Foreign Affairs, and in case his daughter's aversion to marriage to a Lutheran could not be overcome, he also mentioned the Catholic widower who had just been appointed to the brand-new Governorship of Alsace-Lorraine. Then Clara spoke of Gustavus...

Gustavus, at twenty-three, was certainly in love with Clara. Perhaps it became him. Like everybody else he must have had youthful and immortal longings. So far he had had his family's easy way with women, and now he was discovering something else. He believed to be conquering virtue herself, and to attain it too. It is always a pleasing prospect. Even the worst of us would like to change, like at least to think—and talk—of becoming better; the attentions of our reformers are so flattering, and at no other time is the ascending path tripped so lightly as when we are in love. Clara von Bernin, who was so unbending, who when sent by her father to a dance would not dance but prayed, almost audibly, for those present, who did not speak to and seldom was approached by the men of her own age, unbent to Gustavus. She gave him the confidence of seriousness; she spoke with almost *amused* forbearance of what she called his pagan upbringing; the old Baron was a good man, she said, at least at heart—there were many ways of pleasing God. Though for Gustavus there was something finer; she spoke of his immortal soul which nobody had mentioned since the lower catechism. She spoke of what together they might do: for Landen, for salvation, for the poor. Purpose. Elevation. Infinity. It was magnifying, it was heady; it was new. And it was also clear that it was brought about because Clara von Bernin Sigmundshofen found him irresistible as a man. There was something else. Gustavus wanted to get away. Gustavus had never quite belonged to Landen: he often worried about the neighbours, and now he began to see his family in a new light. He did not really seek the Power and the Glory, but nor, like his father, did he wish to *vivre heureux*; he wanted to be respectable. He had the soul of a modern bourgeois, and a niche should have been found for him in a bank. So it was a rather pathetic form of poetic justice that he should have sought to make his escape from nonconformity into the fire of Clara's rigorism and the high politics of Count Bernin. For the present, he was in love with the glass held up to him by Clara, passably attracted by the improbable conquest of her person, puffed above his brothers, and he did love her *beau nom*.

As for Clara! Who can tell? What did she make of it? What did she make of herself? Her contemporaries were surprised when she did not take the veil; I knew her only in old age, and near seventy, in harsh black, upright as a pole, with luminous eyes and a face both tranquil and ravaged, she still appeared the least secular of women. She must have loved Gustavus. It is not imaginable. To me who saw her as the one figure of my childhood who never changed her mind, who did not think of herself, who always was the same, who acted in everything for reasons totally different from those of anybody else, and always could be counted on to act, who always censored, never yielded, never bent to humour, temper, self-interest or circumstance, it is incredible that this tower, this dreaded and derided rock from whom my mother even could not strike a smile, should have been animated once by the most fallible of human emotions. That she gave way to it is not conceivable. And yet she did.

Whatever may have moved Clara proved powerful enough to move Count Bernin. Against her wasteful project, he lined up principles and influences—filial obedience, the duties of the militant, mortification of the will; and priests. Priests calling, priests to stay; priests in conclave in the library, priests casual after tea, priests in the confessional. But there Count Bernin was handicapped, for Clara's confessor, one might have known it, was a latter-day Jansenist. And this good man, Father Martin, looked upon the Count's plan of marriage to a heretical cabinet minister with as much distaste as Clara did herself. The campaign went on all winter and well into the spring, and throughout it they were always on the thin ice of Clara's possible vocation. Clara remained

composed: the alliance, she maintained, was irreproachable. And there of course she had him. For the Feldens by
the standards of their common world were that. They
were one of the oldest families in Baden and their
quarterings at least proved them the purest of Catholics.
The old Baron was a great pet at Court. The people liked
their ways, and they were without knowing it much
loved. In fact they were exactly what Count Bernin
appeared to stand for. Landen was rather mortgaged, but
then few people in Baden, except indeed the Bernins,
were really rich. The boys' looks were considered roman-
tic, and the attachment between Clara and Gustavus was
already being talked about with sentiment. The old
Baron might appear eccentric and old-fashioned, but
however much Count Bernin deplored his lack of public
spirit or was irritated by the shiftless, obstinate, private
way in which the old man went on ordering his life, he
saw that this would not be seen good reason for stopping
the engagement of a daughter to one of the four well-
grown sons of a country gentleman, a less fortuned equal
and a neighbour. If there was one thing Bernin disliked,
it was to show his hand.

Meanwhile the Governor of Alsace was doing very
well without Clara's promptings; Count Bernin daily
found it harder to believe that his daughter ever could
be made to fit serviceably into his plans; at last, wearily
in May, he gave a temporizing consent to Clara's engagement to Gustavus.

They called at Landen. While the young couple walked
about the grounds, the old Baron saw Count Bernin in the
library. In age, their difference was a bare ten years, but
Baron Felden liked to pretend that he was eighty. They
were amiable. The old Baron could never resist the
attractions of his own hospitality; he might rail against

impending guests for hours, but on arrival covered them
with vintage Oloroso and Havanas. Bernin could make
himself appear as aimless as his host. They talked. Of
bird migration and the badness of the times, of a neighbour, old Countess Frassen who had just been convicted
by the new busy-bodies of selling watered wine and
carted off to the county gaol.

"Such interference," said the old Baron.

"An unfortunate incident," said Count Bernin.

"Ah yes," said the old Baron, "watering wine—a great
mistake."

He showed his guest a boat which Gabriel had rigged
inside a bottle and asked him what he thought of the
processes of Monsieur Pasteur. He was at ease to see that
Bernin's enthusiasm for the engagement was no greater
than his own. The Count saw this too, and a deal besides.

In the middle of this visit my grandfather was called
away to see a cow. He happened to be the most competent
veterinary surgeon in three counties and his tenants insisted on his attending their every confinement.

Julius appeared, decorative, composed, and offered to
do the round.

To people's boredom and surprise Count Bernin
talked to them of economics. He foresaw much social
unrest. The North being embarrassed, he told them,
by insuperable problems of expanding industries and low
land-wages, an *ostentatiously* contented rural population
should be nursed in the agrarian South. The idea was not
popular among the Count's landed friends. As he strolled
about his neighbour's grounds, he felt particularly irritated by the fact that the old Baron did in some way
manage to have one of the best run farms in Baden, even
if there were not many profits, and that his tenants

appeared to be better off and better looked after than anywhere else in Germany.

He tried to convey something of this to Julius.

"My father likes them to eat well," said Julius. "He tells them it is foolish to sell their veal and vegetables and dine off dumplings and fried potatoes."

The Count touched on other aspects of the question.

Julius listened with politeness, concealing rather well incomprehension and complete non-interest.

Count Bernin's mind began to work. "Twenty? You said you were?"

He drew Julius out about his prospects and intentions. Count Bernin was very good about this.

So was Julius. He answered with perfect grace, telling nothing.

Count Bernin took this in, too. "And there are four of you?" he said. "Four sons!"

The evenings were still chilly. Julius suggested they would find a fire in the smoking-room.

It was precisely at this moment that the Benzheim authorities, through the War Office, chose to break the news of Johannes's disappearance to his father. The boy had been gone five weeks and must be either dead or overseas. They were not in an enviable position, and they had settled to be straight about it. The War Office was staffed by old-fashioned Prussians who exacted all kinds of enormities from others and themselves; they were able to keep their mouths shut, but like their old Emperor Wilhelm they did not approve of lies. They decided to tell Baron Felden the grounds of public expediency for the sake of which he had not been notified, to admit their mistake and ask him to view the case not as a father but as a German patriot and a member of the ruling caste. The appeal was never made to the old Baron, for it was

Count Bernin who on returning with Julius from the home-farm found Major von Grautkopf, helmet and white gloves in hand, standing waiting in the hall.

"Sir—it is my duty to inform you of some very serious news," said the Major.

"Sir?" said Count Bernin.

The calf was dead, they hoped to pull through the cow. The old Baron had forgotten all about Count Bernin. On his return he found him in possession, and a man in uniform shouting in the hall.

The Major turned on him at once.

"I understand the boy is here!"

"What?" said the old Baron, "what?"

"We were not informed."

"The omission appears to have been mutual," said Count Bernin.

"The boy must be ordered to get ready at once."

"What can you mean?" said the Baron. "Jules, tu as l'air décoiffé."

Julius, in fact, looked five years younger. "Papa, they want to take Jean back to Benzheim."

"*What?*" said the Baron.

"Now, if I might explain," said Count Bernin. It was the first time he had heard of the affair, but in the last half-hour he had listened to rather more than he should. "This gentleman—"

"Von Grautkopf," said the Major.

"Major von Grautkopf has come all the way from Berlin."

"By train?" said the Baron. "Very uncomfortable journey. Not that I've ever been there."

"I do not think—" said the Major.

"All the way from Berlin," said Count Bernin, "on the assumption—"

"He came to tell that Jean was dead," said Julius.

Count Bernin had indeed allowed the Major to proceed this length. The Major was furious.

"Un fou," said the Baron.

"He naturally feels—" said Count Bernin.

"Where is the boy?" said the Major.

"I don't think you quite appreciate the situation," said Count Bernin. The Count, too, and it must be remembered under Julius's eye, had had a difficult time of it.

Slower than his neighbour, grasp came to the old Baron only then. He turned on the Major. "Monsieur l'Officier—this is an enormity. How dare you come here? How dare you reproach me for not having written to you about my son? My son was returned to me from your place three-quarters starved, unwashed—"

"But Baron—"

"And you have the impertinence to ask for him. I hope you'll lose *all* your pupils."

"Baron!"

"Nothing will be gained—" said Count Bernin.

"You would oblige me, Monsieur," said the old Baron, "by leaving my house."

The Major clicked, the old Baron bowed; the Major clicked to Count Bernin, Count Bernin also bowed and very nearly shrugged. Julius was with the helmet by the door.

"*Well,*" said the old Baron and sat down. "Well!"

Count Bernin said nothing.

Presently the old Baron said, "Where is Jean? Jean ought to have heard this. Jules, va chercher Jean. You

E

will stay to dinner, Bernin, won't you? You—and the young woman."

"Thank you. As a matter of fact I should like to meet your son Johannes. The boy must have an uncommon deal of pluck."

"C'est un brave cœur," said his father.

But Johannes could not be found.

All through dinner the old man fretted. Where was Jean? Why was Jean not here? So mal-élevé, so unnatural. Then, when it was time to get out the Bernins' horses, Johannes was reported hiding in the stables.

"How very odd," the old Baron said. "Gustavus, go and fetch him."

Gustavus was talking to Clara; but Gustavus went.

He came back alone.

"Where is your brother?"

"He won't come in."

"*He won't come in?*"

"Oh he's mad," said Gustavus and returned to the sofa.

Julius had gone too. "Papa: he is frightened."

"Nonsense!"

"Oh, is he?" said Count Bernin.

The old Baron went to see for himself, and they followed him. Johannes was discovered in a stall with his arms round a small bull. He was trembling all over and his black curls were matted with sweat.

" Jean," said his father, " Jean!"

Julius, Count Bernin, Clara and Gustavus, Gabriel and two grooms were standing in a semi-circle. Johannes looked through them with dilated eyes.

"Pull yourself together, Jean. Il y a du monde, voyons."

" Jean, please, say something," said Gabriel.

But Johannes only shook.

"Speak to us," said the old Baron.

Clara stepped forward. "Poor little boy," she said and tried to touch him.

Johannes shrank back and bared his teeth at her.

"Oh, do behave yourself, you little fool," said Gustavus and seized him by the collar.

Johannes wheeled and bit his hand.

"*Jean-*" said his father.

"Jean!" said Julius.

"Jean please—" said Gabriel and burst into tears.

The bull stood unmoved, licking his own muzzle.

"My dear, I could not be more sorry for this disgraceful scene," said Gustavus.

"Your *hand*, dearest?" said Clara.

Julius had fetched Zoro. The black dog came bouncing in—looked at his master—looked at the bull—looked at his master, and whimpered.

"Oh you silly," said Johannes and tumbled out of the stall; he threw himself upon the dog and broke into loud sobs.

"I believe the carriage is waiting," said Count Bernin.

Chapter Three

THEY had little peace that summer at Landen. First there was a terse communication from Benzheim.

Kommandantur
Kadettenanstalt Corps Benzheim
Benzheim am Rhein b/Köln
Königreich Preussen

Sein. Hochwohlgeboren   Den 23. 5. 187 . .
Baron Felden zu Landeney
Schloss Landen
Grossherzogtum Baden

Sehr geehrter Herr Baron!
  Durch Rapport des Major von Grautkopf erfahren wir soeben, dass der am sechzehnten ultimo vom Corps Benzheim entsprungene Zögling Kadett von Felden sich im elterlichen Hause befindet u. ersuchen wir Sie hiermit besagten Zögling unverzüglich in das Corps Benzheim einzuliefern.

Gehorsamst,
gez. von Köppen
Oberst u. Kommandant

"Quel. exécrable langage," said the old Baron and tossed the sheet to Julius.

"They say they were told by that major that Jean was at home and would we send him back at once."

"No doubt," said the old Baron, "no doubt. These people seem to have neither sense nor manners."

Benzheim received no answer, but their letter was

spoken of before Johannes; and Johannes, who had been behaving normally again, threw a kind of fit. The first time the old Baron had been shaken, and angry afterwards; now he was only angry. So exaggerated, such lack of *tenu*, had *everybody* gone out of their minds?

Then there was a telegram. Telegrams were rare at Landen. The old Baron had an ornithologist crony at Neuchâtel who was getting on.

"Voilà! on m'appelle au lit de mort de mon pauvre ami. Tout le monde s'en va . . ." He broke the seal with a trembling hand and when he saw the signature, *Benzheim Kommandantur,* he felt put upon, and accused Johannes of shattering his peace of mind. But Johannes was not there to hear; on sight of the messenger, he had made for the woods. Clara, on the other hand, was constantly at Landen. The old Baron began to take against his children. Puzzling notes of hand obviously signed by Julius began coming in: Julius was told it was high time he were at his books again, and he sped back to Bonn.

Johannes's lost watch also preyed on the old man's mind, and he conceived a bright idea. An advertisement. "We'll put it in the papers!"

"What does one say?" asked Gabriel.

" Jules?" But of course Julius was not there. "Oh, one just tells them what it is about, and they put it in."

So Gabriel took the trap into Breisach, where the *Manheimer Anzeiger* and the *Badische Landwirt* kept an office, and explained.

At the time Benzheim was consulting once more with the War Office. The War Office took another look at Major von Grautkopf's report, and Lieutenant-General von Schimmelpfennig wrote himself to his old acquaintance Count Bernin.

"*Lieber* Bernin—"

It was a discursive letter. It touched on the pleasant time spent during the negotiation of the Treaty of Gastein. How well the writer remembered, if he might say so, the *brilliant* resource, the *unfailing* tact, Bernin had shown in his mediation. The Schleswig Holstein Question! It seemed like yesterday. Eight years ago, was it now? *Tempus fugit*. Well—Germans all now. Certain difficulties still to be ironed out; the South did not always appear to *understand* . . . One of their native sons causing something of a small headache just now. Fellow appeared to have taken French leave from one of the new cadet corps. The father must be a neighbour of Bernin's—bit of a rough diamond, they heard.

Count Bernin's support could not always be had for the asking. Under a mass of civilities he returned a barbed question: what was the presence of one small boy at a military school to the German War Office?

The General now dropped Schleswig Holstein. The authorities at Benzheim, he wrote, were anxious about the effect of a, successful, escape on morale; the boy's flight was known to his fellow pupils, a number of whom were new, also, and from Southern families. If the boy were allowed to stay away, the fact might be damaging to the very framework of their educational ideology.

Count Bernin wrote back that he could see their point; but what exactly was he supposed to do about it?

The General's next letter was quite straightforward. The Corps were having trouble with some of their parents; Benzheim considered it essential that the boy should be returned before the summer break-up. Nothing could legally be done without the father's consent.

Pressure seemed not to meet the case— Would the offer of an Order? His Majesty was rather sparing with crosses for civilians. One might approach the King of Bavaria— Was old Felden likely, though, to insist on an Imperial decoration? Could Bernin suggest a line.

Count Bernin replied, truthfully, that his direct influence with his neighbour was nil. He did not tell, what he should have told at that point, that the Feldens were about to become more to him than that. He told the General not to bother about the Order, and he volunteered that Major von Grautkopf had been a mistake.

The General took the point. Yes, he wrote, yes, Major von Grautkopf . . . He appreciated Bernins frankness, but what *kind* of a man would he suggest?

Count Bernin wrote a description.

Captain Montclair, former Bavarian Military Attaché in Paris, was almost a dandy. His clothes were exquisite. The old Baron, to whom friends sent many people, felt guilty about not remembering a letter. "You *are* interested in barometers?" he said.

"Very much so," said his visitor.

Having thus placed him, the old Baron showed his own collection. "This one was designed by the Abbé Nollet; it has an interesting disposition of the Wheel. This one belonged to Lavoisier himself, poor man. The Spiral, now, such an advantage over the Column . . . What is your own opinion, Monsieur?"

"The round ones are not so pretty."

"You are so right," said the old Baron. "Nobody seems to know how to make a case any more. All the same, *without* the Spiral? How would you place your

Rods? Perhaps you prefer the Syphon? Surely you agree with our friend Mercier on the interaction of Moisture and Gravity? Allow me to make you a diagram. You have only got to think of the Pendulum Watch—"

Captain Montclair pounced upon this straw. "Talking of watches, I've been admiring yours, sir."

"What?" said the old Baron. "Oh that. That's no Pendulum Watch."

"No, no of course not, But it is beautiful."

"It is a *very good watch*," said the Baron. "My father made it. There were two of them. My rascal of a son lost the other. Threw it away; so unbalanced. He thought the Prussians were after him."

"Your son, sir?" said Captain Montclair.

"And so they were. My son is behaving like a lunatic, most unlike him. And the eldest one has gone and got himself engaged to the girl of that old busy-body's over at Sigmundshofen, so unnecessary."

"The boy seems to be a little overwrought."

"Poor Gustavus? Oh no, no."

"I mean your young son, the one you said ran away. Isn't his attitude rather unreasonable?"

"So exaggerated," said the old Baron.

"You know, sir, those Corps aren't nearly so bad as your son seems to make out."

"Oh, I shouldn't say that; you didn't see Jean—shocking state he was in."

"I should very much like to talk to you about your son Jean, sir," said the Captain.

"No, no," said the Baron, "we are going to talk about the Professor's new constructions. You must draw them for me. I feel that your visit is going to cheer me up. A tolerable bit of salmon's come in this morning—we will have some Montrachet with it. '58. Not at all a bad year."

"Alas," said the Captain, and explained that he would hardly have the time.

"Not staying here? The inn at Breisach? We must send for your things at once, my old friend Mercier would never forgive me . . ."

Once more the Captain made his excuses; he had to be on his way at once.

"So *very* brief," said the old Baron. "I daresay the Professor needs you."

Captain Montclair went on to Sigmundshofen. Count Bernin was slightly embarrassed by his call. Like the old Baron, he tried to keep it social. He was less successful.

"Well—I was not shown the door," said Captain Montclair.

"Indeed."

"In fact the Baron and I got on like a house on fire."

"Felden is a very charming man."

"Like a house on fire, but I've got nothing to show for it."

How like poor Montclair, Count Bernin later said to Clara, "He always gets on, but he never seems to accomplish his missions." Before his recall, the Empress Eugenie had found him entirely delightful.

"And I couldn't accept to stay at the house," said the Captain.

"No, I suppose not."

"Oh it wasn't that," said the Captain and explained. "Very silly of me."

But Count Bernin did not smile. "You know, if I were you I'd pack up and go back to Berlin," he said.

Captain Montclair, however, returned to the inn at Breisach. Two men in lounge-suits were waiting for him in the tap-room.

"Captain—we should be glad to have a statement from you on The Escaped Cadet."

Gustavus rode over at his usual hour to see Clara. He was much annoyed. "Gabriel has some cock-and-bull story about another man from Benzheim. The house is at sixes and sevens."

"I think papa ought to hear about this," said Clara.

"And does your father think this man came from Benzheim?" said the Count.

"He won't believe a word of it. But Gabriel insists there is a man at the inn at Breisach who has come for Jean. The inn people told our groom that he left a huge silver helmet with feathers and a special case for it on his bed, and he has a white tunic and they saw his sword. Gabriel says its the same man who came to the house this morning in disguise."

"I see," said Count Bernin.

"Do you believe any of it, sir?"

"It couldn't have been that captain who came to see *you* today, papa?" said Clara. "He wore no uniform either."

Count Bernin sat down and wrote once more to Lieutenant-General von Schimmelpfennig. The substance of his letter was, My dear Schimmelpfennig, your Captain Montclair has managed to turn this business into a farce; nothing further can be gained by making yourselves and your emmissaries a local laughing-stock, and I think you ought to desist. Why don't you make those people at Benzheim tell their cadets that the boy is ill or has been sent to another corps or a military prison? Surely their imagination will run to that? Besides I believe the boy *is* ill. A little flexibility, may I remind you, is a useful quality. Always your entire servant, Conrad Bernin.

On the morning of that day, there appeared in two Baden dailies an account of Johannes's escape from Benzheim. As journalism, these copious articles were on the old-fashioned side.

Our Readers will be interested to learn of the gallant escape from the restraint of a certain Military Academy contrived by the intrepid off-spring of one of Lower Baden's foremost personalities, Baron F*_** of L*_**—

But once under way these narratives told a story, and some of the details—supplied by Gabriel's wide-eyed tale—were harrowing. They attracted the attention of circles outside those of the subscribers to the *Badische Landwirt* and the *Manheimer Anzeiger,* and the following morning the facts, in a more astringent form, were published in the *Karlsruher Nachrichten* and the *Süd-Deutsche Courier.* Freedom of the Press in Germany was new then and precarious. On principle anything could be printed as long as it was neither untrue, nor presented tendentiously, nor contrary to public order, morality or the interest of the state. Interpretation naturally was wide, and news and papers were often suppressed on a quibble.

The liberal *Frankfurter Zeitung* prepared a leader and sent a man South for confirmation, Bebel's organ, *Die Neue Zeit*, decided to do the same; the republican *Hamburger Fremdenblatt* telegraphed their Munich correspondent; the more prudent *Kölner Warte* inquired of Berlin whether there was already a *dementi*. The editor of an anti-Czarist revue published in Switzerland arrived himself from Basle. In due course, these gentlemen assembled at the inn at Breisach. Captain Montclair ate his supper in his room.

At Landen Gabriel found himself a quill and scrawled an SOS COME AT ONCE. The weekly hamper was leaving for Bonn: he sealed the note with wax, and put it in the basket with the rack of lamb, the ducks and the green peas.

Early next day General von Schimmelpfennig's ADC and a secretary from Bismarck's Chancellery itself, accompanied by Captain Montclair, presented themselves stiff with travel and solemn with officialdom at Count Bernin's gates.

The count was in his dressing-gown. "Gentlemen, what can I do for you?"

It was simple. To the Count used to thinking on those lines, it was crystal clear. To us, and our perspective as the heirs of this and other more enormous pieces of expediency, it appears futile, shameless and involved. The moves that shape the future seldom shape their own intended ends; the course of self-interest is seen as a bee-line only at the moment, and the history of individuals, groups and countries is the sum of these. On that May morning eighty years ago Count Bernin was told that he had the opportunity of rendering a lasting service to the German Government.

Nearly everybody then believed in the intrinsic desirability of a United Germany. The Empire, in one of those Procrustean phrases by which we force a dehumanized and human imprint on the nature of the universe and cloud our understanding, was a Historical Necessity. Yet everybody up to Bismarck was dissatisfied with the form of the Empire itself. Liberals had worked for Union in the hope of cutting down the powers of the Princes; Prussian nationalists with the intention of establishing hegemony over Austria; Free Traders to get rid of archaic monetary conditions, Democrats to extend the franchise, Labour leaders to unite the working class, Socialists to expand trade-unionism and the Army to expand the Army. The first fruits were the Imperial Constitution of Versailles, new tariffs, anti-socialist legislation, Alsace-Lorraine, Bismarck and the lasting animosity of France. Bismarck had to take a coalition government.

Publication of Johannes's treatment at Corps Benzheim could not fail to raise a question in the Reichstag from members who were pledged to ask such questions. In itself, this was not serious. The Government, or rather the Moderate-Conservative section of its supporters, was quite ready to take a stand and weather what could only be a very minor storm. By an ironic turn it was not those responsible for the cadet schools who found themselves embarrassed, but the anti-militarists who opposed them. Liberal members, though in temporary coalition with the Government, could not be publicly identified with right-wing policy on such an issue without invalidating their mandates. In the event of a debate, a division in the governing majority was thus inevitable. The Government would fall. No combination could hope to form another without Bismarck. Bismarck would find it hard to form another coalition. The Question on The Escaped Cadet must not be asked.

"Yes—" said Count Bernin. "Yes——"

"*If* we can keep it out of the Frankfort and Berlin papers."

"The moment the boy's been sent back by his own father, the bubble's pricked."

"Very likely," said Count Bernin.

"Then we can make those rags print a *diminuendo*. We could get them on distortion, you know. They'll have to say it was all a prank and the boy's been happily returned to Benzheim. Nobody'll dare touch it after that."

"I suppose not," said Count Bernin.

"One would like to know how they got hold of the story in the first place?"

"RC Chaplain at Benzheim's supposed to be an unreliable character."

"Possibly," said Count Bernin with a frosty smile.

"Gentlemen— This is a matter of time."

"Of hours."

"We must be able to issue a directive to the Press."

"It would be best if we had something from old Felden himself. Any chance there, Bernin?"

"None."

"Not if we told him all the facts?"

"Particularly if you told him all the facts."

"A strange attitude. Are you sure now?"

"Count Bernin ought to be in a position to know. Considering their future relationship . . ."

"Gentlemen!"

"Well never mind about a statement. Let's concentrate on the boy."

"*What are we going to tell old Felden?*"

Count Bernin said, "Your Government is faced by a good many controversial issues."

"Forced on us, Count. Forced on us. If you were thinking of the Veto on Ecclesiastical Incumbents— The Chancellor was as much embarrassed by Infallibility—a most ill-advised promulgation—as, let us be frank, many members of your Church themselves. Now there's the appointment of the Bishop of Bamberg . . ."

"*Yes?*" said Count Bernin.

"The Veto here, you will admit, was imposed on us, *ex principio*, by the attitude of the candidate. However, such measures are not always what they seem to be. We are not inflexible . . . In the event of a *de facto* Investiture —I am almost able to assure you—the Bishop's supporters would find little effective opposition."

"This has not been my impression so far," said Count Bernin.

"Oh come, Count, you must credit us with a little gratitude."

"*What are we going to tell old Felden?*"

Count Bernin got up. "We must find a turn," he said.

"*I'd* better not show my face there again," said Captain Montclair.

"Oh I shouldn't neglect pressing a personal advantage, Captain," said the Count.

"Is there anything the old boy might want for himself you can think of, Bernin?"

"He wants his peace."

"Not much in that for us."

"On the contrary," said the Count. "On the contrary."

"Preposterous, isn't it? One spoilt brat in a position to upset the Imperial Government . . ."

Before going over to Landen, Count Bernin spoke to Clara. Gustavus was with her.

"You may as well hear, too," said the Count. "The understanding between you has put me in an intolerable position. And I wish to say this—Clara, if Felden does not agree to send back his boy, I shall not give my consent to your marriage. I shall treat your engagement as though it had never been. I trust that you will not marry Gustavus Felden without my consent as long as I live. And if I know your brother whose aims are mine, not during his life-time either. I am very sorry. But I shall not accept being compromised."

Presently the men from Berlin saw Count Bernin, fully dressed now, to the carriage.

"I can promise you nothing," he said. But when he and Captain Montclair arrived at Landen, Johannes had already very nearly cooked his own goose.

The old Baron greeted them on the stairs. "I am delighted to see you, cher Monsieur. So you *were* able to come back after all?" He took Captain Montclair by the arm. "Come in, come in. I was just about to have a glass of wine. *If* we can find somewhere to sit, that is; I've had such a morning. The house is full of the *strangest* people. But this is such a pleasure. You will find that I've been brushing up my mechanics for you. Not that I've had a quiet moment. Nobody seems to know when to *go* these days."

"What do they want?" said Count Bernin.

"Oh my dear Bernin, I wish you would find out. I don't think they know themselves. I believe they are *impostors*. My children say they all come from Benzheim, Jean's school you know. Well, perhaps they do. *They look like it.* Jean shouldn't have let them come here. *He* is having hysterics somewhere, so unattractive, so unhelpful. Jean's getting out of hand. Do you know, Monsieur, that Jean and Gabriel insisted *you* were from that place. Wait till you see those people! They've all gone to the kitchen. The first time they're in my house, they might have *asked*."

"Did they talk to you at all?" said Count Bernin.

"Oh yes. For hours. Such a morning. Something about Jean's watch. Of course they haven't found it. One of them asked me to contribute to a publication— Perhaps I *will* let him have my treatise on Phosphates . . . And there's a gentleman—quite civil—who says he's from Saint Petersburg. *He* brought his luggage. When I asked him and how is my old friend Countess Troubkine, he told me that he had danced with her at Tsarskoje and that she was a vision. The poor man must be out of his mind. Marie Fedorovna who's been laid up with the gout these fifteen years . . . And they all *would* talk to me about Benzheim. Well I told them what I thought of *that*."

"As a matter of fact Captain Montclair is in a sense connected with Benzheim," said Count Bernin.

"Is he? Are you? What a very extraordinary coin-

F

cidence? How wrong one can be . . . It must be delightful for the boys to have you there."

"The Captain is not actually *at* Benzheim."

"Of course not. He wouldn't have the time. I expect you demonstrate your interesting experiments there occasionally. I wish my friend Mercier had told me. I seem to have got a wrong impression of that school. Jean is an ass. He's very nearly worried me into my grave with his stories . . . Filling the house with those dreadful people too. I can see *they* have nothing to do with Benzheim."

"They are radicals who wish to expose institutions like Benzheim."

"Ah," said the old Baron; "Nihilists. Poor Marie Fedorovna going to dances with them, not that she can of course. What a very odd life she must be leading these days. And Jean letting them come here and getting it all wrong. I don't know what to do with the boy, que le diable l'emporte."

"That is what we have come to talk about," said Count Bernin. "May we go into the library?"

Luncheon at Sigmundshofen an hour later was perfunctory. The men from Berlin had their boxes open beside them on the table and were scribbling.

"Bernin was wonderful," said Captain Montclair. "You should have seen him."

Clara signed the butler not to hand the cutlets again.

Captain Montclair helped himself to Moselle. "Those newspaper fellows were a bit of a break, weren't they? Well, it's an ill wind—"

The young ADC pushed aside his papers. "That's the lot. If you would really be so good, Count?"

"Certainly. My man will take them. The horse is ready."

"Thank you."

"Bernin—may I congratulate you on a not inconsiderable diplomatic victory?" said Captain Montclair.

"I have the station-master at Singen warned to flag the Basle-Cologne Express," said Count Bernin.

"Thank you."

"The man is reliable?"

"Entirely."

Captain Montclair pulled out his watch. "While you are all discussing this excellent brandy, I'd better be on my way. I must not keep my *pupil* waiting . ."

"Clara would you touch the bell," said Count Bernin.

Nobody looked at Montclair as he left the dining-room.

"You expect him to have trouble?"

"No," said Count Bernin. "He is a fool, but he's tough."

"I don't like it."

"Neither do I."

"Neither do I," said Count Bernin.

"It doesn't seem—well, I suppose—straight."

"I suppose there was nothing else—?"

"Unfortunately not."

"I'm afraid you must be right. Well . . And you do advise the night train from Karlsruhe for us?"

"Definitely."

"We've put you to a great deal of trouble, Count."

"Not at all."

But when the Express was stopped at Singen that night, there were no passengers, nor did the gentlemen return to Berlin, for Johannes on hearing his fate had swallowed the heads of several boxfuls of sulphur matches.

Chapter Four

DOCTORS replaced reporters at Landen. The old Baron never could stand them. He believed they brought bad luck. He loathed all illness when it was not connected with animals or could not be laid by a glass of wine and a beef steak, and in his family looked on it as a deliberate disgrace. And he was afraid of death. To have courted it at Landen appeared to him the crumbling of the last brick of sense and sanity. He kept to the library, tossed between terror and fury, admitting no one except Count Bernin and Montclair, certain that the reign of chaos had come down on him.

"Worse than the Great Revolution," he said. "Worse."

Gustavus's entrances were tolerated as he carried messages.

Johannes had been having a kind of convulsions and been very sick. This had taken place in a barn, but the dogs had become alarmed and managed to attract Gabriel's attention. Johannes was given soap-and-water and later had his stomach pumped, and this unnerving experience had left him shocked, sore and weak. Now, he was still in pain, quite out of danger, and lay, drawn in a tight ball, shivering in his bed, banked by hot-water crocks, a prey to Clara's ministrations. Zoro lay motionless stretched flat on the floor, heaving from time to time a deep groan. Clara was trying to talk to Johannes of his great sin. A loud clock was ticking in the room.

Johannes had his face turned against the wall.

Outside, Gabriel was walking about the house, weeping.

"You must never despair," Clara said. "If you allow despair to fill you, you will be alone. You will have shut out God. Offer your suffering to God and He will be with you.

"There is no cause to despair. You must accept your sufferings, you must will them in your heart, moment by moment, as His Will. If you can do this, you will no longer be alone, you will never be afraid . . .

"I will pray for you. Pray that you may understand God's Will. So that you shall be comforted and no longer alone . . ."

But Johannes's mind, clamped in stony misery, darkened by closing waves of non-comprehension, could not hear. And when Julius walked in, fresh from the station with Gabriel clutching at his coat, he found the curtains undrawn, Clara on her knees and Johannes still turned against the bedroom wall.

Clara did not rise, and Johannes did not turn, but Zoro sprang upon him in elastic ecstasy.

"Down Zoro. Dear Zoro. Down!"

At the sound of his brother's voice, Johannes unwound himself.

"Jean, mon pauvre Jean?" Julius said, trying to embrace him. "What in God's name—?" And at last Johannes turned his face.

"Kitchen matches, you know the kind that make that smell, he ate them," said Gabriel. "He chopped all the tops off with a knife and put them in a bowl of cider because papa is sending him back to Benzheim. He read it in *Le Petit Jules Verne Pratique*. Zoro and Ursus came to fetch me. They saved his life. He's had a rubber pipe as thick as that put down his throat. Oh please, please, Jules, tell papa."

"Jean, you idiot, what is all this?"

"Papa says I must go back to Benzheim. Papa wants me to go back to Benzheim."

"What nonsense, Jeannot. Not papa."

"Papa says I must go back to Benzheim."

"Oh Jean, do speak in a normal voice. Papa knows what it was like. He wouldn't want you to go there again."

"Papa wants me to go back to Benzheim."

"I am afraid it's true," said Clara.

The old Baron rather brightened when he saw Julius. "You are *not* going to keep on this coat?" he said.

But when Julius began to speak about Johannes, he was ordered out of the room; and when he persisted, he was ordered back to Bonn. Julius stood his ground. His father turned on him with such violence that he fled, not so much in fear as in bewilderment.

He found Clara. "What is going on here?"

"We have all made a very grave mistake," she said. "I do not think your brother should be allowed to be sent back. The strain has broken his will. He is too young; it would be more than he was meant to bear. If we let him go, he may no longer be able to find his way out of his rebellion and we may condemn him."

"Oh for God's sake, Clara."

"Yes, for *God's* sake, Julius."

"I can't get anywhere with papa. What has come over him? I don't think he understands."

"*I* understand," said Clara.

"What can we do?"

"I will speak to Father Martin. No, not Father Martin. He doesn't get on with my father. We must send for Father Hauser. *If* we can find him."

"Won't he be at the Seminary?"

"That was closed when they were expelled."

"Were they?"

"Oh Jules. We must try Schaffhausen. I'll give you a note. You must go at once and bring him back tomorrow morning if you can."

"Why Father Hauser? *My* father doesn't like priests."

"Do as I tell you."

"You're not going to have the horses out again to-night, Jules?" said Gustavus.

"I suppose they have had rather a day."

"Not all of them," said Clara. "Yours is quite fresh, Gustavus."

"I'll take him then," said Julius, "if I may, and the new mare. I hear she's not been out either."

"I really don't see—"

"Yes, of course, Jules," said Clara, "do take Gustavus's horse."

"Clara! are you out of your mind?" said Gustavus.

"Animals were created the servants of men."

"Really, Clara. Don't you ever think of what your father said to us?"

"How could I not? But dearest—my dearest, we must not be wilful."

"Of course not," said Gustavus, "of course not. But it's all very well for you . . ."

"*Well?*"

"No, no, I mean—I didn't mean—"

"Give me your hand, Gustavus. Oh Gustavus. You

—I— We have this. We shall always have had this. We shall always trust one another. Gustavus!"

"Now Clara, don't cry," said Gustavus.

Father Hauser S.J. sat with Johannes for some time. He patted the dog; he smoked; he talked a little, mostly to himself.

As he was leaving, Johannes looked up and said, "Does papa really want me to go back to Benzheim?"

Outside the bedroom, Father Hauser said to Julius, "I remembered him well. He hasn't altered much. Neither have you. I remember you all. Not that you were with us long—you stayed such a very short while, six weeks was it? to cure you of Newton. Funny now, I should have thought he was rather up your father's street; but you never can tell. It's so much harder for people who follow their own line, one mustn't wonder if they're a little inconsistent at times. Your brother here— he'll probably never make much of a Catholic, but he's all right, he's at one with the brute creation, as we call it. You have something of that, too, but with you it isn't, one might say, fused; it's instead . . . If you don't watch it'll only make you more closed. But of course you don't know how to watch. You will never know much about yourself. Still, remember, it is much to be able to love without expecting return. When you were sent to us, you brought your owl."

"She died three winters ago."

"Haven't you got another one?"

"I have a raven now. Jacques. He came."

"They always will, Julius."

"You are fond of owls, Father?"

"Not really, you know. Not really."

"It isn't true when people say they carry lice."

"I didn't know they said that. So you see. And I'm glad you came for me. It was a long way. He in there, you know: Jean," and Father Hauser used the word the old Baron had used not so long ago, "*c'est un brave cœur.* And he is very ill."

"The poisoning?"

"No. Not the poisoning. And now I will speak to your father."

Gustavus politely ran down the stairs before them. He was the first in the library. "Papa, there is a Jesuit who wants to talk to you about Jean."

"Prussians, Nihilists, Jesuits—" said the old Baron.

"My father is very sorry—he cannot see you, Father," said Gustavus.

"Will you see mine?" said Clara.

"Oh," said Father Hauser.

"I must speak to you first."

"No, Clara. Don't do that, my child. I will do my own asking."

"Father Hauser!" said Count Bernin.

"Conrad Bernin," said Father Hauser.

"Is it safe for you to be here?"

"Quite safe."

"I'm glad. No, they wouldn't want to arrest you; that wouldn't suit their book at all. Still, you had better be careful. There's always some blundering gendarme."

"So you've worked it all out, Conrad? Still at it. Does it ever come out right? Now you know, on your own showing, a blundering gendarme ought to suit *your* book."

"*Hauser*. How can you?"

"Oh I know you'd mind having me in prison. I didn't say you'd call him in. I am one of your inconsistencies, Conrad. But admit I'd serve?"

"There would be the most salutary uproar!" said Count Bernin.

"Accusations . . counter charges . . public lies . . judicial half truths—"

"A man of your reputation and character."

"Never known to have taken part in politics."

"It could mean a turn in the *Kulturkampf*."

"It might lengthen it!"

"It *might* lead to a revision of the Edict of Expulsion."

"And a well-built deal."

"You would return!"

"We would return."

"What are you driving at, Hauser?"

"At what you refuse to see, Conrad."

"Don't you *want* to come back?"

"I? Very much. I can't stand the Belgian climate. And I've allowed himself to become attached to a certain view from our East wing; I like to look on the Vosges. Though, as you see, I *am* here a good deal. Still . . I should be able, for instance, to go to see my old friends at Sigmundshofen without having to wear this borrowed tweed jacket."

"And your penitents? Your pupils?"

"Our penitents, in spite of many excellent priests

available, have taken to analysing their spiritual states by
letter. It is true that this has greatly added to our work.
And we are being sent rather more pupils from German
parents than before."

"Yet the expulsion *was* a wrong?"

"Wrongs can only be redressed by the free consent of
all concerned. The Creation is not a chess-board."

"You are not becoming a Quietist, Hauser?"

"Not a Quietist. But sufficient unto the day, Conrad."

"Such have not always been the views of your Order."

"Members of my Order are subject to error."

"And their products?"

"*And* their products, Conrad."

"And *you*?"

"And I."

"You may be in error now."

"Certain things are knowable," said Father Hauser.

"How?"

Father Hauser did not speak.

"How?"

"That," Father Hauser said, "is a strange question
from a man of Faith."

Count Bernin lifted his head. "There are certain ends,"
he said, "certain ends . . ."

Father Hauser put away his pipe. "*Conrad von Bernin,*"
he said, "*what have you been up to?*"

Count Bernin spoke; Father Hauser listened. Then
Father Hauser spoke and Count Bernin listened. To every
word he had to say. It was a great deal.

"And yet I cannot agree with you," he said at the end.
"I *cannot.*"

Presently, Count Bernin said, "There is too much involved."

And presently, "I can't help it that old Felden hasn't got his wits about him."

"Besides it's too late."

"You are not my spiritual adviser, you know."

"I did not start it. I never liked it."

"*You* know, if anybody does, I am not building for myself. Nor for my time . . ."

"Oh those men. They're still in the house. They are nothing. Automata. Cut off. With their Nation and their duty to the State. They are blind men who must be led."

"Yes, if you like, used. On occasions *used*."

"Pride? *My* pride?"

"But I *can* see the future. I am not interested in the present."

"Nothing has ever been achieved without some cost . . ."

"No, no—there *are* such things as larger questions."

"No. I suppose I never have believed in anybody's happiness."

"Then my service? My *life*—?"

And later again, he said, "Can that place really be so bad?"

Presently Father Hauser said, "Well, good night, Conrad. It's getting late. I shall be back with you tomorrow."

"Where are you going to sleep, Hauser?"

"Oh I'll find myself a place."

"What folly. If you are going to stay, you had better stay here."

"Thank you, Conrad. As you ask me, I will."

Next day, Count Bernin said, "And the Bishop of Bamberg?"

"Kramer is a good man, a very good man, but I doubt that God would let a single soul come to harm because Bismarck will not have Archdeacon Kramer appointed to the Episcopal See of Bamberg."

"He happens to be the one person who is able to get on with His Holiness *and* the Cardinal of Berlin. Now don't you go and tell that to those Government chaps."

"They wouldn't listen," said Father Hauser; "they all but cross themselves when they see me."

Later on that day, Count Bernin said, "Perhaps I haven't done so well by Clara either. Strange girl. Always at Landen these days, with her young man hanging about *here*. I thought I knew her. You are making everything seem very complicated, Hauser."

Father Hauser stayed four days. When he knew that he could get no further, he left.

Count Bernin himself drove him across the Swiss Border. The two men embraced. "Good-bye, Conrad. Pray for me."

"Good bye, Father. Shall I see you again?"

"Clara will know my whereabouts. Give her my love."

Count Bernin returned and faced the men who were uneasily lingering over their mission at Sigmundshofen.

* * * * *

It had become known at Landen that Captain Montclair was to take Johannes away with him as soon as he was strong enough to travel. Captain Montclair, kit and all, was staying at the house now. The old Baron, anxious to see an end of it, had left arrangements to him. Every morning Julius forced himself into his father's presence and tried to speak. The old Baron did what he had never done before, he put his hand to his heart and in a quavering voice threatened immediate stroke. Every day Julius fled.

Gabriel said to Julius, " Jean and I were going to run away together. To America. It is easy. First one hides in a ship, then we are going to hire ourselves out to herd buffaloes in the prairies. Jean would like that. But he won't come. He doesn't listen. He only says papa wants him to go back to Benzheim. I don't love papa any more. Do you? Must we still love papa? I can peel potatoes on the ship and scrub the deck, then Jean wouldn't have to hide all the way and the Captain would give him a hammock and let him have some food. Ship's biscuits is what you get, and pork from the salt-barrel. That's called working one's passage. But he won't come and I can't take him by myself, I'm too young. It would frighten him to go just with me. So you must come too. I thought it all out. You are grown-up and you have money, we could go on trains and it wouldn't be like running away at all. Jean wouldn't have to walk like the last time and have nothing to eat, and nobody could stop you. When we are in America we will write to papa and he will forgive us."

"You *are* a child, Gabriel," said Julius.

In the evening, Gabriel said, "Perhaps it *was* stupid about America. It's too far, and we don't know where the ships are. But you know better. You would know where to take him. And if you think I'm too much I won't come. You'll know best. Perhaps you can take him to your teacher at Bonn, or you could hide him in the house of the lady at Namur papa says you always go to stay with. Namur isn't Germany, is it? I think if Jean were somewhere where he knew nobody could come for him from Benzheim, he would get well. Oh Jules do take him, do. When? *Tonight?*"

"I have no money. Really, Gabriel, I haven't."

"But you're grown-up. Papa gives you money."

"I spent it."

"Couldn't you borrow some?"

"*I did that, too.*"

"Oh well then we must steal it. But Jules, you will take Jean? You *will?*"

"Gabriel—how can I?"

"Clara? Jules must run away with Jean, must he not?"

"No, Gabriel, no. I don't think so. It would be disobedient to your father and cause great trouble and anxiety. It would be a bad rebellious way out."

But Clara went to hold counsel with herself, and that night she knocked at Julius's door.

Julius was in his night-shirt. He had lit four candles on his dressing-table, and he was brushing his hair. He also had a square of Genoa velvet out to look at, bought the week before, and tried to whisk it back into the drawer but it was too late. Clara remained standing in the middle of the floor and saw nothing.

Julius arranged his brushes.

"I know Father Hauser is doing something," Clara said. "I know. But I cannot feel easy. My father is a difficult man, and yours is so very strange. And you know I don't believe—I may be uncharitable—Captain Montclair is a man of conscience."

"He seems a gentleman," said Julius.

Clara sighed. "All this isn't good for your brother," she said. "I think you ought to take him away. Gabriel is quite right. Take him straight into Belgium. You say you have friends there who live in the country?"

"No, no, no," said Julius, "that would be quite impracticable."

"Then this is what you must do. You must take him to Saint-Ignatius at St. Rond. They will be kind to him, and Father Hauser will see to all that's necessary. And you must stay with him; in the state he's in he needs you or Gabriel. I have the money. I brought it."

"Clara, I couldn't."

"Couldn't what, Jules?"

"Well—money."

"Jules: sometimes I cannot understand you at all."

"Everybody is getting melodramatic like Gabriel," said Julius.

"You sound like your father."

"Really Clara, you know— You come here in the middle of the night and suggest my kidnapping Jean from his own house. Have you thought of my father? Have you thought of the servants?"

"May God have mercy on you, Julius," Clara said. But before she left the room she laid a hundred-mark note and two rolls of gold on the Genoa velvet.

Julius put the bank-note in an envelope and addressed it to Countess Clara. He saw nothing he could put the

G

gold in, so he shoved it out of sight beneath some scarves.

The two men from Berlin were not pleased. Count Bernin could read their thoughts. It was very hard on him.

And yet his compromise was one that might even now accommodate all sides. It consisted of two points. Johannes was to be sent back to Benzheim for a brief period only, and as soon as the purpose of his return had been fulfilled, say, in a month or two, he was to be withdrawn for good. The authorities were to give an assurance that considering the boy's state of health they were ready to waive all punishment devolving on his escape. If this could not be promised the boy would not be sent at all.

The officials bowed. "We all do our duties as we see them, Count," they said, and bowed again. They offered, however, to stop themselves at Benzheim on their way and secure Johannes's amnesty from the commandant.

After they were gone, Count Bernin waited. He could not bring himself to speak of his decision to Clara or to anyone; just as before he had not been able to bring himself to speak in time of her engagement.

The answer came on the Saturday of the same week. It was frank. The commandant, impatient with politics and concerned only with the maintenance of the discipline of his corps, had stated that he could not see his way to making an exception of Cadet von Felden. There was a postscript to the effect that it was not practicable, at this moment, to recall the commandant. Count Bernin was in the thick of entertaining members of the Constituary Court of Freiburg; he enquired whether Gus-

tavus was on hand, and was told that he was sketching in
the orchard.

"Do you know when your brother is supposed to
leave?"

"We haven't been told. Montclair is seeing to it. Papa
does not want to know. It may be any time now."

"I can't get away," said Count Bernin, "you must take
this note to your father at once. It is urgent. Quite urgent.
See that he reads it. Say that I shall be over in the evening." Count Bernin lingered, wondering if it were not
safer to tell Gustavus more; hesitated; then let it go and
turned back to the house.

The carriage did not come to the front door. Captain
Montclair and two orderlies carried Johannes to the
stable-yard. Gabriel raised a howl for Julius. Julius
battered at his father's door. It was locked and no sound
came from within. Julius ran out again and saw Johannes,
feet dangling, being lifted in the hired cab. Johannes
neither moved nor resisted, but the dogs were massed
and Gabriel was hammering at Captain Montclair with
his fists. A young groom was trying to set Ursus on the
men, but none of the Landen dogs were trained, and
unused to attacking humans they only yelped and barked.

"Jean—" Julius cried.

Johannes turned his head and looked at him.

Then someone whipped the horses, and they were off,
at great speed down the drive. It had all been so fast that
only then servants and farm-hands began to come
running. Gabriel howling kept abreast with the carriage
and all the dogs were after it in a fury of dust and noise.
Julius stood dazed.

And it was so that Clara, who had been going to the village and had turned half-way on an impulse, found him a minute later, white as paper, standing in the drive.

"Go after him! At once at once— Get a horse, the quickest horse— *Hurry*."

"What good is it?" said Julius.

"Don't let them stop that train— the express— at Singen— if only you get there before them— Don't let the station master flag that train——"

"How *can* I stop him?"

"Order him not to—forbid it—you are the son of the house. Pull him out of the train, or get on yourself, anything, anything, only don't stand here, don't wait, don't waste minutes—Jules do you hear me? Are you a man? Oh! why isn't there a side-saddle in the place—"

"Baron Jules," said the major-domo by his side, "I ordered your horse. It is here."

Julius still hesitated, but once in the saddle he was transformed. He saw his way clear, and he became frantic with anguish—to get there, to pluck his brother from these men, wipe out what he had seen, and he put everything he had in strength and skill and feeling into that ride and all the way he called aloud to Jean. When he got there, they were gone.

"Baron Julius," said the station master. "I am glad to see you. So it was all right? When we stop the express, you know, we like to have it from the family; and there was nothing from your father. And the young gentleman looked so very queer, I didn't know what to think. Still, there he was with an officer . . Well I'm glad you came, that makes it all square now. Baron Julius, there is nothing wrong? *Baron Julius?* Oh Baron Julius——!"

"My poor Gustavus," Clara said that night. "I know, I know. But you could not help it, we all know what your father is like. You could not have made him read that note. He now thinks he did not even see it. Please, Gustavus, do not look like this—you must not feel guilty. It would be a wrong."

Gabriel had run beside Johannes and the carriage as long as he had breath. Then he dropped behind, then he fell. When his heart stopped pounding, he still felt it would burst with misery. He stayed in the fields, swaying, not seeing where he went, not feeling grass nor stone nor hedges. After dark he turned home and crept into the house. He heard his father's, Clara's and Gustavus's voices and went on, up a back-stairs to Jules's room. Jules was not there. Gabriel lit a candle and waited. Jules did not come. After midnight he fell asleep on the chair. When he waked an hour or so later he was still alone and very cold. He paced about for some time, then looked among Jules's things for something he might wear. When he saw Clara's rolls of gold, he took them and left the house.

He walked towards Singen. He knew the goods-train that went North at dawn and he knew the bend below the crossing where it curved and slowed and they had often stood to count the carriages of other trains, and he thought he knew the way to board a moving train. When it came it seemed much faster than he thought it would, the clatter and the draught it made unnerved him, and at first he could not make himself get near enough to

touch and seize. But it was a long train and he had time to
get his bearings; and when he saw another open door
approach and some good bars, he leapt and grasped them.
Perhaps he did not grasp them hard enough, perhaps it
was because he was tired and muddled and exalted, but
before he could find a foot-hold he was thrown off again
and hurled on to a heap of slag. His head struck a stone
and he was killed at once.

*   *   *   *   *

The arrangements consequent to these events were
seen to by Count Bernin. Julius lying ill at Bonn was not
able to come back. Clara with her father's permission and
a doctor went herself to Benzheim to fetch Johannes.
They found him in the infirmary, with the authorities in a
state of uneasy alarm. Return to Landen was not considered advisable, and on Father Hauser's recommenda-
tion he was taken to a doctor in Switzerland at whose
house in the country he remained for several years,
living among animals and the doctor's own small children. They were good to him. Visits from his family,
after one disastrous attempt by Julius, were not practicable. Julius did not go back to Landen for a long time,
and never went back there to live. Clara and Gustavus
were married in the chapel at Sigmundshofen six months
after Gabriel's death, and settled down with the old
Baron. The new Bishop of Bamberg had proposed to
officiate. Count Bernin declined.

Part Three

———

THE CAPTIVE

Chapter One

IN the year 1891, Manet and Seurat were already dead; Pissarro, Monet and Renoir were at their height of powers; Cézanne had opened yet another world. Sunday at la Grande Jatte and le Déjeuner dans le Bois, la Musique aux Tuileries, les Dames dans un Jardin, the ochre farms and tawny hills of Aix were there, on canvas, hung, looked at—to be seen by anybody who would learn to see. And so were the shimmering trees, the sun-speckled paths, the fluffy fields, the light, the dancing air, the water— But were they seen? Were they walked, were they lived in? Did ladies come out into the garden in the morning holding a silver tea-pot? did flesh-and-blood governesses advance towards one waist-high in corn and poppies, clutching a bunch of blossoms? did young men dip their hands into the pool and young women laugh in swings? Did gentlemen really put their top-hats on the grass?

For the age of the Impressionists was also still the age of decorum and pomposity, of mahogany and the base-ment kitchen, the over-stuffed interior and the stucco villa; an age that venerated old, rich, malicious women and the clever banker; when places of public entertain-ment were large, pilastered and vulgar, and anyone who was neither a sportsman, poor, nor very young, sat down on a stiff-backed chair three times a day eating an endless meal indoors.

My father talked little about this middle period of his life. But others knew him, saw him, talked, survived;

and I know that on the French Riviera in the Nineties
Jules Felden drove a team of mules—

Melanie Merz, delicate, soft, pretty, just turned twenty
and exquisitely dressed, sat by the window with her silks
and needle. It was the simplest cross-stitch, coarse flowers
on a square of stuff, and her small sad face was turned
towards the drive and the potted palms outside.

"What would you like to do this morning, my dear?"
said her sister-in-law.

Melanie lifted gentle, round brown eyes and said
whatever Sarah wished her to do, thank you.

"My dear, you *are* happy here? You are enjoying
yourself?"

Melanie said she was happy.

"You are not missing your mother and father? you're
not feeling strange or anything being away?"

"It is very much like home here," said Melanie.

"Oh, is it," said Sarah.

Edu Merz walked in—Edu, not yet forty-five, not yet
bankrupt, still almost at his ease with Sarah; Edu freshly
valeted, wafting eau-de-Lubin, holding field glasses, with
no pressing debts on a fine February morning in the South
of France. "Morning, Sarah; morning, Melanie. Jolly day
isn't it? I'm going to take you out with me to watch the
tennis, and give you a spot of lunch at the *Anglais.*"

Melanie looked up at her brother, gently, intently, as
though he were holding out a nut, or was it a screw of
paper? "Thank you, Edu," she said, "I should like to
very much."

Sarah said that Melanie was asked to Lady De Moses's
luncheon party; and so she believed was Edu.

Oh all right, Edu said; the chef of the *Anglais* would be doing that too, the old girl always had a crowd; he'd take Melanie then and send the Panhard back for Sarah.

The Panhard, Sarah said, had had three punctures yesterday between the *Sporting* and *Les Ambassadeurs,* and she'd rather have the carriage.

"I will get my hat," said Melanie and stood up, chic, exotic, frail; "I shan't be a minute, Edu," and rustled out of the room.

Stunning dress, said her brother. Did Sarah choose it? He shouldn't have thought it looked like Sarah at all; he meant he couldn't see *her* in those large stripes—

They were right for Melanie, Sarah said. Exactly right.

Wasn't it a little, Edu said, a little, he didn't know, he meant to say—Melanie being a young girl and all that?

Stagy?

Yes, perhaps, that was it.

Exactly right, said Sarah. That Commedia del Arte touch. And the girl knew how to put on her clothes, that girl could wear anything. God knew where she had it from. Sarah looked at Edu.

Yes, he said. For a girl who'd never been further from Berlin than Bad Kissingen . . .

"The child was telling me that she finds life on the Riviera like Voss Strasse."

"What rot," said Edu.

"You know I think I will skip Lady De Moses today," said Sarah. "It's such a day. It's you they want anyhow. I'm going to take Melanie for a country drive, I'm sure it's good for her to have the air. We might go up to Jules's." Melanie had come in with her parasol, buttoning gloves. "Would you like to do that, my dear?"

"The young man with the mules?"

"Not so young. He must be my age. At least."

"Not really?" said Melanie.

It *was* a day. Still, blue, very still—and the warmth lay gently across the ladies' shoulders like a blessing. A bee got into the carriage. In the Vallée du Loup the almonds were out among the peach-trees, the young slim peach-trees, rows and rows of them pink and white, all over the hill-sides.

"His villa is not by the sea?" said Melanie.

"It isn't a villa," said Sarah.

It was in an olive grove, at the end of an abominable bit of road, and it was a priory, or what was left of one—a low wing, round arches, the fragments of a cloister.

Julius, wearing a tussore jacket and a black Spanish straw hat, came out to meet them.

They did not go indoors.

Over the balustrade and down the sides of fat oil-jars, great manes of flowering leaves trailed lemon-scented, rose-scented, spice-scented, pure red and tender white. Below, two cypresses formalized the view. Julius shook out a hammock for Melanie. "You will be in the shade," he said. "Not too much. Just enough. It is Tzara's—she is so uncareful about her hair. With this cushion you'll be tolerably comfortable." He stepped back.

"You know—this is a wonderful dress. So *chic*."

Melanie smiled.

He also looked wonderful. Like a man and a gentleman and a lily in the field—turned-out and natural, exquisite and masculine, with a fine profile and sharp nose, tall, balanced, large and light.

"Jules," said Sarah. "I must have your advice on that

Chippendale. Those people have written again. I don't know, their price seems wrong. I brought the sketches they sent me."

"I've something for you to see too," said Julius.

"Such very pretty flowers," said Melanie. "What are they?"

"Oh you know the ivy-leaved kind. I get the cuttings from across in Italy. Cascante, they call them."

"Cascante?" said Melanie.

"Geraniums," said Sarah.

"Geraniums?" said Melanie.

"We are fugitives from Lady de Moses's," Sarah said. "Jules, can you give us lunch?"

"She doesn't ask *me* any more. It took three seasons. I went to Nice this morning; early. You ought to have seen the fish come in—so beautiful. But do you know there wasn't a cat there today, no-one one knew at all except Prince Lichnovsky's kitchen maid. Some vague men from the hotels, no-one from Beau-lieu, not a single chef from the villas, none of the Queen of England's people—though they do eat quite well—no-one at all in the fish-market on the first calm morning after all that wind. No wonder— Well, *we* are going to have oursins presently; they are opening them now. And a loup. Grilled."

"*Oursins,*" said Sarah. "My cook refuses to cope with them. He pretends they don't exist."

"They *are* three sous a dozen. He ought to wear a leather glove. On his left hand. Mademoiselle—would you like to see them?"

"I shall never be able to tell him," said Sarah.

"Yes, please," said Melanie.

Julius brought her a rough, dark-skinned fish, two foot long, and held it up in the air for her to see. "Look at it: a *loup-de-mer,* a sea-bass, though not quite. The best fish there is in these waters. Look how firm he is, how fresh; caught at dawn this morning, look at the gills, feel him . . ."

The fish was compact and supple and marked all over in deep indigo and mat maroon: it seemed to have no scales, yet it shone. In all her life Melanie had not had a young man hold up a whole fish to her in the sun. She blinked at him; put out two finger-tips and touched its side. It was dry.

"And here." He took the basket from the boy. Melanie looked inside.

"They *move* . ."

"Of course," said Julius. "They're alive. They wouldn't be good if they were not. Let me put one on your hand. No—keep it flat; the spikes won't hurt you if you keep your hand flat."

"Oh—" said Melanie, "a black hedgehog."

"No, no, no," said Julius. "No-one would eat a hedgehog, charming animals. Though I believe Gipsies do. Very cruel."

"Why?" said Sarah.

"*Eat a hedgehog?*"

"Why sea-urchins and not a hedgehog?"

"Quite different. They're something in the sea."

"You were just telling us that they were alive. I daresay water dulls the natural feelings. I cannot follow all your fine distinctions, Jules; mind, I don't share your Franciscan sentiments, but aren't lambs as charming as hedgehogs? And I've seen you eat lambs. Of course you'd call it cutlets or saddle. Your position is interesting."

"Alas. '*Les tristes lois de la cruelle Nature . . .*'"

"We could not live on vegetables alone," said Melanie.

"Very true," said Julius.

"I'm glad to see you profit by your lesson in natural history, Melanie," said Sarah.

Melanie shrank back into her hammock.

"I must get us some white wine," Julius said. "Cellar temperature, don't you think?"

Luncheon was laid on bare pink marble under a trellis of mulberry.

There was a loaf of butter on a leaf, the bread was on a board; there was a dish of lemons and there were wooden mills for black pepper and grey pepper and the salt; the china was Eighteenth-century Moustier and the wine stood, undecanted, in a row of thick green cool un-labelled bottles. Julius drew the corks himself; poured, held up, handed glasses. Below the olive trees they could see the valley, the linear terraced hill, and the other slope, soft again, in full sun-light now, feathery with mimosa.

"How good," said Sarah.

"When it is like this, it is like this," said Julius.

"After six days of mistral."

"*Der Süden. . . .*"

"I could never live anywhere else," said Julius.

"I have never been before," said Melanie.

The sea-urchins came heaped in a great armorial pile, sable and violet, tiered on their burnished quills, like the unexplained detail on the hill by the thistles and the hermitage of a quattrocento background, exposing now inside each severed shell the pattern of a tender sea-star.

"With a spoon," Julius said. "Like this."

Presently he struck a match and set fire to the next course. The flames, fed by rosemary and fennel, crackled, aromatic, invisible almost in the brilliant air.

"Like plum-pudding!"

"So over-rated," said Julius. In a flash of silver blades he laid bare the nut-white fish inside the charred, bark-like crust.

Melanie looked for the sauce-boat. There seemed to be no potatoes.

Julius helped her to a few drops of limpid oil.

"Perfection, Jules," said Sarah.

Julius lifted a small bell. "Will you see please that Tzara and Robert are tidied up a bit before they come in."

"They are not back, Monsieur le Baron. They went to the Plan de Grasse this morning. They took a picnic."

"Oh thank God," said Sarah.

"They ought to be back for dessert," said Julius, looking at two watches.

"I will have them sent in as soon as they return, sir."

"Where is Léon?"

"Léon is in the kitchen, sir. He's breaking plates. He is angry because Robert would not take him."

"Tell him to stop at once. Robert is jealous because Léon adores Tzara and Tzara is flattered."

"They all seem to have the most appalling characters," said Sarah.

"Léon breaks a good deal. Have you been to Monte Carlo, Mademoiselle?"

"Edu took her to the kitchen."

"Any luck?"

"I lost two Louis d'Or," said Melanie.

"On what?"

"The game."

"Your *mise*? What did you put it on?"

"Oh. A number."

"Very hard to choose," said Julius. "I have a system. My father taught it to us."

"It is infallible," said Sarah.

"How did you know?" said Julius. "Of course the maximum *is* against one. Would you like me to teach it to you, Mademoiselle? Well you see, you start on the First Dozen, you don't waste anything *à cheval*, nor on the even chances, but you've got to think of the Zero—"

"Yes?" said Melanie.

"Of course that weakens your total; then after you've lost the fifth time running, you triple your *mise*, you see, and change to the Second Dozen."

"It sounds very interesting," said Melanie. "My brother has a system too, but yours is more interesting."

"Jules: I want to go to Le Thoronet," said Sarah.

"You must."

"How does one get there?"

"You've never been? Never been to Le Thoronet? The only perfect Romanesque there is round here? And it is perfect; perfect. Your sister-in-law ought to see it. What *have* you seen? Eze?—rather touched up. Haute Cagne? Cimiez? St.-Maximin? The Islands?"

Melanie looked at Sarah. Sarah said nothing.

"We saw the *Bataille des Fleurs*. And we went to the races, and for a drive on the Grande Corniche, and we saw the scent being made at Grasse."

"Very bad scent I'm afraid," said Julius. "You must go to Les Tourettes, and to Biot and to Valauris; if your head's good you might go up to that Monastery on the Gourdon, most of their stuff is fake—do you know, Sarah, I believe they're selling altar pieces. No, not that pear. Let me choose one for you."

They came in, freshly brushed, wearing woollen cardigans. Tzara went to Julius at once, felt his pockets, and began explaining something to him. Robert stood by with an air of conscious tolerance.

H

"Sit down, Robert," said Julius.

Robert made an ironic little bow to Sarah, and took a chair.

Sarah looked at him without affection.

"Have some fruit," said Julius.

Tzara, leaning against him, took a fig, looked at it, showed it to him, then chewed with assured contentment. Robert pulled up the dish, picked out a Calville apple, put it down again and, looking steadily at Sarah, handled every piece of fruit. Léon appeared, frowning, tiny beside the others, hovered uncertainly. Then he saw Melanie.

He uttered a small cry: was on her lap and flung his arms about her in instant ecstasy. Melanie flinched only slightly.

Tzara opened a palm—a persimmon dropped squashy on the marble. Robert sucked his cheeks.

"You dirty apes," said Sarah.

Léon, lightly on her breast, curled against striped silk, put his little black hand to Melanie's face.

"He loves you," Julius said: "and he is very difficult."

"The dear little monkey," said Melanie.

"Watteau!" said Sarah. "Look Jules, look—Watteau, pure Watteau, of the lightest, most sumptuous period."

Chapter Two

"WHAT would you like to do this morning?" Sarah said.

"Jules Felden is taking me to Monaco to the Aquarium."

"I'm afraid that's out of the question, my dear. You cannot expect me to come on all those strenuous excursions; and I really haven't got the time."

"That is quite all right," said Melanie; "he said he would bring Léon and another lady."

"Indeed," said Sarah.

"We are lunching at Kitty Wolfe's," said Edu, "she's specially asked you."

"That is quite impossible," said Melanie.

"You can't let old Kitty down—she likes to be exactly thirty-six."

"I'm sorry, Edu. I promised Baron Felden. Sarah?"

"Yes, Melanie?"

"Jules Felden says he will give me Léon. Is it not kind?"

"Your mother will be so pleased."

Melanie said nothing.

"Jules Felden is a very charming and accomplished man," said Sarah. "And, you realize, don't you, about twenty years older than you."

Melanie fluffed out her skirts. "I must get ready," she said. "It is time. It isn't good for mules to stand when they are warm."

"Preposterous," said Sarah.

"Well I don't know," said Edu.

"Utterly preposterous."

"There *is* the difference of religion."

"Oh that," said Sarah. "High time some of us were baptized."

"Not while my mother is alive," said Edu.

"What can a man like Jules have in common with a girl like her."

"He seems keen enough."

"For a week; a month. If she's got other ideas, she's going to have a jolt."

"I suppose we ought to find out about his intentions and all that."

"You are mad, Edu."

"Well, I thought *you* might. Felden's your pal."

"I've a good mind to send the little idiot back to Voss Strasse. I'm responsible to her parents, you know."

"Of course—Felden can't have much money."

"Hasn't he? I shouldn't have thought that."

"Well, he lives very simply."

"Not really," said Sarah.

"He inherited some land in Bavaria or somewhere."

"Yes, one forgets he's German."

"Not that there isn't plenty to go round," said Edu, "only if you *are* going to marry a man with a title it doesn't look at all the same, does it, if he's poor, if you know what I mean."

"It's all most unsuitable," said Sarah.

"He would have to get rid of Madame de la Turbie, Sarah—don't tell me you never heard of Madame de la Turbie?"

"Yes, yes. Everybody's heard of Madame de la Turbie."

"They say that's why Felden came to live here."

"Nonsense. What does she look like? I've seen her driving of course, but with all those veils you can't really tell."

"She used to be a stunner. She's getting on now."

"How old can she be?"

"She must be forty. Or nearly. Though it's hard to believe."

"It's what I am," said Sarah.

"Quite different," said Edu.

"I'm supposed to be my own reward."

"How you *talk*. Now who's going to tackle Felden? Melanie's one's sister, damn it all—"

"Edu! I absolutely forbid you."

"Snapping my head off?—what's the matter? Don't *you* think Jules Felden would be a pleasant fellow to have in one's family?"

"A pleasant fellow to have in one's family. . . ." said Sarah.

The mistral sprang up again, and for days swept down the Rhone Valley over the low long-bent patient trees into the sea, whirling dust and paper along the deserted water-fronts. The steam-heating was going full blast at the hotels, and at the villas the windows were rattling and the fire places smoked. In the hills, the women who went *à la corvée des fleurs* came back early after dawn, their hands stiff on the dripping bales of narcissi. At Julius's, Léon and the chimpanzees were kept indoors. Melanie, who was supposed to be still recovering from a bronchitis, coughed again. A doctor confirmed Sarah's order that she must keep her bed.

Julius sent fruit and flowers from his garden with his card and polite inquiries. He did not come himself; and, as far as Sarah could make out, he certainly did not write.

Melanie kept a French exercise book in her bed-clothes.

After a week of it, Sarah stood in the room and said, her eyes on the girl, "One's had enough of this weather, I've decided to cut out March. This kind of a spring cannot be good for you either. As soon as you're up again we are going to shut the villa and go home."

Melanie's small face shrivelled.

Sarah, loathing weakness, loathing power, overcome, goaded by her own position, went on—feeling the moment long, still, touchable almost; hearing the nonchalant words falling and stretching. "I think I shall begin packing up now. Let me see—what day are we?" Melanie did not stir; only those round simian eyes, all brown, moved between the wall and Sarah. Sarah said, "Why, what can it be to you? Jules could come to Berlin."

Melanie did not speak at once. "He does not like Berlin," she said.

"You could always try staying on. I'm sure Lady De Moses or someone would be delighted to put you up."

"Jules would not like me if it were like that."

Melanie was shivering under her eider-downs; yet it was Sarah who, cold with revulsion, could hardly carry herself to the door.

From where they lived, there were no walks. Again, Sarah put down her paper-volume of Anatole France; stood up; turned to the window; tried to read. She was a woman who had to know herself just in all her dealings. She liked few people, had never loved and liked at the same time for long; she could not afford not to like herself. Dignity and conscience were her shell and her recourse. She had presence, she was instructed, she judged, she was too tall; men treated her as she appeared to them, and never, once, had she been spoken to in the way Julius spoke to Tzara, his chimpanzee. Nor was there anyone from whom this could have been entirely acceptable: she sought rectitude, success, character; looks, wit and mind, and had never found them united in one person. Without looks she could not be moved, looks and a civilized façade; mind she was long resigned to finding only among those of her acquaintance who were slovenly and self-interested, or slovenly and indifferent; and at that period of her life she was quite alone.

Once more Sarah put down her book, and faced what there was to face, and saw that it was nothing and that it was irremediable, and saw that if she did not put it aside she would be destroyed. It had no name, no future; it could not be helped; but she could help herself. If one can feel no sympathy, one can at least act with justice; and Sarah saw her way. She went at once to Edu and, aware of the effect of her own presence in the sick-room, made him take the message. The barometer was rising, it had been an absurd idea, the girl was not to worry, of course they were going to stay on; she was not to worry about anything at all.

"Shut up this dump?" Edu said. "Why it's the best idea ever. You must admit it's foul . . Do let's leave. I insist."

"Certainly not," Sarah said; "tell Melanie we're going to stay at least till after Easter." And she returned to *Thaïs,* free for the first time in many weeks of that corrosion, with something of the conscious pleasure and detachment of a convalescence.

"Quite hopeless," said Julius.

"Hopeless?" said Sarah.

"Can't you see? A young girl. Merz's sister. *Avec les jeunes filles cela ne peut finir qu'avec le mariage.*"

"Well *yes,*" said Sarah.

"That's what I thought."

"The step is not entirely uncommon."

"Too soon," said Julius.

"She *is* young. Yet she'll never be much older; you know in a way I think she knows you awfully well, Jules. Well enough for your comfort, that is."

"I mean *I* am too young."

"What do you intend to do?"

"What can I do?" said Julius.

Two days later he said, "Sarah, I've made up my mind. I shall go to Paris."

"Have you thought of her?"

"I think of her all the time."

On Mid-Lent Thursday Edu took his wife, Melanie and Julius to the dinner and dance at the Hôtel de Paris in Monte Carlo. He had meant to make the party eight, but Sarah advised against it. As they were shown to their table the Maître-d'Hôtel saw Julius and said, "I shall tell Gaston *you* are here, sir." Edu had never been served better and he was pleased. Later, Julius apologized for not being able to dance; he was in mourning, he explained, for his father-in-law.

"Father-in-law?"

"My brother's actually. Conrad Bernin."

"The Under-Secretary?"

"His father. Old Count Bernin. He died six months ago."

"Oh I remember. Edu, the one who tried to put that Bavarian boob on the Spanish throne. He must have been an interesting man, Jules."

"Oh no, he was very dull."

Edu rose to dance with his sister; people in the room looked up, and at her dress.

"*Dommage*," said Julius. "Quite impossible. The expense for one thing. You see, I cannot afford a wife."

"Melanie's not poor," said Sarah.

"I suppose not. I am."

"Are you sure? All those things you're always buying . . . Not that I'm not convinced that what you and Edu call my daubs won't turn out the better investments. Still—"

"*Investments?*"

"And you say you are poor!"

"I shall be. Quite soon."

"Jules? You are not spending more than your income?"

"I don't know. I'm spending money."

"Money comes from somewhere," said Sarah.

"It's in a bank," said Julius.

"How did it get there?" said Sarah.

"Old Bernin arranged about the account. You see, I

inherited it. When my poor father died in '82. Not the money, our place. My elder brother ran it, and Clara. Clara is my sister-in-law. I don't think she ran it very well. Then my brother became secretary to her father and they didn't live there any more. They have no children. So it was sold. Old Bernin did it all, actually."

"Have you ever done any work, Jules?"

"Oh yes," said Julius. "I've had quite a hard life. Nearly ten years of it."

"Ten years of what? How little we know about you."

"I worked in an Embassy," said Julius.

Edu and Melanie came back from the floor. The men had some more brandy. Julius talked to the head-waiter about the phylloxera. It was one of his big subjects.

"Phylloxera?" said Melanie.

"The disaster," said Julius. "The American vine louse."

"Another turn, Melanie? Jolly band."

"As you like, Edu."

Sarah said, "Jules, what *will* you do when your money comes to an end?"

"I have no idea," said Julius.

"You ought to think. Doesn't it worry you?"

"Life is very worrying."

"We should like to know what you think of this, sir," said the head-waiter.

Julius tasted. "*All right*, Ricardo," he said. "I haven't come across anything like it these days. I have to send for mine from England, you know."

"Berry Bros. are running low too, I hear."

"I suppose you wouldn't have a bottle or two to spare?"

"I already thought of it, sir. Guillaume has put half a dozen aside; I shall see that they are sent to you, sir."

"That must be hard luck on your other guests," said Sarah.

"Madame—most of our guests have been drinking Spanish brandy under Hennessy labels. It is always a pleasure to serve Monsieur le Baron; Monsieur le Baron pays *attention* to what he eats and drinks."

"Jules," Sarah said, "Melanie is a very rich girl indeed. Didn't you know that? I mean her father is."

"Her father?"

"Yes, Jules, yes. Her *father*. She has got a father, and a mother. All of us have."

"Oh," said Julius. "I am sure they are most agreeable people."

Chapter Three

"*Von?*" said Grandpapa Merz. "*Von?* Got himself baptized, eh, like poor Flora's husband?"

"Of course he didn't get himself baptized," said Sarah.

"They won't give you the *von* if you don't get baptized. Refused it myself three times. Once to the old Kaiser, twice to Wil'hem."

"The Barony in question was conferred by Ottomark the Bear," said Gottlieb.

"How do *you* know?" said Edu.

"I took the liberty of consulting the Almanach de Gotha last time I had occasion to be in your house, sir."

"We have always been jews," said Grandmama.

They were at second breakfast. Second breakfast was laid every morning at eleven-fifteen on a long table in the middle of the *Herrenzimmer,* a dark, fully furnished room with heavily draped windows that led from an antechamber to an antechamber. The meal was chiefly for the gentlemen. They ate cold Venison with red-currant jelly, potted meats, tongue and fowl accompanied by pumpernickel, toast and rye-bread, and they drank port wine. Grandmama sat with them. She had a newly-laid egg done in cream, and nibbled at some soft rolls with *Spickgans,* smoked breast of goose spread on butter and chopped fine. Grandpapa had a hot pousin-chicken baked for him every day in a small dish with a lid; and Cousin Markwald who had a stomach ailment ate cream of wheat, stewed sweetbreads and a special kind of rusks. Sarah had not let Gottlieb add a cover for her; Edu took a glass of sherry.

"You say he isn't baptized, Sarah?" said Grandpapa.

"He was baptized at birth," said Edu.

"Like the Rosenheim children. Bad new habit."

"What does he do?" said Friedrich. Friedrich ate heavily, in a solid, unhurried, unnoticing way, entirely accustomed to what he was consuming.

"He is a gentleman who lives in France and collects furniture," said Edu.

"An art-dealer," said Friedrich.

"Not at all," said Edu.

"He used to be in the Diplomatic Service," said Sarah. Cousin Markwald had been trimming things on his plate. "An early retirement," he said.

"He's not looking to me for a job?" said Grandpapa.

"No, no," said Sarah.

"Felden?" said Friedrich. "Felden? It wouldn't be that whipper-snapper who did the dirty work for old Bernin in the *Kultus-Ministerium*?"

"Politics?" said Edu. "Oh I shouldn't think so. Any rate he's always lived in Spain as far as I can make out, and in France."

"Wise man," said Emil.

"Don't eat so much paté de foie gras, Emil," said Grandpapa.

"Nobody thinks of their gall-bladders," said Cousin Markwald.

"It is very nice paté de foie gras today," said Grandmama.

"*As far as you can make out,* Edu?" said Friedrich. "You haven't made out much."

"The child's too young," said Emil.

"We should all like a good deal more information," said Cousin Markwald.

"He is a very nice looking young man," said Grandmama. "Melanie has his picture."

"A very good-looking young *couple*, ma'am," said Gottlieb.

"They must all live here," said Grandmama; "not miles away in the country like Edu and Sarah."

Friedrich usually looked in on Jeanne on his way home to lunch from his morning hour at the law-courts. Jeanne was then still running her hat-shop in the Nollendorf Strasse. It had one window and was reticently named *modes & chapeaux*.

When Friedrich came in Jeanne sent out the girl to get her dinner, and herself pulled down the shutter.

"Poor Melanie," she said.

"It must have been quick work."

"What did you say his name was?"

Friedrich told her.

"*Jules* Felden?"

"I believe so."

"*Not* Le Beau Jules? That's what they called him in Paris. A friend of mine knew him very well. You may have heard of her? Nelly de la Turbie."

"Sarah does have the most extraordinary friends," said Friedrich.

"He's written to me to engage rooms for him," said Edu. "He says they must be well heated. Well heated underlined. In May. Where does he think this is? Siberia?"

"Edu——I have misgivings."

"He's not going to bring that woman?"

"Worse," said Sarah.

The journey—first class, couchettes—had been long and ruinous. First they had been wildly excited by the train and everything in it; then they had become bored, then fretful, then furious, then fretful again. At each stage they had dismantled something in their compartments. The boy who generally looked after them had gone to get himself a beer and got left behind at Strasbourg.

Edu, on the platform, found Julius impeccable but wan. Julius had had very little sleep and he had had to pay a great many large tips quite often. Nor did he appear free now to leave the station. The porter collected the luggage—half a dozen leather suit-cases, some baby chairs and a net with grubby toys—and settled down to wait. He was whistling.

The conductor handed Julius over to a swelling concourse of officials. Robert offered to shake hands with them. He was ignored.

"Can I not pay now?" said Julius. "I am willing to, you know."

"*The forms have to be filled in.*"

"You see I am so afraid they might catch cold. They are not used to this climate."

He was pressed onward. He was carrying Léon and holding Robert by the hand. Tzara had linked arms with Edu. Edu felt a fool.

"Do up your coats," said Julius. "They lost their scarves." "Actually," he said in French to Edu, "they threw them out of the window at Dresden because the trolley man wouldn't let them have his oranges."

"*Das Reichseisenbahnhofsvorstandsamt—bitte sehr, mein Herr.*"

"In here?" said Julius.

They were kept standing.

There was a row of tables; officials sat behind them. All were writing.

"Sir," said Julius, "may I ask you to be so very kind as to deal with us at once? We've come such a very long way, you see."

The head-official took off his pince-nez; looked at Julius; put the pince-nez on again and went back to writing.

"Really," said Julius.

Edu gave him an imploring look. "*Entschuldigen Sie vielmals, Herr Bahnhofsvorstand,*" he said.

"Now if you will only be good a little longer, you'll be in your own nice beds with a glass of delicious hot milk," said Julius.

Léon whimpered.

"*Name?*" someone said quite suddenly from behind a desk.

"Your name," said Edu.

"*Geboren?*"

"*Geburtsort?*"

"*Vatersname?*"

"*Beruf?*"

"*Mutter?*"

They took an inventory of the damages.

Item) 2 Gas Globes, property of the *Kaiserlich-und-Königliche Deutsche Eisenbahnverwaitung:* smashed;

Item) 6 Glass Cylinders, type 4B, property of the said Company: smashed;

Item) 1 Porcelain Wash-Basin with Lid, property of the *Mittel-Europaeische Schlafwagen Gesellschaft:* smashed;

Item) 1 Water-Bottle & 2 Tooth-Mugs, property of the *Compagnie Internationale des Wagons Restaurants:* smashed;

Item) 1 Enamelled Notice-Plate marked VER-BOTEN, property of the *Preussische Staats-Eisenbahn:* defaced.

Many pens laboured. There was a play of rubber-stamps.

"You will hear from us in due course," the head official said. "You will not leave Berlin, or change your address without previous notice to the Police. And you will sign here—and here. And here. Now the duplicates. Then you may go." He looked up and over his lenses saw what Edu had already followed with a sinking heart. Robert had installed himself behind a desk. He had rigged himself a pince-nez and built a stack of dossiers; he wore a pen behind his ear, gripped an ink-pencil, and was punctuating an imaginary interview with a neat staccato of rubber-stamps. For an improvisation, it was a creditable performance.

"Oh Robert," said Julius, "you must not play with other people's things. How often have I told you."

The head official had risen. Everyone else stood up too.

"He's only a poor monkey," Julius said. "He only did it because he is tired."

They obtained permission to send for Friedrich. They sent for him by messenger and the pneumatic post. Friedrich came and brought a lawyer. The lawyer tried to explain to Julius the nature of the charge. Friedrich and Julius were introduced. Julius took him to be Melanie's uncle, and persisted with that notion. His mother and *sister*, Friedrich said, had been expecting him for four o'clock coffee. Friedrich pulled his watch; Julius and Edu pulled theirs. He must have some brandy and milk for Léon, Julius said; the flask was in his luggage. The lawyer arranged for bail.

They drove to the street with the ornate stucco fronts where Edu had engaged a suite of rooms. A good address, he said. The care-taker tried to bar their entrance; on a landing a woman made a shrill fuss. Edu's horses, long ago, had been sent home. They retreated to the hired cab.

"Palast Hotel," said Edu.

They were not admitted.

"Fürstenhof," said Edu.

The Fürstenhof was full up.

"Try the Esplanade," said Edu.

They drove through the Tiergarten. It was May and it was still light. Julius did not like the look of the trees. "Nine years," he said, "I have not been to Germany for nine years."

They were civil at the Hotel Esplanade. "*Bedauren sehr, meine Herren, bedauren . . .*" But they would not take them in.

"They are as clean as we are," Julius said. "Cleaner. It is true that they cannot take a bath. But they groom themselves all the time, and I brush them with a special powder. It makes their coats so fresh. They never sleep with their windows shut, and they will not eat cooked food."

Edu knew of a discreet private hotel Unter-den-Zelten by the river. They rattled down the Sieges Allee in the twilight. Julius looked at the statuary with distaste. "What are these large plaster figures for?" he said. "Is it some festival?"

The Kings of Prussia, Edu said; and it was marble.

The private hotel did not take them in. They drove up the Linden to the Bristol; they drove to the Bellevue, the Europa, the Gross-Britanien and the Hotel de Russie. They drove to the Deutsche-Hof.

Tzara was asleep on Julius's shoulder. Robert lolled, Léon was crying.

They drove to the Mohren Strasse and tried a number of nameless places.

"*Affen?*" said the matron, "*Jotte doch, det verjrault mir ja die Kundschaft.*"

It was dark at last, but there were plenty of bright street lamps. "We shall have to go home again," said Julius.

"You don't suppose they would let you on another train?" said Edu.

They tried the Potsdamer Station Hotel and the Anhalter Station Hotel; they tried the Gasthaus zum Schwarzen Adler and the Gasthaus zum Bösen Hirsch. They were refused at Haus Temperanz-Blaukreuz and at the Christliche Deutsche Jung-Männer Verbandt.

The cabbie poked his head in. "You ought to try the Kaiserhof," he said, "that's where all those foreign

Emperors and Sultans go. Had the Shah of Persia there last year. They're used to harems and blacks."

"He may be right," said Edu.

The red carpet was out for the Dowager Queen of Saxony. The chief reception clerk returned Robert's bow. They were taken up in the service-lift.

Julius rang for the room-waiter. "I must leave you now," Edu said, "it's too late for you to see papa to-night. You had better speak to him in the morning."

"Speak about what?" said Julius.

Melanie, dressed in a way that was picked on by her relatives, waited for him all evening.

In the morning Edu went to the hotel to fetch Julius. The boy had not arrived. Julius explained that he could not go out.

"The servants here do not seem to be kind."

Edu inquired what he was to tell his parents.

Julius said, "You see, it is only because of Robert. Robert has a difficult nature. He is his own worst enemy."

The boy remained lost for several days. Edu and Friedrich did the telegraphing. Grandpapa was persuaded to call at the Kaiserhof. Julius had just wangled an anthracite stove, the management having refused to re-light the central plant. Julius himself suffered, but Grandpapa found it as warm as his own house. The chimpanzees too, comfortable for the first time, were in an amiable mood; Robert poured Madeira, and Tzara showed an interest in the old gentleman. He gave her a gold-piece, and he went home impressed.

"As good as the Opera," he described at luncheon. "The Opera in the old days."

"There was no message?" said Melanie.

At last the boy turned up.

Julius arrived at Voss Strasse; went up the carpeted stairs; walked through the ante-rooms: Gottlieb rolled back another door,

"Frau Geheimrat—our bride-groom!"

and came upon Melanie in the Berlin drawing-room standing by her mother's chair. The walls were chocolate-brown, embossed; the upholstery magenta; the morning gas-light was burning in the chandeliers. Melanie coloured, smiled, stepped forward with perfect grace. She raised her eyes to him; Julius returned the greeting, but he could only see the house.

Cousin Markwald joined them, and Emil. Presently Grandpapa came in with Friedrich. Each shook hands with Julius, then made for a particular chair.

Grandmama remained spread in hers. "Looks older than his picture," she said.

He was pressed to stay for luncheon. He found he was expected to sit with Grandpapa after it; expected to eat cake with the old lady; expected to chat with members of the family returning from their naps; expected to come back for dinner.

"And what do you do with yourself all day in the South of France?" said Markwald.

"I was there nine weeks," said Melanie.

"Does he play *grabuge*?" said her mother.

"He knows every card-game."

"I believe my grandfather played it," said Julius.

"Hardly a man's game," said Markwald.

Gottlieb and a footman carried in the box; Melanie and Gottlieb settled down to shuffling an improbable number of black cards. *Grabuge* is a game played by two people with one hundred and twenty-eight packs every single card of which is a spade. It is a kind of giant demon, an immensely elaborate simple game; and it takes all afternoon.

"Opposite me," said Grandmama. Julius sat down; but it was found that he could not play. "I will teach you," Grandmama said, but proving almost at once unequal to the task, relinquished it to Gottlieb.

"What's new, Friedrich?" said his father.

"Friedrich goes to the city every day," said Grandmama. While her partner was learning, she availed herself of several successive turns and managed to make good progress.

"Consols are down, papa."

"Always are."

"Why do people never cease complaining about consols?" said Emil. "Yet they appear to have them. Is it a law?"

"It is a safe rule to keep a third of one's investments in that kind of securities," said Friedrich.

"Does Baron Felden agree?" Markwald called across the room, "Do you go in much for consols, Baron?"

"It sounds an excellent idea," said Julius.

"Someone *is* speaking well of consols," said Uncle Emil.

"Someone who does not appear to have them," said his cousin.

"Jules bought such a lovely statue," said Melanie.

"I found it in a church."

"Church?" said Grandmama and Markwald.

"What did I tell you!" said Grandpapa.

"It was in bad condition," said Julius.

"The French are getting above themselves in Morocco," said Friedrich.

"Morocco?" said Grandmama.

"Leather, ma'am."

"Ah yes . ."

"White houses," said Julius. "All white. The Arab houses, at Fez. So beautiful." Julius had become emancipated from his instructor, and Melanie had taken the place by his side.

"How is Léon?"

"Not at all well. I must ask your uncle when he thinks that charge is going to be cleared up."

"The case is going to be heard before the 3rd *Kammergericht*," said Friedrich. "Not this Sessions, though."

"Melanie's fiancé insulted a policeman," said Grandmama.

"It was not his fault," said Melanie.

"And you always go to Paris in the spring, Baron?" said Emil, whistling very gently a passage from *La Belle Hélène*.

Grandpapa took it up more loudly. He always recognized Offenbach.

"Sessions?" said Julius.

"Petty-Sessions. Not before after the summer Recess. The Courts don't sit in August and their lists are pretty heavy."

"I used to give very nice suppers Chez Maxim's, and at the Café de la Paix. Ask the head-waiters," said Emil. "But that was a long time ago."

"When he was young," said Grandmama.

"And rich," said Friedrich.

"I never regretted it."

"You didn't have to," said Cousin Markwald, whom a different course had brought to a similar fate.

"This is Emil's home," said Grandmama.

"Your brother and your cousin made it that," said her husband.

"I am going to have asparagus for dinner," said Grandmama, "Flora's Max sent the first today. There's enough for one." Flora's husband, a recently ennobled banker, had also bought himself a country place. The shoot and hot-houses supplied the tables of his relatives.

"Do I have to stay?" said Julius.

"Unless you want to lose a thousand thaler bail," said Friedrich.

"Was it as much as that?"

"That's what we arranged with your bankers."

"You mean I have to stay? Stay here?"

"Fortunately, there are inducements," said Gottlieb.

"You missed your turn again, young man," said Grandmama.

"I am so sorry."

"Wonder where the Threes are?" said Grandmama, looking at her bottom cards.

"Oh, one *can* look at one's stock-pile?" said Julius.

"Not usually," said Melanie.

It was she who at last took the initiative, and found herself backed by the butler.

"Mama—I don't think Jules really wants to finish the game."

"May I suggest a brief rest, ma'am, before dressing?"

"Melanie, show Baron Felden the conservatory," said Emil.

"I want to finish the game," said Grandmama.

"We musn't let our little pleasures interfere," said Gottlieb.

She rose. He followed her out of the room. His step was light. His coat hung beautifully, his back was non-committal.

Flowers in the house gave Grandmama Merz a headache, but the conservatory was kept stocked by a visiting florist. They stood among the ferns and azaleas in great fear. He saw the threat to his existence, a cloud moving in that would engulf his private, careful life, a threat of which this house, this town, these people, were at once the portents, the tools and the reality. He felt caught up with, brought by the incomprehensible enmeshment of events to the brink, once more, of change; felt he must give battle or become submerged, felt submerged already by his own depression and forebodings. He stood with a smooth face, intent on managing the weight upon his chest and throat; he was then already suffering, or thought he did, from bronchial asthma, and he held himself quite still, coaxing, shifting, balancing the burden with false calm. Melanie moved before him: not anything like pacing, taking small steps from flower-tub to window-seat; her feet were delicate, her dress swished a little, she managed her skirts well. He was not aware of her at all.

Her fear was large and simple. She wanted to cry out, HE DOESN'T LOVE ME ANY MORE, and knew already as clearly as if she had been taught that she must not. She felt that something was missing and did not know what it was; that something was wrong and did not know why; knew that she would fight, and did not know what or how. She was twenty; she had never asked a question; she took for granted what she had been told, that her home was the best of possible homes and hers the best of lives, and if often she had been listless and a little sad, then that was what the best of lives must be. Her mother had wanted some small thing or other at every moment of her many days, whereas Melanie had everything she wanted and had wanted nothing very much. Now her need was entire, and it was everything. She had not heard of the relativity of love, and perhaps what animated her was not relative; her future, or the lack of one, proved it to have been the one directed longing of her body, will and pliant heart. This soft creature was discovering the necessity of courage, and found courage—she pressed aside the immediate claims of her anxiety and turned to Julius with a well-bred smile that bore no trace of either intimacy or strain.

" J'ai tant regretté d'apprendre que vous avez fait un si mauvais voyage," she said in pretty, tripping French. Her ear was good and had retained the sounds of the French governess; in the South Jules had praised her accent; since her return she had worked hard; yet the effort of making this gentle bid was tremendous and her fingers were opening and shutting on the handkerchief behind her back.

He did not notice the switch of language which to him was natural. He said, "Eh bien, ce n'était surtout pas commode pour ces pauvres bêtes."

She realized then that they were not there.

He explained about his difficulties over the right food at an hotel, about their restlessness, about exercising them—

Melanie bent her head and listened. She always listened, to her uncles, to her father, to her brothers . . .

Julius spoke for himself. "The *Tiergarten* in the

morning— people stare so and we have to keep to those
ugly walks. They like to pick their own peaches— The
man said they weren't allowed on the grass, so unfair.
It isn't as if they wore *boots*."

"Nobody here is allowed on the grass," she said.

"Oh," he said, "is that it. Why?"

Melanie did not know.

They dropped this subject.

"Edu and Uncle Emil are persuading papa to let me
have the riding lessons."

"Ah yes," he said, "riding . . Do you get much of it
here?" He had forgotten that it was he who had urged
that course, as he had forgotten that he found it odd that
this was necessary.

She wanted to stretch out her hand, say, My dear,
what is it? Speak to me, my dear.

He said, "The weather has not been good."

"In the South?"

"Here."

"We've not been out this week," she said. It could not
come into her mind that someone so splendid was able to
feel unhappiness, but she saw that he must want his house,
his things, the sun— And when she saw this, she saw
further—it was her habit to love her parents and to defer
to them, and it did not occur to her to criticize them now,
she was merely ready, if at all expedient, to throw her
mother and her father to the wolves.

"It was cold this morning."

"I don't like the cold," she said.

"Of course not."

"It will not always be like this," Melanie said, her eyes
on him. He did not see her, and it was possible. *He does
not like it here. He is not himself.* This smote her. Something else entered in her feeling and, for the first time,

her heart expanded in tenderness. *Do not worry. It will be different soon.* She was less afraid for herself now. *I will find a way. It will be different when we have a house of our own. A house where you want it.* But she shrank from speaking words that included his future in her own. She found it difficult to think of more conversation, and her mind, having got hold of something, was already giving itself to practicalities. Yet they must not stay silent. "My sister Flora has a bicycle now," she said, not adding, since she's married.

Her new-found heroism kept it up, adequately; but when some time later Sarah came in, Sarah everywhere herself, in a smart grey tailor-made, three egret feathers tipping from an enormous hat, Julius turned to her in absolute relief.

Chapter Four

JULIUS borrowed pen and ink from the floor-waiter and wrote to his sister-in-law. He told her that he was entangled with the Prussian law and unable to move, and would she ask her brother, Conrad Bernin, who knew about such things, to do something about it.

Clara and Gustavus, and Count Bernin poised between two offices, were at Sigmundshofen winding up the late Count's affairs. They had not seen Julius since the week when in due course and having lived rather longer than he had expected Baron Felden died and was buried by his weeping tenantry. Julius had arrived from Madrid in time to stand in the autumnal graveyard with Gustavus and the three Bernins. He was overcome, and said a word to Clara afterwards about the untrustworthiness of life. Gustavus was irreproachable, and held himself thus. Clara had masses said all over the country for the old Baron's repose; Count Bernin arranged for an income paid to Julius out of his estate. This was now nine years ago, Julius had returned to Spain but not to his post, and the Bernins only learnt from the German Foreign Office of the vague and definite letter he had sent saying he must leave them.

"The Prussian law? What can he mean?" said Count Bernin.

"We must find out, Conrad," said his sister.

"Of course," said Count Bernin.

Count Bernin in nearly all respects had become exactly like his father. (He even had the same bearing, voice and profile, and their hair was the same grey.) So much so,

that in later years very young and very old people, and
the public who had watched that long career, took them
to have always been the same person. Nevertheless, there
was a difference, and perhaps it was that of being born in
1850 rather than in 1810. The younger Bernin, from the
cradle, had breathed the air of universal suffrage. He was
a shade drier, a shade less high-handed, a shade more
prudent than had been his father—it was all a bit toned
down; and although in the course of years he too became
involved in almost everything that was going, he never
saw himself as a prestidigitator. He was devoted to Clara
and liked to have her about (he never married); and
sometimes he accepted her advice. Clara looked up to her
brother—who was two years younger—and was in his
regard quite without that tinge of misgiving that had so
cleft her conscience in her youth.

Count Bernin also lacked one of his father's most
serviceable gifts—he was no man's fool, but he did not
have the old Count's dead-plumb insight into character
and motive. And this, in his turn, the old man had not
realized. Thus Bernin saw his brother in-law as what he
largely was: dullish, idle, punctilious, vain; not a bad
sort, not incapable of taking pains—Clara's husband,
rather nil, rather decent, mildly useful. The old Count
had seen Gustavus whole, and had failed to impart this
knowledge to his son. Throughout his life, the Count
had had to pay for his repeated failure to communicate an
essential fact at the right time. Here, he had not spoken
merely because he did not know that this was necessary;
he saw Conrad as he saw himself, he did not conceive that
anything he found obvious was not obvious also to his son.

"Why Berlin?" said Count Bernin.

"I don't know," said Clara, to whom one place was
much like another.

"You didn't see him there—the time papa was trying to smooth things for him. *How* he carried on— He could not understand why he had to come at all. It worried him; he had wanted to leave straight from Bonn to London. I can't think what they made of him at the Wilhelmstrasse."

"He never really passed those exams," said Gustavus.

"Oh exams," said Count Bernin.

"London was a splendid first post for so young a man, quite unexpected. I believe he owed it entirely to your father, Clara."

"Poor Jules, I remember how disappointed he was. He had been so certain that it would be Spain."

It had once been one of Count Bernin's schemes to create precedent by inserting the thin wedge of undemonstratively catholic young Catholics into diplomatic posts in countries fidgety about that faith; and indeed Julius had caused no scandal at the Court of Queen Victoria in so far as he had never thought to mention that he was a member of the Roman Church at all.

"He enjoyed it in the end," said Count Bernin. "At least he ought to have, he went down so frightfully well. The English adored him."

"He said he liked the houses and the horses," said Clara; "he said it was all very much like being at Landen."

"He was good at knowing where people's silver and things came from, and he never talked politics."

"Count Helmholz told me they couldn't get Jules to do any work," said Gustavus.

"Well he wasn't expected to do that."

"They also said he was wonderfully discreet."

Count Bernin sighed. "It was his great talent. Quite wasted unfortunately—sheer hypocrisy."

"You *will* help him?" said Clara.

"My dear: does one tamper with the Prussian law? *Que diable allait-il chercher dans cette galère?*"

"I don't suppose one could ask?" said Gustavus.

"Why not?" said Clara. "I will. If you really wish to know, Conrad?"

"Do," said Count Bernin.

To the point-blank question Julius replied one sentence; he was in Berlin because he had been supposed to get married.

"How very, very nice for Jules," said Clara.

"To whom?" said Gustavus.

"In Berlin?" said Count Bernin.

"We must hope that hers is a *solid* faith. Anything less would be fatal for both of them."

"Well, people tend to have that *in partibus*."

Before writing again to Jules, Clara withdrew to the oratory and gave herself to thankfulness.

"We ought to do something to take them off poor Jules's hands," said Sarah, buttoning long gloves. "I'm going to that sale. Andirons and pewter this afternoon. Gothic. Well— Jules said he'd look in if he could manage. I also refuse to have them in the house, but perhaps we can organize something?"

"Why don't you send the girls with Miss Mills, they can go to a bun-shop or the Zoo or something," said Edu.

"I did. It was not a success. Nobody was the right age."

"Tell you what, I'll get papa to take them on his drive. Fräulein von Tschernin can't mind; after all she gets paid."

"Miss Mills minded. She told me."

Grandpapa Merz and Fräulein von Tschernin called for Robert and Tzara in the landau. The four of them drove along the Lenée Strasse and the Viktoria Strasse and the Lützow Ufer; they had bought a bag of nuts, and Grandpapa soon picked up the trick of aiming shells at the hats of the passers-by. Giesela von Tschernin had had a pony and once reared a wolf cub in her mortgaged home by the Vistula, now she inhabited a faded *chambre de jeune fille* on the second-floor flat of a civil-service uncle, and her numbed heart stirred once more with happiness. They bought grapes and ices and a pair of sailor's caps and a celulloid flag, and Robert allowed her to nurse his ears. Later, while she waited, the old gentleman introduced them to his club.

"*There are no such people,*" said Gustavus. "There were some Merzweiler Schleicheggs, but they've had no issue since the Diet of Ratisbon. And there are the Hungarian März März-Glinsky who are mediatized and of course have been insane for a very long time."

"There *are*," said Count Bernin. "Arthur Merz. Merz & Merz G.m.b.H. Phosphates. A sizeable fortune; quite idle."

K

"Israelites," said Gustavus, lowering his tone in spite of himself. "Presumably a papal title."

"Converts," said Clara. "Oh Conrad!"

"*No* title. *Not* converts. I shouldn't think they were christened."

There was a silence.

"Pious Jews—" said Clara. "It is well to remember the origin of our religion."

Gustavus had covered his face. "Nineteen generations of recorded alliances—"

"Can you make out whether it is at all settled?" said Count Bernin.

"Jules doesn't say."

"Knights of the Undivided Vigil . . . Knights of Saint John . . . Knights of the Perpetual Lamp . . ."

"Papa was never entirely opposed to mixed marriages, as you may remember," said Count Bernin.

"Is it to be an engagement dinner?"

"Of course not," said Sarah. "Just an ordinary dinner-party. Smart . . Not too much food . . Jules will take me in, and we'll put Professor Boden on my other side."

"The museum wallah?"

"Yes," said Sarah.

"Oughn't we to have Prince Eitel-Heinz?"

"No," said Sarah. "Above all no royalty, I beg you. Madame Mopurgo on Jules's left—"

"Madame Mopurgo?"

"Yes."

"What about Melanie?"

"Melanie will go in with the French Naval Attaché."

"Won't she mind?"

"Not if she knows what's good for her. Claude Billy is most decorative and he's always managed to live in Persia and places. She's got a new Worth. Sulphur yellow. We didn't think there was time, but Jeanne's done wonders."

"Have you been seeing *Jeanne*?" said Edu.

"Every day," said Sarah.

Count Bernin wrote to Julius's lawyer and to Friedrich; got in touch with one or two people; then wrote to Julius's lawyer again. All of this took time. There did not seem to be much of a case, he pointed out; *if* they let it go as disturbance of the peace, that was; there was still a chance of their bringing it in as contempt of state, *lèse-fonctionaire,* a charge to be avoided. They seemed to feel *touchy* about the business; it would be useful if one were able to tender a statement to the effect that the *primum mobile* as one might say—chimpanzees, was it?— had been eliminated. Was it wise of Baron Felden to live with them openly at the most expensive hotel in town? It was also said that they were being seen in public in the company of the defendant's prospective father-in-law; the authorities appeared to be a little suspicious of the Baron —perhaps he was not creating *quite* the right impression. . . ?

"I don't want to miss the English Derby," said Edu.

"There's no reason why *you* shouldn't go."

"I say, Sarah, I wish I knew what everybody's up to."

"How do you mean?"

"Well, people are sort of wondering. I don't know what to tell them. You know—I don't think he ever really asked papa."

"Your father seems to be under the impression that he did."

"He knows he asked *me* in the South of France."

"Did Jules do that?"

"Through you, I thought."

Clara stood in the doorway of the bare room that seemed arranged as if in perpetual expectation of a board-meeting. "Conrad, we must know who is instructing Jules's future wife. Jules does not tell. Can he be reading our letters?"

Count Bernin was going over estate accounts with Gustavus. He did not look up. "Oh one of the Fasanen Strasse Fathers, very likely," he said.

Clara sighed. "I'd so much rather it were someone like Father Martin. Do you think we ought to send Father Martin?"

"My dear—the poor chap is a very old man."

"He never shirked his duty."

"Oh come on, Clara," said Gustavus, "Fasanen Strasse is perfectly all right."

"Money's at last come up."

"Whom did you talk to?" said Jeanne.

"Friedrich. The old people. Markwald, Emil. Everyone. With Gottlieb in and out. Think of your not knowing Gottlieb. That's enough to make anybody's married life."

"I can't call it that."

"Friedrich was the worst, you know."

"Such a pity Jules *will* go on thinking he's sixty; Friedrich is as vain as Edu."

"I can hardly believe it," said Sarah.

"It was two millions they gave Flora, wasn't it?"

"Yes; but then Max is very well-off himself. I never expected as much as that for Jules."

"Is that how it works? A rich man's *dot,* and a poor man's *dot*?"

"It's not unnatural," said Sarah.

"How much did you bring Edu?" said Jeanne.

"Five."

"That went rather fast didn't it?"

"It went. Well, Emil and Edu thought they'd never make it more than four or five hundred thousand, but I knew that million had stuck in the old people's mind, and I was right. They spoke of it as The Million from the start."

"Then it is a million! Sarah, I am glad for Le Beau Jules."

"There's a hitch," said Sarah. "They can't find anything to put it into."

"Invest it?"

"It's usual to put the *dot* into the son-in-law's business."

"Oh."

"They're quite ready to set him up in one."

"It is their tendency," said Jeanne.

"My dear!"

The two women laughed.

"They mentioned Max's bank. Melanie got to hear of that. One can see how. The way the servants don't have to stoop to key-holes in that house ... She's dead against it. So is Edu for that matter."

"So are you," said Jeanne.

"In this case. Ordinarily I rather like to see a man work. My brothers do."

"It has its advantages," said Jeanne.

"Friedrich's idea was to settle the *dot* on Jules, and let him and Melanie spend the interest. The trouble with that is that a million at two or three percent— the kind of investment they're thinking of—would give them something between twenty or thirty thousand marks a year. It's not enough, Jeanne. Their clothes alone'd come to that."

"Did you point that out?"

"It wouldn't do to be too precise. Emil has seen the truth all the time, and Markwald has sniffed it out. The old people are vaguely puzzled. I really think that if everybody weren't so very vague there wouldn't be a marriage."

"You and I are not vague."

"Jeanne—*why* are you for it?"

"I don't know that I am. A middle-aged woman's instinct for match-making. An exile's affection for her country and someone connected with it. A woman's feeling for another woman. A woman's feeling for a handsome man in distress. *My* feelings about Friedrich's parents."

"*I* could have stopped it," Sarah said. "I could still stop it. And by doing nothing."

"No woman can stop another from getting her man for the right reason."

Sarah said, "She can help her for the wrong ones."

"Of course he'll make her a wretched husband. There are worse things. What makes you think the girl will ever choose better? Or have the chance?"

"She might subside into her own tradition."

"About that money—Sarah, *you* could make them let him have it outright, you know you could."

"I'm not at all sure that I want to. A million is a great deal of money. I should hate not to see them decently provided for, but capital is capital."

"Yes," said Jeanne, "I've been brought up to believe in savings too."

"What I am out to get for them is an allowance, a big allowance. I suggested seventy-five and I think they're going to make it sixty thousand a year. I'm sure that's best for them—it's comfortable, and it's safe. Edu and I will give them the price of a house for a wedding present."

"*Very* comfortable. All the same, Sarah—I don't like the sound of an allowance."

"Only until the old people die. Melanie's share, even if left to her in trust, which of course it will be, is going to be enough for her and Jules to be extremely well off on the interest."

"I see you worked it all out," said Jeanne.

"Yes," Sarah said, "I have."

Grandmama Merz eventually put two and two together.

"Is Melanie going to live in a house with monkeys?"

Fräulein von Tschernin, who had had a glimpse also of Julius, confirmed that this was part of her daughter's radiant prospects.

"We're not going to allow it," said Grandmama.

"Herr Geheimrat is fond of them too."

"Monkeys are all right for bachelors," said Grandpapa.

"I asked him whether he was going to have those

brutes about for the rest of his life," said Markwald; "and you know what he told me? Alas, very likely not, although they did live longer than dogs."

"Dogs too?" said Grandmama.

"Flora's Max brought one," said Friedrich.

"Not in the house," said Grandmama. "Flora told me."

"What does one do with unwanted monkeys?" said Emil.

Grandmama pondered this. "He must give them away," she said. "Hasn't he any poor relations?"

Again Clara walked into a room. She seldom sat down. "I feel I must go myself. I am certain of it."

"You've not been at all well," said her brother. "Besides there's our repository for Corpus Christi."

"Those decorations are not important. I always think they are too elaborate. It distracts attention. And Gustavus can see to them just as well."

"I don't agree," said Count Bernin. "The children of Mary expect *you* to help them; and it *is* important—the mistress of Sigmundshofen has always done the repository, hundreds of people will come in the procession to look at it."

"And there's the Bishop," said Gustavus.

"I do not see it in that way," said Clara.

The first sign that Julius had got down to reading Clara's letters came from Friedrich. Julius had to report once a week at a Police station and Friedrich accompanied him there again on the first Monday in June. Afterwards he dropped in at Jeanne's very cross, and found Sarah.

"I think your precious Felden must be pulling all our legs. You know what he said to me today, in that southern voice of his, 'Your niece *is* a Catholic?'"

"He didn't. What did *you* say?"

"I said we were no Christians if that was what he meant. And he said, yes, no, of course, but did I mean that she was *definitely* not a member of the Church?"

"Oh dear," said Sarah. "I don't think he can mind."

"Mind?" said Friedrich. "*I mind.* I can see why those railway people thought he was impertinent."

"It's that he's used to everybody being Catholic," said Jeanne. "It is like that where he comes from. My father belonged to *La Libre Pensée* and I am what you might call relapsed, but we're all Catholics."

"He thought *I* was a Christian," said Friedrich.

Sarah was seeing Julius that afternoon, and they had a talk which drove her to dine at Voss Strasse.

"It might be advisable not to broach anything until *afterwards*, ma'am," Gottlieb said to her in the hall.

Sarah ignored him, but not his warning. Edu had left for London; Jules had felt entitled to excuse himself that night; she sat almost silent through the cream of chicken, the crayfish in aspic, the vol-au-vent, the calf's tongue and currants in Madeira, the chartreuse of pigeon and the mousseline of artichokes, and it was only after the Nesselrode pudding and Melanie sent upstairs that she disclosed that Jules Felden appeared to think it necessary for his wife to share his religion.

"*He wants her to get baptized.*"

"*The young man with the monkeys wants our daughter baptized.*"

"Who does he think we are?"

"Even Max never suggested anything of the kind!"

"I told you he was a Goy in disguise."

"The poor child."

"*Please* Emil——" said Sarah.

"Well," he said, "of all the cold-blooded, ungentle-manly suggestions——"

Sarah, deciding to let it blow over, had gone home. Next morning she saw Julius again, then Friedrich, then the old man. She had asides with Markwald. The Merz's were glad to vent their feelings but refused to *discuss* the subject, and during the week that followed nobody budged an inch.

"It's like fighting feather-beds," Sarah said to Jeanne. "And it shows how wrong one can be. The old lady and Jules. I never expected any trouble from those two; they're the worst. Jules finds it *odd* that Melanie wasn't Christened, it alarms him. Just says he couldn't marry someone who wasn't a Catholic—it wasn't done—nobody did. Over and over again. Just sticks to that. He *might* have thought of it before. Really now, *I'm* going to wash my hands. I can see the Merz's point. Do you understand him at all?"

"Oh quite," said Jeanne.

"It isn't as though *he'd* ever showed himself the least bit *pratiquant*."

"Nor do the Merz's for that matter. Friedrich goes to nothing—except funerals—and there isn't even the pretence of keeping the Sabbath at Voss Strasse, or not eating lobsters or ham——"

"It is peculiar," Sarah said; "theological dead-lock between non-practising members of two religions."

Edu returned from Epsom and heard some hard words. Jules no longer lunched at Voss Strasse; Sarah talked of summer plans. One evening Melanie put on a thick veil and slipped out with her maid, Hedwig. They entered the Matheus Kirche by a side-door. Hedwig was a well-known face in the congregation; Melanie carried a small purse with gold; Paster Völler was aged. So it was after only a brief interview that she was led into the empty church where water was sprinkled on her forehead and she spoke the words taught to her by Gottlieb, signed the register and was received a member of the Reformed Evangelical Church of Germany.

She returned to Voss Strasse, late, in high excitement, two red circles burning on her cheeks.

The family was worried but already in the dining-room. She faced them.

"It is done," she announced: "I am Jules's."

"The cad," said Markwald.

"What?" said Grandmama.

"Nothing can separate us now."

"Have they eloped?" said Grandmama.

"Worse," said Markwald and her husband.

"Worse!" said Emil.

"Our treasure has been baptized," said Gottlieb.

The same night Edu and Friedrich called at the Kaiserhof demanding immediate marriage. Julius was sitting up, puzzling over the hotel charges. Edu was embarrassed, and spluttered; Friedrich was grim.

He spoke about dishonour.

Julius found his attitude most Prussian, but he consented and the two men withdrew.

A date was fixed for the end of June. The old Merz's, unwilling to see their daughter deprived of pin-money as well as Christian, stated that they would make her an annual allowance of fifty thousand marks.

Clara had sorted out her keys and with Gustavus's help —she was never very good at such tasks—unlocked and locked again plate and embroidered cloth. Then she set out for Berlin. She refused to have the express flagged for her, took a local for Karlsruhe instead, where she made rather a muddle over her changes. She had written a note to Julius, and Count Bernin had telegraphed the Bavarian Legation. (The Badensian Minister was a bachelor, and anyway quite small beer.) Julius booked a suite for her at the Hotel Bristol; at the Legation they prepared a room and sent the carriage to the station. Julius met the same morning train. Clara arrived by a later one. She had sat bolt upright all night in a second-class carriage; now she walked to the exit looking neither right nor left, carrying her own bag, and took the horse-tram to the *Grauen Damen* in the Stettiner Strasse. There she was in time to assist at the end of mass, changed her linen but resumed her dress, had a short

pleasant talk with the Superior and the Sister Porter, and
set out again. She took another horse-tram and went
straight to Voss Strasse.

She sent her card in to Melanie; Gottlieb announced
her without comment.

Clara came swiftly forward, inclined her head to the
old lady in the chair, ignored the men, held out her
hands. "My child—I had to see you!"

Melanie stood wary. All women were her enemies.
But she kept to her pretty ways.

"Tell me? You *are* being prepared?"

"She is going to be married on the 29th," said Grandmama.

"The quietest wedding," said Markwald.

"Then your Reception . .?"

"It's all been done," said Melanie.

"Dearest child!" Clara, her face radiant, advanced
again. Tears stood in her eyes. "So soon! Oh you
wonderful girl. The grace. And I, who doubted your
readiness . . . Will you forgive me? What it must mean to
your instructor!"

"Pastor Völler—"

"Not Pastor, dear, *Father*. We call our priests
Father."

"Father Völler," said Melanie.

"Do I know him?"

Melanie tendered the certificate she carried in her
dress.

Clara, already a little far-sighted, held it at arm's
length. She looked, frowned, shifted the distance again,
looked, her lips moving— Then she emitted a faint
hissing sound, and swayed. Gottlieb was in time with
the chair.

Grandmama proffered her *sal volatile*. Clara stirred.

"A Protestant," she groaned, and to everyone's consternation slipped from the chair to the floor. "On our knees, my child! and may He have mercy on us."

Grandmama signed to Gottlieb. "Bring the poor lady an egg in port wine."

But Clara, who had taken nothing since the previous day, waved sustenance aside. She rose and said in a strong voice, "It is His Will that you should pass through this abominable trial. I may have been sent to lead you out of it. We must not allow heresy to take root in you, we must send for a priest at once. This is an emergency and I believe you will be received. Instruction can come later."

The gasp this time came from the arm-chair. "They want to baptize her twice!" cried Grandmama and sank back into the cushions.

Gottlieb turned and presented the egg-nog on the tray. Grandmama took it.

The Jesuits at Fasanen Strasse did not see it with Clara's eyes and Melanie was not received into the Church on that day, nor the next. The Merz's rallied their wits; Count Bernin and Gustavus were summoned to Berlin; Edu discovered that his family was the laughing-stock of half the town—yet in the general uproar that followed it was Clara's purpose that worked every interest her way. Melanie was instructed and became a Roman Catholic, soon enough for her wedding to be but briefly postponed; the Merz's used the second outrage to bargain for the disappearance of the chimpanzees. Count Bernin, who shared Sarah's financial grasp, was able to increase the pressure. At Hamburg a man

called Haagenbeck was doing wonders in a new kind of
cageless Zoo. Julius met Herr Haagenbeck and liked
him. The two men had some useful talks; Jules made the
donation (half of which came from Grandpapa) of a
heating apparatus with lamps, already in use in the
monkey apartments at Copenhagen, and was only just
prevented from accepting the return present of a seal.
This disposal of the monkeys had been Edu's idea; Sarah
lent her electric brougham, and in this Julius set out on
the snail's pace journey to the Hanseatic port where he
bade farewell to Robert and to Tzara.

Count Bernin indited a statement to the judicature, and
the charges against Julius were dismissed. Sarah and
Clara were going through the invitations together, and
Clara, very simply, told her about Johannes. "There is
another brother. Did you not know? He was ill for a
long time because of a mistake that had been made. He
got better but the doctor said he would never be like
other people. The doctor wanted to keep him, but my
father wished him to be in the world and have as nearly
the kind of life he would have had as possible. He could
not live with us as he must not meet his brothers. It is
part of the illness. Jules went to him the first year, it was
very dreadful. Gustavus never tried. So you see there
wasn't much open to him; the doctor said he ought to be
kept active, and my father thought of the Army. Papa
knew a few people and our old Grand Duchess was very
much attached to the family and there was nothing else
for him to do. So they got him a commission in the
Body-Dragoons. Of course he wears no uniform, and he
didn't have any training. But he's on the Army-list;
and he draws pay like everyone else. Not that he needs
it—his share of his father's estate was put aside for him
and *my* father left him quite a large legacy, he doesn't

seem to spend anything poor boy—but apparently you cannot do things half-way with the military."

She reached for a fresh box of envelopes. "He was put in charge of an Army stud-farm and he's been a great success with the horses. He sits up with them when they're ill. They say he's never lost a foal. Of course there are sergeants and people on the place who run things for him. The farm's the other side of the Black Forest, he is quite alone with them out there; and of course he has his own house. Her Highness died, as you know, but the Grand-Ducal family are being very kind. The colonel is a friend; he doesn't bother him. He hasn't got to report or salute, or see anyone or dine in mess. And everybody is very pleased about the horses. He's a captain now. Papa did not think it wise. But Conrad says it attracts less attention to do things in the usual way; he was due for promotion, being over thirty-five. He doesn't speak; though they say he sometimes does. He looks well, quite healthy and splendid really. He will not eat meat. It is all very sad. He cannot go to mass as he cannot stand being indoors with people, but I'm sure God loves him. I think we'll send him an invitation—his orderly will read it and know he's thought of and put it away."

Clara slid a card into an envelope and addressed it in her rapid, careless hand. "Curious thing," she said, looking up, "we all thought Jean was going to be as tall as Gustavus and Jules, and do you know, he stayed quite short. Stocky-short; more like a farm-hand. You really think we ought to *seal* all these? It seems an unnecessary expense." She held an open flap. "Perhaps Jules and Melanie will have a son," she said.

"Do you think that a good thing?" said Sarah.

Her and Edu's cheque was large. The other presents

came in. Distressing china from Merz cousins, the Landen plate relinquished by Gustavus, the box-ful of jewels that had belonged to Julius's and Gustavus's mother which Clara now insisted on sharing with Melanie. Melanie found the settings pretty, just out of date enough to be wearable again; the rest of the Merz's told each other that the stones did not amount to much. Clara also gave a thin medal blessed by Leo XIII; and Jeanne—who was not asked and thus did not meet Melanie—sent a fan and a mother-of-pearl rosary that was supposed to have belonged to the original of the heroine of *Adolphe*. Both fan and rosary were exquisite. Julius, when reminded of the custom, gave Melanie his father's ring, a topaze so large, deep and clear that for many years the old Baron had not been able to bring himself to disturb that limpid surface by a banal incision, and when at last he had come upon, and sketched himself, a Chinese bird, he found, perhaps to his relief, that the craftsmen capable of executing such intaglio had died out. On his death Gustavus had assigned the crestless stone to Julius who, it having become too ornamental for the men of his day, always carried it in his pocket. Edu had it sent to Friedländer's, where it was competently carved with the Felden arms.

Grandmama parted with some diamonds. The girls' trousseaus—cambric, linen, lace—had been ready for years except for the initials; these with the German Baron's seven-pointed coronet were being rushed through the embroidery department at Braun's. Melanie, single-handed, turned down the near-by spa selected for their journey; the South, she stated, was where she wished to go. Julius had told her Spain; one place abroad was as bad as another; again her parents gave in. Gustavus declared he would be seen dead sooner than in Berlin Cathedral with the Merz's; this and other awkwardnesses

L

at the ceremony were forestalled by Count Bernin's arranging with a Dean of his acquaintance to have the marriage service held at Voss Strasse, a convenience not usually afforded by their own religion which almost reconciled the old Merz's to its taking place. They now said they would give the couple forty-five thousand marks a year, and Grandmama, in a movement of *attendrissement*, lent her own maid Marie for her daughter's going away.

And so in this manner, on a sultry day in July, Julius Maria von Felden and Melanie Ida Merz were made man and wife.

Julius had given his parents-in-law a pair of seventeenth-century Persian china cats. They were large, bright yellow, upright animals with turquoise spots and glinting jewelled eyes, and they were stood on pedestals opposite each other in the first ante-room at Voss Strasse, where they gleamed, monstrous, beautiful and alien, for many years. They were very rare, and supposed to be most valuable. Sarah, who had been given nothing and had coveted them on sight, passed them on her way out after the young couple had left, and felt vaguely mystified and quite cross.

Chapter Five

JULIUS and Melanie stayed on in Spain. They discussed no plans; the future was not broached. Julius took another white-washed house, left the garden and the patio as they were, slowly filled the cool bare vaulted rooms with things—sombre ornamental furniture, great looking-glasses, extravagant statuary, arriving laboriously from Granada by carter over the brilliant roads: carved vermillion folds and gilt scrolls white with dust exposed above the wide-spread horns of oxen; packing-cases from Seville shaped like harps, and packing-cases marked fragile, large as boulders, swaying up the magnolia alley above the invisibly placed steps of an ant-line of pack-mules. From behind shuttered windows, Melanie was watching.

"Oh, Jules, what's that? Where does it come from?

"Won't they drop it?

"Can we have it out at once? Where are you going to put it?"

Julius liked to be alone for the unpacking.

He engaged man-servants, arranged for fruit and fowls; got a pharmacist at Ronda interested in composing weekly a lump of butter for Melanie's maid whose complaints centred round the oil. This butter, a softish fragment of uncertain colour, afloat in a large sealed tank, was borne one early morning up the drive like a tabernacle in procession by its creator, his boy assistant and a crowd. Melanie seemed ready to stay idle. Her maid, also, whom the lower servants assumed to be a lady and the upper ones their mistress's old wet-nurse, was expected to do no work. But Marie, ignoring a prejudice that went against her every fibre, went about a hundred unwanted tasks in stays and starch with compressed lips. Julius felt her as a part of his new burden, wondered if there were no means of making away with her, was not displeased when his valet hinted that there were, yet, his mind on bravos, honestly strove to feed her according to her lights. The slow posts caught up with them and catalogues, dealers' announcements and trade-journals reached him once more, as did the boots from Paris, sherry from the South, shirts from Madrid. He missed his monkeys, but realized that they were happy and active in their larger sphere. He now had a new marmoset, some tame cock-pheasants and a straggle of ailing beasts. The gardener had an angora goat with two white kids; the carrier kept a sty-ful of donkeys. None of these were looked after as they should. Julius went round bribing peasants, arguing with muleteers. He bought off caged rabbits, watered cattle, whisked flies off horses's faces, treated harness-sores—the animals were the one heartbreaking thing in this country, he told Melanie and he told her often. Melanie listened because she liked to be spoken to; she had learnt to look at certain animals with pleasure, she often stroked the golden pheasants by the fountain and she was sure it was all dreadful, but what really frightened her were the beggars. She was much alone.

Julius came and went. He spent the night at Seville, a day or two at Algeciras, stayed at some estate, had an errand at Cadiz, and he looked up startled when she asked him where he was going and when he might return. It was the look that came over him in mid-morning, when they met, both exquisitely dressed, in the latticed penumbra of the *sala* and she never failed to ask him how he had slept.

He was not unkind.

Melanie, sensitive to his every sign, sensitive as the savage to the weather, was not equipped to help him. She was ready to be shaped; at the flicking of his hand. He let her pick up a few tricks of taste. She was easy enough to have about; how easy, having no points of comparison, he did not know; and very pretty; and this, coming in sometime at twilight from the Granada road, he could see again. After the brief greeting, after his bath, after the first glass of *manzanilla* by himself, pale, light, lightly iced, coming down again at that hour when the heat of day still rises from the earth and walls, and cool is divined already in the veins and skin, he would find her in the opened loggia in muslin and ribbons, her shoulders bare, her hair high, the small, shod, pointed feet visible on the chaise-longue, and make his own entrance like a man at the play into his box, during the second act, before the aria by the new soprano.

Sometimes Marie appeared on the terrace where they had been dining, stepped from the bushes in the garden. "Fräulein Melanie, Frau Baronin I should say, I've brought you a shawl." And Julius rose, displayed watches, remarked that, perhaps, it was not too late yet for the Circle . . .

Of course she never went out. Perhaps the course of their life together was really set by Julius's choice of place. The South of Spain in the Eighteen-Nineties was not a woman's country, and emphatically not a lady traveller's one. Julius did not take her anywhere. If it wasn't the flies, it was the dust, the heat— There was nowhere to go, it was not suitable (a word he had lately come to use), she was sure not to enjoy it—

There was the heat. Julius wore a silk veil from the back of his hat at midday, had a system about the windows, compared thermometers; said it was the reason one could not keep a dog. She took to it. It was a very different thing from the Riviera winter sunshine she had loved so well, but it suited her: she was not happy, but she felt in health. She had not forgotten the drives, the pretty clothes, the watching people—the picture in her mind of the South and life; yet here, another layer of her opened to the blanching blaze, the bone-dry, crackling desert air, expanded in the alternate refuge of the siesta, the slow slothful even hours in the dimmed and spacious house. But in the evening she felt restless.

Julius did not seem to know anybody, or at least he said so, though he was always running into people who lived in villas or meeting a man he used to know—ages ago, my dear . . . Madrid very likely . . . yes, yes, en poste; and he was asked to shoot or dine or stay. Melanie was never included. If his hosts were aware that he had a woman living in the house, they took his discretion at its face-value and assumed they were not really married, a view that was also discussed among their own servants. Melanie was placid over these single invitations, she was used to her mother going nowhere, but she would have liked to have her share by being told.

" Jules—Pedro says he remembers you when you were here before."

"Pedro?"

"He used to see you riding."

"It was none of his business."

"He said you looked very splendid and the horse was grey."

"You have not been talking to the servants?"

"No—yes—not really."

"It is most unwise."

"Yes, Jules."

"You do not know this country."

"No, Jules."

"This kind of thing won't do here." In the last weeks Julius had developed something he had never shown before, irritability; and he could not stop.

"It was only because Pedro speaks a little French," said Melanie.

She was at sea about much else. She moved through the days confused by a sense of the familiar, with a twist to it that eluded her experience. Her life had been spent in an atmosphere of selfishness combined with material solicitude. Her family could not be called tender, large-hearted or gay—they were often peevish and generally complaining—but they had the grunting contentment of people settled in their ways, and they were all very fond of each other's company. Melanie had been cherished; and in a hot-house existence the attention of the keepers counts. What they took for granted they took for granted and this gave them solidity, and their daughter had no key to Julius's capricious gloom. In her room now, in Andalusia, stretched rigid on the sofa, when Marie crept in to bathe her eyes, she formed at last the unwonted question—Why?

September too was full summer, though the night fell early. One evening Julius came into the drawing-room and found Melanie on the balcony, the light behind her.

Below somewhere, from under dark trees, from the earth, rose a sudden wail, a splintering spiral of sound, yet a voice.

"Jules—listen .. !"

"The windows," said Julius.

She did not hear him.

"Mosquitos," said Julius. "The screens open, the most dangerous hour. How often have I told them."

Below the voice rent the night, the air, the sinews—

She called him. "Come out! Tell me—this music—?"

"Gipsies." Julius, brought up on Lully, Couperin and a little Haydn, who thought the modern piano *loud*, though he rather liked an organ, stepped forward and shut the windows.

"No," cried Melanie. "No."

"The foreigners always like it," he said.

"Jules—"

"My dear?"

"One could dance."

"They do," he said. "Very picturesque. Such good-looking people. And now you *must* come in."

"Jules."

"Yes?"

"Jules?"

"So imprudent," he said. "Malaria. You'll be having them all over the house. Nobody seems to have any sense. Well I shall have to be going."

"*Going?*"

"You *will* see that everything is shut before you go upstairs?"

"Jules don't go."

"I must," said Julius.

"Don't go—"

"Alas . .—"

"Jules please don't go—"

"My dear." He picked up his hat and gloves.

"Jules!" She wheeled and stood before him, her eyes on his face.

He turned away. She touched his coat.

He disengaged himself.

" Jules!"

He stopped short, and looked at her in consternation. He said, "My dear—do you want me to ring for your maid?"

She sprang at him, blazing. Her right hand, clawed, flew out.

Julius stood still. Then he got out a handkerchief, put it to his cheek, turned once more and left the house. He was still carrying his hat.

Melanie stayed behind and consumed herself in a fury of weeping that turned quite soon to terrified remorse. She waited up for Julius, but when she heard his steps, she had recovered her instincts enough not to throw herself into his arms. Indeed she did not show herself at all, and instead offered him at noon a tempered version of her apologies which he accepted with stiff grace. Julius was shaken and had spent a wretched evening, but he bore no grudge against Melanie; women were supposed to be subject to incomprehensible attacks—as a matter of fact she began to remind him a little of Tzara and one of his father's mares.

* * * * *

Nothing of the kind happened to them again. Julius passed a pleasant autumn and winter in a place he loved, on the track of many acquisitions.

When Melanie was with child, first she was not certain, then she did not tell him. Nor did she mention it in the notes with which she kept her family at bay. At last her maid spoke to Julius and at the same time wrote Frau

Edu. Once he had to believe it, Julius recognized it as the next trick of fate. "Voilà," he said, "tout s'écroule. I knew it."

"You did?" said Melanie.

"The gods—"

He rushed into Granada to fetch a doctor, walked out of his office because he saw it was dirty, was directed to the English doctor, found an old man, shaking and inane, lost his nerve and came back alone. A letter from Voss Strasse crossed with his, urging return.

Melanie saw no reason for not staying where they were.

He told her this was folly; visions of foul stables rose before him.

"You would come with me?"

"Naturally. I shall take you to your mother in Berlin."

"No," said Melanie. "No . . . If we cannot stay here, we could go to France. To your house?"

Julius said it was too small. Besides it was up for sale. The Riviera was not at all suitable, he said; what they wanted now was *un endroit sérieux*.

"Paris?" said Melanie.

Not Paris, said Julius. The country. A place to put one's things.

The idea took root. Among his dealers' letters there was a photograph of a house in the Sologne. It had a brick front, sixteenth-century, but not in the Chambord style he disliked, and a water-piece, and it was to let. Julius took it by telegraph.

The Merz's did not interfere. Flora, their eldest daughter, had not been well all winter, the doctors were ordering her abroad, and they were flustered.

Julius and Melanie had a frightful journey to Madrid, and a better one from there to San Sebastian. Julius was admirable over pillows and mineral water, though himself devoured by a hundred and ten anxieties. At Bordeaux they were met by the French maid he had engaged; Marie, by mutual consent, was put on a steamer bound for Germany; Julius became animated and took Melanie to dinner, he said, at one of the world's two best restaurants. The other was at Brussels. He told her that really he must take her there again when game would be in season, and Melanie repaid him by living only in the present.

Next morning they went on to Tours, where they stayed long enough to see a specialist who told Melanie that everything was splendid, continued to Beaugency, crossed the Loire, and from there by carriage towards Romarontin. Clusters of brown rabbits bobbed up at their passage. The Sologne as the crow flies is only a few miles east of the great rivered valleys of Touraine. It might be hundreds of miles. There is no resemblance to the open calm green rolling prospects between the Indre and the Cher. It is flat, still country of unmoving water and pine-soft ground, a hidden province, unvisited, of serried shallow ponds and scrub enclosed by forest, a water landscape without vistas, the cache of multitudes of small wild harmless animals. The sparse inhabitants raise asparagus and marrows; in many a clearing there stands reflected on the filmy surface of the girdling waterpiece the handsome walls of a gentilhommière in disrepair; but the chief sounds throughout these woods are those of frog and duck and hare.

"Here?" Melanie said.

And at the end of the afternoon, by way of Veilleins, Mur-de-Sologne, le Lude, Chartraine, les Touches, la Dauphinerie; la Ferté-Boisrenard and la Ferté-la Malzone, l'Etang de Vol à Voile and l'Etang du Grand Corbois; by Crouy, Cicogne, les Anges, Bréaux and Lanthénay, they arrived at the Château de la Souve. It was March and they were surprised by the cold. The façade was all that had been promised; unruffled geese were cruising along the sides; there was grass on the drive and thistles on the lawn, the house had long stood empty and, inside, it was damp.

* * * * *

Julius took his wife's condition seriously and she led a careful and secluded life. He began alterations on the house, and again was much away. A long wet spring turned without transition into a summer of close steaming heat. In Spain, life had still racketed below her windows; here all was silence and her view was shuttered by a fringe of pines. Melanie gave herself to waiting.

They were all a little out about the time, and she was delivered one night in September by an excellent practitioner from Blois. Up to the end she had shown few signs of her condition; all was well over by the time Julius returned and she had a quick recovery, making no great case over her part in the whole thing. The child born to them in the heart of France was a girl. They called her Henrietta, after her grandmother, not the lady with the handsome profile and the many languages of whom the Merz's never thought and Julius had not heard. When Clara wrote proposing herself as obvious God-mother, her name with Melanie's was added. Henrietta Clara Melanie was a hideous little thing, underweight, with a wizened face and sparse black hair; Julius had foreseen nothing, and a boy. Her mother looked at it with sporadic bewilderment and limp affection, Julius was seized by passionate interest. Was so helpless a creature meant to live—? He fussed nurse and mid-wife, and would have thought it natural if they had let him have its basket in his room. Melanie reverted to the more apathetic mood of her girlhood.

It was at this point that the outside world might have bustled in on them: relatives, a christening, neighbours, on a newly-married couple, newly settled in these parts (rumour would have them buy La Souve), the natural seclusion of their Spanish journey and the last few months naturally at an end.

Melanie's sister Flora was very ill indeed now and had been taken to Switzerland. Her husband had written to expect the worst. The old Merz's would not envisage that, and thus felt no need to suppress anxiety. They were very anxious and quite miserable.

"Slow," said Grandpapa.

Sarah, who had seen her sister-in-law in summer and then again some weeks ago, looked up.

"I wish I could go with Arthur and Jetta," said Emil.

"You could. Friedrich you *are* going with your parents, aren't you?"

"Papa thinks it would be too much for mama."

"A big journey," said Grandmama.

"Can't see the sense of it," said her husband.

"Well I don't know—" said Edu.

"Papa," Sarah said, "you know that Flora's condition is serious?"

"Too serious for visits."

"Max writes there is not much hope," said Markwald.

"Not much hope . . ." said the old lady, tears trickling

down her puckered cheeks. "Not much hope now till poor Flora's better."

"You know," Clara said to her brother, "I had the trunks out. But Gustavus won't hear of it. Not that *I* don't agree with him. What use are we to a child of that age. Our presence cannot affect the efficacy of the sacrament. I always think it does not matter where very young children are, or who is with them ... You remember we were put out with the wet-nurse till we spoke enough to be taught our prayers. But Gustavus— You would have thought he wanted to make something of it."

"A girl?" said Count Bernin.

"Still—" said Clara. "After the disappointment I've been to him. He didn't seem really pleased *before* we heard. I don't understand him. No Gustavus, I don't understand you at all."

Gustavus did not look up from his sheaf of proofs. He had taken to corresponding with the Baden Herald's Office and they were giving him quite a lot of voluntary work.

"I hope at least that Jules realizes—" Count Bernin began, but did not pursue.

"Now Gustavus, what have you done with that announcement?" said Clara. "Where is it? I want to save it for Johannes; Jules is certain not to think of sending it to him. Look, it's all smudged."

"What on earth do you want to do that for?" said her brother.

"His orderly. He likes getting post. I could try to get it off with bread-crumbs."

"I don't like it," said Count Bernin, as the door shut. Gustavus grunted.

"You shouldn't let her," said Count Bernin.

"None of my business," said Gustavus.

"I shouldn't have minded looking in on Jules and Melanie," said Edu; "I suppose that's all washed up now?"

"I don't think *I* should have gone."

"Why not? Sounds kind of jolly running down to their place and all that."

"Jolly?" Sarah said.

"Paris, don't you know. I shouldn't mind having a shot at Paris with old Jules."

"They don't live in Paris."

"Oh Jules goes up. He belongs to the Jockey, did you know? I thought no foreigner could."

In the Sologne that year autumn set in early. Melanie had used to mind the stillness, now she could not bear the sound made by the wind. She had believed that they would leave when the business of the waiting for the child was over, but Julius made no sign. When he was at home he was easy with her now; friendly, careful, at times almost chatty. It was found necessary to keep fires going all over the house and some of the fires always smoked. This upset him and brought on his asthma, and it occupied much of his time. They had their meals in the dining-room that was too large, and he worked out a way of dealing with the draughts, but the draughts appeared to change directions. They both still took pains about their clothes. A wicker crate arrived, marked

PLEASE WATER, and addressed to Henrietta Clara Melanie von Felden. Inside, on a bed of messy straw and broken biscuits, heaved a fox-terrier puppy. An envelope attached to the crate contained a card. *For Henrietta from her Uncle Johannes,* and a letter. Julius flew into a rage. "What can this mean?" he shouted. Two veins swelled on his temples; he stood shaking. Melanie knew little and asked less. She looked at him, and saw how tall he was. "The letter," she said. "You haven't read the letter."

He did not see it. "What can it mean?" he cried. She had never heard him like this. He stalked off; came back. She was still holding the letter.

He snatched it. He stared at the ruled sheet. Melanie came nearer. "From a soldier," she said. He read the words, addressed to himself. The sender, respectful, sentimental, begged leave to send this fine puppy to the young lady in the Captain's name . . . feeling that this was what the Captain would have wished . . . if the Captain . . . Julius crushed the paper, flung it from him—

"The Captain?" said Melanie.

Later she said, "You could send it back."

"Send it *back*!" He lashed himself. "A *dog*? In a *box*?"

It was put in the stables—Melanie's first order to an out-door servant. Julius went away. When he had been back a few days, he said, "One must acknowledge this— this present."

"Yes."

"You must do it."

"Yes. How?"

"In the third person."

"I will show it to you."

"No, no, no," said Julius.

The dog gradually established himself and became known as Henrietta's dog. Nobody thought of doing anything about the orderly. All October Melanie coughed, her maid believed that she was running a temperature. In November she went down with bronchitis; by Christmas she was up again. Julius told her she must eat. The winter was a mild one, but wet. Downstairs was abandoned; Julius had his dinner laid in the room where he read his catalogues, Melanie was sent trays. At the sound of her window, the wild geese glided into view gathered for their legato dives after any morsel she might choose to chuck them. In January they heard that Flora had died. Julius heard, and could not bring himself to tell her. He locked himself up with the telegram; he thought of sending for Clara, for the curé, for Nelly de la Turbie. At last he asked Melanie's maid to break the news to her. The maid, the new French one, seems to have been a decent enough woman; she did not like her mistress much, but she did her best.

"*Eh bien non, elle ne m'a pas semblée trop bouleversée,*" she reported.

Melanie cried a little on that day, and on every day of that week for poor Flora, and talked of her in spurts of incidents remembered from their early lives.

Julius asked her whether she did not think that her parents now might like to have her with them. Melanie replied that Flora had been away from home these last four years, and she was sure that they preferred to go on as they were.

To her maid she said one evening, "*Je crains que ma sœur n'était pas très heureuse avec son mari.*"

Then the bronchitis came on again, only this time it was pleurisy. Julius said how right he had been about the northern winter. The illness dragged, and the doctor, a local man, was not much pleased with his patient nor the set-up. Julius asked him whether it was contagious, he

M

said he was thinking of the child. The doctor was quite disagreeable over this, adding that there really was no need to wait for contagion in this house . . . Julius had hardly noticed him before, now he took against the man. A rustic, he said. When he told him that Melanie ought to be moved, he put it down to interfering folly. She did recover at La Souve, left her bed, yet was still far from well. The doctor now discovered a tubercular condition and advised immediate departure for the South. Julius believed at once, became frightened and shared the faith in the suggested remedy. Melanie was made to take cod-liver oil, and in March they were able to set out. There were seven of them. Melanie, Julius and the baby, the baby's nurse, Melanie's maid, a woman from the village who had looked after Melanie during the pleurisy and a kitchen-maid from La Souve promoted to act as between-maid. Julius had never been in a carriage with so many women and he was beyond anything.

The house in the South had been sold meanwhile and they went to stay at the Hotel des Anglais in Nice. After a day or two Melanie did not seem the worse for the journey; though to their consternation it was not at all warm. At the end of the week she had the fit of coughing peculiar to her illness, and collapsed. This took place in their own sitting-room but a waiter had been present: Julius coming in from a brief stroll on the front was told of what had passed, in full detail, by the manager. At that time the Riviera was much sought by consumptives, and hotels and their public exercised an almost hysterical vigilance; it could be difficult to stay out a common cold in a pensione between San Remo and Cap Ferrat—*Il y a des malades!* and a place would empty before the evening train. Julius was told his wife must leave the place, on her own feet, within two hours.

He got hold of the doctor recommended by their man in the Sologne, who confirmed that on every ground Melanie must be moved to a clinic. Mentone was suggested. Now, it was to Mentone that Flora had been sent just under a year ago. The doctor said there was also a place at Grasse. They decided on Grasse.

Melanie left the hotel very early next morning in an ambulance. The clinic was quite a pleasant place and there she was considered one of the lighter cases. Presently she was up again; at least for part of the day. Julius had installed himself and the baby at an hotel near-by and spent the time allowed them with his wife. On two or three afternoons they were able to go for a brief carriage drive. They cannot have been very far from his old house. The weather remained bad. Melanie got worse; rallied; had another bout of bed; then got up: suddenly much improved. She was stronger and Julius was able to take her out to tea.

On the night of their removal from Nice he had written to Sarah, a straightforward letter containing all he knew. Sarah's and Edu's instructions were to consult a specialist he named, to leave the old Merz's in the dark at present, and to spare no money.

In April the weather cleared. They had an almost hot spell, though windy, with the mistral whirling up the dust along the roads. Her temperature went up; one morning dressing she had another collapse like the one she had had at Nice. Julius was informed that it was galloping consumption and that the chance of halting it was small. It was the first time he had been told anything of the kind. Edu telegraphed to do everything. This now meant Switzerland. The French doctors were doubtful; Julius hesitated; Berlin pressed. It was getting hot. At last it was arranged to move Melanie to Davos in a private railway carriage. The Merz's sent a courier for Henrietta and her nurse, who took them to Berlin.

The journey to Switzerland was a night and a day. Julius of course went with her. He did, as the phrase goes, everything. He sat with her; and first they spoke little and of nothing very much. He inquired whether she was comfortable, and she talked to him until the end in polite small sentences. He could do nothing for her materially, and at her wish was made to leave the room when they tried to give her nourishment; so he attempted to distract her and it was then perhaps that he first began to tell his stories of the early Landen. Melanie did not improve at Davos; there were no more changes; she was in bed all the time now, generally apathetic and sometimes barely conscious; later there were stretches of deliriousness and during these she babbled to Jules about the South of France in schoolgirl French. In June she died.

The Merz's had a family vault in Berlin. Again Julius travelled in a private railway carriage. One wagon-lits compartment, lined with flowers, held the coffin; in another Julius had his meals, a third was his sleeper. It must have been a lonely journey. In the station in the morning there was a wait while they were being shifted to a siding. When Julius stepped out, upright in his dark clothes, holding his tall hat, to meet Edu and Friedrich, he looked the picture of a broken man.

The coffin had to be lifted through a window. They followed it to a mortuary chapel in the suburbs. After that Edu said, "We thought you had better stay with us—I mean—you know—till after it's all over."

"We think it would be best for our parents," said Friedrich.

Julius inclined his head.

"Your brother and sister-in-law are arriving tomorrow."

"Yes," said Julius.

Sarah was waiting for him. "Oh Jules, there you are. Come in. The poor girl. It's so sad. Dear Jules."

He said nothing.

"Friedrich is coming back after lunch. Did they tell you?—it's for the day after tomorrow. There're still one or two points we'll have to decide on."

"Yes," he said.

"You see: the old people will not be going."

He bowed.

"There'll be a tremendous crowd—"

"Yes?"

He was standing in the middle of her drawing-room. Sarah touched his sleeve. "I'll take you upstairs," she said.

Julius said, "Henrietta—?"

"Oh, the baby," said Sarah.

"My daughter."

Sarah gave him a look. "I hear she's very well looked after," she said.

"I must see her," said Julius.

"Jules dear; I should wait a day or two. My parents-in-law—I don't know how to explain—they think—everybody thinks— It's been too much for them."

"I will send for her."

"I don't think her grandparents would like her to go out."

"*Her grandparents*—"

"You'll find they've become very fond of her," said Sarah.

Presently Friedrich said, "Have you talked to him about the service yet?"

"I couldn't," said Sarah. "Besides what's the use? Baroness Felden will be here tomorrow."

"Better get it all settled now," said Friedrich. "She could hardly—at this moment I mean."

"That woman is capable of anything," said Sarah. "All moments seem to be the same to her. No. We can't go through the kind of thing again we had two years ago. I won't have it. I won't have it for your people; and I won't have it for him either."

"They say at the Stock Exchange—"

"Oh *please* Friedrich. Tell us what Jeanne thinks."

"I didn't ask her."

"But what does she say?"

"She says if she were— if it was her who— she'd insist on Catholic burial but she wouldn't mind having a Rabbi at the grave to please me; and she thinks it could be arranged."

"That's all very well for Jeanne," said Edu.

"I don't know whether Conrad Bernin is in Berlin?" Sarah said. "I don't know where I read he was at the Wilhelmstrasse. I think I shall go and see him."

Two days later, on an urban summer afternoon, Melanie was buried. She had two services and more people followed her funeral than she had ever known. Julius's appearance as chief mourner, walking alone, was much remarked on.

The Kaiser, wishing to do what he could, sent a message asking Julius to a levee in the coming month.

At Voss Strasse, they had not been supposed to know the day, but Gottlieb and some of the maidservants had sneaked out, and so had Emil. Emil was heard to sob. Jeanne also followed the procession (in the closed carriage of some friends). Sarah said to her afterwards, "My dear, *why* didn't you tell me?" But to Edu she said, "Jeanne has such tact."

After the old people had gone to bed that evening, Markwald had to be told about everything. "They left a place next to Flora," he said, "did they leave one for the Baron, too?"

"Poor man. I think I saw a space, but I don't think it was marked."

"The status of the Baron has not been decided, sir," said Gottlieb.

Sarah that week was not an easy hostess.

"I asked him to come to the club," said Edu, "he doesn't seem to want to go. Dash it all, it makes one feel as though one ought to be staying in too and all that. And he's always here."

"Edu—"

"What?"

"Well may you ask."

Edu and Sarah left cards on the Feldens. Clara asked Gustavus when he'd come with her to return the call.

"Must we still bother with those Merz's?" said Gustavus.

"I don't have to go to the Palace?" said Julius. "One hears it's hideous. Besides we shall not be here."

"You must," said Edu and Sarah.

"My father didn't like the Kaiser; not that he knew him."

"It's not the same one."

"Jules's father might not have found him an improvement."

"Is it true that you're to be given the Red Eagle?" said Edu.

"Oh I hope not," said Julius.

"It'll be hard to refuse."

"Do you know I thought of that. Perhaps my brother Gustavus could have it in my place, he used to be fond of that kind of thing. You think I ought to suggest it?"

"Can you transfer a decoration?" said Edu.

"Why don't you speak to Bernin?"

"Yes," said Julius, "he may have heard something about it."

"Jules—about those diamonds?"

"Yes?"

"Melanie's diamonds?"

Jules only just perceptibly flinched at the name. "Oh, those brooches and things," he said.

"They might want to have them for their granddaughter. Nobody's said anything so far, but don't you think it would be a good idea to have them put in a safe? Incidentally where are they?"

"The maid would know," said Julius.

"I meant to ask you about the ring. Wouldn't you like to keep that? The one you gave her? The topaze."

"My father's ring. Yes, I would."

"Jules did you ever buy that house?"

"What house?"

"Your house. The one in France."

"Oh no, it was quite the wrong house."

"Then you could buy one now? You know Edu and I wanted you to have a house."

"Oh but it was as good as having one, the one in Spain particularly—I made so many changes."

"That was taken on a lease?"

"It was rented."

"On what terms?"

"The servants did all that. Pedro. He went to the notary for all those stamps."

"Jules, may I ask whether you have got the price of a house now?"

"The price of a house? Oh, I shouldn't think so. You see, I've been wanting to speak to you about that, there seem to be so many debts."

"*Debts?*" said Sarah, and realized that she spoke too sharply.

"You know—bills for things."

Count Bernin thought Jules's idea sensible. The right gesture—same family, elder brother, after all Gustavus *had* rendered services—and he passed on the suggestion to the proper quarters. His Majesty agreed. The man at the head of the Decorations Department happened to be a general; the old boy looked up Felden and found he was a chap in the Baden Body Dragoons—a bit young, some secret mission very likely, the way they were scattering about Red Eagles nowadays—and in due course the Order of the Red Eagle Second Class was given to Johannes. Gustavus waited; believed himself forgotten; but for once Count Bernin, who was pleased with his own prudence in small matters, refused do to anything about it.

Clara said that Sarah was a nice simple woman and she believed very fond of Jules, and took the horse omnibus out by herself. Sarah was at home.

She rang for tea, but Clara said if she did not give too much trouble might she have a small cup of black coffee, just one small cup, she always felt all in at that hour. "You know how much poverty there is in this town."

The windows stood wide open to the long northern afternoon. A smell of lime came in from the garden. Sarah looked at her Pissarro—a wheelbarrow, a blue dress, insubstantial, in fluffy grass below light fruit trees. "Have you any idea what Jules is going to do?" she said.

He would have to marry again, said Clara. A woman of his own faith.

Sarah remarked that this excellent project could hardly be put under way in the next few weeks.

Indeed not, said Clara.

"And what does he propose to do until this woman—of his own faith—has materialized?"

"Do?"

Sarah sat back.

"Oh, I see," said Clara. "Naturally I offered to take the child meanwhile, my God-child. Naturally. It would not be easy; at my age. I am forty-nine. And my time is not my own. But you know, he won't hear of it? He seemed surprised. He says he's going to look after it himself. He's attached to it already. His father was like that."

"And where is he going to live this parental idyll?"

"Where? oh France I expect, or Spain. Yes, Spain very likely. I should think they'll be leaving us quite soon."

"Baroness," said Sarah, "your brother-in-law won't be at all well off now."

"Jules? I suppose not. There never was much to the Felden property. They are not men attached to money."

"It is what men live on."

Here Clara made the movement of her mouth that had contributed so much to the boredom of Gustavus's life.

Sarah began again. "I don't think you quite realize the position. When Jules was married to my sister-in-law, it was arranged that they receive an annual income from her parents. This was in the form of an allowance to their daughter; no independent provision was made for Jules at the time."

"I'm afraid I do not understand about such matters," Clara said. "If there is anything your husband would wish to say to mine—"

Anger now gained Sarah. She half rose; desisted. Even sitting, both women were tall; both would as lief have stood. "I see it's no use," she said. "What do you expect them to say to each other—?" Then she subsided. "I was trying to help . . ."

Clara flung out her fine hands. The swift gesture from

that rigid body brought out something excessive. "Forgive me— of course one must speak. It is only that I do not understand about settlements. What is it that you want to say to me?"

"I don't know," said Sarah.

"Jules will have less money now than when his wife was alive? That is not hard to say."

"I never thought she would die," said Sarah.

"*Didn't you?*"

Again impatience swept her. "Let us keep to the point," she said. Then, "Less money? Possibly none."

"He'll still have his own."

"That was gone long ago."

"No, no. How could it?"

"It wasn't a great deal to begin with and he spent too much."

"He spent too much," said Clara. "One does do that."

"I believe you're the most frivolous woman I've ever met," said Sarah.

"Then you say Jules will be in actual want?"

"*Your* words." Sarah thought of Frankfort; of her father: in his study explaining to them all exactly where they stood. Questions—answers. She looked again at her Pissarro. Her father would *not* have bought it. She had never liked Frankfort.

"Do you like this picture?" she said.

Clara stabbed her lorgnette in the direction of the wall. "What is the subject?" she asked.

"A farm-yard in Normandy, if you like."

"I do not see the use of these things," said Clara. "Is it not insisting on error, this making images of what is itself illusion?"

"What?" said Sarah. "Is that how you see it? All of

it? Illusion. You may be right; for me it is *this* that can make a farm-yard real."

Clara made another attempt at looking. "Surely not? Oh I cannot believe that—this is a *harmless* painting. We could ask him to live with us at Sigmundshofen only that the house is to be shut up. It's so very large. Now that my brother is to be in the cabinet again—he doesn't want me to talk about it, but why not? as it is true—we shall all be moving to Berlin. Yet I don't see why we could not leave some rooms open for Jules, and the child. There'd be the caretaker. The farm is rented, though we seem to be getting eggs— I'm afraid there wouldn't be any actual *money*. There're so many claims on mine— Gustavus never seems to have any either; my brother has been very generous but I really don't think I can come to him again . . . I daresay Jules will be all right. There's the Catechism and school I built on the grounds, that will be convenient later on. We'd be coming down every year for the *Landtag* Elections, perhaps Jules could give my brother a hand— In Lent we open the house to the Saint-Eustatius Association for their retreat."

"Has Jules stayed with you before?" said Sarah.

"We asked him; I don't think he ever came."

The next day Sarah took him to Voss Strasse. On their way in she stopped. "Oh look at them! So beautiful. Your cats."

He seemed taken aback. He glanced at the yellow creatures on their pedestals. "I'd forgotten about them," he said.

"They give me pleasure every time. I really must see that they're left to me."

"Oh I shouldn't," he said.

"I ought to have warned you. One is not supposed to mention anything, anything that's happened. I find it ghastly. But don't."

"Naturally," said Julius.

They all lunched together. Afterwards Jules went up to the nursery.

In the evening Sarah said to him, "You really enjoy, do you, the company of this baby?"

"Well, *yes.*"

"They'll never let her go. You see they are afraid."

"It's my child; I could take her away."

"Perhaps you could. I see great trouble ahead. They connect abroad with illness— The child's a German subject. They could do many things. Perhaps these places were not healthy—"

"What can I do?" said Julius.

"How sad you look," said Sarah.

He stood facing her. She got up. "I should wait a bit," she said, turning to the window. "On Wednesday they're all leaving for Bad Kreuznach; it's their date for the cure. Why don't you go with them?" She pulled the curtains. "It's not a bad little Spa . . . They've taken a whole floor . . . They might as well begin to get used to you."

Chapter Six

TOMORROW, and tomorrow, and tomorrow... Life, in the neat sad dry little French phrase that bundles it all into its place, Life is never as bad nor as good as one thinks. *La vie, voyez-vous, ça n'est jamais si bon ni si mauvais qu'on croit.* Never as bad, never as good ... When? At the instant of calamity, at the edge of fear? when the bad news is brought, and the trap felt sprung, or the loss strikes home? At low ebb, in tedium, in accidie? In the moments of renewal? the transfiguration of love, the flush of work, the grace of a new vision, the long-held now? Or later, when the doors shut, one after another, and regret moves in the heart like a steel coil? Never as good, never as bad, but a drab, bearable half-sleep banked by a little store of this and that, subsiding after visitations and alarms, a drowsing, often not uneasy, down the years, an even-paced irreversible passage—life, the run of lives, the sum of life? Is it consoling? is it the whole truth? Is it inevitable?

The years that followed the death of her husband's sisters cannot have been happy ones for Sarah—Edu's gambling, Edu's waxing debts, Edu's unchanging nature: the whole repeated cycle that had pressed her into a graceless self-reliance; she was growing old; time was passing; everything that happened, or not happened, could be seen as adding to the final shape; and as we know her she must have been living on her own close terms with disillusionment. Her children were growing up. Into stiff, matter-of-fact, secretive girls, unlike the girls of her own youth, curiously out of sympathy with their parents and their time. When they had been small she had looked forward to the future when they would be old enough for her to love them; meanwhile, she had seen that they were given everything she believed they ought to have, had indeed watched over them with almost compassionate concern, prospecting their evolving looks as one scans a company report. She had a great fellow-feeling for women and was resolved that her daughters should have everything from straight backs and teeth to interests, to prepare them for their lot; now it was found they could not love her. What she had done to Edu, she had largely done for them; perhaps they judged her, took their father's side; she could not tell. What did they say about it to each other? did they talk? did they get on? There was about these young creatures a hardness and sufficiency that puzzled and intimidated Sarah who did not know that it was said to come from her. She admitted to herself another disappointment—their minds had not grown interesting. Yet what grieved her most was that she saw in both of them signs of the sources of her own frustration.

Of none of this she spoke. Few people were at ease with her; nobody laughed *with* her at her jokes. For the two or three eminent men who came to her house, and for the painters who dined with her and whose studios she visited, she was too rich, too idle, her manners remained too uncompromising, to think of her as anything but a hostess or a patron. They blossomed under her Midas's touch; *her* most intimate conversations were with her brother-in-law's mistress, and her most refreshing talks were with lawyers.

Yet throughout her troubles Sarah never took her hand off Julius. When they were both in Berlin he was her constant companion. Whenever her consciousness was startled again, as it occasionally was, into attention to his idiosyncrasies, he exasperated her and she showed him the impatience one shows to an otherwise well-kempt and handsome dog who has once more dragged the same old bone into the drawing-room. Yet as a rule his presence soothed her; she liked being chaperoned by him in auction rooms, she had come to see him as the pleasant person to have in one's family, and she could assure herself that she had shepherded his existence into a predictable, and not intolerable, course. He had his flat in Paris, was courted by the dealers quite as much as she was, took a house in February wherever he wished to, in Morocco, in Corsica, in Spain; seemed attached, as far as she could make out, to a series of agreeable women. Had the old Merz's not continued to pay Melanie's allowance year in year out, quarter after quarter, into his account, and not as much as mentioned it? Had they not once or twice paid a mild miscellany of debts? He spent less time in Germany than she did. He stayed at Voss Strasse for Christmas and in summer followed them *en villégiature*; otherwise he came and went as often or as little as he believed he must or dared, and to see his daughter, the ugly, cosseted, ignorant little girl, wrapped in muffs and ermine, on whom he seemed to bestow the same exaggerated devotion already bestowed on her by Emil, Gottlieb, Marie, Grandmama and Grandpapa.

At times, rather wistfully, Julius talked to Sarah of remarriage. He still saw himself as tragically widowed, and had come to look upon the married state as a haven of liberty and safety. He had got it into his head that if only he produced a mother he would be allowed to take his child abroad and live with her there for ever after; and one year some such project actually came up. He told Sarah he had decided to get married to a Frenchwoman

N

of his own age with a child of her own. Madame Dupont her name was, or so Sarah believed she had heard him say; he conveyed that he had known her for some time, and said that with her he would be *comfortable*. Sarah took this to mean money.

The old Merz's pounced on the fact to their advantage, the existence of another child. Julius told Sarah that this was most awkward as Madame Dupont—was it Dupont?—for whom life no longer quite held all it used to hold, was looking forward precisely to making a home for her own girl.

This had puzzled Sarah with her sense of house property. "She cannot be looking to you for one, Jules? Did I hear you say she had an *hotel* Avenue du Bois? and a place at Cannes?"

"You see," Julius said, "it hasn't been *convenient* for her so far to have the child with her."

"Oh the convent system," said Sarah. "Clara Felden once explained to me about that."

"*En nourrice*—" said Julius.

"Those Catholics," said Sarah, dismissing it from her mind.

The step-sister alarm at Voss Strasse put a quick end to Julius's plan. For a long time afterwards, however, he remained insistent and quite sad, telling Sarah how comfortable they would all have been. Grandpapa, betraying an awareness of money passing, increased the amount of it that was finding its way into Julius's bank.

"You know what?" Edu said to his wife, "it's now up to what it was before Melanie's second Christening, and he's only one now."

"Your words," said Sarah, "are food for thought."

When Julius and Sarah both were fifty, Voss Strasse staged a joint celebration. The idea was thought to have originated with Gottlieb.

Their birthdays fell within a few months of each other. Sarah had believed Jules to be about a year or two older than herself, a view that was not generally shared; Julius had not envisaged the question of her age at all, though if asked would readily have given her a decade more. Voss Strasse had kept count.

"Perhaps the Eumenides *were* rather like the Merz's," said Sarah.

Julius looked at her with distaste. "Must we?" he said, "do we have to?"

"Attain to this noticeable age? We must. And we have."

"Not I," said Julius. "Not until July."

"It's in the *Kreuz-Zeitung*," said Edu. "Milestones."

"This *fête*—" said Julius.

"You will be hard put to cling to your conviction, Jules dear," Sarah said.

As they came up the stairs the number 50 large and round greeted them from everywhere. Festooned with paper garlands, framed by leaves of extraordinary deadness, gloss and durability, in icing, in marzipan, in electric candles, in candied fruit; 5 and 0 cut out in tin foil and wired between the antlers of the nineteen-ender stag sent, not shot, by Max from his Silesian estate, a trophy that reclined on the carpet in the antechamber at the foot of an altar of offerings, attentions to Merz from Merz connections—poultry in their feathers, hares in fur, strings of partridge, a dozen brace of this and a dozen brace of that, cray-fish clambering weakly through damp seaweed, Westphalia hams, snake-lengths of smoked eel, great glistening lumps of sheer boned goose flesh sewn into its own faultless skin, five-pound tins of caviar afloat in silver coolers, Strasbourg terrines large as band-boxes, hot-house asparagus thick as pillars, fifty plover's eggs in a nest of bronze twigs, and rising Pelion upon Ossa, tier on tier, crested at the apex by the plumes of massed heads of pineapple, corbeille upon box on box on case on satined case, Port and Havanas, Arabian Mocha, Smyrna figs, grapes in cotton-wool, Turkish delight, Marrons glacés, Sacher cake and Karlsbad plums. The presents proper were laid out in the ball-room; and through the salons to the dining-room there stretched a buffet displaying the substances of the antechamber at a stage nearer to, indeed already surpassing, the customary degrees of commestibility. Supremes and Fondants, Velours and Claires, Masques and Glazes, en Bellevue, en Chartreuse, en Savarin, en Bouquetière, Surelévés and Richelieus, Figaros and Maintenons, Niagaras and Metternichs and Miroités—en Grenadin; en Favorite; en Chambertin; en Financière; en Chassé, en Croisé, en Frappé, en Triple-Eau, en Glissade, en Diadème; en Sainte-Alliance, en Belvedère, en Ballonné, en Demi-Deuil and Demidoff: Gramonts, Chimays, Souvaroffs, Albufera and Tivoli.

"There's a corner of France for you, Baron," said a guest.

"By way of the Eastern Empire," said Sarah.

"I beg your pardon?"

Henrietta, dressed as Hermes, recited some verse in honour of the celebrees; Grandpapa made a speech that began with *nel mezzo del cammin* and ended in safe harbour. Both were almost word perfect. Their efforts had been composed for them by the Poet Jubilate, a literary gentleman, now of advanced age himself, who had officiated at such functions in certain Berlin circles as long as anybody present could remember. This status was non-pro, that is he did not publish (although some of his *vers de circonstances* occasionally found their way into the social columns) but was rewarded in the manner of some eminent consultants at the door by an enveloped honorarium changing hands between him and the master of the house. At the end of the day another well-known face appeared, and presents, food and buffet were cumbersomely photographed from under a black veil.

It was at the end of that year that Sarah set about to pay her husband's debts for the last time. During the same winter their youngest girl was caught having tea in a public place alone with a young man, a trotting-horse trainer from a nearby course. The girl, not yet fifteen, was alive to the enormity of her conduct and relieved rather than anything else by being packed back to school in mid-holiday, but Sarah who had wished to meet the man—a near-gentleman found to have been dismissed for laziness and betting—felt she had seen a ghost.

Once she had completed her arrangements, she settled down to waiting for what she knew was bound to come. She foresaw the mechanics; saw that her course would not be popular, was convinced of its justice and necessity, and a little concerned about the fascination it revealed to hold for her. Months, a year, another year, passed in the expectation of this full-dressed shape, this half-conjured future, and as she waited it was not always with composure. Once or twice she believed it to be imminent; often, she hoped so; but when one morning in May Edu came home from the club having left behind him that enormous I O U, when he came through the door into her room to tell her, she realized she had been certain it would not be for that summer. The temptation came to her that she could still leave everything unhappened—quickly take out the cheque-book, write the figure, bid Edu to be gone, see him streak out—and she in her light room with her pictures and the tray, the tea hardly less warm than before. . . . What she said was, "Will you please go away now, I want to get dressed; I shall be ready to speak to you in half an hour."

Everything thereafter took place much as she had envisaged it. But that long rehearsal did not spare her the emotions of the performance, step by step, and the staleness, the sense of *déjà-couru,* did not lessen the indignity of the stings. One or two points surprised her; the length of the unrolling—there was so much more of everything: conferences, talk, paper-work, waiting, waiting for the courts; and it was spread over more time. And she was baffled also by the tenacity of hope; she had believed to have discounted Edu, yet when Edu showed himself without a shred of either grit, grasp or change, she felt desolate.

When all was over they went abroad as she had also known they would. Beyond that point she had not looked, and she became alarmed at once by the sudden and utter flatness that encompassed her. Edu moping at the villa was offensive; when he was gone, she cast about for a way of keeping herself running sensibly, and decided to provide the necessary astringents for her life. Two facts came to her aid—her recent dealings had left her with a taste for the workings of finance; it was now the 1900s, and the prices of the Impressionists were going up. Sarah was still a very rich woman; a share of Kastell

Aniline profits came to her annually; her sources of information were excellent; she trusted her own skill. She left the South for Paris with no expectations and two resolutions, to make a certain sum that winter in the stock market and to buy a Monet, a large garden scene, already negotiated for by the Musée du Luxembourg.

* * * * *

Late love has this in common with first love, it is again involuntary. In the event, Sarah did make a large sum of money by playing the French *Rente*; she did not get the Monet, but she bought another, and she also bought a Seurat, yet these achievements hardly weighed with her at all: if she had chosen them to keep herself employed, diverted and absorbed; employed, diverted and absorbed she was that winter—rapt in discovery, borne on laughter, freshly, involuntarily, magically absorbed. She was also something else, she was happy.

"Do you know anyone who can help one to get a telephone?"

"Telephone?"

"T e l e p h o n e ."

"A most disagreeable instrument, I hear," said Julius.

"Obviously you're no help."

"A friend of mine has one. Somebody put it in for her as a surprise. It is used for ordering oysters when it's too late for sending a *petit bleu*. But the *petit bleu* is quicker."

"Extraordinary housekeeping. Your friend could

hardly be willing to wrench it off her wall and give it to me? We must get our benighted Embassy to do something. You must speak to them."

"I?"

"The brother-in-law of the Foreign Minister."

"Oh, poor Conrad; I don't think of him in that way."

"It's the way that best bears thinking about. They say it takes three weeks normally. I want it now."

"The telephone?"

"*Yes,* Jules."

"Whatever for?"

"To talk. To talk to one's friends in the morning."

"Sarah?" said Julius. "You are not expecting me to talk to you on the telephone?"

"No," Sarah said. "Not you."

A few days later on she said, "I've got it. By my bed. It's heaven. Though when they cut you off, it's not. I don't know what I ever did without it."

"That invention—?"

"Among other things."

"I've come to say good-bye," said Julius.

"Where are you off to?"

"Berlin of course."

"Haven't you just been?"

"Not since the New Year."

"I've hardly seen you."

"No," said Julius.

"When will you be back?"

"In February. I hope."

"Oh yes," said Sarah.

"You see, I didn't go the last time Henrietta had a cold. And now there's Edu's being away too."

"Edu is doing very well on Corfu," she said quickly.

"Yes," said Julius.

"I may ask you to do one or two things for me up there."

"*You* are not going?"

"You know I've shut the house, Jules."

"You could stay at Voss Strasse. I do."

"I have no intention of going away," said Sarah.

Most of the men stood. Talk hung fire. Sarah's dinners usually went at a certain clip, but this one was not under way. Of course there were no cocktails. Julius pulled his watch. "Sarah," he said taking an intimate's privilege, "who are we waiting for?"

"Someone you don't know. She is often late."

"A fault," said Julius.

Sarah smiled absently.

Presently the butler came in and spoke to her. "Not at all," she said, "it doesn't matter in the least."

A rustle went through her guests, most of whom were French.

Julius pulled his watch again.

"Well what time *is* it?" said Sarah.

There was a flurry by the door, the swish of thrown-off furs, and there came forward into this overlighted room a young woman in her early beauty. Her dress was the colour of night-deep violets, her face was a clear oval, veiled and alight with an expression of untouchable serenity, and there was snow in her hair.

"Caroline—" said Sarah, and rose.

"Darling—monstrous." Her look, like her voice, was quick, warm, yet it was withdrawn; the regard was unseeing. "How can you ever forgive me? That endless Brahms— you know the way that never stops. And then of course no cabs, there's a blizzard—" She faced the company with easy, absent animation.

They closed on her in a general converging twitter. "And what did you make of the Debussy?" "Do you suppose we'll all soon be used to it?" "I must confess it hurts my ears." "Ne préfériez-vous donc pas une vraie mélodie?" "Cependant le Naturalisme—" "Une salle de concert n'est pourtant pas un bord de mer!" "Peut-être Madame est Wagnérienne?" "Have you seen the Ballet?" "Which night are you at the Opera?" "Do you skate?"

Dinner was announced two times.

Julius quickly went up to her. "I believe I am taking you in," he said. "My table," Sarah tried to say but Julius had already borne her off.

From her end, through the conversation of her neighbours, Sarah again and again looked at where they sat in a closed circle. She saw the neck and shoulders glow like fruit and marble; the shining auburn hair a little damp now though still light as feathers above the narrow band of sapphires; the still, transported face. Julius was chattering without stopping and ate nothing. She sat hugging silence, sometimes bubbling to the surface in a splash of talk. Once she picked up a truffle peel from Julius's plate and ate it.

"Dinner parties," Julius told her, "so unnecessary. Large ones. So many people eating together. The after-dinner faces—it is so unbecoming to the women."

"How like Lord Byron."

"The poet?" said Julius with the recklessness of someone trying a very long shot.

She smiled at him, all on the surface now. "Lord Byron, the poet."

When the voice behind them said, Mouton '64, she gathered herself like someone who hears the Anthem struck for an instant of respectfulness.

"You really like claret?" said Julius.

"I love it."

"It is unusual."

"For my under-privileged sex? I daresay. My father taught me. He was very fond of it, poor dear. I was an only child you see, and I suppose papa had rather have me drink up his claret than let it go to his cousin."

"Why to the cousin?"

"Because our place would go to him."

"Was it mortgaged?" said Julius.

"Entailed."

"So you drink claret with your father. It is a good way."

"Not any longer. I am now—do forgive the Hans Andersen word, one can hardly use it at table; one can hardly use it at all; but what else does one call it?— I'm an orphan."

"You have no father and mother? and no brothers and sisters?"

"That sounds quite different. Much better. Also much worse. It's not usual to be without them at my time of life; no, I'm afraid at my age, the word *is* orphan."

"An orphan?" said Julius. "That must be rather a nice thing to be? Is it?"

"Not nice for those who died. In India, of one of these unbelievably quick things, four years ago. No, they were not governing it; my part of our family is rather past that stage. They were travelling."

"So the cousin has the claret now?" said Julius.

"The cousin has the claret."

Presently she said, "You know you're so like Sarah describes you. I've heard so much about you. We talk of you a great deal."

"Have you? does she? She's never told me about *you*."

"Well, she's only known me for such a very short time."

Later on, when they had a moment, she said to Sarah, "Your Jules is rather a pet. And *so* funny. And of course outrageously decorative; I'm so glad you produced him at last. He's going to take me riding. Francis never rides now. Oh Sarah . ."

"My dear."

"And I wanted to say, I don't see how you can forgive me for tonight. It was unpardonable. But you know—"

"My dear—it was *not* Brahms this afternoon, it was Schumann. I know: because I was there."

"*No?* What a lark." She smiled at Sarah with her eyes. "Darling, then you're able to say that you saw me."

"Please, please, my dear, be careful. Oh I beg you."

"I might. A little. To please *you*—to throw something to the gods."

"And were you supposed to have changed into this dress in the cab?"

Her look turned inward again as if to meet a memory.

"Should you even talk so much about going alone in cabs?"

"*Not* alone."

"I am frightened."

"I am happy." The face became drawn; then her eyes met Sarah's fully, she very lightly touched her hand with her hand. "Sarah—I am so happy. The world—"

"It does not make you invisible. Nor invulnerable."

"But it does," said Caroline, "it does, it does."

Julius drew Sarah aside almost forcibly. "Sarah, Sarah, Sarah, do you know? She knew Robert."

"Who?"

"In Hamburg. She was waiting for a boat. His name was on the grille. She bought him a tangerine but he wanted her to give him her ring. So unlike him; he must have liked her. Who is she?"

"A Miss Trafford," Sarah said repressively.

"Miss?" said Julius.

"Yes, yes."

"A great mistake. Unless she really *is* in a Circus? She doesn't give that impression at all."

"Oh Jules. She's English."

"Oh, authentic Miss."

"Yes."

"Miss for unmarried? *Unmarried?*"

"Yes."

"She does not give that impression either. Did you say she is not married?"

"Not married. But my poor Jules, not for you. Not for you."

"I shall ask her tomorrow," said Julius.

Part Four

———

A FREE AGENT

Chapter One

"Why?" I said. "Why, mummy? Why?"

"Is it an idle question?" said my mother, keeping a hand on her book; "is it wise? Don't you know that you may have to stay for an answer. And I may bore you. I don't like boring people."

We are said to re-invent our memories; we often re-arrange them. Did we hear this *then*? Do we *remember* saying that? or do we remember being told we said it? Did this happen at one time, or is this clear-cut scene, that amber moment, a collation, a palimpsest, a stereographic recording of many others? I see the lime tree, see my mother in the long dress, at her tea-table, alone, the parasol beside her—or is it the lady by the bushes and the ribboned hat in the picture upstairs?—I see the gramophone with the funnel horn set for striking up *Vesti la Giubba* by the master's orders, the horse-shoe outline of the park beyond the lawns; hear the tone of her voice, bear in me the mood of the afternoon, always long, always hot; smell the lilac——

"Why—everything?"

"Now you *have* stopped me. Before I'd begun. And I did want to talk. What are you after? An outline of the Aristotelian method? the Copernican system? Not Genesis, I take it; I know you only talk theology with the natives. A thirst for knowledge is very well—it wears off so early—but you must be more selective in your inquiries, duck. There is nothing so fatal as a good vast subject. You know, the man you try to talk to about crop rotation and who says Atlantis is more exciting. Well, it

o

isn't. I want your mind—if you turn out to have one—
to be concrete and fastidious."

"Yes, mummy."

"You have already formed this wish yourself? You
have grounds of hope for its fulfilment? Or do you merely
concur?"

"Concur."

"I must be boring you already. Go away and play."

I did not want to play. I had been playing all afternoon, batting the tennis ball against the coach-house wall.
"I like to stay with you."

"*How* like the young men one used to know. It's not in
the least flattering unless you also make yourself agreeable. Girls of course are never sure of their welcome at
all, or that was what one heard. I should try to forget it.
Do I alarm you?"

"Sometimes."

"Not now?"

"Not now."

"Explain."

"I like it when you talk like this. Not *to* me."

My mother did turn her attention on me. "Hm . . ."
she said.

"I like listening to you."

"Your papa used to say that. But do you understand
what I say?"

"I like the words."

"That's what's known as the argument in a circle,
duck; *petitio principii*. Talking is words. *La poésie s'écrit
avec des mots.*"

I squealed.

"There you go roaring with laughter. It may be an
approach to education."

"Not for funny. For nice."

My mother gave me a sweet look.

"Are these strawberries?"

"You ought to do better even at your age," my mother said; "how old are you? (no, don't tell me, the last thing I want to be reminded of is years). Do you see why?"

"Because we know they are strawberries?"

"How would you feel if you had friends to tea and what they'd say was, 'Is this bread-and-butter? Is this your mug? Is this a chair?'"

I pondered this. "I think I should like it. Nanny says things like that. Papa, too."

"Does he?"

"Not questions. Papa says, 'This fruit is not entirely bad. This is not an uncomfortable chair.'"

"Go on," said my mother.

But I veered. "Nanny says in the park one makes acquaintances by passing the time of day."

"The Park?" my mother said sharply.

"Not ours. Nanny's last charge's. It's full of children and other nannies. Do you know it?"

"Oh yes — Full of grown-ups, too."

"Nannies are a kind of grown-ups. I should like to have children to tea with me saying those things. It would be a way to get to know them, it is conversation."

"If that's the kind of hostess you intend to become, I mustn't interfere. I only hope I shall find an excuse for not having to dine with you. Oh well, I'll most likely be dead by then, or living in the East."

"Not dead," said I.

"Darling, such a conventional reaction. It comes from thinking of one's own death. That's why people so rarely dare wish it on each other; I'm sure even here nobody positively wishes mine."

"No," I said.

"What?" said my mother, "do I catch a note of doubt? Oh *do* tell me."

I stood silent and her look was drawn; I knew to my horror that she now shared my sense of being on thin ice.

I feigned ease, but to make matters worse my hand went to my forehead and touched the scar above my eye-brow. I still do this at times; though the scar is hardly visible any longer as a scar and no-one knows now the meaning of the gesture. I saw her seeing, and turned scarlet.

I am certain that my mother never experienced an instant's embarrassment in her life; what moved her then must have been dismay, concern . . She cleared a space in front of her on the table, then faced me. "Now darling," she said, "you know what that was. It was temper. You know that no-one wished your death, no-one wanted to kill us . . A number of people thought they had cause to feel very angry about us and they lost their tempers—perhaps they were right, perhaps they got it all a bit muddled, we shan't go into that now, one day you will hear about it and then you can decide for yourself. Now it *is* frightening when people are angry, whether we know them or not. These people were not particularly thinking of you . . *You've* lost your temper, you've chased a chicken—"

"Never," said I. "Throw a stone at a *bird*?"

"I'm glad to hear it," said my mother with the sudden note of exasperation in her voice that I feared. It was the voice I sometimes heard coming through the house. "Very meritorious. Only that was not the point. I used the chicken—bird—to make you realize something about the nature of anger, and the things one does in anger, and you, like a parrot, side-track by pleading the specific—*I never chase birds.*" She sat up straighter, and she seemed to address the trees, "There's no surer way of fobbing off reality than this sleight of mind, this pulling of the small, true, irrelevant, literal fact, no surer way of shutting yourself out. Lie, if you must, *lie*—as long as you remember you are lying; it's more honest, less stupid, than this niggling shuffle with the general and the particular." Now she swooped on me, "And for goodness' sake don't let's make too much of that absurd episode—it was no flight to Varennes. My grandfather, your great-grandfather that is, faced the Luddites. If you'll ever get to doing lessons you'll hear about that." Then with sudden reversion, "Oh my poor little parrot, fowl or bird, you have much to learn . . . And now I *have* alarmed you."

I had been grateful—I still am—for the trouble of her careful first words; yet they did not touch the core of the unease. I would have liked to re-assure her, tell her that she had got it wrong, that what disquieted her for me did not disquiet me, I knew it wasn't anything—an anecdotal outing, the cobble smashing through the glass in the closed carriage—nothing to what Red Indians were up against any day. And I had not been frightened. Excited: interested in the amount of blood I was able to shed, How many stitches, nanny? I never thought of it, or not in the way I felt my mother to mean; but to tell her, the grasp, the technique, the freedom, the whole concept of telling her, were outside my powers as some distant magic. To tell her that it was not that, that it was—what? Something about the arranged words? the talks that stopped, the servants' looks? Papa. Nanny's exaggerated lightness; her general disapproval, her pity? The almost extra-sensory perception of a grown-ups' disturbance,

the whole cloud of uncommunicable knowing of something wrong. . .?

"Duck," said my mother, "come and sit by me. We'll
talk of something else. You were asking me something.
What was it? You were asking me about *everything*."
(You never knew with *her*, the housemaids said, "Never
notices a thing for weeks on end and then all of a heap it's,
'Lina, that's the fifth of that set you've smashed this
month, do you aspire to the full dozen?'") "What is
your everything, duck? What did you want to know?"

Everything. The garden, the stables, the house, the
servants, the animals I knew, my parents, the other house,
my games, the pony; Fanny. When nanny was very cross
she said, *If I could talk,* but more often she said that I was
a fortunate little girl; and from the books she read me I
knew that this was so. My possessions and surroundings
were what they ought to be; my routine conformed
recognizably with that of my coevals in literature; my
family was requisitely complete. Yet there were devia-
tions . . . There was the fact that we were living in Germany as nanny was never tired of rubbing in. My mother,
I sensed, did not make quite the right kind of mummy in
fiction (young and beautiful of course was standard), and
she was so much away. Papa did not fit at all. The tall,
sad, glossy gentleman who was never either stern or jolly
but addressed one in phrases of grave politeness and
sometimes offered one a sweet upon his stretched-out
palm; I thought of him as belonging to another kind of
story. *He* was the Unlucky Prince who had been changed
by the sorcerer into a hare or stork, only the spell was
such that nobody could see he was a stork and so he could
not be found by the person who was to set out to change

him back. Parents, perhaps, were not a serious matter. Henrietta was. *She* was too old. It was bad enough to have no brother at school, but to have a sister, one's only sister, who was practically a grown-up, worse than a grown-up. She played with me as if I were a doll, and she tried to dress me up. *Mademoiselle, regardez comme le bleu va bien à ses yeux. Je voudrais tant la coiffer; avec des boucles elle sera ravissante. Tiens, je vais te faire un collier.* And when I snarled, she said, "*Tu ne devrais pas faire des grimaces, cela abîme les traits.*" It was a lapse. But the worst, the most inadmissible, was Fanny. Surely no child one read of had ever been inflicted with a fiend like her? The whole business of my mount did not bear going into. The pony was an angel; but he was big and strong and, like our saddle-horses, was not allowed these days outside our gates. It was one of the things one did not ask about. There was a paddock, and one could ride in the park though it was frightfully overgrown, or one could trot round the lawn, but the horses were stuffed with oats and clever—my mother herself had been thrown—and the pony, without any malice of his own, generally tried to bolt. This seemed a great worry to papa, and it was not often that I was allowed to ride. To console me, he bought Fanny. Fanny was looked upon as safe, sweet and small. Papa loved and trusted Fanny, and Fanny venerated him. She ate from his pocket, and would take a lighted cigar from his hand and blow a few puffs of smoke. She liked him best in formal clothes, and he always tipped his hat to her; but above all she loved a top-hat, and he sometimes wore one to give her pleasure. She was also fond of music full of brass, and it was for her benefit that the gramophone was set a-trigger at tea-time under the lime tree. Fanny had not come that day; she did not care for my mother, though she knew better than to show her open enmity; there was merely a mutual coolness between them, two charmers who had no use for each other. I had been prepared to love Fanny full tilt; but, above all people, Fanny detested me.

She was exquisite to look at. She was a small, grey, high-bred Egyptian donkey—no longer young—with delicately shaped limbs and the finest markings. Papa had bought her from a passing circus, and he liked to tell of the scene of ceremonial leave-taking when the staff from clowns to ring-master and director had lined up to kiss her. Now she belonged to me. Every day she and I were made to spend long hours in the park together by ourselves. Nobody but I knew that Fanny could not be ridden. It was her secret. (It was found out later on that it had been her life's career. Her turn had been to throw people from the audience, led on by a wager to try her round the ring, and she had thrown them—men whose feet almost touched the ground, jockeys, Sunday riders, cavalry officers and all.) We would leave the yard, Fanny with a trim little saddle, I on her back, and jog off. When we were out of sight she shed me. She simply toppled over on her side and I was in the grass. When I tried again, she rolled me. She rolled very hard. First I would not give up—I really longed to ride. It tired her. One day she did not topple, she bolted—with surprising speed— into the orchard where the new apple-trees were low, and there we cantered to and fro, I face downward flattened against her mane under the grazing branches. I never bothered her again. Hereafter I dismounted at her sign, loosened her girth and bit, and was left to my own devices until it was time for our joint return. The arrangement seemed to suit Fanny, but I knew that she despised me. Sometimes, to put me in my place, she would chase me down a lane, catch the slack of my dress and shake me savagely. As she liked to find papa whenever she felt like it, she often came to seek him in the house. The floors were too slippery for her to manage, so a set of felt over-hooves were made and kept outside the front-door. Fanny, who knew how to make her wishes felt, would stop an out-door servant to strap them on for her; I never got used to the sudden sight of Fanny turning a passage on a bedroom floor.

I had another function in Fanny's life; both my mother and papa thought it proper that I should groom her entirely myself. Fanny submitted to the necessary mini-strations with the alert impatience of Madame du Deffand having her hair brushed by a dull niece. Only one thing I did could please her—our house was in a still dry valley without natural waters, nanny often talked to me of the seaside and my mother of the sea, and I felt delicious only in the cool water of my tub. I was sure that poor Fanny must feel the same, so I sponged her, squeezing the good fresh water over her nostrils and behind. The first time there was a furious tightening, hoof twitching for the ready kick, then a surprised and pleased relenting; and from then on she always lifted tail and muzzle with grati-fying confidence to my sponge.

Perhaps I might not have fallen so much under Fanny's domination had I had other company. We had no visitors, we do not entertain the servants said; I had met no living children. Everyone I knew was as adult as my poor donkey. There was the grandmother I had felt comfort-able with—I remembered cosy drowsy days sitting to-gether in a warm room sharing good things to eat—though that was far away now and I was outgrowing her, besides nanny told me she was not really my grandmama. The maids I held in affection, and sometimes they would play. But their moods changed often. They all came from the village—a place of great allure—they were with us to get trained, and they were least unwilling to let me have their time when they were new. I longed to hear about their home life—how many in that litter? had dad made up his mind to plant rye for fodder? were the turnips lovely again this year?—they usually told me they had sweet-hearts. They also took it upon themselves to enlighten me as to my religion (I had not known I had one). And here too, I found out, there were some grave shortcomings. I did know the Lord's Prayer, but I knew it with an ending so wrong and wicked that it made them flinch to hear it and use a word like mummy's words, heresy. I had no rosary; I had never heard of the Magnificat. The family ate meat on Fridays. (One didn't have to look for whom to blame for that.) All my people, I was forced to conclude, and especially my mother were on some grounds or other in a state of mortal sin. No doubt was left on where this must ultimately lead them. It was debated whether it was permissible for me to eat the Friday meat. Abstinence, they said, was only a Commandment of the Church, and Obedience came before those. Yet was I not bound to own up and ask them to dispense me from the latter? It might go to their very hearts, it might. Since when, said someone else, was Confessorship obligatory when it was known it was a Grace? The highest below Martyrs. Martyrs and Confessors— It was agreed that the course would be an advantageous one for me. The Remissions! A thousand years at least off Purgatory. The final concensus seemed to be that I would be perfectly *en règle* if I ate what was given to me but did not ask for a second helping. My own solution was to secrete my Friday bacon and give it to the dogs. The aspiration I myself most cherished was to be an acolyte. Practice for this function filled some of the time supposed to be spent with Fanny. I was told such future was not possible because of my being a girl; yet virgins had served mass in the Catacombs, all one needed nowadays was a Dispensation from a Cardinal. It was suggested that I should ask my father to write to one, or better still, ask my God-mother to see the Archbishop.

"He wouldn't say no to *her*."

"*Wouldn't he though now—?*"

A light had sprung to their eyes, and it was at such a moment that our butler, a kind Frenchman, would disperse us by being of a sudden present. I regretted this, but knew that he was right. In return he'd ask me into the pantry and teach me a game called *Pigeon vole*. He told me many friendly and delightful stories, and I never minded his keeping an eye on me. It is to this gracious man that I owe the intimations of that sense of lighter heart, of deep-grooved pleasures, daylight and proportion, that sense of inalienable benefits received, the lines of that sustaining love I was to feel thereafter for his country.

One did not ask anything of my God-mother, who was also my Aunt Clara, one submitted to being asked by her. *What* she did not ask one— I knew the answers that would satisfy her, but they were things impossible to say. She always believed one. She did not come to see us very often, but when she did she was everywhere. Before, Henrietta and Mademoiselle went about the house putting away things like Fanny's gramophone; papa often stayed upstairs, and during these visits my mother was nice to him. I did not find Aunt Clara frightening, she only embarrassed one; and though she took no general notice of me, she always insisted on a private talk. I knew that my mother tried to stop her.

"*My God-child—?*"

The only one of us who came out on these occasions as herself was nanny. When she thought it was enough, she appeared and marched me off. The admiration of the house was with her.

"I should be sorry at my time of life if I didn't know how to deal with dowagers. Papist or C. of E., if you ask me, their bark's worse than their bite."

This I felt did not at all describe Aunt Clara nor her powers; the results however were on nanny's side. The pragmatic method, as my mother would have said.

The presence that I welcomed was the other tall lady's, my mother's friend in the wonderful clothes, such as she sometimes but by no means always wore (I could admire clothes ideally, contemplatively—feathers, jewels, silks, unconnected with coverings for such as myself); when she was here my mother was different and the afternoons were not so slow. I loved to watch them as they sat together under the trees, or upstairs in my mother's draw-ing-room, the one that had the French windows and the picture that was like another garden, look at them, some-times hear their talk—

"I *could* take up Greek again— I'm reading *Faust*. Of course you haven't. I've never met a German yet who has. Perhaps my circle is not entirely representative."

"I must have a generous nature after all. The way I'm not holding it against you to have been so unpardonably right—"

"The ball, as my poor mother would have said—she really did say those things, you know; I was just begin-ning to mind, when she died—well, the ball *was* at one's feet... Poor woman, *she* was right too. I would have held it against her. Yes, of course, my sweet, you may have cream."

The splendid lady looked impatient.

"Sarah—this is your one great fault," my mother said. She hugged the King-Charles. "Oh, you meant the child? Is she here too? All the time? Do go away, duck; go and learn something."

I could learn but little. Various people had tried to teach me to read, and the various phonetics had left me confused. For I had no language. Or I had too many; acquiring and forgetting them with great rapidity. My mother talked to me in English, and so of course did nanny, who spoke it even to the servants who seemed to get her wishes the way I got those of Fanny. To papa my mother mostly talked in French, or in what I knew was Spanish; he addressed me in French at the times I knew it, and otherwise in Southern German which, as he talked it, was not like the German spoken sometimes by my sister and always in the other house, and which resembled, but was not really like, the patois of the maids which was a language of its own. Mademoiselle, who came from Neuchâtel, was supposed to keep me up in French and the village priest had started me on Latin; yet without the steadying recourse to books the ebb and flow of my attainments was erratic. And to add to the confusion I had an Italian name. I was called Francesca.

"Mummy—I've got it."

"What?"

"The question."

"Let's hear it."

"Mummy," I said, "why are you here?"

*   *   *   *   *

Jules had proposed to Caroline Trafford on the morning after meeting her. He was turned down, stayed
another half hour when he had heard his fate and came
away in high good spirits.

This mood held through all that winter and the spring;
enough of it was left to trundle him, not unpleasantly,
through August and July when Miss Trafford was in
Ireland and he in attendance at a German Spa. In Paris in
the autumn it flowered forth again. There seems to be a
tide in men's existences when they are contented and at
peace with their condition against all reason and certainly
their own, almost against their wills. Jules believed he
loved Miss Trafford, had tried to tell Sarah that life
without her was impossible; he had been refused, and
refused in a way that left no doubt that she could not as
much as think of him. Yet there he was, not only comfortable, merry as a grig, going about evening and day
running errands, sighing, enjoying himself, complaining,
he also felt carefree; for the first time in his adult life he
did not probe his fates, he forgot them.

To Sarah, borne more consciously on the same wave,
Caroline said, "The French National Archives were no
idle lie—I *have* a great deal of time. *An elderly man replete
with knowledge*— But Sarah, so alive! much more alive
than I. Always fresh, always round . . There isn't a dry
corner anywhere. And *so* just. The miracle of holding so
much and holding it so lightly. Nothing's too complex
or too small. He turns to it, no he doesn't do that—he's
there—he *is* attention, with his tolerance, his good humour, the fantastic learning he sports like a nosegay he's
just plucked from the hedges, his impeccable human
values, and, of course, his powers of feeling. Whatever he

touches becomes more. Whole. And every time, you know, it's done as if it were the first. A man who's spent his life trying to understand men, action, the world, and who's still moved! He makes other historians look not just cast-iron, but breezy.

"And he works, you know. We have no idea, you and I— He thinks one has to, one must pay out what one takes in. So there he goes, day after day. To add six lines to a page. And I wait. No, it's not waiting; I like the time. I like the space. To turn round the moment . . In the street —standing still, sleep-walking in the Tuileries—"

"Caroline," said Sarah, "you should not cut yourself off so entirely. You are seeing nobody but him and me. And Jules."

"Ah yes, *and* Jules." Their eyes met over this. "He protects my sleep-walking. I'm very grateful to Jules. Do you know people are beginning to talk about him and me? Can it be the reward of innocence?"

"You should sometimes see your own people," said Sarah.

"Francis is that. In the only permissible sense."

"You should see those who are in a narrower one; and you should see them publicly."

"And it was *you* who told me to be careful. *They* might not be talking about Jules. In London, this time, I thought I caught some rather queer looks; you know, the face that dares not speak its question. Oh intangible. Straws in the wind— What surprises me, is my paying notice. People have always talked about me; I can't say— can I?—that I haven't given them cause. Oh don't let's think about it."

"Caroline," Sarah said, "I wish you'd reconsider about staying with me when you're here. Please don't say no again at once."

"Darling, I *am* grateful. But no . . . It's better as we are. I'm not cut out to be a guest, no more than you are, so we don't have to make bones about that. We don't like other people's roofs; even our best friends'. As for the rest, you must know that half the women in my family have died alone in undusted villas in the Brenta."

"You have not reached that stage."

"Oh no," said Caroline.

"Meanwhile—"

"The Hôtel du Rhin is a fortress. You've only got to look at the American visitors—such youth, such ostentatious nonprotectedness, such *open* virtue. The least one can do is believe in it. No, Sarah, don't make your point. Remember my trump, remember that I have Brown. I may be alone in the world, I may have no hearth nor home, I'm still chained to that sacred presence, an unsackable family servant. Brown does as well as the American women's faces."

"I've been thinking of taking a house," Sarah said. "I'm tired of this ghastly flat. I should like to feel settled where you are."

"Oh no, don't do that!"

She had said it quickly in a direct young voice. Sarah, used to the deliberate, the teasing manner of her friend's speech, was startled.

"Let's all stay as we are. No plans."

"But my dear, why?"

"Because— well, because," she was herself again, "it seems to be something I have in common with Jules. I am superstitious."

Sarah, restless, unused to not carrying out her projects, bought a motor.

"But you had one?" said Caroline.

"This one's faster."

"I see. It must be so worrying for the horses."

"What horses."

"On the road."

Sarah shrugged this aside. There was a silence filled by Caroline's looking at some aspects of her friend's existence. A little later she said, "I ought to mention, my dear, that we have coal mines. One coal mine."

This was clearly an *amende honorable,* but for once Sarah had not followed.

"To tell you that we also—we—my family—I—at a cost, well, let us say to more than horses, are drawing profits from what we might call progress."

"Why not?" Sarah said in her dry tone. And this expanded into another silence; presently interrupted by herself. "These are sentimentalities . . luxuries . . ."

"Ah! but they are not."

"My dear child."

Caroline could take this. She could see herself as the young woman who lived abroad, made Fabian points, spent her money and did little about anything. She could also see over her shoulder. And the descendant of Whig humanists said with the serenity of a collective emotion, "Sarah, *not* luxuries."

Sarah waited; almost patiently.

But Caroline lacked the heart to break her mood. She was still young enough in experience to be met by many things for a first time. She was stricken by the lack in Sarah, affected by her own revulsion, lamed by a sense of

P

general recession and an intimation of large loneliness, and her nature was not well equipped to deal with these. An idea came to her rescue like an arrow. They were to have met at seven, now they must meet at once: she knew where to find him. She had made up her will. "I must go," she said.

Sarah said, not without gentleness, "What do you reproach me for? I have not made this order."

"You don't mind enough," said Caroline.

There was again a pause.

Then Sarah shook it off. "That's hypocrisy, my dear. Lip-service, typical—" she stopped.

"Of perfidious Albion?"

Then almost at once they looked at what they had done, at the newspaper world they had let into the room; they both stared at the carpet as if they expected to see bits of crockery lying there. Caroline knew it up to herself to find the word, and felt the seconds going. Then she heard Sarah.

"My dear—we'll be talking about the Naval Race next." She said it rather well.

Caroline rose. "Oh, aren't we all strangely and fearfully made," she said in great dejection. "And now I really must go; I'm already late—which won't surprise you." This was her token of return to their accustomed manner, and Sarah accepted it as such.

"Would you ring for a cab for me?"

"I'll send you in the motor," said Sarah. "It's at the door."

"Oh, do," said Caroline.

This motor seemed to make itself a place. Whenever, later on, Caroline tried to think about that period of her life, she saw Sarah's motor. Sarah's motor (it was its sole identity) with herself in it going somewhere at great rate; Sarah's motor being sent for her, Sarah's motor waiting at all the doors. It solved and created many of their problems—being in two places at one time, or almost; then failing altogether to get them to a third, and it seemed to impose its pattern on their days. The motor, Sarah made known over the telephone, should be taken out, could not be taken out; she started to pursue her painters down the Seine, and at times they got as far as Giverny. It must have been one of those wonderful Octobers, so much longer too, that people used to enjoy in Paris in those days.

"There's Jules."

The motor having kept them waiting, they were caught by him on Sarah's door-step. He swung his hat to them.

"I suppose this means one ought to ask him . ."

Jules took it up with simplicity. "We must take a picnic," he said.

"*A picnic,*" said Caroline.

"Very well. I'll get them to put up something."

"Let *me* see to it, may I?"

"If you don't take all morning."

"Does he actually penetrate to your kitchen? Is he good at that, too?"

"Oh wonderful," said Sarah.

"I wish we could make use of him for Francis. Poor wretch, he's monstrously fond of good things."

"Plenty of those in this town; without our exertions."

"Ah, but it's these men who keep them up to the mark." Jules returned, looking thoughtful. "*Mon Ténébreux,* tell us the secret of your basket?"

"They carved the chicken," he said

"We were not going to devour it whole," said Sarah.

"It's not the same," said Caroline.

"Not the same," said Jules.

"Can we start?" said Sarah.

"Would you mind if we stopped for *one* minute Avenue Victor Hugo?"

"Yes."

"You mean it's all right?"

"No."

"Sarah: what a very uncompromising mood. Can it be family life? And you two only so very slightly connected."

Sarah made no answer.

"Were you any nicer to him before? You *did* know each other?"

"Oh do get whatever it was you wanted, Jules," Sarah said in a rallying tone.

While he was in the shop, Caroline said, "Darling, *six-pence* for your thoughts."

"Jules's all very well, only such a bore—you do realize that he's almost thirty years older than you? And one can't talk."

"Oh I just go on, no-one stops me."

"He would have—in fourteen years."

"That does seem long." Caroline gave Sarah one of the quick smiles that sometimes entered into their run of talk.

"It did " Sarah said with sudden lightness of heart.

They went through the Bois; but it was only after the Saint-Cloud Gate that they began to see the trees. At Saint-Germain-en-Laye Sarah herself suggested that they should stop to look at the fruit. And after that they were three people on an outing on a fine day who took much pleasure through their eyes. Jules said it was Ile-de-

France weather and that the clouds, the shape of the whole sky, were different in Normandie, and Sarah agreed with him. Caroline now wanted to be shown this change, and they told her it came beyond the plain of Mantes, though Sarah said she would really have to wait until the hill three miles this side of Vernon.

The motor disposed. While the chauffeur dealt with whatever might be the matter, they found a farm, half café, wine-shop, grain-shop, where under a trellis in the garden they could eat their lunch.

"Now we can have their bread," said Jules.

He went himself to fetch a loaf. Caroline took it from him.

"It is warm," she said. She broke off a piece and held it out to Sarah.

"Don't tell me you found that sausage in *my* house," said Sarah; "I never have anything like it."

"It's what they get for themselves," said Jules.

"French servants are superior beings," said Caroline. "Would you like me to find some for you?"

Sarah sat insulated as if by a haze of time; she saw Jules's offerings and profferings, the oblivious, the accustomed ease of Caroline's acceptance; she wished all women were able to be like Caroline, but she wished it with a tender heart, and she had a sense of enrichment almost from the meaningless poignancy of the scene.

The owner of the place also ran a market garden, and presently invited them to do the round.

"Sheer Sisley," Sarah said. "One does see where they get it from."

Outside the potting shed stood a large box of freshly dug garden earth. Jules looked at it.

"Feel it," said the owner.

Jules took off a glove. Caroline, originally gloveless

(she was apt to be a little careless in these matters) had her hand already in the box.

"Awfully good," said Jules.

"Loam," said Caroline, "see how crumbly .. it's got a spring to it." She took another handful. "Sarah, look– *Where* are you?"

Sarah was standing at some distance with her hands folded.

Caroline took in this figure. So one might take a photograph; at the time she only saw it in a very brief succession of astonishment, reproof and pity. And when after a number of years they talked again about this day, Sarah said that she remembered it very well, though nothing about a box of garden earth; the motor had not broken down, they had never been even near Vernon, but had picnicked, as they had meant to, at an inn on the edge of the Forest of Fontainebleau.

Caroline was away again. Jules knew that she had gone to Venice.

"Does one? at this time of year?" he said.

"Apparently," said Sarah.

"Wouldn't you like to? Then I could join you. Is it a good idea?"

"No."

"I believe you *may* be right," he said.

Sarah let this go.

But he lingered; and in the door he said, "I have an impression that Miss Trafford's lover must be a married man."

Sarah enjoyed taking this apart in a letter. But she did not send it. She often tore up the letters she wrote to Caroline; it was something nobody had to know but herself.

The next time Caroline came back from London she said to Sarah with stiff lightness, "They do know now, it was unmistakable. The houses we were asked to together, and the houses we were not— Not that I ever saw him. Well—hardly. I suppose Venice, even in November, was a mistake. A menace the way people seem to travel these days. Of course we went on to Ravenna quick enough—the *cold*—but one forgets one knows all those Italians. Well, someone must have blown it." She had spoken as if she were reciting a lesson to the wall. Now she glanced at Sarah. Sarah showed nothing. She took a breath and went on, "Oh, nobody as yet has cocked an eye-brow. They are waiting—you could hear it tick—which way the cat's going to jump. And Sarah– I know that too now."

Again their looks did not meet. "Do you think I might have a glass of water? Just some water. I'm not going as Jules would say *me trouver mal*."

Sarah went for it herself, and held it to Caroline almost clumsily.

Caroline drank the water. "Better now," she said. "Such a nuisance." Then in a stronger tone, "I don't want to talk about it. Now: yes. Not again. Sarah? you saw it all the time, didn't you? *I had no idea*."

"Caroline—"

"It never occurred to me that once it was out it would be all up." Here she held Sarah's look, as if to dare her to smooth this down. "Extraordinary, isn't it?" she went on, "I, who always think of myself as knowing everything. I didn't think it could make any difference to us what people said, or knew. In these cases what *is* knowing? Appearances. My dear—they're never conclusive, unless one's been exceptionally foolish or reckless, or unlucky. One just doesn't admit. If one's front's good enough one can get away with anything. What's in one's favour, actually, is that it's considered so enormous for a girl to go to bed with a man—yes, darling, that *is* what it amounts to. People cannot believe it. Unless they're pushed to. It's only those poor brave things who go about breaking lances for Free Love who cop it; and that's what they went out for, so really they are all right too. Oh I'm not saying it doesn't tell against one, the appearances, in some quarters; that one isn't in for some sticky moments—some people seem positively predisposed to belief. Here's where old front comes in. Shall we say one gets away leaving a few feathers? But *ruin*— No."

"A lucid disquisition," said Sarah.

"It was this I thought you were afraid of for me."

Sarah let it sink in. "It was part of it. I should have said more."

"Could you?"

Sarah considered this, with her own lucidity.

"There are so many things always between two people," said Caroline.

"What?" said Sarah.

"I felt you did not like him."

"I did not know him."

"Ah—but you could have admired! You were rather

tight-fisted, you know. And you must have seen him for what he is if you saw that he would not let his wife, nor me, become exposed to what is coming on us now?"

"I saw that such situations are not tenable."

"As he cannot protect both me and her, he will do the only thing he can. Abolish the situation. Simple, isn't it? A simple piece of arithmetic."

Sarah looked stricken.

"Oh but not yet," said Caroline. "*Not yet*. He doesn't know what's going on, thank God. Aren't the people most concerned always supposed to hear last? I must do everything to keep it off, I must try to get him somewhere safe. Perhaps we'll go to Ireland . . Our last host there was convinced I was my mother. What a fool I've been! Because he's always had mistresses, because he's rather like me in all this, *open*— Once, early on, when we'd managed to get away and there I was first at the inn on a Friday afternoon with a dog and no luggage, he came into my room with a book and a basket of apricots . . . I thought— Oh I don't know what I thought. That he'd take it like me, that he wouldn't mind. Now I see that he cannot . . He cannot leave me to face the talk, and he cannot leave her to hear it. He likes her immensely, you know. She is very nice. Yes, I might say I know her. I've seen her. Oh before; years ago when I was first out. She's forty-five now. I'm glad I did. It seems to make it easier now—*not* an unknown face. I don't think she'd remember me. *She* must not have a face and name thrust on her. He's always been plain about what she can count on from him."

"I suppose so," Sarah said.

"We talked of it. Of course. How we can never marry each other— or really go off together. He *cannot* leave her.

If they'd both been younger . . . But for a man of his age to leave a woman of hers—it would be barbarous, unthinkable."

"And *you,* do you really feel this?"

Caroline raised her face. "I do."

"That gives her a queer champion."

"I know, Sarah. There's that too."

There was silence.

"I've often wondered."

"Yes?"

"The things one wonders about. What it is like at forty-five? What *one* is like; what one does want, what one feels? I never dared ask you. I am not asking you today . . Today does not count."

"Caroline," Sarah said, "have you never been jealous?"

"I thought of her being dead."

"Have you wished it?"

"I have not let myself. I don't want it. It would have struck at everything. One could not live in such a world. It would have struck at what binds him and me. If I had not managed to keep clear of this I should go insane now."

"It strikes at oneself," said Sarah.

But Caroline's mind was not on Sarah. "There was never any choice in it for me. I'd do the same again today. One does not not take the crown of life."

"My dear," Sarah said, "you are still very young."

"That," Caroline said, giving herself a little shake, "may yet be the worst of it. I wish, I wish it hadn't come so early." She put her hands to her face.

Sarah brought herself to ask. "What will you do?"

Caroline uncovered her face, the beautiful face, all smoothed now for an instant by surrender, "I don't know."

Sarah had a definite, a physical sense then of a want that could be filled. And it came to her what she must say. When, whenever the moment comes, I will take you away. To the East, round the World, to China . . . We will stay away for two years, for three, for more. For whatever time it will take until you can bear to return, to go back to your country and the life you must have there and which is before you. ·

I can do this. I will leave my daughters to strangers and my husband to his pursuits. They do not need me.

I will do it so that you shall be numbed; stunned by movement, people, impressions, by quick changes and fatigues. You will be bound to and borne by a huge apparatus of travel.

I will do it so that the voices you shall hear will be Dutch, or French, or the voices of Orientals. I will see that there are men whose admiration you will be able to absorb without awareness and who will not remind you.

If you want dangers you shall have them; if you want to do things that are not often done by women I will arrange them. If you want art, great art, not tasteful objects, which will astound and live when we shall long be dead, I will teach you. I am able to command people and you do so by your presence. Everything that can be done in countries such as these for a woman such as you will be done for you. And to you it will be dust and ashes and great emptiness.

You will not be interested; you will not be pleased. You will be very unhappy. But the time will pass. I will wear it out for you. I will drive the time for you. And there will be your youth, your curiosity, your habit of taking life with full hands. You will find ease. And one day you will be ready to go back to all that is still yours. And you will not have been harmed.

She felt herself filled with certitude and strength and a great wave of love for the young woman before her. "Leave it to me. I will see you through. I will take you away." The words were in her and she knew that Caroline would seize what was held out to her, as a child accepts to have itself led upstairs from a room of wreckage. But she hesitated; held back by the sense of how paltry, helpless, conventional and meagre her plan must sound to Caroline—held back by the consciousness of her own joy.

Then Caroline spoke again and the moment had passed.

"It is rather a problem isn't it?" she said in what Sarah had called Miss Trafford's about to ride against a six-barred gate voice. "As, technically, I shall be alive. I'm not the kind that dies. Not like the dogs who starve on their master's grave. It would have to be the front-door. They howl, too, and that would be so *mal-vu*. How does one dispose of a life when there's so much of it left? It's going to be a long twenty years. It's not that I propose to die at forty-five—*her* age—but *en ces cas-là ce ne sont que les premiers vingt-ans qui coûtent*."

"I had thought—" Sarah said.

"There's one thing I'm positive about, I shan't go back to England. I could not bear that. No . . . Fortunately there's nothing for me in England now that I haven't even got a home any more. I shall never want to live in England again."

"Never—?"

"I needn't go back even in order to hold my head high,

it's never been bowed. There isn't going to be a scandal. I could still marry the next Prime Minister but three. I don't want to; Francis has put me off politics. I'm spoilt for a politician's wife. Oh Sarah, for what am I not spoilt? We have read all the books . . . Who would not be unbearable to me now? I could not bear any of the nice young men who were always hanging round. *No one* young. And I couldn't bear an imitation— An author with pretensions and no looks— some don without fresh air. I couldn't bear anyone solemn, or uncouth, or smart or clever or unkind. And I cannot bear to hear a man talk! What *is* left? Hunting, I suppose. The one thing I love and he does not. How I shall miss him." She stopped. "I just thought of something. Of something rather frightful. I don't think I want to say it, because I might feel bound to it. I had better say it. Perhaps you will call me a fool. That would be a help. And I know you want to help me."

"What is it?" said Sarah.

"Only that I must not make him go to Ireland with me now to gain time. I feel I must keep things between him and me intact; if I plot now I should lose— I can't explain—call it the sense of rightness between us. So I must not lie now— I see how much lying it would have to be. Oh God, I may even come to feel that I must *tell* him what I know. Is it not frightful? Is it nonsense? Would *you*? Sarah, would you tell him?"

"Yes," Sarah said, "I would. For my own sake."

"I was afraid you would see it in that way. Thank you, Sarah, you always understand."

Sarah turned away.

Caroline said, "I want to ask you something. I should like him to see your pictures. I want him to see the Monet, the wonder. Would it be possible? soon?"

"Bring him any day this week; at tea-time. I shall not be in."

"Sarah," Caroline said once more, "you always understand."

A few weeks later Caroline told Sarah over the telephone that she had decided to marry Jules.

Chapter Two

"HAVE you a prejudice against baptism?" said Jules.

"It can hardly be a marked one," said Caroline. "I remember the ado about it among papa's cronies. But that was in the Nineties."

"No prejudice yourself?"

"Well—no. As long as it isn't those wretched heathens. I'm sure it's more convenient. What is your view? I love you to have views, Jules."

"Then you would not mind?"

"Are you being cryptic about something, *Cher*? What is it? I hope you are not thinking of our children? When I haven't decided whether we are going to have any. In fact I have decided. You are such a wonderful father to Henrietta, it could hardly be duplicated."

"Henrietta is getting older," said Jules.

"Not noticeably," said Caroline.

"It is not the same," said Jules.

"So you were talking of our children!"

"No, no," said Jules, "of baptism."

"Whose?"

"To find out whether you had the prejudice. I rather thought you might not."

"Not?"

"Have the prejudice. It is very strong in some people."

"What prejudice?"

"Against baptism."

"Oh Jules, do begin in the middle."

"Only because it has always been like that. We have

always had the same. So perhaps you would not mind being baptized?"

"*I?*"

"The same religion as one's wives. You see?"

"Oh *clearly*. But my dear Jules, are you an Anabaptist?"

"Oh, no. At least I don't think so? Clara would know about the theories."

"Such an odd sect for the sister of the German Foreign Secretary. With us it doesn't have quite the same standing."

"I believe poor Conrad's father had some difficulties. Can it have been with Bismarck?"

"Jules—I cannot see you walking to the fount."

"I was taken when I was a week old."

"So was I," said Caroline.

"You mean, you *were–*?"

"Goodness, yes," said Caroline.

"Then you *are* a Catholic."

"My mama would have said so. She was an Anglican. Very keen on the Apostolic Succession."

"I don't think we have that," said Jules.

"We?"

"Hasn't Sarah told you?"

"Perhaps she didn't think it was sufficiently to your disadvantage. Whatever it is?"

"We have always been Catholics."

"Oh darling! good old R.C.s? I should have known. I thought it had to be Lutheran. You know, Elisabeth and her German Garden. Discovery on discovery .. It's getting better and better—an R.C. foreigner, what would my poor mother have said? And now you want me to enter your church. That's always *de rigueur*, I know. To be received into the Church of Rome .. It sounds rather well. That's what you'd like me to do, isn't it?"

"Yes," said Jules with an air of having unburdened himself.

"I have no objection," said Caroline. "My father was an Agnostic, if the word is familiar. I shall look forward to my Instruction. I must have a Jesuit .. I'm sure Sarah will be able to produce the very best. No– Sarah is being so unhelpful. We will go to Clara; your sister-in-law is our woman. Oh Lord, I suppose it all means getting married in Westminster Cathedral—not the Brompton Oratory, you think?—well it'll be a change . . ."

"It isn't—" said Jules, "it isn't that I don't think—" he left the window-sill against which he had been leaning, "Ce n'est pas que vous ne soyez pas parfaite, Caroline." He raised her hand and kissed it. "Vous êtes parfaite."

He took a breath. "You know, I believe I should not mind at all what you are. It is only because of Clara. She can be difficult about these things."

"How I long to meet her! Are you afraid of her, my pet?"

"No. But one does what she wants when she really wants it."

"Like me?"

"Different," he said, and there was a smile on his face.

"Like Sarah?"

"Not like Sarah. One is afraid of Sarah, but one does not always do what she wants."

"You *are* coming on, darling," said Caroline. "Though your theology is a disappointment. I believed all members of your church, except Trappists, were accomplished casuists. Did you really think one had to be baptized?"

"It is necessary," said Jules.

"No, my oaf, it's not. Christian baptism never comes

off and it's good for all the branches. If you change, you are received; not re-baptized."

"I'm afraid you are wrong," he said politely. "I know. I've been through it."

"How?"

"When— Henrietta's mother."

"My predecessor! Oh Jules. *Was* she? Oh of course, I see. How did you bring her to do that? How did you put it to her? Oh, I wish we'd call her by her name. You ought to talk about her; you really ought. Do. What was she like? How did you feel about her? Speak."

Jules remained silent.

"Why can't you speak of her? What is the matter? Jules! please."

He made a tremendous effort. "Because," he said, "because she is dead."

"Oh my dear. You know that is no reason. One day I'll make you see it. Nous devons changer tout cela. Let us begin. How did you talk to her?"

Jules looked puzzled.

"Well, easily? did you make jokes? did you talk to her about yourself?"

"We talked."

"In what language?"

"In French."

"Was her French good?"

"Very good."

"As good as mine?"

Jules considered this. "Melanie's accent was better."

"Bravo. Bravo, Jules. *But—was it*? Her accent? What's wrong with mine?"

"It is not so French. But I like it. I told you, you are perfect."

"Ah, my pet, far from it. Far from it. All the same, do you know, oddly enough, I shall try my best."

"You will be pleased to hear—there may be a valid impediment."

Sarah sighed.

"Money."

"Ah, well."

"Is that all you've got to say about it?"

"What's the use of my saying anything," said Sarah.

"It's rather serious," said Caroline.

"Yes?"

"It appears that he's entirely dependent on his parents-in-law. Your parents-in-law."

Sarah attended to her flowers.

"They won't be his much longer."

Sarah said nothing.

"I wish you'd stop looking as if you'd seen the Medusa," said Caroline. "*Whose* raft is it? Have you any idea what Jules is going to do?"

"Has he?"

"I wouldn't know. I suppose I ought to talk to him about it; I don't feel like it."

"The whole thing's preposterous!"

"Not at all," said Caroline.

"Because you choose not to see it."

"Sarah, *please*."

"What will you do?"

"There you are."

"You have money," said Sarah.

"Oh that, yes. Not what *you'd* call money. Enough."

"Enough," said Sarah.

"I'm sure Jules's not thinking of it!"

"Thinking is not the sole approach to money."

"He'll be ruined, in a sense, by marrying me."

"Ruined?"

"Lose his independence."

"Jules's independence . ."

"Relative independence. It matters to me."

"You surprise me," said Sarah.

"Must I say it? If one's going to marry a man because one cannot get the other one, it doesn't feel at all the same, does it, if he also hasn't got a penny. Do you see? Oh Sarah, what is it *now*?"

"Nothing. I thought I was reminded of something. Everything seems to remind me of something."

"You take it too much to heart," said Caroline.

"You don't know—"

"There's nothing more to know," said Caroline quickly.

"I have written to Berlin."

"Have you?"

"A *letter*," said Jules.

"Indeed," said Sarah.

"I thought I had better."

"Very likely," said Sarah.

"Because of the new expenses."

"Yes?"

"Caroline."

"Yes?"

"I shall need money for Caroline."

"Jules, what did you tell them?"

"You see, I thought I'd better write because of my *allowance*."

Sarah said almost humbly, "Don't ask me to help you. Don't ask me to do anything."

"I don't think that will be at all necessary," said Jules; "I only asked them to be good enough to increase my allowance as I was getting married."

Chapter Three

THEY were married shortly after Easter; and they were married in Berlin. A friend of Caroline's aunt's children came down with measles in their London house a fortnight before the settled date. Caroline called it providence. "I'm not going to have it put off, and I'm not going to be married from my own ex-home as they're now suggesting. My first reprieve— You don't know how I dreaded it. Berlin will be different; I find myself positively looking forward to Berlin. Only think of meeting all those wonderful Merz's. Sarah—I'm afraid you've got to marry me from your house. It's inevitable. You remember how you used to press me to stay with you? Now I'm asking you for the shelter of your roof."

"I never thought it would be that one."

But Sarah returned to Berlin, summoned Edu and reopened her house.

Jeanne came to her during the first hour.

"How I've missed you!"

Sarah started.

"It's been a long eighteen months here. I envied you. Now that you are back, have you come to stay?"

"Yes .." Sarah said. "I suppose I shall stay."

"You'll find some changes."

"I thought I saw a great many uniforms on the streets."

"I haven't noticed. They say there's rather more of that."

"How is Friedrich?" said Sarah.

"The same."

"Edu's arriving tomorrow." Sarah took stock of her old friend. Jeanne had always been a pleasure to look at; now she looked much like everybody else. An elderly lady, smart.

"Little we thought—" said Jeanne. "When you left; that you'd be coming back to this house for a wedding."

"I must see about getting the presents out of the customs. I must make lists. Where are those addresses? where do I keep my paper? I seem to have forgotten my own house."

"You can count on me," said Jeanne. "But first I must hear all about it. What is she like? is she pretty? Is she taken with Jules? How is *he* bearing up? Was it all your doing? They met at your house, didn't they."

"By accident," said Sarah.

"That was enough," said Jeanne. "Our Jules is a creature of habit. They call her The Englishwoman at Voss Strasse; they don't know what to expect. Gottlieb and Henrietta are ready to worship her, Emil says she was quite a *well-known* actress. It's taken ten years off his age. Markwald's convinced she is a governess. And of course they're all in a state about the child, they'll do anything for her as long as she won't take Henrietta away from them."

"They're not helpless," said Sarah.

"Friedrich says Jules has been quite unlike himself this year. Sarah, where is it going to be?"

"Berlin Cathedral."

"Ah, *yes* . . ." said Jeanne. "A big wedding."

"Her uncle's coming over to give her away; and I don't know who else. Jules's asked Bernin to be his best man."

"Does Jules know what he's let you in for? Do *you*? Sarah dear, forgive my asking, is it wise? A function of this kind? so soon?"

"What *do* you mean?" said Sarah. "Oh I know; I shan't be allowed to forget it. The house of an undischarged bankrupt. It happens to be my house. It never belonged to Edu."

"There's so much bad blood in this town," said Jeanne.

"Always was," said Sarah. "I don't see what they've got to complain about; there's been no undeserved hardship. Edu's not my sole obligation. I'm not going to spend the rest of my life in a mouse-hole. And I will *not* think of everything."

Jeanne looked at her quietly.

"I *shall* have to think of whether to have Henrietta or not, and of getting her something to wear."

"They have left it all to you," said Jeanne. "Is she helpless, too? You know that you haven't told me a single thing. Is it true that she is quite fast? Is it true that she's been to Italy alone with Jules? I don't even know whether she's thirty or seventeen. Voss Strasse believes both."

"If you *will* listen to Voss Strasse."

"I don't," said Jeanne. "I can't. You know I only hear what Friedrich tells me."

Sarah softened. "*You* will like her," she said.

A week later Caroline arrived. She was met by Jules and Clara. "I am very glad to see you," Clara said in a tone that held no regard for a station platform. Caroline lunched with the Feldens and Count Bernin at the Wilhelmstrasse. Clara apologized for their not being alone—she was merely her brother's housekeeper. The guests, three or four men one of whom Caroline knew in

London, seemed to have no apparent connection with each other. She sat between Bernin and an old boy determined to talk compliments to her in English. Bernin was extremely agreeable, conveyed an easy welcome, seemed to know exactly who she was and did not ask a single question about England. It could have been anywhere in the world; except in a private house. She saw Bernin keeping a light hand on the table, saw Clara taking no notice of anything, yet being part of it all the same by providing the note of detachment; she saw Jules and Gustavus sitting side by side at the other end, and saw the kind of likeness that is always disconcerting. The food was almost ostentatiously perfunctory and, if it was not, appeared skimpy. Caroline, used to this kind of occasion, was now indifferent to her own relation with it or effect, she, too, was quite detached; the spring to seize, connect, relate, had become slack, and she received the scene before her, the room, the lives, the people, not shaped in terms of judgement or analysis, Thackeray or Trollope, but as an integral and direct impression of something composed of several levels—smoothness lying over painstaking elaboration, an order covering and engendering chaotic agitation and beyond it nothing. The impression was without words or thought and it was as solid as a cannon ball, and it was extraordinarily disagreeable. She turned to Jules, and he was outside; from him there came immobility, not stillness, the immobility of someone asleep and yet at bay. It lasted but a flash. Clara addressed her and she was pulled back by personal antipathy, yet a sense of a malaise persisted. After luncheon Bernin took her to see his office. There he asked her to remind Frau Merz that he was sending out a secretary to settle details of the seating at the ceremony and the nuptial mass. He was afraid there had to be some slight alterations in the music. "Of course you don't know St.-Hedwig's? It's not Chartres. Though you will find it large. I advise you to have a look at it. Tomorrow morning? Eleven?" He made a note. "Someone will expect you in the main sacristy; east entrance." Then he mentioned her uncle.

Something made her say, "Only by marriage, you know. He married my mother's sister."

"But he is coming over?"

"Oh yes," she said.

"I always read his speeches."

"I heard *one*."

"I wonder whether he realizes that fundamentally he and I are of the same party?"

"You have so many . . ."

"The Centre is the actual liberal party."

"I thought there *was* a Liberal Party."

"There is a party of that name."

"We haven't got the room," she said, "members would have to stand in the middle of the floor."

"The Reichstag is more accommodating," said Count Bernin. "Do you think there is any chance now of Jules's wanting to come back to us?"

"To you?"

"The Foreign Office."

"Did you find him so suitable?"

"That was a long time ago. I never had anything to do with him then." He added, "You must be aware that you could make any man's career?"

"I'm not so sure that I hold with careers," she said, "though this is hardly the place to say it."

"There are careers," said Count Bernin, "and there is service. This place has seen both. Jules nearly did come back once. He was a bit at a loose end at the time; we got him a secretaryship in Paris, the very thing he'd like one would have thought, he seemed rather pleased, then he turned it down. You know why? It had occurred to him that he would be representing Germany in France, and he said he couldn't do that. Not Germany, not in France. He has strange ideas about Germany."

"I'm afraid he's not unique."

"I believe Jules really hates it. He asked whether he might not be given another country to represent. Like a commercial agency."

"Did Jules really do that?"

"He's an obstinate fellow. Not that there isn't something in that notion of his. One does one's job where one happens to be placed, one does one's best for the firm, but the firm itself is subordinate to the general economy. I changed firms. Like my father I began by representing the corner of the earth I was born in, Baden; later it was Germany. But whether Germany or France or Montenegro, the true statesman is a steward entrusted with the welfare of the larger whole."

"Has this ever been a working concept in international politics?"

"There is a leaven. In many quarters. Among men in all kinds of positions. We are all placed to serve the greater end."

"Abolition of Armies and Navies?"

"That may well be one of the aspects."

"Social justice?"

"Helping the poor is always a rich man's duty," said Count Bernin.

"When there are no more poor?"

"Are you not putting the cart before the horse?"

"You have not told me: what is your horse?"

"Spiritual unity, without which there can exist no other. Re-establishment of our Faith. The old Faith, to which *you* have just returned. I regard it as a happy omen."

"Count Bernin," said Caroline, "are you quite mad?"

He smiled. "I said re-establishment—there are times when one can only go forward. I do not expect the English people as a whole to return to the Church of Rome. Yet the Church of Rome might well receive the Church of England. There is nothing inherently impossible in the conception of a Universal and United Catholic Church, a Trinity of the Roman, the Greek and the Anglican Branches, each one, each whole, each equal. With *certain* adjustments. The Anglican Branch might be expected to unify her liturgy— On the other hand, one need not necessarily envisage Disestablishment—"

"Romanism without popery?"

"In the sense interpreted in your country."

"And the *Pope*?"

"That would depend. As you know the Sovereign Pontiff is not born but made."

"Tell me—is all this quite orthodox?"

"It is not for us to say. In the event, a Council might pronounce."

"Is that the way you talk to Cardinals? You know you have shocked me."

"I hope not. Do not allow yourself to be," said Count Bernin. "All vast dreams are shocking. To small people. I do not look at you as small."

Then Gustavus came in and led her back to another room where she found Clara standing by herself who said, "You will let me help you?"

Later, Jules took her to call at Voss Strasse.

"She's very pretty," said Grandmama.

"Reminds me of Fräulein zu der Hasenheyde," said her husband.

"Please can I be your bridesmaid?" said Henrietta.

"Oh I must congratulate you," said Grandmama.

"We must congratulate *ourselves*, ma'am."

"You have nice jewels, my dear. I must give you some more.

"Aunt Sarah said I was to ask you."

"Too good for Jules," Markwald said to Emil.

"Too *good*."

"I hope you will let me show you something of the town?" said Friedrich.

"I can see to that, my boy," said his father.

"I'm going to have a new dress," said Henrietta.

"Have you decided where you will settle after your honeymoon?" said Friedrich.

"You haven't got a home?" said Markwald.

"You need never fear to remain without one," said Emil.

"That's papa's ring," said Henrietta, "I know what the stone's called. Did he give it to you?"

"A habit," muttered Emil.

"I hope you are getting enough to eat at Sarah's," said Grandmama.

She visited the *Schloss* with Gustavus and saw the Law Courts and Panopticum with Friedrich Merz. Sarah said, "Wouldn't you like to see the gallery at the Museum? it's really quite first-rate."

"I don't think I will," said Caroline.

She took Henrietta out to a bun-shop. Clara called to have another talk. Sarah felt she could do no less than ask Jeanne for tea.

Henrietta said, "You will be my mama?" and Caroline answered, "Don't you think it's a little late in the day?" To Clara on her second visit she said, "Why do you want to know? I don't believe you're in the least interested in me."

"I am interested in every Christian soul," said Clara.

Before she left she took Caroline's hand and said, "We do so hope you will let your first child be born at Sigmundshofen."

After Jeanne had been to tea, she said to Sarah, "You must forgive my prying and prattling the other day. I did not realize."

To Caroline, Sarah said, "You did not like her?"

"Why?"

"If you did, you didn't show it. She's a nice woman."

"What's the good of my meeting nice people now?" said Caroline.

Friedrich, taking her down the *Linden*, said, "Sarah's been making a great mistake if you ask me, bringing up her girls abroad, never letting them near their grandparents. Out of sight, out of mind you know. No wonder they're only interested in Jules's girl now. Pity she's so plain. Well, I suppose it doesn't matter half so much in an heiress."

"She's not plain in the least," said Caroline.

"Her young step-mama can afford to be magnanimous," said Friedrich.

"Jules and Edu are off to Melba tonight," Sarah said; "I didn't think you wanted to go. Should I ask someone in, or shall we be just by ourselves?"

"As you like," said Caroline.

Later on, breaking the silence, she said, "What do the Germans make of Bernin?"

"He has no following," said Sarah, "everybody mistrusts him."

"Such a good reason for being in office."

"He's considered a man alone, he's a recognized universal lesser evil. The Socialists have been using him for some of their reforms but they loathe his guts, and they'd like to break him; to the Herren-Club Conservatives he's a sort of utopian radical they push forward when they want to look broad-minded. He's a great embarrassment to his own party, and of course the Kaiser eats out of his hand."

"People in England say he'll be Chancellor."

"It's quite possible. Unless something stops him. My people regard him as a menace; he'd be a disaster financially, he'd spend simply everything he'd lay hands on. He has no interest whatsoever in capital development, and he's much too high-handed."

"The Roman mission . ."

"Oh, that's more of a private hobby," said Sarah.

"*Jules's families.* Did you know there is also a loony brother?"

"I meant to talk to you about that," said Sarah. "He'd be so much better off in a home. Who told you?"

"Clara. That woman has no small-talk. It is rather a joke or isn't it? One's brother-in-law who's a German officer and an uncertified lunatic."

"A typical piece of Bernin folly," said Sarah.

On her third day Caroline tried to go for a walk by herself in the town. It was an April afternoon, turning twilight, with the street lamps being lit and the shops still open. For some time she walked rapidly, her face unguarded, moving to the momentum of her thought, finding herself unseeing a path along the pavements. Gradually she became sensible of an undercurrent of intrusion, a brush of whispers, glances, of steps according to her own.

"Gnädiges Fräulein—"

"Du schönes Kind, wohin—?"

A white tunic shone before her, a braided arm grazed her dress. At a corner two hatless women laughed. Near her the tip of a sword struck stone.

She moved on, as one moves through a jungle in a dream.

A boy whistled in her face; a couple of youths tried to bar her way; an eye-glass caught the light; coming to under a waxing insolence of stares, she checked her pace. At once they were upon her with more gross obtrusions.

"Gnädigste gestatten! Gnädigste—"

She cast about her. She did not know where she was. She tried to stop a cab. It was not a cab. She saw a woman with a net bulging leeks and cabbages, and turned to her. She tried for some German, "Ich bin verloren."

The woman slowly bared her mouth, guffawed.

Caroline turned away.

When at last there was a cab, a man tried to get in with her. They were under a lamp and she was able to see his face: a youngish face, pasty, with a fair moustache, above too high a collar. Panic ebbed, and she found herself held up by rage. "*I've never seen such manners*," she said in English. The man fell back. She pulled the door. She tried to give the name of Sarah's suburb; the driver did not seem to understand her. Then he refused to go. They were still under the same lamp.

"Voss Strasse 9," she said.

"Frau Geheimrat is resting," Gottlieb said, "but Herr Baron has just come in."

The house was very warm; filled with an opaque quietness through which the gas jets hissed.

"Don't bother to tell anyone," she said; "I only want you to get on to Frau Edu's chauffeur for me. I shall wait here." She sat down.

"We shall have him at the door in twenty minutes,"

said Gottlieb. "Meanwhile, may I suggest some slight refreshment?"

"I could do with a nip of brandy," she said.

"It will be a *pleasure*."

"I do believe you are the kindest person in this town," said Caroline.

At Sarah's, she found Jeanne. The two were unpacking presents.

"It was so good of you to send me a card."

"Not at all," said Caroline.

"I'm sure you're going to look ravishing. Who did your dress?"

Sarah did not look up.

"It isn't ready," said Caroline.

"They never are," said Jeanne.

The next day was a Sunday and she was lunching with Jules. "For God's sake can't we go somewhere quiet?" "There is a place. If you don't mind going to a private room?" "I *don't* mind."

They came in by a street entrance.

It was a very small room and the furnishings were fake French. Oysters, brown bread-and-butter and Chablis were already on the table.

"Where are the waiters?" said Caroline.

"The waiters only come when you ring the bell."

They sat down on the banquette.

"It's Edu's favourite restaurant," said Jules.

She put aside her napkin.

"Would you like me to open the window a bit?" he said.

"Yes please."

"I'd much rather go to Borchard's; but Borchard's have no *cabinets particuliers*."

"Jules," said Caroline. "I cannot go through with this."

She felt him go stiff, as a dog goes stiff in mid-run.

After a moment he said, "I always knew it was too good to be true."

She gave him a look. "I did not mean it like this, I'm not trying to jilt you. Is this how they do it? I was not thinking of you."

He waited.

"I cannot go through— all this. The nuptial mills— Berlin Cathedral— That is one aisle I do not wish to walk up. And I will not," she took fire. "I can do many things. There're things that are impossible for me to do. And I'm perfectly clear as to those!"

Jules said, slowly, gently, "Is it because of the previous attachment?"

She gave him another swift look; then she allowed a silence. "Jules, you are the most extraordinary man. *Yes*. At least partly. I don't know. I've taken an independent dislike of aisles."

He said gravely, "One is not happy at these ceremonies."

"Jules." She held his eyes. "I'm going to ask something of you. Do not say no too quickly. I am asking you to go away with me, now, soon, at once—before this ghastly date."

Jules listened.

"Let's get on the train to Spain and clear out. Get me out of here before I lose my mind."

"How can I?" said Jules. Then, "Yes—I could, I *can*." His voice changed to a high, reciting tone and he went on, "I can take you away, I shall get you away. Tomorrow?"

"You *are* wonderful," she said. "You've given me confidence in myself, I was more right about you than I knew. And Jules—I shall never forget this—*you* will be able to count on me too."

"I only want to be with you," he said.

He poured her a glass of the wine and she drank it, and she also ate some of the bread-and-butter.

"And now that's settled, we might as well do some thinking. We had better get married all the same, don't you agree? Rather an unnecessary act of folly if I were to run off with you at this point."

"Whatever you prefer," Jules said; "unmarried lasts longer."

"Give me some more bread-and-butter. Like poor Jeanne. *Has* it with you? I always heard you were so flighty."

"Over twenty years," he said. "Of course with interruptions."

"And never a thought of wedlock?"

"It would not have been suitable earlier on. And when one might have, there were obstacles. It would have been very comfortable. Now I'm glad."

"Sarah says you almost married a French widow."

"Not a *widow*," said Jules.

"My pet, I must tell Sarah myself. You will have to explain or fail to explain to everybody else. I'm leaving it *all* to you. I suppose then a quick job at a registry office? There must be such a thing. We have three days. At least you know the language."

"Clara?"

"She'll have to lump it. *I* shall have to telegraph my uncle. He ought to be grateful for being saved from

Bernin. Poor Uncle John has such a boyish nature; I feel at last I'm standing guard over his career."

"Clara would mind our believing we were married when we are not."

"Of course! civil marriage doesn't count in your—in our—church. Oh dear. I don't think we can do that to her . . Well, we must find some friar in a village in Spain soon and send her a post card or the certificate."

"Two marriages . ."

"*Darling.*"

He got up, and found the bell.

"Yes, do order some lunch," she said.

"The oysters have got warm," said Jules.

"I ate mine."

They were married by a priest in the ante-room at Voss Strasse in the presence of Clara and Gottlieb. The Merz's had been persuaded not to appear. They sent a hamper to the train.

There had been one more hitch: Caroline had pensioned off her Brown at the time of her engagement, and the new woman suddenly refused to travel. "I shall have to sleep in my clothes," she told Sarah. "It won't be easy to find someone here," Sarah said. Finally, Grandmama offered to lend her own maid Marie, and Marie said she did not mind if she saw Spain again before she died.

After it was over, Caroline said, "This room looks strange? Oh, it's Jules's cats."

"I asked them to remove those idols," said Clara.

Caroline shook hands with the priest and with Gottlieb. Clara kissed her. Then Clara and the priest left. Jules drew his watch.

"Do go up to Henrietta," said Caroline.

In the carriage, they looked out of their windows.

"In Rome one throws a coin into that fountain," said Jules.

"I am cold."

Half-way to the station, Jules said, "Sarah asked me to give you a message. It's about your present. She's giving you one of her pictures."

Caroline waited.

"The large one you know. The two women on the bench."

She went white.

"I was to tell you: as she did not know where you would be, she left it in Paris for you; it is in a strong-room in a bank in your name."

"She shouldn't have done that. *No*—"

"You like that picture, do you not?" said Jules.

She shut her eyes. "What it must be like to be able to give something like that . . . Scaring."

"Now it belongs to you."

Caroline burst into tears. "Sarah has given me her Monet— the beautiful Monet—" She wept loudly, more like a boy sobbing over a dead rat than a lady driving in the morning through the streets. "I've been beastly to Sarah, beastly— And now I can't even tell her. I've behaved like a monster— Oh Jules." She took the handkerchief from him. "Clara is right. She says I am wilful."

Chapter Four

WHEN they had been in Spain for six months Jules bought a horse for Caroline.

"Do you think it will please her? It is a surprise."

"I am sure it is a very fine animal."

"*You see*, the weather is getting cooler. Shall I have him brought round to the patio?"

"Frau Baronin is resting. Frau Baronin said she was not to be disturbed."

"Oh of course not," said Jules.

Marie moved to go.

"Did the English books arrive today?"

"No, sir."

"Do you think they could be *lost*?"

"It would not be surprising, sir."

"What can we do?" said Jules.

"If there is nothing else, sir?"

"Send me Pedro, will you?"

"Pedro's gone into town with Frau Baronin's letters."

"Oh, yes. Perhaps if we sent someone to Gibraltar?"

"Gibraltar, sir?"

"There must be English books at Gibraltar."

"I am sure I don't know, sir."

The distance of humped hills lay drained ivory at that hour. Caroline was standing in her room.

Tu réclamais le Soir; il descend; le voici.

"And then," she said. "And then . . ."

"Oh is that you," she did not turn. "What time is it?"

"Getting on for half past five, ma'am."

"It can't be; the sun's down."

"Well, the days *are* drawing in."

"We seem to be dining just as late," said Caroline.

"Herr Baron has been in some time."

"I think I'll have my bath now. How's the water?"

"Herr Baron has had the second cistern filled today."

"No; it's too soon. I shall wait for a bit later. I'll ring."

"Very good ma'am."

"Marie—do you ever have headaches?"

"Oh no, ma'am."

"I think I have one now."

"Ma'am ought to be lying down."

"I have been lying down."

"What is it?"

"It's me, ma'am. Herr Baron is in the East loggia. Herr Baron wishes to know if Frau Baronin will join him in a game of dominoes and a glass of wine before dinner?"

"Oh, all right; I'll be down presently. What are you fussing about?"

"I'm putting out ma'am's clothes."

"Oh I'm not going to change."

The carriage was in the drive. Jules had been ready this half hour. "We shall be late," he said.

"For the fireworks," said Pedro.

"There'll be fireworks three days," said the coachman.

"The Procession," said Jules. "The Procession is always so beautiful."

Pedro sprang to open the front-door.

"Frau Baronin is not coming. Frau Baronin has changed her mind."

"Not coming to the fiesta?" Jules said. "Perhaps it *was* tiring the last time." He turned to the house.

"What is it?"

"The horses are getting restless."

"Why?"

"The horses in the carriage, sir."

"Oh, tell them to unharness. I am not going."

"What is it?"

"It's Marie. I've made you a cup of chocolate, sir. Pedro has shown me the way Herr Baron likes it."

"We have been asked to Alcantarra again. For the shoot."

"So we have."

"Will you go?"

"And sit in a drawing-room with forty women and their cream-puffs with the shutters down."

"You could be more with the men."

"*The men.* Oh I suppose the men are all right. As long as one doesn't have to talk to them."

"Then you will go?"

"No, Jules."

At the end of the autumn Jules asked Caroline if she

would prefer to spend some time in Madrid. Caroline said, what for?

"Perhaps you would rather go somewhere else?"

"I didn't know we were to move. You organized it all so well here." He said nothing. "Haven't you?"

"I thought *you* might like to," said Jules.

"Oh, I."

"Robert and Tzara used to be like that."

"Robert and Tzara?"

"When we stayed in Paris too long."

"So you took them to the country?"

"Yes," said Jules.

"How very unselfish."

He said nothing.

"I don't think they were *so* much nicer than I am."

"They could not help it."

"How I loathe patience. I wish I were a man."

"Oh, no," he said. "Why?"

"To run away to sea."

"In a tiny cabin, inside a ship? and never go anywhere by oneself—you wouldn't like that at all. Someone else I knew talked about going on a ship." He turned his look on her as if to find some sustenance. "He tried to run away."

In his boyhood Jules's imagination had been much impressed by a circus turn called the *salto mortale*. Now, he had the sense of his dreams of forty years ago, of being at the trigger second of the anguish and imperative to leap—through the blazing cupola into saw-dust, safety, light. "He was my brother," he said. "You know, I had a brother?"

"Oh, of course," said Caroline.

"Perhaps," Jules said, "it is not so bad to die?"

"Not to be had for the asking," she said. "What am I supposed to do in Madrid?"

"Madrid?" said Jules.

"What am I supposed to do in Madrid?"

He gave her a helpless look.

"Then why suggest it?"

"It is a town," he said.

"Nothing would surprise me in this country."

In January Caroline suffered Jules to make the change. She liked nothing about it. It was bitter cold; a cutting wind from the Guadarrama blew across the squares; if beauty of walls and stone had failed to strike, urban ugliness could only swell oppression. The floor Jules had been able to take for them had mildewed hangings and was exposed to a hundred draughts, and it displayed a number of rather startling inconveniences. Again she submitted to the days within the lines of least resistance. But here, passivity meant balls, drives, theatres, trades-men, streets; they were besieged by callers. She was chilly, generally bored, and often not too comfortable, but she did not have a moment to herself, and she was —an achievement in that city—always a little late. One morning she woke, looked out of the window, laughed at a quarrel, ordered her horse, learnt that her saddle had vanished, and told herself that misery was a habit and like all habits can be broken. She returned at tea-time.

Doña Nieve and her daughters, she was told, were in the *sala*.

"Seven? Did I hear you say, Pedro?"

"Five, your Excellency."

"They cannot go on waiting all evening? Go slow on the refreshments." She went to find Jules.

"You look wonderful," he said.

"How can I? In these rags."

"Not the clothes," said Jules.

"My poor darling. How true. I think I *will* see Doña Nieve. I shall ask her advice. They will find that so placating."

"Oh I shouldn't do that."

"Placate her?"

"Go to her dressmaker."

"My dear: she looks perfectly gorgeous to me."

"Passably," said Jules.

"Where *shall* I go?"

"I will tell you. I shall find out exactly."

"From whom?"

"Someone you don't know."

"Well dressed?"

"Oh yes," said Jules.

She sat down and laughed. "I see such a neat joke against myself. I am so slow. I do wish I could share it with someone."

"With me?" said Jules.

"I don't think so."

"Don't come to the ball tonight—you know how you hate it."

"Someone must go with you."

"Nonsense, *Cher*; you forget Doña Nieve and her seven dwarfs. They eat out of my hand."

"Who will see you home?"

"You know I shall be scandalously late. Oh Mendoza, or someone."

"That would not be suitable."

"Really, Jules . ."

"You do not know this country."

"I've got a pretty good idea."

"One must be very careful," he said, "in our circumstances."

"What can you mean?" said Caroline.

"Mendoza *is* your lover?"

"Since you ask."

"Forgive me."

"Not at all. Oh, *darling*." She held out a hand. "I'm so glad you're still able to surprise me. You do, you know. You must have had the most un-Victorian upbringing."

"And Zuñega de Valdafuentes?"

"Is *that* his name? I've only heard him called Zuzu. Yes."

"All of them——" said Jules.

"Oh no, no. Not all."

"No, not all. Mr. Symington?"

"Mr. Symington and I talk. I'm very fond of Mr. Symington."

"Like me."

"I am *very* fond of you, Jules. Much fonder than of Mr. Symington."

"Yes," said Jules.

"My dear," she said, "I suppose I ought to say it, though the moment is really too horribly pat, you know: if you want to call it a day, and I don't see how you can want to do anything else, it's up to you of course. I shall do whatever seems least intolerable to you—separation, divorce; I need hardly tell you that it's been all my fault."

"Not fault."

"You are generous."

"Life is very difficult," he said.

"It is what we make it."

"You do not know the dangers," said Jules.

"Oh dangers . ."

"You are not afraid."

She brought her attention to him. "You are?"

"There is always reason," he said.

She considered this. "You know—I will try to bring you luck. As I cannot exactly make you happy, I can at least try that."

"You do not want to leave me?"

"I was thinking of you."

"Of me?"

"For once."

"Oh *no*."

"In that case," Caroline said, "in that case I'll tell you what we'll do, we'll have one more summer in Andalusia and get ready to move over to North Africa next winter. I daresay on our way to Persia."

One evening in the spring (Jules had already left for the South to get their house in order) Caroline came home and found Mr. Symington sitting in the dismantled gallery in the twilight rustling newspapers.

"Oh, Symie," she said, "have they been looking after you?"

"For the last few hours. Always so instructive, seeing the local Press. You know who's here? They call him *El Ilustre Sabio Ingles,* in two columns, look—" he handed her *El Madrileño*. "No-one at the Embassy had the slightest idea."

"Here?" she said.

"Do you see the French are giving a reception for him—typical."

"In Madrid?"

"Madrid is not Somaliland."

Of what happened next Caroline once spoke herself.

We met. At once. I don't know how. I must have got rid
of Symie . . I must have sent a note . . I don't remember.
I who cannot bear to wait, who cannot manage suspense.
I wasn't there at all. *I* was suspended.

Then he was there.

A most extraordinary thing happened, the thing one
had always heard being said. It was as if we had never
been apart for a day. No search, nothing aside, no double
thought, no lag—It was he, it was I, it was us: it was *all
right*. Flowed into place as when the lights have just gone
up . . . An instant easy rightness, oh absolute rightness;
and immense, immense relief. One breathed again and
whatever still might happen, one knew it could not touch
one. He was there—all as before—quick like a simple
miracle.

And of course everything he did went right. He had a
carriage waiting at the door, he was living in a house
someone had lent him, we were in the country the same
evening. We did not leave each other during these first
hours. It was inevitable, it had the touch of the prodig-
ious one sees in skaters on the ice, in birds—

Then something else happened. Again it was unexpected and undeniable. It was as if for the second time in
forty-eight hours we had been brought before the
presence of something we, ourselves, had given shape to
at some point of the past. A confrontation— The next day
it was different. Time *had* passed between us; we *had* been
separate. We weighed, we watched, we waited. We felt
the past, we had to include the future. It was no longer
the same: in fact it was over. It was still the best that could
have happened, but it had happened. I had walked in as
into an open garden; one does not enter that way twice.

I knew more about myself, about needs, about life in
time. I realized the high impersonal pitch between us

—his lack, the voluntary, cultivated lack, of possessiveness—and saw that it was not maintainable for me. I was no longer as civilized. And I knew the gap that comes later between admiration and sustenance. I saw that if it did not end here it must change, and what the change must be.

For a week we saw each other every day, all the day. We did not speak of it. I had learnt that too. We were gentle; like ghosts. I often thought of Jules— of his more naïve attachment; I thought of him with more than gratitude, and I was very sorry. For it was clear that the end of Francis also meant the end of Jules.

At the end of the week she left. She took a train out of Madrid. He was staying on for a few more days. She left in sadness; she felt flat, chilled, emptied; she was alone. But she was also free. And she was upheld by the clean sweep, a quiet grim sense of being alive still, stripped for a new existence. She knew precisely what was to come, and what she had to do. She looked at her actions of the last past year, at the impasse she had forced her way into, and it was not flattering. She saw the use she had made of Jules, and where it would have led them; and she was struck by the narrowness of the escape. She looked at it all most coldly, amazed by her own disregard of the realities, and it appeared folly, pig-headed, childish and absurd, but already her view was tinged with impatience; she could no longer understand, and she turned away.

Caroline's Spanish friends had seen to it that she and her maid had two compartments in a special carriage attached to the fitful south-bound train, and so for her the long slow journey was eventless and secluded. During the first night she did not go to bed; she sat up, her lights turned off, the windows down to the streaming air. She sat—looking out, looking out, drinking in the night-air with full lungs. The night was milky, shot through with sudden lights; the countryside but outline. The train ran in and out of patches of darkness, charged walls sharp-angled as backdrops rearing near in relief and shadow, flew across a clearing: the sectioned, linear planes of a station yard. Now and then, two posts, a stanchion, the tracings of a girder, flashed into sight, stood detached, postulated a shape, luminous and concrete, rose, slid and were passed. They had also passed through her. She and the night were the medium and the motion and these shapes– these signals– this permanence– were of them. Quick-silver lengths of rail streaked out beside her, spread, flowed forward, converged, ran on, were sucked into darkness. The train swished by an empty lamp-lit platform, she knew that her father and mother were dead, she had a flash of non-existence. They died with strangers, before their time: it had reached her; she took the loss and her own, and then she was weeping for her parents' death with fresh first grief. When she had wept she was calm; as the night wore on serenity filled her, she was exalted by a sense of gaining distance, of moving swiftly towards the future. There came a point when her actual destination already seemed to lie behind her, when she asked herself what she was doing here, and her errand in the South (the tidying-up action, she had called it) a shell and repetition. Might it not be long— She thought of herself once more in England. The empty ship . . And there opened a sudden joyful hunger for mere return. The West—! Paris first, foretaste, itself fulfilment, lingering—and then, and then, she would see and walk and sniff the streets of London. She saw an old man in a clearing bent over a switch, he was tapping something, now he straightened up, he had seen her. She smiled to him, she felt the smile he could not see, it bound them. She took her purse from beside her on the seat and opened it out of the window; the golden sovereigns, taken short by the wind, settled, unheard, upon the tracks, paler than the clinkers, disappeared ... The old man was already out of sight. Someone will find them, she said. And then she thought her wish.

Jules was not at the station. As nobody seemed to be certain whether their train had been seven hours late or a day early, it was not surprising. Leaving Marie to collect some vanished boxes, she went on in a hired cab. Pedro opened the door. She went through the house, from room to room, looking at everything with careful interest. So one might visit a villa at Pompeii. She was still in her travelling clothes when Jules came in.

"I was just thinking what a lovely house this is," she said.

He kissed her hand.

"How warm it is already. Let me look at you."

"I'm afraid," he said, "I've been gambling rather a lot while you were away."

"A tiresome male habit. Have you lost very much?"

"How did you know?" said Jules. "You see— But first you must have some lunch."

"Oh yes, lunch first," said Caroline.

It was then that they brought her the telegram.

She flushed.

"It came yesterday," Jules said, "I signed for you."

She felt chiefly anger. "How messy it looks," she said, staring at stamp-marks and erasures on the envelope.

Then she saw that it had been addressed to her care of

s

the German Embassy in Madrid, and forwarded. She ripped it open. It appeared to be in English; some of the words were run into others, and most of them were misspelt, but after a few seconds a message became intelligible.

```
jules   brother   shot   by   acci-
dent   urgently   advise   immedi-
ate   return  °  sarah
```

Caroline's special carriage (and Marie) were still in the station, and the guard found it the most natural thing that they should occupy it. Jules lay down as soon as they had started. Caroline sat opposite with a novel by Edith Wharton still fresh from her travelling bag. Towards evening Pedro, who was lodged somewhere in the bowels of the train, produced some sherry for them and a sandwich meal, and Jules began to speak. Before he had only said two things.

"Gustavus — Oh, the poor man."

And then,

"You *will* come with me?"

After that he had left everything, down to his own packing, to Caroline and Pedro. Now he talked and talked. Caroline, who knew little about such things, wondered rather uncomfortably whether he could be ill.

"My father— I am sure you would have liked him. He would have liked you—

"The winters were not nearly as cold as they say now. We had fires lit in our bed-rooms before we got up shooting— but that was more because it was so pleasant—

"When Jean danced with the bear, the bear loved it. They do not usually—

"Poor Gustavus. I don't think he can have been very happy—

"Now there is no one left. Only I, and Jean. Caroline—I must see him now. Do you think he would see me?" And again he said, "You will come with me?"

Presently he said, "I went once— after— when that thing had happened to Gabriel."

"Jules," Caroline said, "you must not distress yourself."

He leaned back.

"All a long time ago, wasn't it?"

"Not really," he said.

And presently, "We had everything we wanted—When you came into the hall you could smell the bees' wax—

"When I came back I brought a lemur—

"They did not know what that place was like. I knew. He told me."

"Jules."

"I don't think Gustavus ever minded. When he was sent back— He *was* sent back."

"Jules!"

"Caroline?"

"You'll bring on your asthma."

"What will it be like seeing him now? *Tell* me?"

"My dear," she said, "you don't realize that I know hardly anything about it. You never told me."

"What it was like there— And the men who came— Papa did not know— You are so like Gabriel. I will tell you."

Caroline sat on the seat opposite, numb, tired-out.

"You do not know what he looked like— You do not know—"

Once Pedro was at the door and she slipped out. She

had wired to Madrid, now there had been a stop and arrangements were confirmed; an official had boarded to tell her that they were going to be coupled on directly to the San-Sebastian Express. Changes at the border, and again at Bayonne, then straight through—Angoulême —Poitiers—Paris—Liège—Aix-la-Chapelle—Cologne. "You will be in Germany the day after the next day, if God so wishes."

Before midnight Pedro again turned up bringing a bottle of medicine he had borrowed from a lady fellow passenger. Valerian, Caroline said, she knew the smell. Together they measured out a few drops. Jules kept hold of her hand.

"Even if he has changed it will be best to see him won't it? We will see him. We will go as soon— as soon as we can go— Papa never let anyone touch the trees— how you would have liked them— and wax, wax for polishing, wax from our own bees—"

When at last he had dropped off, Caroline left him and crept into the compartment she now shared with Marie. She pulled off her clothes without turning on a light, got into the bunk and was asleep at once. Some hours later she waked with a start. It was not quite day-break, the train was standing still. Two things leapt to her mind. The wording of the telegram was most peculiar. She was probably going to have a child.

Chapter Five

It was again morning when two days later they were across the German frontier. At a stop Caroline heard something being called outside, up and down the platform below curtained windows, vaguely disturbing. When they pulled out she knew what it had been.

Fel-den. . . . . . Fel-den. . . . . .

She got up, and dressed. Presently a sheaf of telegrams were brought to her. They were all for Jules; he was, she hoped, still asleep, and she put them aside.

When they drew into the first large station, she was with him. Jules had just waked up, Pedro was fussing about him with a spirit-lamp; it was raining, and Jules said so. Again she thought she heard his name. They did not expect to see anyone they knew before Berlin. She leaned out. Some men came up and asked for Baron Felden. Who are you? she meant to say, then she knew they were reporters. "My husband is not well," she tried to fill the casement; "what do you want?" But Caroline spoke no real German then, and her sentences did not command attention. They crowded under the window. "There he is," one of them said.

"What is it?" Jules called from his bed in French.

"Please go away," she said; "I will come out and talk to you."

"Is she the French or the Jewish lady?"

Caroline caught this. Intent on nouns and grammar, she said, "I am the English wife."

"The one who didn't have the wedding—"

Pedro came up to raise the window; she stopped him.

"What do you want?" she said.

But one man was already in the corridor. The door opened behind her, he stepped in. "So, you people think you can have it all your own way for ever—"

"Good morning," said Jules. He was wearing a dressing-gown and holding a cup of china tea on a light silver tray. The compartment smelt of *cuir de russie* and fresh air.

"Doña Carolina, do I throw him out?" said Pedro.

He had kept a lighted cigar. "Sorry to trouble you."

"Is there any need for you to speak to us like this?" said Caroline.

"I see the Grand Duke's myrmidons haven't turned out to protect you."

"Est-ce la Révolution?" said Jules. "Cela tombe bien."

"Your friend, His Royal Highness the Grand Duke of Baden; this is Karlsruhe, in case you haven't noticed."

"You come from His Highness?" said Jules.

Just then there was a commotion in the corridor. Two more men appeared in the door-way. The wagon-lits conductor was nowhere to be seen, but Marie was trying to ward them off.

"Shame on you," she said.

"Perhaps she also has a commission in the Body Dragoons?"

"We represent the German people," the man with the cigar said to Jules.

There Caroline turned on them. "Gentlemen—" she said and let fly in English. It might have been impressive had they not begun talking all at once to Jules. Jules fainted. So it was only later on from Marie that she heard what he heard then, that Captain Johannes von Felden had been shot by a soldier of his regiment.

It is not my aim at this time to recount the Felden Scandal. Even if I wished to do so I should hardly be competent. One phase of it was over before I was born; the next, I lived through without knowing it. My knowledge of the institutions, government and temper of the Kaiser's Germany is sketchy, conventional and instinctive, full, no doubt, of inaccuracies and gaps; it is also retrospective and so indelible as to be almost impervious to subsequent correction. It is lurid knowledge, of the kind one might acquire of a house through which one has made one's way with a candle in one's hand. The Bernin Papers have never been published; and are now believed to have been destroyed. Newspaper files of the period are probably still extant. I have not looked them up. I doubt I ever shall. What I learnt came to me, like everything else in this story, at second and at third hand, in chunks and puzzles, degrees and flashes, by hearsay and tale-bearing and *being told,* by one or two descriptions that meant everything to those who gave them. Also, by putting two and two together. I have never been to Spain; I only know the Paris of before the first Great War in which my mother as a young woman crossed the Seine to talk to Sarah and walked with Julius in the Tuileries from words and pictures; I never went back to Germany. With one exception, the people of that time had passed out of my life before I was out of childhood: I did not see them again. They are all dead now. Their houses are no more. Their few descendants must be dispersed over three continents. Had I a mind to, I should be hard put to find them. It is a finished story—immobile in the unalterable past; untouchable, complete, as if sunk inside a sealed glass tank. For me, it was never a new story. Every second hand had touched a first; to every fragment there had floated up another—this phrase had been the key to a remembered look, this fib belied an earlier one, this hint illumined words once overheard, this tale resurrected the mood of a whole winter. Which memories are theirs? Which are mine? I do not know a time when I was not imprinted with the experiences of others. In a sense this is my story.

The Felden Scandal was remarkable for the extraordinary ill-nature of the emotions it aroused. Public scandals, scandals during periods of relative stability, that is, when many may wish to have a whack at, but few are ready to pull down, the existing structure of society, follow a certain pattern. Something, an abuse, a crime, an instance of gross injustice, becomes known by leakage or design and is taken up. The régime, that is supposed to have tolerated, committed or otherwise abetted the abuse, tries to deny or explain away the facts exposed. If these facts happen to be very much at odds with what the general citizen has come to expect from his established rulers, if they are irregular, or disreputable, or sensational enough, or presented to appear so, or if the citizen is simply very poor or very thwarted or very dull, the public scandal will indeed be public and it will be on. Motive will be everything, but motive as usual will be scrambled. Some of the accusers will be prompted by faction, and some by principle, others will think of morality or self-advancement or their friends and enemies, and most of them will think a little of these all; and nearly everybody will believe he is thinking of that so complexly constituted entity, a man's conception of his public duty. The men in office, too, will be animated by

loyalty to faction or each other and a sense of the useful-
ness of their careers to their country and themselves.
There will be a measure of honesty and a measure of
truth, and often more than a measure of good will, but
there will also be very large measures of the opposite
things. And when the hue and muddle are all over, when
heads have rolled, and ink and printer's ink have flowed,
and voices have been raised in anger and pretended
anger, when many people have been made to feel self-
righteous and a few have been made to feel afraid, when
the test-case has been decided and the commission sent in
their report, when every side has gone as far as they
would go and time has been worn out, there will very
likely be some justice done and a little guilt brought
home: this innocent man will have been re-instated in his
place and his detractors been deprived of theirs; that
practice discredited, and that borough the last to put
through their contracts in that way; but the borough
council know, and others know, that they were not the
first; the innocent man in being vindicated has been
through the gutter, and there are those who think that his
innocence was a great nuisance and those who have not
been convinced of it at all, and those who speak in private
for the men who are out, knowing that the day must
come when it hardly will be necessary to do so in public;
and of those who were so loud and happy against the
doers, how many are there who did mind the deed? A
score has been chalked up; it will bear interest; and all in
all the world in that country has become a little muddier
than it was before.

For all that, there is usually a generous element in such
upheavals. A murmur of tolerance, some staunchness
among friends, desire to obtain better things for others;
clamour for a hero as well as devils and the scape-goats.

In the Felden Scandal everybody seems to have turned, almost indiscriminately, against everybody else. Of course it must have been true that nobody had much of a leg to stand on, but there was also this: the events that caused this outcry against the existing order—sequels to an irregularity in a backwater enacted over thirty years— were not representative of it. They may have shed a queer light on the Wilhelminian era, certainly not a characteristic one, and indeed people must have asked themselves how it could have happened here. And yet the howls went up, and no-one ever, anywhere, seems to have been heard to laugh.

The Colonel of Johannes's regiment had retired. (He was not the kind that is made general.) The next man was a new broom from the North. He looked at his lists and found that he had a captain in charge of a stud-farm by the forest who had not yet turned up to report. He asked, and was told that the captain never did. He asked more, but there seem to have been no answers. "It had always been like that." "They had never seen the captain." "The major would know." The major unfortunately was absent on long leave; his health had been running down and he was wintering on Madeira with a wife. The Colonel, much displeased about a great many things, declared in mess that he would send for the captain.

"Oh I shouldn't do that, sir."

"Pray, why?"

"He wouldn't come."

"*Captain* von Felden?"

"Well if you really want to know, sir, he's supposed not to be quite all there."

"The *captain*?"

"That's what they say."

"Unheard of."

"It may be just because he's getting on sir. He's been out there since before anybody's time. He must be frightfully old."

"A *captain*? No, no, there must be some mistake. Can't get round the retiring age, you know."

"The Grand Duke's supposed to take an interest in him. His mother used to."

"The Grand Duke?"

"Our Grand Duke, sir."

"Ah, to be sure."

A young subaltern piped up; "Perhaps he's the Man in the Iron Mask?"

"I shall send for him at once," said the Colonel.

"I should write to the major, sir, I should."

"Write abroad? About something going on twelve miles from here?"

So the Colonel sent for the captain; and when Johannes did not come, he sent again, a second-lieutenant from his own province this time, and a corporal. Their names were von Putnitz and Schaale. Johannes's own orderly had been rattled by the Colonel's first inquiry, and he tried to dress him in a uniform. Johannes appeared frightened and resisted. He flung himself on the floor and tried to roll the tunic off his back. The orderly at once helped him out of it and managed to calm him down. He then left him in order to ask the Colonel's messengers not to see the captain today as the captain was not well. The lieutenant looked at the orderly, who was dressed in breeches and a striped jacket, and told him that his orders were to *see* the captain. The lieutenant and the corporal then entered Johannes's room. The lieutenant brought his heels together before a superior officer and announced himself in accents Johannes might have been supposed to have forgotten. Johannes, teeth bared, sprang at his throat. What happened then has never been quite ascertained. The attack must have been savage as well as sudden, and von Putnitz cried out. The corporal always maintained that the cry had been explicitly for help; Putnitz testified that this was not so, but once admitted he could not be sure. The corporal drew a revolver and fired two shots, and by the time the orderly got into the room Johannes was dying. The lieutenant, wounded and bleeding, was jabbering with shock; the corporal stood staring at the weapon in his hand.

It was a difficult position for the Colonel. He did not see it so at first. He had Lieutenant von Putnitz put under arrest and the corporal in irons, and arranged for a court martial. He might have had at least one of them shot out of hand next day, had not Johannes's orderly, Faithful George as he came to be dubbed, lost his head and bolted. Two hours after the deed he appeared on his bicycle in his own village, beside himself with grief and terror, and tumbled into his parents' kitchen with the cry, "They've murdered my Captain!" He then went on to Sigmunds-hofen, the address of the lady whom he knew, who had come to see them and who had always written to the Captain like a sister. The house was closed, but as it happened Clara was there, having come down for her annual eight days' spring airing. Clara had turned sixty, and her health was not good; she had always been merciless with herself, and her frame could not produce the strength she constantly expended. What she had to hear was terrible to her. "It must have been God's Will," she said. Then, "A judgement." "Did he have a priest?" she asked. "Taken like a child . . . Ah yes . . ." The orderly, who was weeping, saw the confusion of that scene, and wept more loudly. Clara failed to recognize his need. She asked for an hour in which to recollect herself; the orderly found his way to the village tavern with his tale.

Meanwhile the Colonel had a warrant out against him for desertion. And when he with Clara and a young priest from Sigmundshofen-Dorf, whom Clara had commandeered, stepped off the local train at the garrison he was arrested on the platform. Clara tried to interfere; then went off to add the orderly's arrest to the long messages she was sending to her husband, to her brother and to Jules over the public telegraph. Jules's got lost in Spain. Desertion carried a death-sentence, which, in peace-time, might or might not be commuted. The Colonel later explained that his warrant had been a matter of routine.

When the Colonel was informed that a female relative had arrived at the dead Captain's house, he did not like it at all.

"She's the sister of the Secretary of State," his second told him.

"Is she? I daresay. Another irregularity no doubt." Then he bethought himself that what with three culprits now at heel, Felden must be regarded as a deceased brother officer and the victim, and he decided to express his condolence to the lady. Before he could do so, Clara was announced.

She cut him short. "There has been grave negligence," she said. "How could you have allowed him to see soldiers?"

"Madam—" the Colonel said.

"We, also, are to blame. It was a mistake to leave him here. We ought not to have trusted you."

What he learnt from Clara was devastating to the Colonel. Could this be the same service he had dovetailed with so happily at Stettin and at Schwerin and at Lüneburg? It addled him, and he did not want to hear, but he could not stop her. When at last she left him he was so upset that he broke his rule about regimental concerns and then and there wrote out a report—a string of pained questions—to his brigade. (He had cause to be grateful; this report, as it turned out, did not save his career but it did prevent his being cashiered on the spot.) Later the same evening he was told of the presence of reporters from the town. He gave instructions to send them packing. The reporters got hold of a conveyance and took themselves off to the forest and the Captain's house. And so, between them, Faithful George, Clara and the Colonel got the story into the morning papers.

At first it appeared a desultory sensation at the breakfast tables. It was called the Dragoon Officer Murder for a day or two; of course that label had to be abandoned, yet it somehow set the tenor of the public mind, and none of the alternatives ever became really established.

Then, before the week was out, the story was given direction by the appearance of the first of a series of leaders in the new Socialist daily *Fortschritt*, above the signature of one of the most ruthless and accomplished publicists of the day who wrote under the pseudonym of Quintus Narden. Narden was not a young man, and he had been for years the spokesman of the Anti-Militarists, the Army was almost his monopoly—that overgrown body of sabre-rattling drones, that state within the state, that romping-ground of insolent and idle aristocracy, that waxing incubus . . . The article was called *A Family*. He would attempt, Narden wrote, to give an outline of the careers of three brothers. Three Barons. Pleasure-loving men brought up in the lap of luxury, though men of but small fortune. How, then, did they provide for themselves? Were they given professions? did they condescend to learn a trade? did they envisage work? They *were* provided for. By whom? By their noble connections, by their wives, by—the German people. By way of the Government Services; by way of High Finance; by way —well might the reader's credulity feel taxed—by way of the German Army. Let him take the eldest of the three first. His course was simple. When he reached the age of twenty, he married the only daughter of one of our wealthiest statesmen and settled down to live in her father's country house, his own patrimony, some neglected and indebted acres, having been sold up, and had lived there ever since. He would still be there, had he not recently changed that abode for the one occupied —*temporarily*—in this capital by the Count, his brother-in-law, in whose wake he had followed upon the latter's acceptance of a portfolio in the Government. In return for nearly forty years of hospitality the Baron had obliged his father- and brother-in-law respectively with a little paper work, of a nature, perhaps, not to be entrusted to functionaries sworn and trained? The second brother had aimed higher. No stay-at-home, he had himself propelled —without discernible qualifications—into the Diplomatic Corps by his brother's father-in-law (the same late statesman, and father of the present Minister). After adorning this service for a few years with his recognizedly graceful presence, he had nonchalantly left it, having secured for himself a still more desirable sinecure in the form of a matrimonial alliance with our Israelite plutocracy. Neither the general unsuitability of the match (unsuitability according to the tenets of his own caste), nor the partners' disparity of age, the bride being a girl twenty years his junior and in failing health, nor the evident reluctance of her parents, had deterred the intrepid Baron from his purpose. He set out once more upon his travels, taking with him the young wife. She soon died. Unencumbered, yet affluent, the Baron always contemptuous of his native country settled in the French metropolis to an existence the particulars of which would hardly make fit reading in these pages, and from there continued to pay assiduous, and no doubt rewarding, court to his ex-in-laws. Unequal even to the duties of a father, he succeeded in saddling these old people with the one off-spring of his brief union to their hapless child. Bounteousness, it might be said in passing, all the more remarkable on the part of a Jewish house itself renowned for a reluctance to meet the liabilities of its own scions; although perhaps less astonishing when seen in the light of the championship of another lady, also Jewish, also of great wealth, and herself connected by marriage with the family mentioned, who had proved for more years than it would be polite to reckon what might be termed a fast friend and protectress of the Baron's, an accord that sustained a rift only with his recent second venture in matrimony.

The current partner was, he understood, an English lady influentially connected and of course of ample means. There could be little question that the Baron, who did not bestow his favours lightly, had not chosen well. And yet it might be doubtful whether this self-styled cuckoo would find among the practical and more tight-fisted inhabitants of Albion quite the same tenderness of treatment afforded him by gullible, good-natured Germans?

Here Quintus Narden paused to beg his readers' pardon for having worn out their patience with so banal a story. Now, he must come to the third brother. Little was known of this youngest of the three beyond that, boasting no particular aptitude or education, and lacking apparently in the pushfulness particular to his elders, a place was found for him in the Army. Nothing unusual in this, nor, given his relations, in the fact that he seemed to have started his career in the Land Arm of the Realm point-blank with a commission in a crack cavalry regiment. So far, so ordinary. But as the years went on this prodigy lost his mind. He became disordered, feeble-minded, non compos. Still not a very remarkable development—it might well have been that the boredom, the utter idleness, the dissipation, lack of purpose and frivolity of his existence wore away what little faculties this rather blank young man had once possessed. (A contingency which upon investigation might be found to be not infrequent in His Majesty's Services.) And here again, he wrote, he must hesitate—he doubted whether his pen was able to render intelligible facts at once so spare and bald. The officer's condition did not improve. He must have been insane, it was now revealed, for on to twenty years. Where did he spend them? In the safe keeping of one or other of his brothers or their foster relatives? In a private home? In an institution? In a manner of speaking, yes. The officer spent them in the Army. For twenty years, until his violent removal by death, he remained in his regiment; he drew his pay; he wore the Kaiser's uniform; in the course of seniority he was promoted to a captaincy. It had never been the present writer's opinion that the military were ideally constituted for the detection of failing mental powers—but two decades! Narden broke off, declaring himself too bemused to venture on a reasonable construction of the facts; he hoped he wrote, to 1ecover his wits sufficiently by Monday to discuss some aspects that disturbed him under the heading of UNDIS-COVERED? OR COVERED-UP?

T

This article forced attention. "What are we supposed to have done now?" they asked at the War Office.

"Better find out."

"Can't have Quintus Narden tell us who's fit to hold a commission."

"Better find out."

This proved a baffling business. An officer of that name had indeed been carried on the Army List for the last thirty years; but nobody had heard of him, except a handful of local people, and these were not in positions of responsibility. There were no records. There had never been a report. All the Captain's colonels were dead (except the one before the last, and they had not yet heard from him). The Secretary of War spoke to the Chief of Staff and decided to have the court martial of Lieutenant Putnitz and Corporal Schaale adjourned.

"The regiment has telegraphed, are they to bury the officer with full honours?"

"Of course. No. Perhaps not. Have it held over; yes, have it held over."

"Not our pigeon," the Government whips said to each other. "Let the generals nod over it."

"I shouldn't be too sure; it's *us* who have to get the credits through."

"Awkward, about Bernin—the fellow who got himself shot is his sister's husband or his brother-in-law or something."

"Don't say you've read the filthy sheet?"

"Just glanced at it."

"Bernin's a seasoned old bird."

"Wish one could say the same of the Government."

"It *would* have to come before the budget's in."

"Can it be true?" they said in the clubs.

"That chap off his rocker all those years . . ."

"Bit stiff."

"Oh it's just a mare's nest of old poison-pen's."

"Narden's always been careful; in his way."

"*Well*, if there's anything in it, all I can say is it doesn't look at all well."

At a hundred and twenty trade-union meetings over the country, the chairman said, "*Comrades——*"

"Who is Baron Bluebeard?"

"*All* those heiresses."

"Greedy."

"One is all right per family—second brother's job."

"How *did* he do it?"

"*Our* taxes."

"That's right."

"*Our* savings."

"Hear, hear!"

"The working man's pence."

"*That's* where they go!"

"Lunatics in luxury."

"Did you see—Jews got their fingers in it too."

"Whenever there is something rotten in the state of Denmark . ."

"The Army daren't do a thing about them, or they wouldn't get the steel."

"Krupp isn't a Jew, Uncle?"

"The Jews could stop his money."

"Of course."

On the Sunday night that followed the publication of Quintus Narden's leader, a garrison near Magdeburg reported that a mob had forced their way into the regimental mess dragging with them an individual decked out with the insignia, cuirass and plumes of a cavalry officer, bearing round his neck a placard with the inscription, ME TOO. This guy having been deposited in the gentlemen's card-room, the mob noisily withdrew. The individual, who upon investigation proved to be incapable of speech, was later claimed as their town idiot by a near-by community.

This form of officer baiting caught on, and for many years remained a favourite Sunday-night sport in rural Germany.

It was on this first Sunday that Jules and Caroline arrived in Berlin. It was evening, and the station looked empty. Caroline had half hoped that they would not be met. But there was Sarah. Sarah had come out to meet her friend. She had brought a footman and a car, and was wearing the longest pair of foxes' furs and a huge hat.

"*You*——"

"How is he?" Sarah said.

"I don't know. You will see. He thinks he's got bronchitis."

Sarah said, "They are hoping at Voss Strasse that you will both stay with them. You are expected."

"Oh Sarah, what a horrible idea; you can't mean it?"

"You *know* you can always come to me, only—"

"I thought we'd go to an hotel."

"I should go to the old people's," said Sarah, "really I should."

Julius emerged, having been settled into his over-coat. He greeted Sarah. "It is cold," he said.

"Jules," Caroline said in a tone which Sarah noticed was loud and almost coaxing, "Sarah tells me that the Merz's want us to stay with them."

"I always stay at Voss Strasse. I've come to see Henrietta. Where is Henrietta? Why isn't she here?"

"Well, it's rather late," said Sarah.

"Henrietta is grown-up now," Julius said in a peevish tone.

"It is a bit cold," said Caroline.

"It is *very* cold," said Julius.

"All right," said Caroline, "I suppose we might as well go there. For a few days."

In the car they said little. Julius was shivering ostentatiously.

"It was good of you to come out all that way, and you're not one for stations. I was prepared for Gustavus."

"My dear, it was nothing." Sarah did not say that Edu had implored her not to go.

"Does one *really* wear these now? Your hat. I can't take my eyes off it.

"*Beginning* to wear them," said Sarah.

"The courage! I wouldn't dare show my face under them in the street."

"You will," said Sarah.

Further on she said, "I hope you didn't think my telegram interfering?"

"I had already left Madrid when it came," Caroline said. "It seems a long time."

"I only sent it because—"

"It was the only telegram we had," said Caroline.

They crossed the Wilhelmstrasse. "Clara's not here," Sarah began.

"Oh, is that it."

"She's still away; down there. By herself. You see they're waiting." She glanced at Jules.

"Waiting?" said Caroline.

"To be able to have the funeral."

Caroline looked up. "We thought that would have been all over."

"No," Sarah said, "*not all over.*"

"You must make my apologies, Caro. I shall have to go straight up to my room," said Julius. "I'm not at all well." He coughed. "I will have my dinner on a tray; Henrietta can come and have hers with me. I want Pedro to come up; not Gottlieb. You *will* tell them?"

Quintus Narden's column the next morning began with an apology. His attention had been drawn to a number of errors in fact, and he hastened to correct them.

(1) Baron Felden had not been doing paper work for his brother-in-law, the present Secretary of State for Foreign Affairs, as had been incorrectly stated here last week. "Oh, I sometimes see to who's going in first at the

dinners, Conrad's a bit slack about precedence," the Baron was reported to have said on the subject. It was also not accurate that he had never been engaged in remunerative employment. Baron Felden had been assisting the Heralds' Office of the Grand Duchy of Baden in an honorary capacity for a number of years, and was now drawing a modest salary for his knowledgeable contributions.

(2) Baron Julius von Felden's present match was not what it had been made to appear. The writer had been misinformed as to the lady's actual position in her own country; at the time she made the Baron's acquaintance, she was living in relative obscurity in Paris. Her personal fortune was merely adequate.

Both the Baron and his wife were at present in this country.

(3) It had been stated that Captain von Felden had become insane while serving in the Army. It was now established that he had been totally non compos when he entered the Army twenty-seven years ago.

"What is it all about?" said Grandmama Merz. It was second breakfast.

"Jules must sue for libel," said Emil.

"Damages!" said Grandpapa.

"Fine son-in-law," said Markwald.

"We emerge not unscathed, sir."

"Has someone been spending too much money?" said Grandmama.

"It's about Jules's brother, mama."

"The Regimental Tragedy, ma'am."

"Unfortunate young man . . . Mustn't mention it to Jules."

"*No, no.*"

"Sarah will," said Grandpapa in a crowing tone.

"How beautiful Caroline looked last night," said Emil.

"I don't think there's anything to be gained by dragging it through the courts at this moment," said Friedrich.

"The Feldens would have to show defamation of character," said Markwald.

"Markwald," said Emil, "are you Quintus Narden? I've often suspected it."

"*Cui bono?*" said the Chancellor, "would anyone mind telling me that? *Cui bono?*"

"Provision for a younger son, Excellency? As has been suggested."

"Poppycock. I should leave that to the Social-Democrats."

"Her late Royal Highness of Baden–?"

"A most virtuous, and a most constitutional old lady. We never had any trouble with her. Someone has overreached himself badly, I'm afraid. But *why?*"

Correspondents managed to press a staff major responsible for public relations. "He only looked after horses," said the major. A statement which when duly printed was ill received by both the cavalry and infantry.

"Caroline–"

"Oh, don't begin mincing words with *me*, Sarah. And you do it so badly."

"This *foul*–"

"It's all largely true? Isn't it?"

"To think that I had that man for dinner!"

"I always told you so," said Edu.

"Told me what?" said Sarah.

"Yet it hardly sounds like Jules, does it? Though I can't say that I find it at all unlike Gustavus."

"Your long-haired chaps," said Edu.

"This one's very soigné."

"I don't understand it any better than Narden says he does," Caroline said later when they were alone.

"It *is* a strange mess."

"It is horrible."

"Yes, now that one thinks of it."

"I must say something. I believe Jules tried not to for thirty years; then he tried to tell *me*. I didn't notice. Too absorbed. Too absorbed in my well-loved self— Too late now."

"Late is the word," said Sarah.

"Oh Sarah—how could it happen?"

"Well you do know who's to blame?"

"All of us, Sarah."

"The Bernins."

Caroline sighed.

"Do you know why Bernin never married?"

"I wondered."

"And I do believe he wanted sons badly. They say he has been keeping himself eligible for the Church. In case— For what a Red Hat can lead to."

"*No?*"

"I'm not altogether sorry Bernin is being shown up now for what he is."

"Are they talking about the Bernins?"

" Everywhere."

The *Fortschritt* leaders gave rise to one of the few al-
truistic gestures during this affair. Within the next days
Julius and Gustavus each received several hundred letters
from unknown Army officers of all ranks offering to call
out Quintus Narden on their behalf. Julius's were opened
by Caroline who wondered whether acknowledgements
—printed cards?—were not in order; some of Gustavus's
found their way to the authorities. Someone acted with
promptness, and commanding officers everywhere had to
instruct their gentlemen that Herr Narden was not of
duellable status. (Narden, when he heard of it, professed
himself amused by his Untouchable's position and
poured much scorn on the 300 Mandarin Lieutenants in
his column, inflaming many an honest bourgeois' heart.)

"Friedrich, what's the news?"
Friedrich Merz flung a bundle of papers on the table.
"Riots at Hamburg, riots at Leipzig, dockers's strike
threatened at Kiel. They're insisting on Corporal Schaale's
having a civilian trial, and the Army won't give in."
"That's always so hard for them," said Caroline.
"A trial by jury for manslaughter."
"Schaale's become a ruddy hero," said Edu.
"Riots at Bremen, riots at Dresden, paving stones
thrown at the police at Stuttgart, riots at Karlsruhe—no
those aren't for the Corporal; it's Faithful George they
want down there."
"The Army must give in," said Markwald shrilly.

"I thought Clara had the poor fellow out by now?" said Caroline.

"My dear lady," said Friedrich, "there isn't the man in Germany today who'd dare lift a hand for Clara Bernin Felden."

"He sent me Foxy. When I was a tiny baby. My uncle's orderly, Faithful George. He came in a box. *You* remember Foxy, Uncle Edu?"

Edu, in whose house the animal had spent it's life span, said, "Oh yes, Foxy . . . By Jove, did he? What? Faithful George? *How?*"

"*Henrietta?*"

"What are *you* doing here?"

"Who told you?"

"Surtout pas devant—"

"My poor Emil, the child's French is so much better than yours," said Sarah.

"Your uncle sent you a dog?" said Caroline.

"Only I didn't know it. And it wasn't my uncle. He couldn't you see." Henrietta's features were very Merz, but her manner of speaking was Jules's, with something of her Grandmother's in it too, and Caroline now saw this.

"But you like dogs?" she said, and she had the sensation that her own life also had come to an end.

"We cannot have a revolution because the Army has to have their face saved," said Markwald.

Sarah said, "We really don't want you here."

"Very well," said Henrietta, "I shall go and see Gottlieb."

"That's what all the reasonable people are saying," said Friedrich.

Caroline said to Sarah, "That boy must have been her age then . . . Jules's brother."

"They'll never give in," Sarah said, "and they wouldn't mind putting down a revolution."

"Where would that leave *us*?" said Friedrich.

"Oh, quite."

"The Government's got to do something."

"The Government?" said Sarah, "I wouldn't give the Government a week."

"Surely the Corporal would also be acquitted by a court martial?" said Caroline.

"The people don't think so."

"Not with Putnitz's evidence."

"There's someone whose shoes I shouldn't want to be in."

"They want to tear him limb from limb."

"Someone more unpopular than us?" said Caroline.

"He denies having cried out for help."

"Berlin is quiet. So far."

"Berlin has got the evening papers."

"Is *nothing* going to be done about those?"

"Apparently not."

Quintus Narden had left fat pickings to the tabloids.

"I'd no idea Nelly was as rich as that," Jeanne said to Sarah. "I knew she had done well. But—real estate avenue du Bois de Boulogne . . ."

"Very likely lies."

"'One of the most prominent figures of the half-world thirty years ago.' She was that."

"Thirty years is cruel," said Sarah.

"And unjust. She outlasted La Païva."

"Well, *she* doesn't have to live here."

"My old friend has been successful."

"Of course they have got it all wrong; to my certain knowledge Jules hasn't set eyes on Madame de la T°°°°° these fifteen years. And there was never any question of marrying her. You remember, there was the quiet widow with the child, the old people were so upset about? I wish to God now he had married *her*. What was her name?"

"I never knew," said Jeanne.

"Dupont! The mysterious Madame Dupont."

Jeanne could still blush. "Nelly de la Turbie's *real* name is Dupont. You see one used to take these fancy names at that time; I believe it's going out, only the stage do now."

"So she almost did live here! The mills of fate. Think of *her* ending at Voss Strasse."

"Not her," said Jeanne. "It would have been the end of Voss Strasse as far as Jules's concerned."

"Mills of fate again," said Sarah. "And the child–?"

"That was quite a business; she thought she was in love then. The child is the Spanish Count's. Not Jules's."

Narden made no further allusion to the Feldens' private affairs in the *Fortschritt*, but the morning after episodes from Julius's French life had appeared in other papers he mentioned that the Foreign Office had offered a secretaryship at the Embassy in Paris to the Baron in such and such a year, and that it had been turned down. In the Civil Services where promotion functioned like slow clock-work and Unterministerialdirektoren and Regirungsrate sat ticking off the assiduous years, this glimpse created more concentrated bad blood than anything that had gone before. No plodder had ever liked Bernin, now opposition to the Count became open, solid, almost dedicated.

Julius and Gustavus had not seen each other yet. Julius was kept in by his cold and asthma, and with Clara absent the brothers seemed to be bereft of means or need of communication. This weighed on Caroline.

"He *never* comes here," said Sarah.

"Gustavus? Oh, good Lord."

"And it's not such a pleasure going out these days."

"Don't tell me they *both* stay in?" said Caroline.

"Very likely. Men mind so much more."

"Poor Jules, he thinks he is an insect turned into a brown leaf. So transparent."

"But alone."

"Oh yes, quite alone. Poor Jules."

"They must get it over. You know, their meeting," said Sarah.

"I don't know what it is between Jules and Gustavus. Jules was almost light-headed that night on the train . . . And how I wish they'd have the funeral."

"That will make a difference."

"It will help Jules."

"He won't go," said Sarah.

"But he must."

"Nothing we do or don't matters a scrap now."

Caroline said, "Sarah, tell me this, is it—is Jules like this because he has been living with the Merz's for so long?"

"No," said Sarah.

"I don't want to understand it," said Caroline.

"You were very good at understanding in Paris."

"Don't let us speak of Paris."

"Your Monet is still there."

"I cannot believe it."

"Don't change," Sarah said passionately.

"I'm not very good without— Not very good by myself," said Caroline.

Sarah got up and went to a window, a thing she always did in her own houses. The window gave on to the court-yard, and all the windows were the wrong size at Voss Strasse.

"This is only a kind of crisis?" Caroline said with a lapse into her younger voice. "Sarah, isn't it?"

Sarah turned to her, but without seeing. "Crisis? There are no crises. It's all a chain, a long chain. Oh yes— it will pass, this crisis."

"It was the wrong question," said Caroline.

"Twelve gentlemen to see Herr Geheimrat."

"What do they want?"

"Desire was indicated to impart this themselves, sir."

"Twelve?" said Grandmama.

"A deputation, ma'am."

"Will they've had luncheon?"

"After a fashion, ma'am."

"Gottlieb, what is all this?" said Friedrich.

"The Israelite Retail-Trade Association of Greater Berlin, sir."

"Why not say so at once."

"I did not believe it was material, sir."

"I will see them," said Friedrich.

"Send them away," said Markwald.

"Show 'em in," said Grandpapa.

"I understand they wished to see Herr Geheimrat by himself."

"Here we all are," said Grandpapa.

"They don't want us to get up," said his wife.

"Perhaps *I* should," Caroline said, doing so. "I believe you are right, Baronin," said Fräulein von Reventlow, and followed her. Gottlieb held a door for them. The deputation filed in by another. They carried their top-hats and looked round respectfully.

"Herr Geheimrat! Frau Geheimrat! Gentlemen!"

"'Morning," said Grandpapa.

The head-man plucked a document from his coat.

"Why is he reading to us?" said Grandmama.

"An address, ma'am," hissed Gottlieb.

A member corrected him, "A petition."

"Can't understand a word he's saying—"

"Speak up," said Grandpapa.

"The volume is not at fault," said Gottlieb.

"We're *compromising*—?"

"The community, ma'am."

"*Community*—?"

"Of interests."

"Ah yes."

"*We* are not in retail hosiery," Emil whispered to Markwald.

"We have touched pitch."

"Interfering asses," said Emil.

"*Harbouring*—?" said Grandmama.

"A form of invitation, ma'am."

"*Assim*—? *assim*——?"

"Assimilationists."

"Must be one of those semi-precious stones . . very unsatisfactory. *Implicate*—? *Co-religionists*—? *Shipwreck*—?"

"Hush, ma'am; they would like us to listen."

"Why don't they sit down?"

"Did we ask them?" muttered Emil.

"*Gentiles—?* Where?"

"Ma'am . ."

"*Eliminate—?*"

"Kick out," supplied Markwald.

"That's what I mean," said a member of the deputation, "let Goy eat Goy."

"WHERE—?" cried Grandmama.

"Moritz Bluhmenthal!"

"Herr Geheimrat?"

"I knew your father before he had a pot to piss in."

"Oh Herr Geheimrat."

"Were you by any chance referring to my son-in-law?"

"Well, Herr Geheimrat—"

"Go home, my boy, and mind your own business. And you can tell the same from me to the community."

"Papa—"

"I have my family live with me if I please, and," the old man looked about with satisfaction, "I send packing whom I please."

"Yes sir, of course sir, only— We shall all be suffering for this, we know we shall . . ."

"True words," muttered Markwald.

"Merz & Merz among the martyrs," said Emil.

Questions began being raised; once again Count Bernin's hand was discernible; the awkward problem of Johannes's funeral was met by an unannounced quiet burial at Sigmundshofen. There were present, besides Clara, Gustavus and the priest, two officers from

U

Johannes's regiment, Faithful George and a number of elderly villagers from Landen who remembered him as a boy. The Foreign Secretary, detained by the state visit of the Crown Prince of Bulgaria, had been unable to leave Berlin. The private character of the ceremony was after-wards derided as weakness on the part of the Army; there remained, however, the unspoken face-saver that it had been due to the wishes of the family.

Three days later Corporal Schaale escaped.

The Kaiser cancelled his yachting trip; the long-awaited interpellation took place in the Reichstag; and on that night there were crowds demonstrating outside both the War Ministry and the Wilhelmstrasse. The Government was expected to fall in the morning.

"What if he *did* just manage to make off on his own? Things do happen that way. I should have tried to in his place, and nothing surprises me about that Colonel."

"The country must be in very bad hands," said Mark-wald.

"No authority," said Friedrich.

"I shouldn't have said that," said Caroline.

"Ladies are born anarchists."

Clara was back, and Caroline went to her on that after-noon. It was round the corner but she drove there in the Merz's Landau. The entrance was thronged and there were a few jeers at a woman in her kind of clothes. She was shown into the same upper room in which, a little more than a year ago, Clara had asked her to let herself be helped. She had not seen Clara since her own marriage ceremony, and she felt that it was she now who had come to proffer something to that worn and upright figure. Gustavus was there.

She made her apologies for Julius. "I should have liked to have gone myself," she said.

"You did not know him. There was no need."

Gustavus said, "Do sit down, Clara."

Clara ignored this.

Caroline, on what was actually a horrid little chair, came as near self-consciousness as she ever could. She felt too smart, small, young.

"There seems to be so much misunderstanding. My brother must explain. People would behave differently if they were told what really happened."

"Clara dear—" said Gustavus.

Caroline looked, and realized how little she had seen of him. She was held anew by the likeness between him and Jules, and by the difference. Gustavus was more solid physically than his brother—it was not vitality, but he was there—and he was quite without that extra-human fineness that made Jules felt sometimes as only half a presence in a room. Both men appeared younger than they were; Jules *looked* younger, Gustavus had acquired the fussy boyishness of the permanent A.D.C. "What really did happen?" she asked.

Clara told her. "And now Conrad won't say anything. He says it had nothing to do with him, he says he was not there. That is true of course. Conrad was en poste in Rome during those years. When he came back Jean was already settled. It was papa who arranged it. When papa died, everybody was charitable and it just went on. What with being so much older and leaving home so soon, I don't believe Conrad ever knew Jean."

"How monstrously unfair," said Caroline.

"What did you say?"

"It is unfair."

"*Unfair*—what a curious term."

"So then it is all true?" said Caroline; "Jules told me some things, but they seemed so very queer."

"Jules did not know everything," said Clara.

"*And they sent him back?*"

"We all tried to prevent it; according to our lights. My father, too. When he was able to see what it would mean, he tried to undo it. There was a very good man—a priest —he is dead now. Papa was too late. Now I know that it was something that had to come to Jean's father. Though the rest of us had to go on doing our best; you see, Caroline—it was our duty."

"But the Army? Clara, the Army?"

"We did not see it in that way. Papa did not. It was only a farm . . One of our local regiments . . It seemed less sad."

Caroline looked hard at Clara, with awe and something like a nascent admiration. For the first time since her arrival in the town she did not feel desolately apart.

Clara said, "Perhaps everything was rather different in papa's day. It is very dreadful that we should give such scandal now. Conrad must speak. Gustavus—"

But Gustavus, they found, had left the room.

The Government did not fall next day. Bernin said nothing; but the Chancellor got up and spoke a few firm quiet words. He spoke of mountains out of mole-hills, he spoke of self-seeking propaganda; he pledged investigation of the matter under debate, but doubted if it was of a nature to perturb the workings of a great realm; he under-took to guarantee that justice would be done and a certain fugitive discovered; and he promised to maintain order.

This speech had a wonderfully calming effect. Solid people felt they had been carried away too easily.

"It could peter out now," Sarah said.

The week passed. Schaale was not found. In the towns, police were omnipresent but reserved; the people began showing signs of tiring of the riots.

Then Quintus Narden sprang the fact that Captain Felden had been decorated by His Majesty.

"*My* Red Eagle!" said Gustavus.

"Ruritania," said Sarah. "Such a pity it isn't more noticeable."

All over Bavaria a bulletin appeared on the house-fronts, purporting that the Kaiser had been non compos since 1902, and in some localities the Crown Prince was proclaimed Regent.

On that day Count Bernin resigned.

Chapter Six

"HE had the Corporal hidden in the Foreign Office."

"He was found there?"

"That's just *it*—he was not. They took him down to Baden with them. He was smuggled out in a trunk."

"No, not in a trunk, he left bold as brass by the main-entrance dressed up in priest's clothes. The sister did it."

"My dear chap, you've got it all wrong: the Felden Murder was *used* by Bülow—very clever of him actually—to get rid of him. The Cabinet had got on to his naval deal."

"The Englishwoman was the go-between. Baron Bluebeard was the cover. He got paid for marrying her."

"He promised the bishops in the House of Lords to get our Naval Estimates cut down, then the bishops were to sell out to Rome."

"I heard it had been the Zionists?"

"Oh, the Zionists too."

"The Baron ratted; he never married her. Preferred to stick to Frau Shylock. He got some kind of a show put up in their cathedral; man in my department knows some-body who was there, he said there was so much incense you couldn't see your own hand, but there was no bride."

"They'll have to close that chapel on their place; he's been excommunicated, though he won't let on. The Holy Father sent a secret bull."

"He left Germany. On foot."

"Little good that will do him. He's to be locked up as soon as he gets there. In the Vatican. He knows all the Church secrets."

"Will he be a monk then?"

"A state prisoner."

"*Have you heard?* Count Bernin is to be indicted for High Treason."

"Friedrich, what's the news?"

"Putnitz has been cashiered. Cowardice."

"What will he do?"

"Oh, a bullet, or the colonies. Here he is, in a lounge suit. 'Ex-Lieutenant's Comment'. The 9-*Uhr Abend* nabbed him in the station. '"It was all a mistake," says von Putnitz.'"

"I wish Clara had heard him," said Caroline.

"The Doctors' Association are asking for an inquiry into Army medicine, there is to be a commission."

"A humdrum day. Anything else?"

"The market's up. Very rum."

"Not at all," said Sarah. "There's not going to be another peep out of the South for a long time, a victory for industry. It's about finished all those Catholic peasant parties."

"You're not expecting a *boom*?"

"Oh yes."

"Anything else?"

"Only rumours."

"The Eighteen-Months-Service Bill is to come up before recess."

"The old Jesuit's gone; but we are to be left helpless."

"Poor Germany."

Indeed, the troubles, public and internal, of the administration had not been lessened. Too many questions had been left unanswered, and substantial people throughout the country were acting on their conviction that something, somewhere, had gone very wrong. In Government offices, inquiries were shuffled on to sub-departments and everybody was furious with the fellows down the next corridor; the ruling caste was divided by the sense that they had let each other down, and they blamed the Kaiser in their hearts.

"H.M. has always been unfortunate in the choice of his friends."

"It couldn't have happened under the Old Man."

In all this, little love from any quarter was lost upon the Feldens; and through the whole of that summer the gutter press, scot-free, poured forth what it pleased. They were fair game.

"What does she do with herself all day?"

"She has her own sitting-room, you know, upstairs. I go to her; she comes to me. She insists. She insists on going out at least once every day. She does her shopping, she goes to the Zoo, she rides a little in the Tiergarten. She's talking about sending for their horses. And she reads . . ."

"*I* know. Two novels a day. The next stage is chocolates."

"She reads mostly history," said Sarah.

"They ought to leave!"

"Where is there for them to go?"

"Leave Germany altogether," said Jeanne.

"I don't think she would do that, she'd call it running away."

"You ought to tell her, Sarah."

"*I?* She did say to me she couldn't slip off to England–like Edu."

"I should have thought of her as more, I don't know–" Jeanne said.

"More what?"

"Worldly—? feminine—? spoilt—?"

"It comes as a surprise. Caroline is an English gentleman."

"The two or three one used to know in my time drank horribly. But I know you don't mean that."

"No."

"There is no sense in her staying, Sarah."

"She doesn't like it any better here than you do."

"I've got used to it."

"I hate it!" said Sarah. "With what Quintus Narden calls the notorious lack of patriotism of my race."

"He doesn't notice my existence," said Jeanne. "I'm only fit for the 9-*Uhr*. 'The other Foreign Concubine.' My poor grey hair . . Though it's also taught me the small use of an actual husband."

"Jules doesn't read the papers."

"Isn't he *tempted* to?"

"It doesn't occur to him."

"That's *my* idea of a gentleman."

"He's started coming down to meals again," said Sarah. "To some of their meals."

"Of course she has the child," said Jeanne.

"What child?"

"Jules's."

"I believe she's trying to educate her. That's lost on Henrietta."

"The girl ought to be out of it all. Sarah—is it beastly? The streets?"

"Berlin's a big place. The only really bad spot is the door in Voss Strasse. And seeing that it doesn't make the slightest difference to anyone in that house except to her and me, and of course poor Friedrich—"

"I'm afraid Friedrich uses the back-entrance," Jeanne said, looking her friend in the eyes.

"You do love him," said Sarah.

"He loves me."

Sarah said nothing.

"You can understand that?"

"*Yes*," she said. "No. Yes. You know I think my girl is going to marry that violinist."

"Will you let her?"

"It's that, or her running away. I'm sure she'd much prefer the latter. Not he though, as I read him; he's at the house all day, she thinks it's so brave of him. When I have a couple of men from the Watch & Ward outside."

"I read that," Jeanne said.

"My body-guard. They're the same people we use at Kastell at the works."

"I read about that, too."

"I wouldn't do it for my sake—I didn't do anything

the other time—but I won't have my guests insulted at my own door."

"The violinist?"

"I didn't think of him."

Jeanne said, "You *are* fond of her."

"I wish she'd never met me!" said Sarah.

HOLE-AND-CORNER WEDDING BUT—
A FOOD ORGY
Judo-Aristocrats Feast As Unemployment Soars

"It *must* be a fake," said Caroline. "When I didn't share so much as a sandwich with poor Clara. Anyway, that's *you* with Jules in front of the Neronian spread, not me. It's familiar though— I have seen these hams and antlers before."

"In the family album," Sarah said. "Jules's fiftieth Birthday, and mine. I have not forgotten it."

"Extraordinary backcloth. It isn't real–?"

"What?"

"The edibles?"

"Quite real," said Sarah.

"Frau Baronin, I did not wish to disturb Frau Geheimrat, but should we send out some soup to them?"

"Do you usually?"

"It has been our custom to dispense some charity."

"Then I suppose so. Oh, by all means."

"My dear child," Markwald said, "they're shouting for venison."

"Not very realistic of them," said Emil.

"Seeing it is not in season, sir," said Gottlieb.

"All the same, perhaps *not* soup?" said Caroline.

"They've come neither to be reasonable nor to be fed," said a voice from the door.

"Frau Eduard," announced Gottlieb.

Sarah was carrying a parasol. She looked cool, but cross. "Who said Prussia was a Police State?"

"Do you think they'll keep it up, Gottlieb?" said Markwald.

"We might envisage retirement for a night's rest, sir."

"It was like walking through a bad Breughel," said Sarah.

"Their afflictions are impressive, ma'am."

"It's no worse than Spain," said Caroline.

"I didn't know we had so many in the town."

"Nobody ever does it for fun."

"If I may be permitted to quote Marie, ma'am," Gottlieb said, "Marie says they are the chorus from Boris Godunov."

"Edu got it this morning."

"What's Edu to Hecuba?"

"His debts."

"Well, he's not here to hear."

"No judge is ever going to give him a discharge now, he'll be a bankrupt till his dying day. I suppose one must take it as a blessing in disguise."

"But darling, the *disguise*."

Sarah said to Caroline, "Jeanne would like you to come and see her."

"That's very good of her."

"She would come to you, you know, if she could."

"She and Gustavus——"

"Do go," Sarah said.

"She must remember that I did not the first time I was here; it would hardly be a service to her if I did so now."

"Am I mad? Are they mad? Are all the Feldens mad?" Sarah picked up the newspaper.

MONKEYS FIT COMPANIONS
Baron's Choice For Jewish Bride

"This one says the chimps were part of a Southern-Separatist plot to bring dishonour to the country from within. That poor brute I spoke to once in a cage at Hamburg?"

"Caroline, you oughtn't to be here."

"My place is by my husband's side, isn't it? You should see the letters I get from home. They all make a point of writing to me. About the delphiniums and Mr. Asquith's Budget and Mrs. Patrick Campbell, and they're not addressed to me at all—it's as if I were already dead and buried."

"Has it occurred to you that Jules most likely wouldn't be here at all if it weren't for you? And for my telegram."

"Sarah, I *cannot* make plans now."

"That is unlike you."

"I daresay."

"You've got to decide something."

"I said I could make no plans."

Sarah said, "My dear, don't make it any harder for yourself than you can help."

Caroline said nothing.

"I have an idea," Sarah said.

"Oh don't insist."

"We can't stay here all summer. Do you never think of time? We'll soon be in August."

"I don't see why *you* stay," said Caroline.

Without a change of tone, Sarah said, "For one thing I happen to be a mother; just at present it would be difficult for me to leave without my daughter accusing me of dragging her away."

"How's that going?"

"Not well," Sarah said.

"Don't listen to her. No-one knows what's good for them."

"And I know?"

"Forgive my temper," said Caroline. "We all have our troubles."

"Yes."

"They're always one's own."

"Caroline—there isn't anything else?"

"Of course not," said Caroline.

Pedro, the man-servant who arrived with them from Spain, had become a problem. When he was with Jules, he was contented enough and they talked about the things that interested them. But he had to go to mass, and he had to have his day off, and he didn't know the town and he didn't know the language, yet he was getting known himself in the drinking cellars of the neighbourhood, and he was very bored, and often he came home late and incoherent. Marie who had rarely had a good word for the man in Spain, had established herself his guardian angel here; she saw to it that rice was cooked for him that was not rice-pudding, she made Gottlieb see to his daily wine, she fretted. When she was in an unbending mood Pedro called her *Tia*, and she liked it.

One hot Sunday morning Gottlieb, Marie and the flock of servants had returned from worship early; not so Pedro. Gottlieb served luncheon in the dining-room; when he came to sit down to his own dinner, Marie, already in her bonnet, would not let him. She seemed to know exactly where to go; yet Gottlieb, whose intercourse with Marie was respectful, dared not chaff her. At the third *Spelunke*, as she called these taverns, he found Pedro (she of course had remained outside). Pedro was standing lightly on two tables; he had been given white-beer to drink spiced with potato spirits; someone in the audience who knew about as much French as he did had constituted himself link and compère.

"What did the first wife do?"

"The first wife she weep all day." Pedro curled up on the boards, impersonating a lady moping on a chaise-lounge.

"And the second wife?"

"She weep all day, too." (The *liar*, Caroline said.) Pedro posed himself into a graceful figure pining by a window.

"Now tell them why these poor women weep."

Pedro drew himself up. "Because my Master is very Magnificent Man."

The old people and the house were getting ready for the annual departure to the spa; Sarah had called as usual, she and Caroline were upstairs in the latter's sitting-room.

"I wish there was a dog," said Caroline. "Did you see, Faithful George has resigned the Service. After thirty-one years. 'Orderly says Army not the same without his Captain.' I hope he'll get his pension."

"Bound to," said Sarah.

"We ought to do something for him."

"Clara will have been seeing to that."

"We can't leave everything to Clara. And now there'll be all that money."

"You are speaking of Jules's and Gustavus's inheritance?"

"How convenient the papers are. We don't have to tell each other anything."

"Jules ought to see the lawyers, Caroline."

"I can't even ask him to. I dare not mention his brother's name."

"Something should be done," said Sarah.

"Don't I know? The money must be refused. Or given away . . . Could *I* get a power of attorney?"

"I'm afraid not for such a matter. Unless— Jules *is* capable of transacting business?"

"Oh yes, yes. If he wishes to."

"He asked my father-in-law for an advance. Did you know? It appears he's absolutely penniless."

"*How?*"

"He lost a year's income at Granada, just before you left."

"Good God," said Caroline.

"And he isn't even fond of gambling. They do it absent-mindedly."

"It was while I was away."

"Perhaps he was lonely," said Sarah.

"The forms of consolation—" said Caroline.

"It seems the Madrid bills aren't paid."

"I thought *I* had paid them."

"Bills have a way of coming in."

"And now this money . . . Not what it's said to be, but a good deal."

"The Captain's savings."

"Sarah—do you know how he lived? Clara told me."

"He had a house to himself, hadn't he?"

"There was nothing in it. Sarah—nothing; no possessions, hardly any furniture. Curtains, and a few cooking things. He never owned anything, he never bought anything. He preferred to sleep on straw, clean straw . . . And there was his food; he seems to have lived chiefly on oatmeal and carrots and milk. Faithful George saw to his having plenty of warm easy clothes. But nothing else . . nothing ever . . . Can you imagine it, Sarah? can you see the years? Faithful George was very good about everything, he saw that he wasn't cheated. No wonder he hardly touched his pay."

"And there's what his father left him, a third of the estate. What Jules had."

"I gather Jules spent his early."

"On a lovely place off the Grasse road, on travel, on Madame de la Turbie . . ."

"You remember when I was here last spring? I never thought of him then. I could have gone with Jules to see him. He would be alive now. No, Sarah I have to think of it. Have you thought of something else, have you ever thought that he might have been cured? I've

x

been reading about that. Sarah, when he was found dead he had a card for my wedding in his house."

Sarah kept silent.

"And now I cannot speak of him to Jules. I can hardly speak to Jules at all."

"I know his total eclipses. It's time he re-appeared. There's that other thing."

"That can only be ignored," said Caroline.

Unspoken, the words stood in the women's minds.

BARON'S YOUNG WIFE DIED OF HEARTBREAK

NEGLECT OR WORSE—?

Damp House— French Maid's Testimony

"Her parents have not read it, thank God for that. But her brothers have. Emil has, Markwald has, the servants have. Her child may have—"

"It is poison," said Caroline.

"Melanie was a queer girl. If only there were an occasional word from Jules."

"He went out with me the other day. I made him. He hates my going out, but as he can't discuss it— I took advantage of that."

"What was it like?"

"Ghastly. They're pretty bored with me by now, this was the first time they set eyes on *him*. He was rather wonderful; never moved a muscle, just a little more stiff. I suppose that is what men look like on a battle-field— I had an uncle who rode at Balaclava. Jules never said a word. Nor did he say a word afterwards. I see now what Clara means by retribution."

"When did you see so much of her?"

"I saw her three times during the two weeks she was

here," said Caroline. "I'm afraid, if anything, my outing's made Jules worse."

"Then someone must act for him; I agree there ought to be a gesture about the inheritance. It'll be complicated —generally is with intestates—I understand everything's been invested, in a conservative sort of way though not at all badly. There's also the settlement the Captain had under the old Count's will."

"I expect that reverts to the Bernins," said Caroline.

"Not at all," said Sarah. "*You* ought to see the lawyers. It's to go to the Feldens. In trust to Gustavus and Jules, then outright to Clara's children, if she'd had any, and to Jules's. That'll be Henrietta at twenty-one."

"I wouldn't let a child of mine touch it!" said Caroline.

"The law would prevent your doing that."

"You mean to say that any children I might have would inherit that poor boy's money and I could do nothing about it?"

"Any children in wedlock with Jules—certainly."

Sarah went on. "It is extraordinary, people never do know. They seem to know all about how they ought to be tried for murder and about illegal arrest, but when it comes to property . . It makes everything so vague."

"Sarah, I must know something. You have known him for a long time. Will Jules— will he, will he be himself again?"

"He has never been anything else." Sarah had answered at once. She spoke in her coldest tone, the one Caroline so seldom heard. "Jules is a rock. India-rubber, but a rock. He's kept himself wrapped in untouchable delicacy—and he *is* untouchable. Jules has never known what any other human being felt. Jules will outlast us all."

"You are very bitter."

"I feel rather anti-Felden this morning."

Caroline looked away. "*What* we have dragged you into," she said.

"*You?*" Sarah raised a face to her friend in which there was no hope. And in the manner of someone who has let go all care of good opinion, she said, "You might as well know, you must have been wondering with every newspaper blaring it, I was in love with Jules, and he was rather taken with the little Merz girl, so I made the marriage— To save my face to myself— To look magnanimous— Not so much in love either, enough to touch *l'amour propre*. It's all so long ago that it's hardly true any more. Yet, *I* made that marriage, I'm good at arranging things, as good as your Clara in my different way." Her mood collapsed. "But—" she gave full weight to her words, "I did not arrange yours."

"No . ." Caroline said, "no . ." trying to think. Appalled more by the sound, having hardly taken in what she had heard, she tried, "It'll never be what it was . . . paying is not buying back . . . let's not open doors to further desolation . . . let's be what we are, wiser perhaps, not better women."

When two days later Sarah entered Voss Strasse she was shown into the Herrenzimmer. "You have heard our news?"

"My parents are so pleased."

"We are all so pleased."

"Jules told us last night."

"*He* is pleased."

"She only told him yesterday."

"Henrietta is to have a little brother, ma'am."

"Early in the next year."

"Jules said January."

"Or February."

"You must go and congratulate him."

"Where *is* Caroline?" said Sarah.

"Upstairs."

"She hasn't come down today."

Sarah hesitated.

"Frau Baronin just went out, ma'am," Gottlieb said; "Herr Baron put her in the carriage. Herr Baron wanted her to have the air."

Caroline, as a matter of fact, had decided to call on Jeanne. Perhaps she did so in a spirit of New-Year's resolutions, she hardly knew herself. At any rate she went.

Jeanne was now living in a very pretty flat in a non-descript street.

Caroline looked at it with new eyes. "What a charming room," she said.

"One does what one can," said Jeanne. She only saw her visitor. Conscious always of beauty in a woman, and the possession of it in a woman's life, she was moved.

"Of course Sarah's house is lovely."

"Sarah does everything à l'anglaise," said Jeanne.

Caroline laughed.

(Jeanne already heard herself saying, She is not only beautiful—she is radiant.)

"Not her pictures, though."

"No, not those," said Jeanne; "I'm coming round to them."

"I was round. But I never really saw them until Sarah. *She* taught me."

Jeanne rang for tea. "Tell me," Caroline said, "does

everybody spend the summer in Berlin, or only everybody I know?"

"I'm a bad example. Friedrich likes to be where his parents are, and I'm not much of a one for the country."

"No—?" said Caroline.

"It makes me feel lost. I have a little house, a villa, at Travemünde—that's the seaside—I don't think I spent more than three days there half a dozen times in ten years."

"It seems a waste."

"I didn't buy it to go there. It seemed a sensible idea— you know, safer than the bank."

"It's by the sea?" said Caroline.

"Oh yes, the sea's there. Though it's not a wilderness, you can put your foot to ground without getting your ankle turned, the walks *are* paved. It's quite a coming place." Something made her add, "Would you like to go there? The house is empty. There's a little garden, and it's really not too bad. Why don't you try it, and see whether you can put up with it? It's not far, you and your husband could drive there. And it would give me such pleasure."

"What a very sweet thing to suggest," said Caroline.

"Don't say no, think it over. It would be a change. Not a big change . ." She smiled. Then, bethinking herself that there was some point in being sixty, she said, "Will you let me say something? I really wish you were going back to your own home."

"Where?"

"Aren't you thinking of going back to Spain?"

"Oh no!" said Caroline.

"Travel, then . . Some kind of move . . You should not stay here." She said it very kindly.

Caroline said, "You see, I am enceinte."

"My dear." Jeanne made no pretence of taking it entirely in her stride, yet she kept herself in hand. She said warmly, "Yes, that will make a difference. I am very glad for Jules. It will be the greatest help to him."

"He seems to take it in that way."

"And you?" Jeanne said.

Caroline made no answer.

"You are so young."

"Not so young; most of my friends have children."

"Many women," Jeanne said, "have children before they want them; or they wait and it is too late. That is the way .. But one can never tell."

Caroline said, "This is not a good moment."

"No, my dear, no. It will help you, though, to put it behind you."

There was benevolence behind Jeanne's words, benevolence and compassion, but there was no suffering; the suffering Caroline half knew that she put on Sarah with almost every word she said. For once she had the sense that her meaning did not sink away into layers of emotion and despair, or glance off, bootless or alien, as it did with Jules or Clara, but bounced back to her, clear and aired, like coins rung upon a counter for what they might be worth. She answered as she had not meant to speak, "I am afraid. Of the very thing you implied, I'm afraid of what it may be to him. You must know that Jules is not the best man to bring up someone."

Jeanne said, "A son will change him."

In a voice strong with revulsion, Caroline said, "Am I to provide him with a lost brother?"

Jeanne saw much of it, if not all. She recognized the cry from the heart and she effaced herself. She waited till the sound of the young woman's words had faded, then she said, "Jules loved Henrietta as his child."

"While she was a child."

"She is still that."

"Not in his eyes. And there is what they've made of her."

Jeanne said, "There were circumstances . ."

"I know. Money; Jules's own queer position; the girl's future."

"That seems assured now."

"It had better. After no childhood and no parents, and being shut up in a stuffy house for fourteen years . . She ought to live with Jules."

"Friedrich says they still would not let her go."

"Not out of Berlin?"

"No; they only have this feeling about abroad."

"That's what *I* thought," said Caroline.

"Do you know one thing, my dear, you will soon be committed to so much thought about yourself—*cela change les idées.*"

"That's the nicest way I've ever heard it put," said Caroline.

Jeanne said, "Things have not been very happy for you lately."

"Well, no."

The elder woman opened her arms. Gratefully, naturally, Caroline gave herself to the embrace.

In the door she said, "I know now what we're going to do. I've just made up my mind."

"Don't make it up too fast."

"Dear Jeanne. Plans always make me cheerful."

Chapter Seven

ONE day all things have an end, and when autumn had set in and the holidays were over and the Reichstag met again, the Reduced-Military-Service Bill was not passed and the budget was, the new Secretary of State was dun-coloured, there seemed to be threatening once more a deal of trouble in Morocco, a mysterious crime had taken place at Hanover, the Kaiser and the Kaiserin announced a Court Ball, and there was after all a brand new battleship. Putnitz was farming, and so was Faithful George; the Colonel, some majors and a brigadier were in retirement; Corporal Schaale remained unfound; the papers, and so perforce the public, dropped their interest in the Feldens and their connections and concerns; the Merz's house was like any other house, people came and went, and the passers-by went by.

Caroline wrote and answered letters; went here and there; travelled South, found Gustavus knowledgeable, saw at last what she wanted.

"You are decided?" Sarah said, a week later.

"Absolutely."

"It will be a tie."

"What is not? One might as well have a home."

"At the border of Alsace? The world is larger."

"Not for me," said Caroline.

Sarah shifted her ground. "If you *will* sell out all your capital—"

"Not all. Just a few shares. They won't let me touch my trust fund. I shall have to raise something on the income."

"It'll cripple you."

Caroline shrugged.

"Jules hasn't even seen it," Sarah shifted her ground again."

"He can't help liking the house. I do. You will." She smiled.

But a month later everything was still unsigned; Caroline ought to have gone to England, and the house was certainly not ready. "Now I shall have to leave it all till afterwards," she said; "I knew it."

"The first house is always the hardest," said Sarah.

"Those poor animals arriving from Spain almost any day now."

"*Who?*"

"The horses. I had so hoped to have everything ready for them. You know what Gustavus said to me, the booby, 'You and Jules are *not* thinking of riding?' Sarah, you have no idea what it's like down there, their lives— total gloom. I sat through one meal. Bernin behaves as if he hadn't turned a hair; but he's desperate, *so* bored. There's talk of his going to South America. Do you think he will be Emperor of Brazil after all? Clara moves among her poor; Gustavus used to go into Karlsruhe every week to help making people's family trees, he's been pushed to give that up; now he hardly stirs. Yet everybody in those parts seems as friendly as can be, if a bit curious."

"Your chosen neighbours," Sarah said.

"My dear, not at all, it's hours and hours in a very slow train from the Bernins' place. Seeing that neither Gustavus nor Jules will take a train lightly—"

"You'll have Clara on your neck."

"She is my sister-in-law. Clara's had a good deal to put up with."

"Caroline, don't snap. Edu used to say *I* did."

"I must have got it contradicting Gustavus. You haven't heard the half of it yet. He suggested—I admit he hummed and hawed—that we should call the boy Landeney, that's a title they have, at least during his minority, and as we were about it I was to change my name, too; he said I ought to call myself Baroness Landeney. He said I would find it more comfortable."

"A pity he can't offer it to Edu," said Sarah.

"I don't think I'll let the horses go to Sigmunds-hofen."

At the end of the week, she said, "Have you ever heard of lawyers as slow as mine?"

Sarah said, "I still don't see why my father-in-law—"

"You know there can be no question of that," said Caroline.

"Then I wish you would let *me*."

"There seems to be a run on buying a place for Jules. My turn."

"At least, let me do some investing for you. Try a few thousands, I'll double them for you in a month. I could— oh never mind."

Caroline said, "I *am* grateful. Very. But again it has to be no."

"And I'm so good at it," said Sarah.

Instead, Caroline let her find them a flat.

"Here? Yes, I suppose so. Why not? No point in moving to anywhere in particular now. I have to think of Jules, he doesn't know *l'Affaire* is over. Nobody knows how to tell him. Darling, do get us something quick."

After Caroline's child was born, Jeanne went in to her. "Do not upset her," said Jules. "Try not to let her talk," said Sarah. Caroline said weakly, "Is it all right?"

"Yes," Jeanne said, pianissimo.

"Yes?"

"Shsh .. Yes."

"Ten toes and all?"

"Yes, yes."

"It was a boy?"

"No. Yes."

"Which?"

"You must rest, dear," said Jeanne.

"It is *alive*?"

"Oh yes."

"OH MY GOD, WHAT IS IT?"

"A girl."

"Rather a mercy?" said Caroline.

Ten minutes later she opened half an eye. "We won't have to call it Julius Augustus then," she said.

At the end of a few weeks, she said, "This place is not one of your best efforts, Sarah. And look at these," the sofa was covered with estimates. "They are waiting for the spring to look at the roof, it beats English workmen. Meanwhile we'd better all move back to the flesh-pots."

"Can you bear that?"

"It'll please the old things to have us a bit longer. One really couldn't do less after the way they stuck to us."

By the time their own place was ready, Julius had procured a motor-car, and Caroline an English nanny.

"They're pretty good sport," Edu said.

"I think of it more for travelling," said Julius.

"My dear chap, you won't find the time."

This was of little moment in the years that followed,

and Julius was able to keep to his original idea. During the whole of its existence this car had no function other than that of conveying Julius, and Julius and his man alone, bi-annually to and from Voss Strasse and his country home. In the intervals between this accomplishment the vehicle was out of mind, indeed of sight, resting on its elegant high wheels on the premises of a mechanic at Colmar.

Caroline and the two children always took the train.

When she had begun to think of Henrietta's coming out and her own baby was just under three, Corporal Schaale suddenly turned up and was re-arrested. His story was simple. He had not been spirited away. Terrified by the prospect of his trial he had broken out of the cells he knew quite well, having guarded them himself, and skipped into Switzerland where under another name he found employment and obscurity. His return was a visit due to home-sickness. He was tried by the military at once, almost overnight. Putnitz again denied having cried out for help ("I cried out because I was startled"), Faithful George was a very damaging witness ("The Captain never hurt a fly"), there was no evidence that Johannes had been dangerous, indeed, no doctor having seen him, no proof of his insanity, and Schaale was sentenced to death.

There was an immediate flare-up. The story was revived, and for a week emotion blazed again. Caroline was in Berlin then; she was driving out with her small daughter and the nurse, in the Lenée Strasse crowds recognized her coupé and some stones were flung at them. Two days later the Kaiser reprieved Schaale by commutation.

The Corporal was taken to the fortress where he was to serve a life-sentence. Popular conscience was appeased.

Schaale's parents, some private advocates and the League for Human Rights tried for an appeal. Disliked by the authorities, suspected by the people and their fellow champions, bereft of aid or comfort from their husbands, Clara and Caroline joined them.

It looked rather hopeless from the first. They were kept dangling; nothing new was coming up about the case. As reasonable people put it—a man had got rattled and shot another, it was pretty certain that that man had been a lunatic, even so, if it was not exactly murder, it was hardly a reaction to be condoned altogether by society; the man who had pulled the trigger was a soldier and ought to have known better, besides detention in a fortress was not the same as penal survitude.

Sarah rather subscribed to that opinion, but she gave a cheque to Caroline.

After two years the appeal was finally turned down.

"We can never drop it," Caroline said to Clara. "That man is still in prison."

"That is not for us to think of. We cannot know the reason. It may preserve him from great temptation. It is *our* duty to work for his remission. We need not decide about the result."

Gradually the revisionists lost heart. The Corporal's parents refused to sign any more papers; the advocates dropped out. At last only a bishop—a man of charity who trusted Clara, a clerk in the office of the League, Kastell-Aniline money, Caroline and Clara kept the movement going; Caroline with almost superstitious fervour.

"I believe I am supporting the entire League for Human Rights," said Sarah; "they cannot remember having ever been so prosperous."

"Well, *good*," said Caroline.

"It comes expensive," said Sarah.

"Darling, go and play the market," said Caroline.

"I could just as well have paid Edu's debts; it might have come cheaper."

"I suppose one could *manage* an escape?" said Caroline.

"I shouldn't advise it."

"It wouldn't be the same."

"A pardon," said Jeanne.

"What I want is full legal release," said Caroline.

Jeanne said, "The papers are your only hope. Couldn't you get them to take it up again?"

"There's nothing new. Clara tried the Swiss doctor he lived with for some time; he's dead. One of his daughters remembers something about it."

"That's not enough," said Sarah.

"Get them to stir up something," said Jeanne.

"With Quintus Narden for our Zolà!"

"I would go to Narden, if it were any good," said Caroline.

"My dear," Sarah said, "the Felden Scandal is as dead as mutton."

*   *   *   *   *

"That's rather a long story, duck," my mother said. "Perhaps one day— Some of it— I'm afraid I don't come out of it very well."

Part Five

———

A REPRIEVE

At the end of our sixth winter at Voss Strasse, Grandpapa Merz died. He died in his sleep. In the morning knowledge of it seeped throughout the house in the same soft stealthy way. My mother was sent for. The house was full of women; governesses, the companion, house-maids, nanny, Henrietta, Marie, but as it happened my mother was the only grown-up woman of the family. She went in alone to the old man and his wife, into the ground-floor bed-room none of us had ever seen.

Later on we were all bidden to go downstairs. But first my mother came to me in the nursery. Henrietta was with her in a tight dark dress; she looked frightened. I was already in my hat and over-coat.

"It is sad, duck," my mother said, and kissed me. "One always feels it is. But he had a long life and liked it."

"That is good?" I said.

"For some people."

"*We* are going to spend a nice long day at Frau Edu's, ma'am," nanny said; "I telephoned."

"Her father is already there."

"Won't the garden be lovely!"

"I don't see any need for that," my mother said. "Come down and sit with your Grandmama Merz, duck; she's specially asked for you."

I turned to nanny, "Will I have to say anything to her?"

"You'd better look after Henrietta, nanny," my mother said, "she says she has a headache. Would you like to stay here?"

"Yes please, Caro," Henrietta said.

Grandmama was in her drawing-room, sitting in her usual chair, wearing her usual garb. Her hands were in her lap, but there were thick, slow, round tears rolling down her face, seemingly without her knowledge as she did nothing to wipe or stop them, and the spectacle fascinated me. I settled on the floor.

"Something young is best," she said, patting my cheek but looking at my mother.

After a while, she said, "Where are the gentlemen?" My mother signed me to ring the bell.

Gottlieb came in, his eyes were swollen and his voice was unrecognizable. "The gentlemen are breakfasting with the mourners, ma'am."

"Ah yes."

After another while she said, "Bring your chair a little nearer, dear." My mother obeyed.

"You are fidgeting," my mother said to me.

"Yes."

"Didn't you bring a toy?"

"*In the Presence of Death?*" but I did not say it aloud.

"Here we are all three and none of us has been taught to knit," my mother said. "I've often regretted it. Have you?"

"Knitting is very dull," said Grandmama.

"It's not too late for you to learn, duck," my mother said.

"Too late," said I.

"Shall we try a hand of demon?" My mother had introduced this briefer game some years ago.

"Not before luncheon, dear," said Grandmama.

Later on, I managed to slip out. The *Herrenzimmer* was filled with people. Most of them were men, and many of them were crying. They were sitting round Friedrich who was hunched on a chair, weeping bitterly into a handkerchief. Emil and Cousin Markwald were sitting next to him, and Markwald also was convulsed with sobs. Gottlieb stood by the door, announcing more people.

"Herr Kommerzienrat Veilchenfeldt!"

"Herr Doktor Herzberg; Herr Prokurist Stern!"

"Herr Schiffahrts-Direktor Warburg!"

"Herr Rechtsanwalt Wolff!"

"Herr und Frau Schwabach; Herr Bank-Direktor Reichenheim!"

"Herr Sanitätsrat Goldschmitt!"

The newcomers all made straight for the son of the house, shook hands and spoke something. Edging near, I caught it. *"Beileid—herzlichstes Beileid."*

A footman and my father's young Alsatian, Plon, were handing trays with coffee, port, sandwiches and cake.

The ante-rooms were filling too; I went out and took up a stand in the hall.

"Frau von der Waldemar!"

"No, no—I am sure they do not wish to see me today, I only came to put my name down."

But Gottlieb firmly propelled her in. I followed the lady; and saw my mother come out of the inner drawing-room to speak to her.

At noon a very old gentleman appeared. He wore a fur-lined coat with silk lapels. He was led straight into Grandmama's.

"Herr Handelskammer-Präsident Simon!"

"Mein ergebenstes Beileid."

Grandmama said, "Someone had to go first."

It was a free day and at one point of it I found myself in the kitchen. Cook, too, had been crying, but she said it was a time to rejoice. I felt doubtful. As doubtful as I had been feeling all day. "You do know where your Grandpa is now?" "Yes," I said, pretending to be interested in the flour-bin. I did not say that the answer in my mind was Purgatory.

In the *Herrenzimmer* once more, a grown-up turned me round. "What are you doing here, little girl," he said, "in a blue frock?"

Emboldened, I said, "In the Presence of Death?" aloud this time.

"Why, you wicked child—!"

I fled to my post in the hall.

But when I saw Edu and Sarah coming up the stairs, I hid behind a hanging. Sarah was wearing a short black veil; she was walking very straight; Edu was behind her. He stooped. Gottlieb stepped forward with outstretched hand. Edu seized it in both of his. "*Innigstes Beileid*," he said. The two men broke down. Sarah walked on.

In the afternoon I met my mother in a passage. "What do you think of it all, duck?" she said.

I thought. "I like it," I said. "I think it is nice. I like the crying. Everybody is kind today."

My mother looked at me. "You're not so wrong," she said.

"Is it always like that?"

"Not at all. And sometimes people aren't there."

"Like if we had been in our other house and only heard by post? Is that more sad?"

"Different."

I usually knew when my mother had done with me, but now I was too full of it. "Sarah didn't cry. Was she cross?"

"It is not unlikely," said my mother.

"Mummy—"

She waited.

"Henrietta says one death brings on another."

"What rot. She hasn't been reading statistics?"

"Papa told her."

After tea I hoped to unburden myself to Plon. But the day had gone to Plon's head.

I said, "He died without the sacraments."

"He didn't have to have them. They do it all different here."

"I know," I whispered, "*heretics*."

"Oh I wouldn't go so far. The catechism doesn't tell you everything. He had this party instead. You *see*?"

It was the time we usually left for the country, but we postponed it for some weeks.

"There will be changes," Sarah had said to Caroline.

"I suppose so. One doesn't imagine them in this house."

"There soon will be no house," Sarah said; "it is all folly!" She allowed herself a dramatic gesture. "You are aware of the will?"

"One could hardly avoid it," said Caroline.

Grandpapa Merz's will was dated at the time of Edu's bankruptcy. Except for a mounting list of codicils the instrument was straightforward enough. Legacies and annuities to the servants, legacies and annuities to Emil and to Markwald, token legacies to Edu and Sarah's children, a large legacy to Friedrich and a scarcely smaller one to Jules, and a life annuity to each; a hundred thousand marks and some emeralds to Caroline by codicil; the chief of the estate to the old man's wife for life and thereafter to their grandchild Henrietta. The jewellery, also, went to Julius's daughter. Sarah, Sarah's daughters, Caroline and Caroline's own girl, were each to choose a ring.

"They've all got a shock coming to them. I saw it for

years. Do you realize how they've been running things–? I'm not speaking of this house, we all know what that's been costing with the servants positively proud of the princely bills rolling in. Do you know how much they spent a year on butter?"

"It can't be more than what we do on Francesca's cow. I'm prepared to weep, though."

"You saw about all those charities in the obituaries? Edu and I thought it must be a hoax. Not at all. *It was Gottlieb*. He had a special fund, which he used at his discretion. But I'm not thinking of all that—flea bites— though it's perfectly ludicrous. Do you realize the amount of cash that went out every year in these allowances–? They're not pocket money. Friedrich is most comfortably off, Jules has a rich man's income, a relatively rich man's—"

"He's rather cagey about his affairs," said Caroline. Sarah told her.

"He *took* that? *Every* year?"

"His last raise was when the child was born."

"And *I* pay nanny. We generally seem to be short— It's supposed to cost two-and-six a week to live down there the way we do, but it doesn't."

"Then of course there was Edu—I knew they were supplying him in one way or another for years—I'm perfectly aware that Edu has been playing sub rosa; heavily, too. Well, take a thousand one day, and two the next week, and occasional extractions of five from his father, add it all up and you'll see what it means in terms of capital."

"Sarah, I thought they were so very rich," said Caroline.

"What happened is what always happens when people cease to control the sources of their income. All the old man did in Merz & Merz for the last forty years was to vote himself more dividends. The works are still all right, though suffering badly from depreciation . . . The partners let him do as he pleased, knowing he couldn't last for ever. Trouble is he very nearly did; they'll get his shares dirt cheap now. The banks made the same calculation, there is a huge overdraft.

"As for what there *is*, none of it comes to as much as it looks on paper. My father-in-law made some exceedingly silly investments, and then forgot about them. Moreover, he liked a flutter now and then. Friedrich advised him. Very badly. Friedrich cannot bear to sell anything once he's bought it, whichever way it goes. He hasn't got the temperament, and he always tries. If he's got too little pluck, the old man had too much, and neither of them knew the first thing about it. And they were *slow*; when I gave them a tip they treated it as something that would keep till after the flood.

"Sarah—were all the Merz's gamblers?"

"Yes. Except Markwald."

"He lost his money too."

"Yes."

"What was it?"

"Lack of suitable occupation," said Sarah.

"What does it all mean now? what you've been telling me?"

"That it cannot go on."

"There is nothing left?" said Caroline.

"We shall have to sell out the shares and some of the other stuff to meet the overdraft and pay those legacies . . And keep the old lady and all the rest of it going for another five, ten, fifteen years . . *And* find the principal for the life annuities. It cannot be done. My dear—*Jeanne must not be left in want in her old age.*

"Of course I am leaving her something. But that . . . in the normal course of events . . . And it is not the same. If it ever comes to her it must be a remembrance from a friend—not provision. I believe she has some savings; so has he—if he's kept them— but again that is not the way it should be, or she deserves. So I've *got* to see that Friedrich gets his inheritance. And naturally the servants; and the two old boys, but that's no problem."

"Jules will refuse his," said Caroline.

"*Well*—" said Sarah, "if he *would* take half? That would be a help."

"He will take nothing."

"That's nonsense," Sarah said. "He had a right to expect something. And he couldn't afford it."

"I forgot to say about my own legacy," said Caroline.

"My dear, a mere drop. And it would look so bad. The old man adored you. There is one thing that can be done : we must sell the house. The city's been wanting it for ten years; nobody can afford to live in that kind of house any more."

"Poor old lady."

"She need never know. Nobody will know except you and Friedrich and the lawyers. I am buying it."

Caroline checked a gesture. Presently, she said, "So it *will* go on."

Sarah said, "I never thought I would come to this one day. I remember coming here for the first time. I was engaged to Edu."

Caroline had a flash. "When I decided about Jules that winter, it was this that was in your mind?"

Sarah said, "I did not want to see you here."

"How you must have hated it; always."

"The house—yes. And you?"

"Another waiting-room," said Caroline. Then she added, "So Henrietta will not be an heiress?"

"Well hardly *that*," Sarah said.

That week nanny left for her holiday. "Where are you going, nanny?" I said.

"Home," said nanny.

She had asked permission to take me with her. My mother seemed to like the idea; hesitated; then said no. "I will take her myself one day." Nanny was annoyed.

I was allowed to see her off, though. After I came back from the station I gave the slip to Marie; I was upset and tried to lose myself in a game I had, called racing. I galloped round the ante-room—one part of it was the straight, the corners had to be taken closely and it was also good to shut one's eyes. I crashed into something and before I knew where I was yellow china was tumbling about my ears. I had broken one of papa's cats. I howled.

Servants came; my mother was fetched. I was still sitting in the china when I heard her at the door, "Am I to appear now every time the child breaks something?" She came in and she changed colour. She stood quite still. "Sarah's cats," she cried. "Oh my God. It's the one thing she likes!"

She stooped and picked up bits, trying to hold them together. Then she picked up something else. It was a newspaper, very old and thin and dirty. "What's that?" she said.

"It fell out."

"*Where?*"

"Out of the poor cat. When it broke."

My mother stood still again. She was turning the newspaper in her hand.

"It was inside?" she said.

"Inside."

She called Gottlieb. "Can we lift the other one?" she said. "I want to see something." Gottlieb called Plon; and they carefully got the cat that was whole off the pedestal, and turned it upside down.

"Do you remember whether they were both the same? All solid? No holes?"

"They were identical pieces, ma'am. We took them off once a year for cleaning."

My mother looked furious. She still had the newspaper. "What is it?" I said.

"*The Staffordshire Clarion* of August 16th 1879."

"I didn't do it on purpose, mummy," I said, but my mother had walked out of the room without seeing me.

We left for the country soon afterwards. My Uncle Gustavus, Clara and her brother were spending Easter with us. My Croquet Party, my mother said. Easter Sunday was a fine day, though windy, and the grown-ups had their tea out-of-doors under the lime tree. I was with them. Fanny came to see us. My father and Gustavus were playing dominoes. Fanny nuzzled their coats. "She wants your note-case," my father said; "she likes to count a man's money, it's a trick she has. Give it to her." Gustavus fished out his note-case and held it out to Fanny. It was a big fat one, and the leather had a smooth polish. "I see you still have yours," my father said, "so have I. They last for ever."

Fanny stretched her muzzle and one by one pulled out the bank-notes without making them wet.

I squeaked.

"How she enjoys showing off," my mother said; "Clara, do you think it's good for donkeys?"

"A goose we had could do it too," said Gustavus.

Fanny opened another flap in the note-case with her lips. "Eh—" said my uncle. Fanny clenched her muzzle and jerked the note-case out of his hand. "You mustn't take other people's note-cases," said my father. But Fanny shook her mane, cut a caper and cantered off a few paces.

"Starved for an audience," said my mother. "Get it from her, duck."

I got up with an air of resolution. "Fanny, please," I said, standing in front of her. Fanny looked at me with her clear large eyes. She took a corner of the case between her teeth and shook it, the way she sometimes used to shake me: money, photographs and bits of paper blew over the lawn.

"Oh you clumsy creature," cried my uncle.

"Catch them," cried my mother. I ran. I was quicker than the wind and retrieved handfuls before anybody else. Aunt Clara picked up something by her feet. She held it at arm's length, "That must be yours, Conrad," she said, "it is your writing." Count Bernin and my father were the only ones who had stayed sitting in their chairs. Count Bernin glanced at it, "No, it's not," he said, "it's papa's."

"Give it to me!"

We all looked at Gustavus then.

"May I not see it?" Conrad Bernin said quietly.

"Give it to me—" my uncle said again, and I can see him. I had never seen anyone stand so still.

My father rose.

"Please stay, Jules," said Count Bernin.

Then he spoke. "This is a note my father wrote to your

father, Gustavus. We've all heard about it. Your father is supposed to have burnt it. Unopened. Unread. This is what you told him and my sister at the time. Would you care to explain, Gustavus?"

Clara made a movement. Bernin turned to my mother. "Caroline, will you be good enough to read this to us? I should very much like your opinion; everybody's opinion here."

My mother looked at Clara. Clara inclined her head. My mother looked at the piece of paper, drew a breath, then slowly in her very English voice read the German words.

> DEAR FELDEN,
> Please give your whole attention to this.
> Your boy must not be sent back. Father Hauser tells me he might lose his reason. Hauser, as you may remember, practised medicine for some years before he entered the seminary. He has convinced me. A political issue is at stake and Montclair & Co have been deceiving you. This is most serious; I cannot come over now as I'm detained, but I hope to be at Landen this evening and deal with everything. Meanwhile let Julius keep an eye on his brother.
>
> In great haste, yours ever,
>
> B

When she had finished, Clara spoke first. "Our father wrote this, Conrad," she said. Her lips moved.

"I have never heard of it," Julius said. He was trembling.

"You were not there, Jules," Clara said. "It was after you went off that we were told about the note; it was the night Gabriel was killed. My father was supposed to have warned yours by sending him a note which he refused to look at and put on the fire in the envelope. But the old

Baron told me he had seen no note that day. I always felt that both my father and Gustavus knew something about that note they would not tell. I was never sure the note had existed. In my heart I believed that Gustavus had been trying to be good to my father, and I knew that the lie would be forgiven him. Now may *I* be forgiven."

Julius said, "Caroline . . ?"

She said, "Did Jules's father read this note?"

"Yes, Gustavus," said Clara, "tell us what happened. We can hear it now."

Gustavus was sitting again. He looked no longer rigid. "Oh I hardly remember," he said, "so much happened that day. Yes, I suppose papa did read it, and got angry, yes, and then he put the envelope on the fire . . . Yes, I remember it all now."

Count Bernin's eyes were on him.

"He was good to his own father!" Clara said.

Caroline said, "How did the note get to Jules's father? Who brought it? Who was the messenger?"

"Gustavus was the messenger," Clara said.

Julius said, "On the fire? It was July. You see, there were never any fires laid at Landen in July."

There was long full silence.

Then Clara said, "Tell us the truth now."

"The truth!" said Count Bernin. "I believe my father always knew it."

"You never delivered the note," said Clara.

But no-one looked at her. Julius had covered his face.

Then Caroline said, "But why? For God's sake, why?"

Clara gathered herself. She said with a great effort, "My father feared to compromise his career; he had told us that if Jean were not sent back he could not give his permission for Gustavus and me to marry." After a pause, she said, "He did it for me."

Caroline cried, "Say something. Someone must speak! Gustavus— Jules—"

Count Bernin rose to his feet. His face looked horrible. "*It was you,*" he said, "*you—!*" but he could not control his voice. "You, who brought this on us. Much is clear now—the way my father treated you in his house, the way he never let you have office— Oh why did he not tell me? It was you who destroyed our work— his— mine— *You* ruined us. Now it is your turn."

I had stayed, biding my time to get away unnoticed. Now I seized the chance and fled. I reached the house by way of the orchard, as I approached it another figure went streaking by. It was Gustavus.

"Go to him, Jules," Caroline said. "Shake him, hurt him— if that's what you feel like doing to him, but say to him whatever is in your heart. Go *now*."

Julius fitted the dominoes into the box. "There is nothing to say," he said.

It happened half an hour later as my mother was about to come into the library. When she heard the shot, her hand was on the door. She went in, saw, called for help; but it was too late for help. When the doctor arrived his main use was to give a sedative to Clara. Clara had fainted when she had been told.

Later in the evening, Count Bernin went to Caroline in her sitting-room.

"I've come to ask you something."

Caroline gave him a chair.

"When you found him—he was already dead?"

"Yes. It was as the doctor said. He died at once."

"Caroline : my sister must not know this."

"Will not the doctor tell her?"

"I spoke to the man. He's a Catholic."

"*You spoke to him already,*" said Caroline.

"I will protect my sister. Where I can."

She said, "Will you not explain?"

"Yes, I expect I have to explain to *you*."

"I never pretended to be what I am not. Beyond politeness, that is."

"I was aware of that," he said coldly. "It is very terrible to us; that he died the way he did—without the sacraments."

"Poor Clara. Oh, Conrad–" She looked at the old man, for he was that, and saw herself and him, two people alone in a bright room in a house in which unspeakable things have happened.

"There is another chance, the chance we all have; it is independent of the presence of a priest. It is contrition. If before our death we have an instant of contrition, one flash in which we realize the nature of our deeds and repent of them, not in fear, but for the love of God, if we have but that one instant, God can have mercy on us. 'Between the stirrup and the ground—'"

"Yes," Caroline said, "I *can* see that. Rather wonderful. . ."

"But there must be time," said Count Bernin. "Consider that he died by his own hand. His chance could only have come *after* he had pulled the trigger."

Caroline said, "He was dead when I came into the room. I am sorry."

"Without that fraction of time he cannot—do you hear me?—he *cannot* be saved."

"*You are very certain,*" said Caroline.

"So is Clara. Assuming your point of view, which I
z

do not, assuming we *could* be wrong, it would make no difference as it would not shake Clara. You know her. If she is told that her husband died at once, she will know that he did not have that time. She will know that he is damned."

"*Conrad.*"

"There's no need to be squeamish, Caroline. *De mortuis*—there is no more foolish saying. Thousands of souls are damned every year, every day . . It is a fact. It is presumption even to talk of being saved. All we have to believe in is the chance."

Caroline said, "He was practically a boy when he did it— In a moment of panic— A young man terrified of not getting what he wanted— How many of us—? And he carried it with him all his life. *Think* of having kept the note—"

"This is your way of looking at it," said Count Bernin.

"Did she see him again? Before— after what happened in the garden?"

"She did."

"She spoke to him?"

"Yes."

"And it made no difference?"

"It made *the* difference."

"She reproached him?"

"In a way. She did a very foolish thing. It is of no moment now."

"What was it?" said Caroline.

"There is no need to go into it again."

"I wish you would tell me, Conrad."

Count Bernin said reluctantly, "She threatened him with public exposure."

"Clara?"

"It was an idea she got into her head. She thought that

if her father's letter were published it might revive
interest, well, in that man's case. She thought it might be
the chance they had been looking for. She told this to
Gustavus, she told him that setting free the Corporal
might be *his* chance of atonement. Then she came to tell
me."

"And you?"

"I told her I would do everything in my power to
oppose such an intention. The first result has justified
me."

"*Poor* Clara."

"Will you help me to help her?" said Count Bernin.

"Can a woman of her spirit be sustained by a theological quibble?"

"Hope is more than that. Without it we shall have
destroyed her last chance of peace on earth."

"Conrad—she did love him?"

"I do not know," Count Bernin said harshly. "It does
not concern me. She had duties to him as his wife; and
she was responsible for their marriage."

"If we tell her—this story—must she not, on your own
showing, find out the truth later on?"

"She will have what support she may need then. It
does not regard us here and now. As you do not believe
it does not regard you at all."

"So I am to invent the scene of Gustavus's death-bed
repentance for your sister."

"You are asked nothing of the kind. I merely want you
to say that you believe it possible that after you opened
the door and went for help Gustavus was still alive. I
want you to say this to her if she asks you. As I know her
she will ask you when she wakes tomorrow. She will
believe you, as she knows you are ignorant of the
importance of the question. Will you do this for us?"

She said, "I do not think I can."

He waited.

"*There have been too many lies.*"

He still waited.

"Now it must have a stop. It is a feeling I have. It is choking me. I feel if there were one more lie we should all perish."

"That is superstition," he said.

"Perhaps. Do we know where superstitions come from? The Greeks were superstitious. I *know* that we must break this pattern." In a different tone she added, "I know you're right about Clara. I'd do anything to be of help to her. Only, do not ask *me* to set up the next lie."

"That is the only way you *can* be of help to her," he said. "Perhaps you are asked to do this, to set up the next lie as you call it, in redemption of a past lie of your own."

She gave him a clear and gentle look. "So you knew about that? I wondered. I did not choose that to be one. But of course you are right: I allowed it to become that. There were other people involved at the time; it seemed best so. It does not weigh very much now, there's been payment."

"I don't know what you are talking about, Caroline," said Count Bernin. "Do I understand you to say that you *have* lied for the benefit of others?"

"You argue well," she said.

"Will you draw the conclusion?"

"No, Conrad; no. It does not work in that way. It cannot be manipulated; even one's bad actions, it seems, have to be spontaneous. Not a wrong for a wrong . . ."

"Is telling a white lie to save a fellow creature from irrevocable anguish that? To you? You must have a strangely constituted conscience."

She said, "I know that I must not do it. I know as if I saw it written before me."

"*You are very certain*," said Count Bernin.

"What can I do?" she said sadly.

Count Bernin said in a low voice, a voice that seemed to be speaking only for itself, "Nothing is knowable to man left to himself . . . to man who believes himself alone . . . the mind creates its own illusions . . . the spirit that has never asked outside itself is alone . . . there is a knowable reality . . . a link . . . for those who are far from truth . . . who will not see: compassion."

Caroline said, "If Gustavus were to have had the time he did not have, can we believe that he would have used it?"

"The mercy of God is infinite."

Alert, she said, "Did you ever feel that yourself?"

"It is what I believe," said Count Bernin.

"Ah—" Then she said, "It's no use, Conrad. I'm sorry." And then, "It must be getting late."

But Count Bernin stayed.

Presently she said, "If this mercy is so infinite why was he not given the time he needed? why was the bullet not made to go another way? why was he not prevented from doing what he did at all?"

"These are the questions of a pagan and a school-child. There is free will, and there is a law."

"Ah yes," she said, "a law."

At one point she said, "If I will do this thing you ask me, will *you* let Clara, will you let me, do what we can about the Corporal?"

"The man who killed your husband's brother?"

"*He* is not that man."

"You realize what it must mean once more? To Jules, to me—to all of us. To the girls."

"To all of us."

"You have been a disturbing presence amongst us. You are asking a great deal now."

"No Conrad, don't worry—I am not asking it. I'm not asking for anything. No deals . . I did want to get the Corporal out, but not in that way, not at that price . . ." Then she changed to a smile. "We both know that if Clara has set her mind on it, she will do it anyhow."

Count Bernin said, "As you are so reluctant, will you let me do it for you? I would tell Clara tomorrow that I asked you at once—she will understand that—and what answer you gave me. She will not ask you again. Will you consent to that?"

She said wearily, "I cannot make you see. It would be the same. It would be worse. Oh I don't want to be churlish—and I don't want to be hard, above all—"

"I have always been interested in you," said Count Bernin. "There was a time when I was able to wish that your child might be a boy . . I might have treated him as a son, made him my heir . . Jules could have been brought round. As it turned out I have no need of an heir."

Presently he said, "Could you not have been mistaken? An error in observable fact—a human possibility."

"You forget the doctor," said Caroline.

"Who will be kinder tomorrow."

She sighed.

He looked at the picture on her wall. "That is what you like, isn't it? I suppose it would be what one'd turn to, if one went in for that side."

"Art?" she said.

"Not all art. This." He read out the name-plate, "Claude Monet. I can see that this is—" he paused "persuasive."

"Did you never succumb?"

"I liked Shakespeare as a boy," he said.

Caroline said, "Conrad, you have lived so long, more than twice as long as I have. Such strange gleanings . . ."

Count Bernin said, "Nobody has ever understood me."

Presently, he said, "My father made one mistake. In which I followed him. He believed one had to fight heresy from above. The real menace of this century is irreligion."

Presently he stood up, "You would call yourself a humanist, would you not? I beg you to consider what I've asked you in that light."

"Oh what I call myself . ." she said. "But whatever it is, don't you see? is against you."

"I shall leave you now," said Count Bernin. "Remember that my sister will ask you first thing tomorrow morning."

Caroline remained alone for some time; the night was still mild, though dark; then she went uptstairs and knocked at Julius's door.

"I know it's late," she said, "and we're all worn out, but I have to speak to you. Now. I cannot deal with this by myself.

"For once, I am going to treat you as what you might be to me—an elder brother."

Julius was in his dressing-room. All the lights were on and he was still in his clothes. The lamp he used for diffusing some liquid in the air against his asthma was burning; a ledger was open on the table, but he was not writing.

When Caroline came in, he was standing with his back against the curtained window. "Have they gone?" he said.

"Who?"

"Are they not going? They must! They cannot stay here, not in this house. They must take— everything— back to Sigmundshofen."

"*Tonight?*"

"They must go. Make them go, Caro. You've been speaking to them, they must have told you when they are leaving."

She controlled herself. "Jules, this cannot do," she said.

"You are not on my side," he said.

Again she made an effort. "I need you," she said.

He went to the decanter and poured her a little brandy. "I cannot smoke tonight," he said, "because of this," he touched his chest.

"Jules, Conrad wants me to tell Clara that he did not die at once."

"*No,*" he said, "*No, No.*"

She looked at him and saw that his face was grey. Something went out from him that she was not good at recognizing; yet she had known it in horses, it was that kind of fear.

"I have been alone all evening," he said.

"There was much to see to."

"I would have sent for you, but I thought you were arranging for them to go. Let us have some piquet." He fetched the cards.

They drew. "Your deal," she said.

She took up her hand, discarded, picked up five. She stopped. "It isn't possible," she said, and saw that Jules had dropped his hand, too. All their cards were spades.

Julius recoiled.

"A practical joke," Caroline said. "A rather nasty one." She turned them over. "Not *at all*. They're

grabuge cards; Plon must have brought them by mistake
from Voss Strasse. Shall I try to find another pack?"

"Oh no!" said Julius.

She remained sitting at his desk. He stood before her.
"Don't you think that we must speak? We need not
speak of my predicament, but we must speak of what has
happened."

He put his hands to his ears. "Don't speak of it to me,
don't speak of it ever."

She looked at him intently.

"I've got a good mind to go away," he said off-hand.

She wished to calm him. She matched his tone, "Yes
that might be a good idea."

"A long journey," said Julius.

"Then we could shut up the house."

He said suspiciously, "There is no reason for
that."

"You know we shall have to do it sooner or later," said
Caroline.

"Who says so?" said Julius.

"We should have talked about it before. I did not want
to while we were under their roof."

"You have been talking to Sarah," said Julius.

"Of course."

"The lawyers think it's entirely preposterous."

"Jules–?"

"One must not let Sarah interfere about everything."

"You don't mean you are going to insist on that
money?"

"I know nothing about it," said Julius, "I know nothing about money. It was left to me. It has nothing to do
with you or me. The lawyers will see to it."

"*Jules.*"

"You are not on my side," said Julius.

She got up swiftly and went to the door. "Stay," he said. "There is no point," said Caroline and went out.

As she walked down the stairs she had the sense of the house asleep and not asleep : of Clara lying held under the drug, of the wake kept in the library by the men-servants and the women from the village, of the nursery, of maids uneasy in their dreams, of people alone, wakeful and watching. On the last step it came to her what she must do.

Count Bernin was writing in the downstairs drawing-room.

"I have decided," she said.

He bowed his head.

"I shall go away. Now. At once. The uses of my presence here are at an end."

"Yes; but when you come back?"

"I shall not come back," said Caroline.

In her room, she sat down to write the letter; then she saw that it must not be so. She went herself to Jules. The lights were still full on, he was standing in the same position by the window. She had not realized that less than ten minutes had passed.

"I am leaving you, Jules," she said; "this time I am. There is nothing I can say now. I shall send for the child in a few days; anything else we can settle by letter. This place is yours, I gave it to you."

Julius said, "I always knew you would leave me. It was too good to be true."

"No Jules, it was not that. Not for many years— I know you have come to resent me. I've been but poor protection."

He said, "You are not leaving *now*?"

"Yes."

"What folly."

"You showed me that it was possible to leave your house at this hour."

At the door she said, "I had meant to ask you one thing—did you know that the cats you gave to the Merz's were fakes?"

"Oh yes," said Julius. "I was taken in. I was young then, but I knew it after a week. It was one of my worst mistakes."

"And what made you give them as a present?"

"I did not like to look at them. What could I do? You see, they were beautiful—they were very good fakes."

I waked. Some light was coming in through the open window from the park, and I was able to see the outline of her face bent over me. "Are you going away, mummy?"

"Yes, I am going away. I shall send for you, duck; nanny will come for you soon.

"Are you taking a train?"

"It will be a milk train, I suppose."

"Where are you going?"

"England."

"England is good? Nanny says so."

"At the moment I feel rather prejudiced in its favour."

"I will be in England with you?"

"Yes. You must go to sleep now."

"Promise?"

"I promise," said my mother.

* * * * *

But nanny never came. My father found some letters in a book and sent them to the lawyers and my mother did not get my custody. After some time my father sent me a note asking me not to mention her name to him again; this rather hurt me as I should not have spoken of her anyhow. Her room, the one with the picture in it, stayed locked. My father and I lived in our country house in summer, and in the winter with Grandmama Merz at Voss Strasse. I now travelled there with my father in the motor-car; he said we were ruined and could not afford to buy railway tickets. He often spoke of our ruin, and there were some signs; he had sold the horses and refused to get beer in for the servants, they were made to drink up the older wines. And I soon had no more clothes. Blankets and overalls were best for small children, he said, and I liked this well enough. We had no more servants from the village; my father had them come from France, and forbade them to go out or speak to the local people, it would give them revolutionary ideas, he explained to me. When we needed things that had to be delivered, my father sent for them from a catalogue and they arrived in parcels. Our butler had left soon; it was to get married, but I believed he missed my mother. I had no new nanny; but one or another of the housemaids always looked after me. My father still went to auction sales. The new servants told me that we were not really poor; I knew myself that my father had come to a settlement about his Merz inheritance and that we also lived on some of the capital that had been left to him by his brother Johannes.

When we were in the country my father and I had all our meals together. He told me stories about what he used to do when he was a boy, and about furniture, and he also knew about fruit-trees and vegetables and how to grow vines, and he taught me. We were never silent, though I found it always a little difficult to talk to him myself. He had much trouble in these years with his asthma, and I knew it worried him. Henrietta did not come to the country with us any more; Grandmama was lonely and she stayed all the time with her. My father said it was much better so.

"I hope you will never trust a young woman," he told me.

Later on Henrietta also stayed away because she was engaged. It was to the violinist who had once been engaged to Sarah's youngest girl. Sarah first said that it was a mercy, and then she said it was not, because her own girl had run away with another young man.

"He's worse, *if* that can be possible," she said.

We did not see much of Sarah. She did not call so often at Voss Strasse now; though Edu came every day. My father had taken against Sarah; he called her a false friend who had brought great misfortune on us all. Sarah's eldest girl was training to become a hospital nurse. Edu said Sarah was quite cut up about it; but he said as soon as a chap'd come along there'd be an end of it. Sarah said chaps only came along for the other one.

I also knew that Sarah had paid Edu's debts.

"Why not?" she had said. "It'll make all those old gamesters sit up. I seem to have become so very rich lately—I see no point any more in keeping it up. I forget why I ever started it."

Grandmama Merz said to me every day when I came down to say good morning, "When shall we see your beautiful mama again, dear? I miss her very much."

As my father seldom was downstairs at that hour, I did not really mind.

I was not sent to school; my father was not for it. Also it might have been awkward for a while. My Aunt Clara had been right—the Bernin Letter, as it came to be called, together with the fact of Gustavus Felden's suicide, roused interest again. People seemed to feel this time that Corporal Schaale really would be better out of prison. The authorities became tired of the fuss; the Corporal's trial was not re-opened, but he was given a full pardon and released.

We never saw Aunt Clara.

In November 1913 my father caught bronchitis as we were driving up to Berlin. We reached Voss Strasse; but the bronchitis had affected his asthma, and the asthma affected his heart. It was a struggle for him to breathe, and the more he struggled the harder it became. They gave him morphine to relax the tension, but when he lay still the bronchitis choked him. Presently pneumonia set in. He did not want to die and he was sure that he was meant to, and these weeks must have been very terrible for him. I had become afraid of such things, and tried to avoid having to go in to him. Emil and the servants helped me in this. When he asked for me at the end I did not go.

They buried him in the Merz's vault, next to his first wife, Melanie.

Shortly afterwards I was told that I would be taken to my mother. I was to be met at the Dutch border and one of Grandpapa Merz's former companions was to take me for the German part of the journey. When it became known that my mother herself would be meeting me in Holland, Marie offered to come with me instead.

Marie and I arrived at the border station, dressed in black clothes. We went into the stuffy waiting-room, but my mother was not there. After a while we went out again. It was very cold. We had seen from the train that it had been snowing.

"Always late," Marie said; but she said it with pleasure in her voice.

Then she was there. "Frau Baronin is as lovely as ever," said Marie.

My mother bent to kiss her. She was in furs and a little veil. I had thought of Marie as a robust and bulky figure, and of my mother as small. Now I saw that it was not so. Marie was frail and old. "You must have been over-estimating the ravages of three years," she said; "but I wish you'd call me Trafford; as you always used to at first in Spain, do you remember?"

"Ah Spain—" said Marie. "Oh Miss Trafford!"

"Well perhaps not exactly *Miss*?" said my mother, turning to me. "Now let us see what you look like," she said. "Do you still speak English, duck?"

"No, yes, I don't know," I said and found that I did.

"*Your garments*—" said my mother.

"That is only because they are new," I said. "It is not what I usually wear."

We went to another platform. There was not much time.

"I brought a letter from Frau Edu, ma'am," Marie said.

"Oh, give it to me," she said. "*How* is she?"

"Getting on, like the rest of us. If you ask me, ma'am, she's been badly cut up by Herr Baron."

My mother sat in a compartment and read the letter, while Marie saw to my things being put on.

"I must send her an answer," she said. "Duck, do you travel with note-book and pencil? I thought not." She opened her own bag.

The guard began banging doors. "Oh never mind,"

she said. She went to the window. "Give her my love. Will you? Oh, and there is something I must answer. Marie, are you capable of remembering a message? Will you tell Frau Edu, with my love, that the letters that were found were inside *The Correspondence of Gustave Flaubert*; they were letters in Spanish of no importance to me—have you got that? unimportant Spanish letters— I put them there myself; I thought Jules never read." We were pulling out now, I was on the step hugging Marie. "Tell her," Caroline said, "tell her I was wrong about that too."